SERIOUS BUSINESS

Larry Gibilaro was born into a family of Italian musicians settled in London, where he has lived for most of his life. He has five surviving children from a long marriage which ended in 1998 with the death of his wife. Currently Professor of Chemical Engineering at the University of L'Aquila, in Central Italy, a post he previously held at University College London, he now divides his time between Italy and the family home in Clapham. He has published a technical book, *Fluidization-Dynamics*, on his research interests. *Serious Business* is his first novel.

Larry Gibilaro

SERIOUS BUSINESS

PISANEDDA
PUBLICATIONS

Published by *Pisanedda Publications* in 2006

www.pisanedda.com
e-mail: books@pisanedda.com

A CIP catalogue record for this book
is available from the British Library

ISBN-13: 978-0-9551977-0-3
ISBN-10: 0-9551977-0-8

Printed in L'Aquila, Italy by
Stabilimento Linotipografia Gran Sasso

Prince of Wales College occupies nearly all of the rectangle in Central London bounded by Torrington Place, Kepple Street, Malet Street and Gower Street – respectively to the north, south, east and west. A certain amount of redevelopment has been necessary in order to accommodate this major addition to the family of University of London colleges, rivalling in size that of its near neighbour, University College London. The basic topology of the area has nevertheless been preserved. This has been achieved by simply pushing Malet Street eastwards, so that it now runs to the back of the British Museum close to its east, rather than its west, face. Almost all the previous occupants of the rectangle have been relocated: the School of Hygiene and Tropical Medicine to the abandoned premises of a major London teaching hospital, closed as a result of National Health Service restructuring; and RADA (the Royal Academy of Dramatic Art) to a riverside, architectural-prize-winning complex on the Isle of Dogs. Only the bookshop remains, its skilfully extended neo-Gothic facade lining as ever the entire Torrington Place boundary.

Chapter 1

It was on a cold, rain-spattered November evening, getting on for three years ago now, that I was to witness a dramatic event which brought home to me that there was something seriously amiss in the affairs of Nigel Grandison. At the time it appeared only a distracting interlude, quite unconnected with anything else that was going on in my life. That perception was soon to change.

I had been working that day, as I had been for some weeks, on what had turned out to be an intriguing problem in fluid mechanics. Analysis of this type can become an absorbing diversion, exercising a soothing role on a troubled mind. I had come to rely on it in the last year, following the unexpected breakdown of a long relationship which I had thought indestructible. The particular investigation initially concerned a rather narrow academic oddity, stumbled across and shelved some years before when it seemed I had better things to do with my time. Now it came to serve its purpose, providing several hours respite each day from the enveloping emptiness in which I still found myself. The fact that for weeks it appeared to be getting nowhere was of little consequence, if anything a consolation: a comforting rut with no end in sight. But then it all started to come together. During that afternoon it had reached a critical stage and I stayed with it while time slipped away. By evening an astonishing result of unbelievable generality appeared to be emerging, accompanied by a growing feeling of excitement and a parallel sense of fear that some careless error was propelling me to an absurd conclusion. Time it seemed to call a halt, to come up for air.

I left my desk and walked to the window, leaned on the sill and collected my thoughts in the comforting current of warm air that issued groin-high from a grill above a concealed radiator. My office, on the first floor of the School of Engineering Science, faced across a narrow thoroughfare to the block on the Malet Street boundary of Prince of Wales College that housed the Goldburg Centre. As I stood pondering the significance of the unexpected direction in which my work was leading, my eyes came to rest on the window directly opposite, that of the Centre reception area which was in total darkness. Suddenly it burst into light, as though my gaze had somehow triggered a television receiver. And an instant later, by way of emphasising the analogy, a dishevelled character entered left and staggered to the centre foreground. He was clearly in a highly disturbed emotional state: his head rocking violently, lips mouthing agonised exhortations, clenched fists pumping the air then beating on the sill in front of him. I stood transfixed, feeling some action was required of me but having no idea what this could be. Then, quite suddenly, the performance was over, the protagonist regaining some control, gripping the sill and staring fixedly and apparently sightlessly ahead. It took a moment or two for me to realise that it was not the ravings of some demented intruder I had been observing but those of a man well known to me and my colleagues, among whom he was variously disparaged, admired, feared and detested: the legendary Nigel Grandison, Deputy Director of the Goldburg Centre.

After a while his eyes appeared to focus on me as I stood there, frozen like an idiot, our respective roles of object and observer effectively reversed: two rigid, illuminated figures facing each other in silence across the darkness. In vain I sought for some sign of recognition I might make to break the impasse, but nothing even remotely appropriate came to mind. So I just stood there, motionless, until he turned away, quite composed by now, and returned with his

8

customary dignified limp to face whatever it was that had driven him to the edge. As he exited left, as suddenly as it had been lit, the screen turned black.

I remained at the window for a while absorbing waves of warmth and speculation, my thoughts switching between the enticing possibilities emerging so unexpectedly from my work and the scene I had just witnessed across the way. The Goldburg Centre – Grandison's undisputed territory by this time, which he ruled over in the manner of a feudal lord – gave every impression of thriving, despite the harsh climate which had the remainder of the college wilting in despondency. No funding shortages there, it seemed; the lavishly maintained facilities positively bustling with urgent activity; bushy tailed personnel and earnest visitors striding in constant streams through its imposing portal. And although people spoke disparagingly of the quality of the Centre's open-literature publications, it was generally understood, and indeed widely and emphatically promulgated by Grandison and senior members of his staff, that these represented an insignificant element in the output of their labours: their real work was not for public scrutiny at all but for the august organisations that funded the programmes, insisting from the onset on a total blackout. The headaches such secrecy can engender in an academic institution, where tradition has it for people to shout their mouths off at the first opportunity, are not difficult to appreciate, and could well be thought to contribute to Grandison's habitually tortured appearance – more usually associated with his sickly constitution, the myriad, for the most part undefined, physical disabilities to which he was subject. They could even provide some clue to his temporary breakdown of a few moments earlier. Sympathy was perhaps in order here; but any twinge of this I may have felt was overshadowed by curiosity at what lay behind his outburst; and, no point in denying it, a degree of satisfaction, glee even, at the prospect of cracks appearing in that great edifice, widely proclaimed a model for all to emulate, exemplifying the inevitable future direction of academic research.

Life, it appeared, could be becoming quite interesting again: a transformation long overdue. Something, however, was beginning to feel not quite right, which I soon interpreted as suppressed hunger: I had not eaten since early morning. Even more urgently, I needed a drink. I went through the motions of tidying my desk (avoiding the fleeting temptation to check over the final stages of my work, which I was able to persuade myself required a refreshed mind, but in fact was more to do with fear of uncovering the fatal flaw), put on the stylish overcoat given me the previous year by Julie, shortly before she left me for good, and set off to satisfy these emergent cravings. I locked my room and descended the dimly lighted stairway, the evening heavy with unfocused possibilities and promise.

Outside the Engineering Science building a fine drizzle, visible only against the few still functioning sodium street lamps, had glazed patches of the paved thoroughfare to a rich golden sheen. A cat walked purposefully into the deserted recesses of the college interior as though it owned the place. The silhouette of irregular vertical tubes of the notorious Goldburg Fountain stood still and silent as ever against the night sky. Seeing this reminded me of the tentative arrangement I had made with Karl to meet him somewhat earlier that evening in the Goose. No doubt he would still be there. As I passed the Centre forecourt, heading for the main gate into Kepple Street, the quiet of the evening was broken by the sound of a slamming door, causing me to look over to my left. There, through the pipes of the fountain, I watched the unmistakable figure of Grandison limping away from me in his long, cloak-like overcoat towards the college boundary with Malet Street. This contained a gate which had once, in a previous, less-security-conscious era, provided a convenient shortcut into the college. As far as I was aware it had been locked and unused for years. But it opened on his approach; and a large woman, dressed in what appeared to me to be some sort of high ranking nurse's uniform, came through to meet him. Solicitously taking his arm, as one might that of an extremely fragile, ancient relative, she led him out into the street to a white vehicle parked at the kerb.

The rain had completely stopped as I crossed over Oxford Street into Soho, heading for the Goose where Karl was likely to be well installed by now. Although it was certainly premature, I was eager to talk to someone about my as yet unconfirmed findings, and that person had to be Karl Dembowski. Years before he had been my PhD advisor at Franklin, subsequently persuading and then actively helping me to publish sections of my thesis in major research journals. Although his role in the work had been pivotal, directing me through to the most significant of the conclusions, he had stead-fastly refused to have his name included as an author. This attitude was in stark contrast to many I saw around me, and was worrying at the time as I suspected it of being a consequence of how little he valued the work. Later, when I came to know him better, I was to learn that he was in fact well pleased with the way things had turned out but wanted this used to kick-start the academic career of someone he saw as a promising future collaborator in the varied enterprises – ranging from the highly prestigious to the undoubtedly dodgy – to which he was constantly drawn. In any case, his reputation was such that he could, as he once put it to me (false humility never having featured among his many vices), amply afford such generosity. Single authored papers in the serious research literature are something of a rarity; and it was almost certainly as a result of those publications that I secured the lectureship at Prince of Wales College. But although my career had since progressed reasonably well, I often felt I had failed to live up to those early expectations. In spite of (or, more likely, because of) the friendship that was to develop with Karl, this was sometimes to bother me.

The Goose was packed, its open doorway framing a vibrant tableau of the joys and pitfalls of alcohol abuse. To my right as I entered, Michelle, the most glamorous of the resident transvestites, was entrapping an unsuspecting northerner, probably down for some sporting event, seemingly unable to believe his luck. At the bar three salesmen in suits were regaling each other, amid spasms of uncontrolled hilarity, with tales of the gullibility of their clients. Over the din a cracked, cultured voice could be heard directing eloquent obscenities at the portrait of a recently deceased celebrity: an ex-patron of the Goose of some notoriety. All in all a reassuring indication that nothing much had changed in the place over the last thousand years or so.

I edged my way towards the counter, peering intermittently into the exuberant mass blocking from view the corner from which Karl liked to hold forth. It was only after I had managed to get served, and was working my way into a space with enough elbow room in which to drink, that a small gap opened up somewhere in that general direction. Through it I glimpsed the profile of a strikingly beautiful young woman with an enormous mass of unruly jet-black hair piled high on her head and sticking out in all directions. She was seated in deep conversation with someone still hidden from view. Something about her appearance caught me off-guard, awakening something inside, triggering a fleeting blend of emotions: longing; inadequacy; despair at the realisation that in barely two years I would be forty and indisputably over the hill; envy of the unseen partner on whom she was focussing rapt attention. Then the gap widened, possibly as a result of somebody falling over, revealing her companion to be Karl Dembowski.

Karl, I noticed with a further twinge of envy, cut a ruggedly handsome, debonair figure. He was then in his mid-fifties but looked considerably younger; a notorious womaniser, currently progressing through the final stages of a messy third divorce. Seeing me, he at once waved me over; and with much weaving and squeezing, almost all of it unpleasant, I made my way to their table.

'At long last! Daniela . . . this is Paul, Paul Harrison. Where on earth have you been? We'd just about given you up.'

She fixed me with a friendly, familiar gaze, her lips set in an expectant half smile. And then I recognised her. We had met some months before at a college reception for academic visitors and new staff, which it had been my turn to attend as a member of the host contingent. These occasions can be quite trying, particularly early on before the sherry has had time to kick in. I had somehow managed to get drawn into a group of seven or eight inhibited looking males trying desperately to show interest in what Matterton, the Deputy Registrar, was saying. An ex-military man, his unvarying tactic in these situations was to demand little more than name and number from those he managed to gather around him, and then embark on a sustained monologue on anything that came to mind. This served the purpose of stopping anyone else getting a word in, thereby preserving continuity and maintaining order. The Japanese mineralogist on my right was nodding away like those dogs you see in the back of Ford Mondeos; and the Czech mediaeval historian opposite was steeling himself, after several failed attempts, to submit his views on something for general approval.

This had been going on for some time when I saw her arrive in the hall through a side door, looking ill at ease and vulnerable. She had been worried, I was to learn, about not knowing what to expect, nor what she should wear, and was embarrassed at arriving late. For a while she hovered unnoticed around the various established groups, none of which offered any obvious opening. Not waiting for a break in the flow, and resigning myself to remaining forever in ignorance of Matterton's view on the impending strike of railway workers, I muttered a hasty 'excuse me' and disengaged myself with a clear conscience to answer the call of duty.

She was clearly grateful for my intervention. We moved to the drinks table, and from there to a sheltered corner conveniently close to bowls of peanuts and other like delicacies which the straitened budget for such events could still stretch to. In the few minutes we spent together I learned that she was a biochemist on sabbatical leave from a university in Argentina – where her maternal grandparents had emigrated from Italy; that she had been educated at an English school – hence her fluency in the language; and that, after only a couple of weeks in London, she was already disillusioned with what she had seen of the work of the Goldburg Centre, where she was supposed to spend a year. There was something refreshingly open and responsive in her manner, which made me warm to her immediately. But before we had been able to progress far beyond the necessary dry exchanges, she had been spirited away by Trowbridge, one of the Goldburg Centre's 'senior group managers' (titles of this type regularly appeared and mutated in that organisation), to be presented to some personage of note on the far side of the room; and when I looked around for her later that evening she had gone. I had expected to run into her in college in the days that followed but she appeared to have vanished completely, leading me to assume she had had second thoughts about her secondment and had fled home.

'She's come all the way from Argentina to work with Nigel Grandison.'

Karl's tone left no doubt to his feelings for this arrangement. He was well known as an implacable foe of Grandison's, a position which secured him widespread admiration as well as some localised enmity.

'I'm sorry. I didn't recognise you under the hair.'

It had been tied in a neat bun on that previous occasion, which together with her rather staid clothing had created the desired academic impression. Now she looked quite wild.

'You can't imagine how intimidated I felt when they took me off. I had to put up with being cross-examined for hours by a group of important old men. I'd no idea what it was all about. I came back to find you when I could, but everyone had gone.'

'You don't look as if anything would intimidate you now.'

This was certainly true. She appeared quite regally composed and in control.

At this point Karl, anxious to regain the initiative and safeguard himself from possible association with the set of important old men, rose athletically to his feet and put himself to reorganising the seating arrangement in order to accommodate me at the table. This he managed to achieve with his customary charm, inconveniencing a number of drinkers, who nevertheless shifted bums and chairs without complaint. As a result, I was able to insert myself on a bench between Daniela and a convivial stage-Irishman, sporting a green lapel badge indicating membership of some religious or perhaps terrorist organisation. When the arrangements were fully to Karl's satisfaction, he set off purposefully to buy drinks, skilfully executing the complex manoeuvres entailed in reaching the bar and catching the barman's eye; leaving me with Daniela.

'You completely vanished,' I said after a few moments of silence. 'I thought you'd returned in disgust to South America. Don't tell me you've been locked away all this time in the Goldburg cellars.'

'Certainly not the cellars. My security clearance doesn't extend below the first floor.' At the time I thought she was joking, responding to my flippancy. 'In fact they sent me to Coventry.' She gave a wry smile. 'Seems that's a big joke to the British. Anyway it was hell. I only got back last week.'

It turned out that, following her cross-examination on the evening in question, she had been despatched to an industrial suburb of Coventry, to a former technical college for farm workers and apprentices to which the then Thatcher government had granted a university charter. That the acclaimed Goldburg Centre should associate with such a place was a mystery to most people but not, as I was later to learn, to Karl. He had discovered that the Head of the newly

15

established Department of Biological Sciences there owed his position directly to Grandison's undercover machinations – which had also led to his membership of a key research funding committee and a government advisory panel reporting on current developments in biotechnology: the deliberations of both these bodies frequently concerned matters of direct concern to Grandison and the Goldburg Centre. The reason given to Daniela for her temporary transfer was that it would provide her with basic experience in advanced experimental techniques, supposedly of relevance to her programme of study. In fact, she had spent her entire time there instructing technicians in the operation of vastly expensive state-of-the-art equipment, which nobody in the department had any idea what to do with.

I looked round to see what had become of Karl, who seemed to have been gone a long time. He was now approaching, gradually extricating himself from a convivial gathering encountered along the way, his large hands enfolding a cluster of full glasses. There seemed just time to broach a matter of some interest to me:

'How on earth,' I asked, 'did you and Karl get to meet?'

She looked uncomfortable for a moment before replying:

'Oh, we go back a long way.' And then, after a pause: 'In fact, it's because of him that I'm here.'

'I see.'

She was about to say more but was interrupted by Karl's return. He was clearly bubbling over with something he wished to impart, but first concentrated on distributing the drinks. These included a pint of Guinness for the Irishman, giving rise to a protracted display of gratitude. After it had run its course and further optimistic remarks had been exchanged, Karl was able tell us what he had learned during the course of his return journey from the bar. Plans, it appeared, were afoot to dismantle the Goldburg fountain and replace it with something altogether more traditional. He pointed out the sculptor, Ben Palmer, among the group he had just left: a slightly-built, middle-aged man, with a red face sandwiched between a brightly coloured silk neck scarf and a large brimmed hat. His original brief had been for something 'excitingly modern and dynamic', which was somehow supposed to encapsulate the achievements of the Goldburg Centre and provide a focus for the college as a whole. It could well be argued that the disastrous event of the fountain's inauguration fulfilled the essence of these requirements beyond the wildest of expectations. This, unsurprisingly, was not Grandison's view. He had seen to it that the final instalment of Ben's fee had been withheld, and had steadfastly refused to allow any modification to correct the fault which had resulted in his public humiliation. The fountain had not functioned since that day, and he would countenance nothing short of its complete removal. Now, according to Ben, he was negotiating in Italy for something along the lines of 'bare breasted nymphs in a tranquil pool'. Karl was ecstatic. Twice he nearly fell off his chair with laughter. Together, the three of us composed a pompous letter to the Times, quoting from memory the Centre's own pre-inauguration hype, demanding the preservation for posterity of this unique example of late twentieth century public art.

It seemed, as I made my way to the bar, that God was in heaven and all was well with the world. Over to my left, Michelle was transporting her companion, quite comatose by now, out into the street. The three salesmen were locked in furious argument, one of them having seemingly come to identify himself as the victim of one of the others' outrageous scams. Malcolm, the landlord, with a resigned raising of the eyebrows, broke off from trying to pacify them to come over and serve me. As a friend of Karl's, I could always count on privileged treatment.

Karl and Daniela were engaged in intimate conversation, which ceased as I returned with my round. The silence that followed was broken by Karl enquiring after the progress of my work, which I had briefly described to him some weeks before, when it appeared to be getting nowhere. I responded with a bogus display of diffidence, which he saw through straight away; and then, with his prompting, began to outline the steps in the analysis and the conclusion to which they seemed to be leading.

Karl became quite enthusiastic at this stage, and started to question me on various points. The ease with which he was able to enter into detailed discussion, assimilating tranches of complex analysis solely on the basis of my jumbled verbal account, was truly impressive, reminiscent of his inspired interventions in my doctoral and post-doctoral researches at Franklin some fifteen years earlier.

The conversation, I realised with some embarrassment, had turned opaquely technical, quite unintelligible to anyone outside the field. I turned to Daniela to apologise, only to find her smiling at us contentedly, seemingly quite unconcerned at her exclusion.

'We seem to have got carried away. I'm sorry.'

I then suggested to Karl that we continue the discussion some other time, but Daniela would have none of it:

'Please, please carry on. I'm really enjoying it. I haven't heard ideas treated with enthusiasm since arriving in England. It reminds me of home. All they ever get excited about in the Centre is funding. Oh, and impressing people who understand absolutely nothing about the work. And going on and on about the importance of the Centre and what is done there without ever saying what it is. There's certainly nothing of any importance going on that I've seen.'

She looked suddenly sad and, for the first time that evening, a little lost. Karl reached over to her, pulling her head to his shoulder, in what could be interpreted (but was not by me) as an avuncular fashion, and holding it there as he spoke:

'Not even in the basement labs?'

'I've no idea what goes on in the basement labs.'

'Then we're going to have to find out. Aren't we?'

Although he had spoken softly, affectionately even, there was a note of determination in his voice, which I recognised from past occasions signified a commitment to action.

18

We sat without speaking, absorbing the change in atmosphere. Another phase of the evening had slipped away and yet another was emerging into which it seemed I was being drawn. Without identifying the cause, I felt a nagging discomfort at this prospect. This, the effect of drink and lack of food and something else as well, something to do with Daniela, combined to shift my mood abruptly down to the familiar depressed state in which it had become accustomed to cycle since the departure of Julie from my life. I was the one who eventually broke the silence, insisting to Karl that we postpone our discussion, and excusing myself from joining them for a meal later that evening. He made no attempt to dissuade me, simply suggesting a time to meet in his room the following day. Daniela, on the other hand, made a convincing show of disappointment as I rose to leave; and it was with the feeling that I was in some way letting her down that I eased my way through the crowded bar and out into the street.

It had started to rain quite heavily. Sufficiently so to clear the pavements of all but those seeking shelter or in hurried transit to somewhere else. The bars and cafes were packed, fumes and a cacophony of music and frantic conversation escaping through their doorways into the sodden night air. I stopped at a nosh bar in Old Compton Street for a salt beef sandwich and apple strudel; then, feeling a little better, headed for Charing Cross Road and the tube that would take me to Brixton. My arrival at the platform coincided with that of the train – a rare occurrence; and I managed to make it to the only remaining unoccupied seat just ahead of a heavily pierced and tattooed youth with a shaven head – perhaps things were starting to look up again. I shut my eyes and tried to make some sense of the evening's activities. There was the question of my work, which I had the feeling Karl would discover some fault with. This worried me less than it might because knowing him as I did I felt confident that we would find a way to a perhaps lesser, but still significant, conclusion. And if he didn't? This possibility was immensely pleasurable to dwell upon, engendering a warm glow of self satisfaction, which if I didn't watch it could make me unbearably smug for a while. It would also justify the promise I brought with me to Prince of Wales College, and about time too.

Then there was the vexing question of Grandison. Our association, I had to remind myself, extended back a long way, back to school days in fact. And yet I had never got round to telling Karl about this, very probably because of Grandison's extreme reluctance on the matter. I had tried to bring it up at our first post-school encounter at a conference in Switzerland years later, but he had resolutely blocked all reference to his past, a past for the most part shrouded in mystery, which was clearly how he wished it to remain. Which was why, I suppose, I had withheld from Karl and Daniela the account of Grandison's tortured antics of earlier that evening. Pity really: it would have made a good story over a pint in the Goose.

A sudden surge of activity alerted me to our arrival at Stockwell, where I had to change trains. I alighted amid a disorderly group of young Afro-Caribbeans en route from a West End gig to something apparently more exciting nearer home. Lost in introspection, I crossed with them to the crowded adjacent platform amid boisterous jostling and shouted exchanges. The train, after a considerable delay and to jeering applause, entered the station hesitantly, as though weighing up the wisdom of stopping there. As I boarded it for the brief last leg of the journey, my thoughts turned to Daniela in an unfocused, wouldn't-it-be-wonderful sort of way. And there, with only occasional interruptions, they remained, as I left the station and wove my way through the still throbbing streets of Brixton to the flat I once shared with Julie and used to think of as home.

Chapter 2

There have been a number of occasions in my life when I have had reason to feel grateful to Nigel Grandison. The first, it shocks me to realise, was getting on for a quarter century ago, when I was barely fifteen: an ungainly schoolboy trapped in a stifling, authoritarian hive, portrayed as a microcosm of the awaiting world beyond. It always comes as a surprise to me to hear adults speak of their school days with anything other than relief at having put that extraordinarily unpleasant period of life behind them. I have no reason to believe that my experiences in this respect were in any way out of the ordinary. But on walking through those gates for the last time, having so it seemed paid my debt to society, the palpable sense of relief was overwhelming. Almost immediately, that phase of life appeared blurred and distant, and very soon I ceased to think of it at all.

The memory of one episode, however, buried along with all the others, was to surface many years later, emerging as sharp and clear as if it had occurred the day before. The setting was the annual prize day at St John's, the Roman Catholic boys' school I attended in East London. The main hall was packed: parents and other well-wishers occupying the raised benches along the two sides; the masters, a sprinkling of notables and the 'celebrity' (a minor television personality and 'old boy') appointed to distribute the prizes seated lined-up on-stage; the boys standing massed together, filling every inch of the remaining space. It was a welcome event, if for no other reasons than that it broke the tedium of classes and signalled emphatically the

21

approach of the long summer break. There was also some interest in possible outcomes: in who would be honoured and who disappointed – both eventualities offering the potential for satisfaction. The downside was the physical discomfort and inevitable speeches which had to be endured.

The proceedings started to unfold predictably enough. First, the distribution of academic prizes: books, for the most part destined to remain unread, delivered with patronising smiles to regular bouts of applause and the occasional ironic cheer. A prize for every subject in every class, starting from the bottom of the junior school and working unremittingly through to the upper sixth. Despite my assumed air of cynical detachment (I was fifteen at the time and well into the rebellious mode), I experienced an unpleasant jolt during this stage. I had fully expected to receive the fifth form mathematics prize, and so felt annoyed as well as disappointed to see it bestowed on someone I had consistently outperformed throughout the year. These emotions, however, were soon to be overlaid by others of an altogether more disagreeable nature as the apparent reason for my exclusion began to emerge. But that was after the sporting awards, the undisputedly major part of the whole business, heralded by an excited buzz of expectation, which persisted throughout the presentations, bursting periodically into spirited, at times tumultuous, applause.

Then came the turn of the headmaster, Brother Oswald, one of the few remaining monks of the religious order which, up to ten years or so earlier – before the disincentives of a life of poverty, chastity and obedience had finally dried up the pool of potential recruits – had undertaken all the teaching and general management of school affairs. Brother Oswald possessed more than sufficient of the trappings appropriate to his role: elegantly handsome in his flowing cassock, with a seemingly permanent sun-tan glowing beneath a head of tight greying curls; a great favourite with the boys' mothers, whose purrs of approval as he moved to centre stage could be clearly identified among the general hubbub. He had been, so it was said, an academic scholar of some distinction, and was now widely regarded as a saintly man. His demeanour at prayer in chapel was certainly a model of saintliness, much remarked upon and only very rarely caricatured.

One of the persons uninhibited by this customary reticence was standing just beside me that afternoon: Barry Skinner, a fellow fifth former, destined for fame and untold fortune in the murky world of public relations. Some days before the prize-giving, he had passed around a 'holy picture' of the kind employed by the monks to mark key passages in their missals. These typically featured episodes in the life of Christ or the Virgin Mary; or else portraits of the saints, often embellished with picturesque depictions of the instruments of torture with which they had met their deaths. Barry claimed to have found this particular one under Oswald's pew. It consisted of a seemingly unexceptional sepia portrait of a holy man at prayer. What made it extraordinary, however, was the remarkable resemblance that it bore to Oswald, both with regard to facial appearance and attitude in chapel: the way the right hand lightly touched the brow, leaving the left free to turn the pages of a sacred tome; the odd angle of the head, allowing the gaze to be switched from holy text to the heavens by the merest rotation of the eyes; the short tight curls and expression of intense religious fervour (enhanced in the picture by halo and radiating shafts of light); all contributed to an overall impression which would have been difficult to better.

I was pondering this extraordinary likeness and its significance (Had he consciously studied it and rehearsed the pose?), not taking in the spoken words, as Oswald went about his usual business: extolling the virtues of school, church and country; praising the winners in the day's event; spurring on the losers to greater effort; and the rest of it. It was after much of the same that an alteration in tone alerted me to the fact that something different was afoot. This was confirmed by the arrival at Oswald's side of Brother Ignatius, the deputy head, an event which triggered a muted rendering of the reception conventionally accorded the pantomime villain. For just as Oswald exemplified the beneficent, transcendental aspects of the religious calling, so Ignatius had come to represent its darker side. Tales of his sadistic proclivities and of his tenacity in seeking out and humiliating transgressors, however minor and remote in time their supposed offences, were legion. I had had a number of brushes with him that term and was well aware that he had it in for me. There he stood, hunched and uncouth, in utter contrast to the poised figure of the headmaster at his side: woollen football socks sagging around his ankles, showing from beneath his grubby cassock; tiny, furious eyes scanning the hall through pebble glasses to still the disturbances to which Oswald appeared quite oblivious.

What this was leading up to was the inauguration of an important new prize to be presented to a boy selected from any part of the school following prolonged consideration by the senior teachers. The name of the winner would be inscribed each year on a roll to be displayed prominently in the main hall, alongside that of the head boys. As was usual for Oswald, he took his time getting to the point. But what was unusual this time was his frequent reference to a bundle of notes held in his left hand (the arm angled, I could not help noticing, in a manner reminiscent of that of the holy man in Barry's picture), and his recourse to prompts from Ignatius, who had clearly scripted the whole thing.

The gist of it all was that the criterion of outstanding achievement in the classroom or sports field, by which the previous prizes had been awarded, failed to accommodate those who – through no fault of their own: as a result of genetic impoverishment, birth injury, lack of some essential nutrient at a critical stage of development or other impossible circumstance – stood no chance whatsoever of achieving anything. And yet numbered among these unfortunates were those who, though fully aware of their limitations, nevertheless strove un-relentingly to do their best. The negative implications were obvious enough to everybody present – except to Oswald himself, who appeared blissfully oblivious of any possible problem with this heartfelt expression of decency and Christian values.

The reason the announcement of this new initiative took, even by Oswald's standards, an inordinate amount of time to deliver was that it included copious examples of the type of activity to be considered in making the selection. It was with growing horror that I realised that a number of these appeared to relate to me, and I became aware of Ignatius's triumphant gaze beaming in my direction. It was at this point that I recalled the unwritten rule for these occasions: that, in order to spread satisfaction as widely as possible, no boy was to receive more than a single prize; and the reason for my previous exclusion fell into place with a sickening finality. Barry, who had kept up an irreverent banter throughout the proceedings, had turned silent beside me as I stood frozen, waiting for the worst. Oswald was approaching his climax, radiating joy and goodwill, Ignatius smirking jubilantly beside him.

'Brother Ignatius has been kind enough to draw up a short list of contenders for the first Pius XII Award.' (In honour of a pope not, so far as I was aware, unduly impeded in his pursuit of advancement.) 'After careful consideration, and following prolonged consultation with the brothers and lay teachers throughout the school, we have arrived at the unanimous decision that the winner this year should be . . . Nigel Grandison of the upper sixth.'

I threw myself ecstatically into the applause that greeted his nomination, clapping till my hands hurt, a torrent of relief lifting my spirits, tears welling around my eyes. With hindsight it may have seemed easy enough to dismiss my previous anxieties as paranoia. But the fact remained that certain of Oswald's references could only have related to me, and indeed could only have come from Ignatius. Interestingly enough, it emerged that I was by no means the only one to have been targeted in this way. The post-mortems that followed identified four others, including Barry, who admitted to severe discomfort in the lead up to the declaration, and there could well have been more. On disinterested reflection, one could not but admire the skill and perspicacity, not to mention dedication, with which Ignatius had stage-managed the whole thing. For quite some time afterwards he could be seen chuckling away malevolently to himself as he went about his affairs and attended to his religious observances.

Grandison's reaction to his award provided a good indication of his extraordinary resilience and ability to make capital under the most unpromising circumstances. It was well known throughout the school that there was something wrong with him, though opinions differed as to precisely what it was. His warm clothing, donned at the merest whisper of inclement weather (hand-knitted cardigan, scarf in school colours but thicker and much longer than the standard item and worn wound twice about his neck, sturdy boots and woolly hat), were all in clear contravention of school rules, but tolerated in his case in acknowledgement of his special needs. As he limped his way towards the stage, in much the manner he would display later in life after the loss of a leg, the crowd parted respectfully and a lay master hurried forward to support his arm as he mounted the steps. The strained expression on his pale face, telling of suffering endured, remained fixed and unsmiling as he accepted the award with quiet dignity from the somewhat marginalised celebrity. Then, in an unprecedented move taking everybody by surprise, he turned to the body of the hall and, raising his right arm in a mute appeal for silence, prepared to address the assembled company.

The effect was electric, the bustle subsiding abruptly into stillness as though at the flick of a switch. Ignatius, visibly perturbed at this unscripted assumption of authority, appeared on the point of intervening physically, and may well have done so but for Oswald's hastily extended hand on his arm. And thus they remained: two disparate robed figures, frozen together as though participants in the children's game when the music stops, waiting anxiously to hear what Grandison would have to say.

They need not have worried. Nothing in the remotest way contentious was to emerge. He merely thanked everyone – the brothers (in particular Oswald and Ignatius), lay teachers and boys – for the kindness and understanding they had shown him in his struggle with ill health throughout his attendance at the school. This period of his life was now drawing to a close, but he would be thinking of them all as he faced the even greater challenges of the world outside. And so, with a polite bow to Oswald and Ignatius, he made his way painfully off the stage to an ensuing applause which more than matched in duration and intensity anything that had gone before.

With that he moved out of my life as swiftly as he had moved in, and more than ten years were to pass before he would unexpectedly re-enter it, and again give me reason to be thankful for his presence. A colleague at Prince of Wales College was to remark much later, with a mixture of bitterness and grudging admiration, that when it came to saying nothing there was nobody who could do it more impressively than Nigel Grandison. His presence it seemed was enough. A presence which, in an indefinable way, drew heavily on his frail physical condition, guaranteeing him sympathetic attention and shielding him from criticism.

Chapter 3

The morning after my evening with Karl and Daniela in the Goose, I awoke early from a confused dream in which Julie was back in the flat, pottering about in the kitchen as she used to, everything the way it had been before she left. It came as no surprise at all, however, to find that her appearance had changed: although she was still quite undoubtedly Julie, she now exactly resembled Daniela.

My first decision of the day was to put a stop to all this: to stop fantasising about Daniela. She clearly had something serious going with Karl and nothing but trouble could come from pursuing my train of thought in that direction. Such interest as she appeared to show in me could in any case be attributed to mere Latin politeness to Karl's friend. My second decision was to get into college early that morning, before a crush developed on the tube. This was an unusual move for me as I had no teaching duties that day and am not by nature an early starter; but there was some work I wanted to get done before talking to Karl about it in the afternoon.

The college appeared pleasantly tranquil as I entered the main gate: just a steady trickle of early birds heading mainly for the Goldburg Centre and a few night cleaners coming off duty in the opposite direction. I switched on the hall lights in the School of Engineering Science, then made my way through the deserted corridors to my room. From the window I could see that the Centre reception area was already busy; its guardian, the fearsome Miss Brown (out of sight to my left), apparently harassing a small group of visitors who were staring fixedly, as though mesmerised, in the direction of her desk. On an impulse, it occurred to me to confirm her presence there, which would entail moving to a location sufficiently to the right to provide the necessary angle of vision through the reception area window. It so happened that adjoining my office was a narrow store room – once the personal laboratory of a long dead former occupant – possessing two windows well positioned for this purpose. By simply shifting aside a small cabinet I was able to enter this area through the connecting door, and was rewarded with a direct view, through the Venetian blind, of the bull-mastiff-like features of Miss Brown scowling over a pile of papers. She had been part of the scenery for as long as most people could remember, originally employed by the Professor of Biochemistry (at a time when there was only one of these), with whom it was widely rumoured she was having an affair. This seemed to me about as probable as Karl's contention that she was tethered to her desk by a chain, which could be released in an emergency to set her on to troublemakers.

From where I now stood I could see the Goldburg fountain set back in the concourse fronting the Centre forecourt. On moving to the other window, the one further from my room, the main entrance itself became clearly visible – as did the locked gateway to Malet Street beyond it, through which I had seen Grandison escorted the previous evening. Close by, in the far corner of the building, was another doorway I had not noticed before, and which appeared to lead directly to the ground floor laboratories: probably another emergency exit, in addition to the ones opening on to the roadway immediately below me.

Having wasted enough time, I returned to my desk and set about checking through the workings leading up to where I had got to the previous evening. The last stage had involved a number of convoluted algebraic manipulations, nothing particularly difficult but easy enough to slip up on. The first thing I did was to work through these again using a slightly different route, thereby reducing the chances of simply repeating a stupid error. So far so good. Then, in some trepidation, I took the whole thing further, and was relieved to find that it led eventually more or less to where I had told Karl that I thought it would.

It was coming up to one o'clock. I had missed breakfast and internal rumblings were telling me it was time for lunch; my appointment with Karl was for three. There were two consistency checks I needed to make; one would take an hour or so, the other much longer. While trying to choose between getting on with the first one or going to find something to eat, the phone rang. I answered it, but the line was dead. Hanging up and without thinking further, I got on with the first check. By now I had built up a good head of steam and it made sense to try to profit from it. In little over an hour the final result had passed effortlessly through the first filter, intensifying the glow that had ignited earlier when it first materialised on paper. Previously held imprecisely in the mind, a jumble of vague concepts, there it stood: a beautifully compact mathematical relation, carrying implications which would send waves well beyond the narrow academic boundaries within which its origins had been conceived.

As I was putting my papers together and gathering up other bits and pieces to take with me to Karl, my attention was drawn once again to the view through the window of the Centre reception area. There was something different about the confident, businesslike manner in which the new occupants were now comporting themselves, their relaxed interactions leading me to believe that Miss Brown had been unaccountably called away. But then she came striding into view, conferring earnestly with a superior, pin-stripped individual, all traces of harshness erased from her features, which now displayed an almost girlish willingness to please. While I was taking in this transformation, a flurry of motion signalled the imminence of an event the occupants were clearly anticipating. Those nearest the window shuffled closer to it, others further away moved back, the net effect being to clear a corridor through the centre of the room which they all faced, standing in silence as though awaiting a bride and groom. A few moments later I could just see, between the heads of Miss Brown and her recently acquired soulmate, the figure of Grandison making his way slowly and painfully between the onlookers towards the door to the stairway leading down to the main entrance. He appeared his usual sickly self, perhaps even more so: eyes puffed and red, shoulders sagging under the weight of unimaginable burdens. There was somebody with him who, in the few glimpses I was able to get, looked very familiar, though in some other, quite separate context which I could not immediately identify. As they moved out of sight to the right, clearly intent on leaving the building, I thought I would make use of my recently discovered vantage point to get another look at him. I entered the adjoining room and viewed the entrance of the Goldburg Centre through the side of the blind in the timeless manner of the old woman spying on her neighbours. Almost immediately, the main door opened to discharge a purposeful young man, who surveyed the surrounding walkways, nodded at two individuals I had not noticed before standing some distance away to his left, and then – apparently satisfied that the coast was clear of rabid dogs and armed terrorists – turned and beckoned to those waiting behind.

And then I saw him clearly as he emerged and peered guardedly around, at one moment seemingly straight at me. He appeared older than in his frequent appearances on television, in which he was fast gaining the reputation as the safest pair of hands the government could call upon to deal with importunate newscasters in times of trouble. Following him were two attentive young men with whom, together with the one who had preceded them, he made his way to the gate on the Malet Street boundary. This was opened with a flourish by a further member of the team, who had been standing there erect, arms folded, awaiting his moment of action. At the precise instant at which he stepped through the gate, a gleaming

31

black limousine drew up at the kerb; doors were flung open, and Frank Hepplewaite, Minister for Health, folded himself inside to be whisked away with his entourage to wherever further matters of state had been deemed important enough to require his attention.

Just as I emerged from the building, heading circuitously for Karl's room in the Physics Department via a kebab house in Store Street, the autumn sun broke through the clouds throwing dazzling reflections off the Goldburg fountain, projecting broken shadows across my path along the walkway. I had been quite sceptical about it at first, attributing Karl's enthusiasm more to his loyalty to Ben Palmer, a long time drinking companion, than any aesthetic consideration. Then it became part of the scenery, clearly at one with the clean vertical lines of the Centre facade. The fact that it had never functioned, except during initial trials and only once thereafter (hilariously at its inauguration), had ceased to matter – except, understandably enough I suppose, to Grandison. I turned to take it in again, seeing perhaps for the first time how perfectly it composed the approach to the Centre forecourt, drawing the eye through its structure to the imposing edifice beyond. Jets of water would only be a distraction. Perhaps – the absurd thought skimmed through my mind, accompanied by an image of Karl and Ben Palmer in drunken conspiracy – it was never intended that it should work in the first place.

I was about to continue on my way when I became aware of a woman watching me from a second floor window above the Centre foyer. It was Daniela. She waved when she saw I had noticed her; and as I responded, with the raising of an arm and an involuntary tightening somewhere low inside, blew me an expansive kiss over the Goldburg fountain. I was already late for my meeting with her lover. As I turned away, to take my chance with the salmonella and whatever was to follow, the clouds moved over blocking out the sun.

Chapter 4

The visit of the Minister for Health was by no means the first expression of Her Majesty's Government's interest in the affairs of the Goldburg Centre. Hailed from its inception, seventeen years earlier, as a model for the future direction of university research, it featured prominently in ministerial pronouncements claiming credit for this far-sighted initiative. In fact it was the brainchild of the newly appointed rector at the time: Charles (shortly to become Sir Charles) Hardcastle. His selection from a wide band of eminent candidates was a pioneering move, paving the way for others of a similar nature throughout the country. For although a highly successful public figure, even his best friends, if he had any, would have been hard put to lay claim to any trace of academic distinction on his behalf. Nor would he have thanked them if they had. The son of a Yorkshire mineworker, self-taught and self-made and justly proud of the fact, he had risen to eminence in the world of commerce through, as he saw it and was fond of pointing out to others, hard work, plain speaking and common sense – values seemingly at odds with those prevailing in the institution he had been chosen to lead.

His surprise appointment could be largely attributed to the desperate state of the college finances – bequeathed by his distinguished predecessor as he slipped seamlessly into the House of Lords – and the evolved composition of the Court (the college's governing body), which over the years had come to be dominated by worthies from the world of business and finance. What had particularly attracted them to Hardcastle was his performance in his last job as chief executive of Appletons, a national grocery chain. He had taken this on after a string of ardently heralded financial wizards had successively failed to reverse the fortunes of the once thriving concern. Within two years he had things looking up; and after five, Appletons had become the clear market leader, leaving its competitors in disarray. Analysts attributed this success to a growing public perception of the superior quality of its merchandise, rather than the more quantifiable value-for-money factor, and this consideration could well have weighed with the Court. Further analysis, which revealed this perception to be quite groundless, would not have been available at the time, but spoke even more forcefully for Hardcastle's Midas touch, hinting at something rather more behind it than the folksy attributes he preferred to display.

One of the first things he set his mind to on attaining office at Prince of Wales College was the matter of research funding and direction. He foresaw substantially increased contributions from the world of industry, which in return would secure unimpeded access to this powerhouse-of-expertise (Hardcastle's chosen term, preferred to the trite and discredited centre-of-excellence employed by his predecessor), at present frittering away its talents in unprofitable, if not downright useless, activities. In this his views coincided with those of the government of the day, for whom the idea of part of the tab being picked up by the private sector held obvious appeal – as did the presentational possibilities of a substantial slice of the research being redirected to the pressing needs of the country's wealth creators.

Hardcastle then approached the Goldburg Foundation, an organisation with which he had had previous dealings, which both sides preferred not to talk about. After prolonged negotiation, and subject to numerous conditions, some unusual, many never to be made public, tentative agreement was reached on the establishment of the Goldburg Centre. The Foundation's contribution to this enterprise, though substantial, was to fall well below the projected budget. The shortfall could only come from public funds, but this had been ruled out of the question during initial soundings. Armed with his full reserves of plain speech and common sense, together with a mission statement, reams of estimates, projections, business plans and the like, Hardcastle returned to the fray. He pressed the case that the withering away of public support, to which both parties were irrevocably committed, could only be achieved if preceded by a massive injection of primer funds. This, he argued convincingly, would lead to immense medium and long term savings, serve as a model for the entire university sector, and bring untold credit to the government which had grasped this major initiative. At an opportune moment, as he felt some wavering in the opposition, he played his trump: he had secured the willingness of Max Warlberg, the for- midable Nobel laureate, to head the Centre, thereby guaranteeing the flow of industrial funds which would soon render it viable.

And so the go-ahead was given. The government contrived as ever to have its cake and eat it: loudly proclaiming its support while making no new money available at all – simply transferring funds wholesale from other, already hard pressed, research pools, to hails of protest which were duly ignored. The college suffered over two years of dust, noise and turmoil as the demolitions, construction and landscaping took their course. During this time the infighting among the diverse groups, who saw their futures transformed in the lavish facilities taking shape alongside them, reached fever pitch; and Warlberg, understandably enough, had second thoughts about his appointment. By this time nobody seemed to care. All that mattered now was securing as large a share as possible of the dream palace rising inexorably from the rubble.

From the start the biological sciences were regarded as the prime focus for the new enterprise. This was as much to do with the wishes of the Goldburg family as anything else. Ebenezer Goldburg, the Foundation's creator, had apparently set out to read biology in *his youth, abandoning his course in its second year in order to devote himself uninterruptedly to his first love of making money. He nevertheless retained a vestigial interest, which was to blossom in later life, assuming obsessive proportions in his dotage. When the full name of the institute, The Goldburg Centre for Bioscience and Biotechnology, agreed upon after months of wrangling, was relayed to him on his deathbed it was said to have comforted his final hours, softening his hostility to family members gathered, as he put it, like vultures around him, easing him contentedly into final oblivion.*

Professors of biochemistry walked tall, bought new suits and were to be seen everywhere striding self-importantly between meetings. Biologists and pharmacologists likewise considered themselves legitimate heirs to the impending fortunes. Other less obvious contenders vied tirelessly to get in on the act. Physicists, on discovering that the work of an eccentric member of their department could be classified as biophysics, went through the motions of assembling a research group under that title. A band of marginalised chemical engineers, who delved into sewage treatment and suchlike unedifying processes shunned by their colleagues, came to realise that they had been biochemical engineers all along, and felt better about it. These and like readjustments were aired and argued over interminably at college meetings, to the unconcealed amusement of disinterested onlookers. At one, the Dean of Modern Languages made reference, amid general hilarity, to an initiative in bioItalian, only to be forcefully rebuked by Hardcastle, clearly angered and perplexed at a flippancy never before encountered in his dealings with grocers and other serious men of commerce.

As the first phase of the development approached completion so the infighting between rival factions intensified, sowing the seeds of jealousy and suspicion which were to characterise relations of the Centre with much of the rest of the college long into the future. Endless acrimonious meetings failed to establish workable links with the various academic departments with which the Centre would have to share facilities: laboratories, animal houses and workshops; as well as academic, technical and secretarial staff. Very little of this detail had been given more than cursory consideration during the planning stages, and even less had been settled by the time the new, luxuriously appointed reception areas and offices had become ready for occupation. There followed an unseemly scramble for possession in which the newly installed director (a professor of pharmacology, reluctantly prevailed upon by Hardcastle to accept the appointment following the withdrawal of Warlberg) lost all semblance of control. He finally succeeded in extricating himself irreversibly from further involvement by succumbing to a spectacular heart attack at the climax of a particularly heated exchange – seemingly on the point of degenerating into physical violence. In the period of mourning that followed, Hardcastle was able to reassert some measure of authority. The temperature fell, but the tarnished image of the whole enterprise became exposed to intense scrutiny and adverse comment. The situation was hardly mollified by the appointment of a stopgap director: an elderly professor of biochemistry, Miss Brown's putative ex-lover, just two years off retirement. For the Goldburg Centre the prospects could hardly have appeared more bleak.

Chapter 5

I had just about finished my kebab (salad with two sticks of what could just possibly have been grilled lamb packed into pitta bread) as I re-entered the college main gate, heading for the Science Block and my appointment with Karl. A shabby door at the end of a second floor corridor, much in need of refurbishment, bore two inscribed plaques: one in brass with 'Department of Physics' in quaint italics, the other in black plastic with 'Departmental Office' in stark white capitals. Stuck below them with adhesive tape, a yellowing type-written sheet set out in some detail, with let-outs and reservations, the periods during which the facility could well be open for business. Along the wall to its right, a massive notice board displayed a jumble of timetables, notifications of cancelled lectures, seminar announce-ments and other, for the most part out-of-date, information. Beyond it, a door bearing the name Professor Karl Dembowski in bold lettering stood ajar.

Expecting to find him there, I tapped and walked in. He appeared to have slipped out, leaving his pen open on his desk next to a stack of notes which looked as if they could relate to the work we were meeting to discuss. His office was spacious and businesslike in an unpretentious, well-used manner: two walls lined from floor to ceiling with shelves filled with books and journals; a row of filing cabinets under further shelving carrying box files and stacks of papers; a computing area with impressive looking equipment; a low table in the middle of the room surrounded by worn, comfortable looking chairs. Two windows overlooked Gower Street to the terrace of one-time-grand Georgian houses, now functioning almost exclusively as cheap hotels. On his desk, alongside the cluttered working area and antiquated anglepoise lamp, facing away from me to his chair, stood a picture frame: a familiar feature. It seemed that Karl carried it around with him on his travels. When I first knew him in California it contained a portrait of his second wife, later to be replaced by the third. It could well have once housed the first, the design, perhaps by choice, being such as to facilitate easy replacement of the contents. On an impulse I picked it up to see if number three had gone the way of her predecessors. She had. In her place was a head-and-shoulders portrait of a young girl, about fourteen years old, quite beautiful, with plaits and something oddly evocative about her quizzical half smile. Although in no way indifferent to the attractions of young women, Karl's tastes, so far as I had been aware, stopped well short of paedophilia. No sooner had I started to reassess this perception than it came to me with a start that the photo was of Daniela, and her words of the previous evening, 'we go back a long way', took on a sharpened significance.

Further speculation was interrupted by Karl's return. Clearly amused at my clumsiness in replacing his picture, he was nevertheless in a hurry to impart a more absorbing concern. Allowing himself no more than a hasty 'beautiful child wasn't she . . . still is I suppose', he launched into an account of the prevailing Common Room gossip concerning the meeting I had witnessed that morning:

'The only thing known for certain is that a number of senior executives and their lackeys from three, at least three, of the major pharmaceutical companies had nothing better to do this morning than call on Grandison. Why on earth should anyone want to do that? And, in particular, why all together? They're supposed to be competing with one another, so it could hardly be to do with specific projects they could be foolish enough to be funding.'

Karl's belief in the inconceivability of Grandison being involved in anything of any significance whatsoever was absolute. This had always seemed a trifle unfair to me. And anyway, wasn't there more to the Goldburg Centre than just Grandison? The image of Trowbridge came floating into mind, persuading me to abandon my inclination to inject a note of balance.

'What is revealing,' he went on, 'is the *consistency* of the rumours concerning the gathering coming from seemingly different sources. The whole thing is so obviously orchestrated. Now who do you think could be responsible for that?' He paused for a moment, looking at me, eyebrows raised. 'Officially the Centre are saying nothing, playing down the whole thing. Just a policy group meeting. Nobody's business but their own. And yet the rumours obviously stem from there, probably from Trowbridge; he's certainly a source, though no way the primary source. As you know only too well, Trowbridge wouldn't pick his nose without first clearing it with Grandison.'

I had no idea what the rumours were about and so asked him.

'Sorry, I thought it would have got to you by now. Everyone's talking about it. You know, the usual thing: the wonder drug that's going to revolutionise the treatment of some incurable disease. Generally leaked to harmonise with bonus time in the pharmaceutical industry. It helps if it can be said to be based on some cosy natural material – like sheep's bollocks or larch bark. The media splash it over the front pages, use it as happy endings for news broadcasts, the punters rush out to buy shares, up goes their value, up go the bonuses and everyone's happy. Especially the fat cats at the top. Then you hear no more about it.' He paused, motioning me to a chair and settling himself in one next to me before continuing. 'It's cancer this time; which is particularly strange, seeing that there's no serious base to draw on in that area, neither in the Goldburg Centre – surprise, surprise – nor even in Biological Sciences. They got out of all that years ago, when is became clear that the big players had it all sown up, were in any case the only ones with a hope in hell of being able to fund it to any practical extent. And now, out of nowhere, we're suddenly getting all this interest from the pharmaceutical industry and unattributable puffs that a breakthrough has been made, or is imminent, or could be imminent. What is still very much in the dark is who on earth is supposed to be behind it. Whoever they are, they've certainly managed to conceal their lights under a bushel pretty thoroughly up until now. Trowbridge's team? Pull the other one.'

'Frank Hepplewaite was at that meeting this morning, you know.' I had been waiting for the opportunity to get this one out. 'I saw him leaving.'

'You're kidding?' He looked thoughtful, far away for a moment. 'Well, they really are playing this one then. Or maybe . . . or maybe they're being drawn into something else . . .'

I broke the silence which followed this pronouncement by going on to describe the events I had witnessed a few minutes before, including Miss Brown's transformation, which in the normal course of events would have delighted him. But he was stuck elsewhere:

'Just what the hell is going on there?' He smiled having said that, as though switching away from wherever it was that his mind had wandered, then shrugged dismissively, returning to normal: 'The usual empty hype from that place. No substance to it, we can be sure of that. The strange thing though is Grandison throwing away his customary caution and risking exposing his empty hand. That's not like him at all. It's what makes me wonder whether something else could be behind it.'

'Maybe Daniela knows more.'

Karl's features softened momentarily at the mention of her name.

'It's just possible, I suppose. Anyway, we can ask her. She'll be meeting us tonight in the Goose.'

'Us?'

His smile managed to convey a gracious blend of apology and invitation.

'Well it seems we are going to have a lot to talk about when we finally get down to it.' He indicated the pile of papers on his desk. 'The pub is probably as good a place as any to round that off.'

So he had indeed started working on my problem. It was difficult to understand when, what with appointments occupying most of his morning and Common Room gossip taking care of the extended lunch break. It could only have been last night, after leaving the Goose with Daniela. I wondered what she had thought of that; but then she would be well adjusted to his prodigious working habits by now.

'And anyway, Daniela was particularly keen for you to come along tonight. She was hoping you would join us for something to eat this time.'

'Thanks. I look forward to it.'

I was reminded of a previous occasion long before, when Karl had effectively propositioned me on behalf of his stunningly beautiful wife – the second one, not long after their marriage, certainly well before the break up was in sight. I had heard about such things but regarded them as belonging to a different universe to the one I inhabited. The offer was well intentioned. As advisor for my doctoral research at Franklin, he clearly regarded pastoral matters part of his remit. Following a convivial evening at their home, when I had drunk far too much and gone on embarrassingly about my emotional entanglements, they deduced that something important was missing in my life and kindly offered to provide it. When out of cowardice I declined, it was shrugged off good-naturedly. Afterwards I often regretted the missed opportunity.

The conversation returned to the Goldburg Centre, which notwithstanding Karl's antipathy for Grandison had by now come to be generally regarded as a reasonably thriving concern, drawing in industrial funding and constantly in the news. This emergence from its unhappy beginnings, some twenty years earlier, resulted from the replacement of the original, stopgap director, on his retirement two years later, with a dynamic, American-based biophysicist: Charles Lauder, headhunted by Hardcastle with inducements rumoured to be unprecedented in the history of British academia. Lauder was in fact a British citizen, who had been snapped up by a prestigious university in Texas soon after completing his doctoral studies at Cambridge, and had remained there ever since. He and Karl knew each other quite well. They had mixed socially and professionally in the United States, and it seemed at first that this association would become reinforced as a result of Lauder's appointment at Prince of Wales College. They would have made a formidable combination. Hardcastle had long sought to involve Karl in the Centre's activities, knowing it would boost its prestige. Karl, however, had other ideas. Soon after Lauder's arrival he embarked on a sabbatical secondment in the United States, and appeared set on transferring there permanently. Eventually a deal was reached by which he retained his chair in London concurrently with another at the University of Franklin in California. Incredibly, this arrangement worked out well, both institutions getting good value from his services, and Karl apparently thriving on the hectic schedule, which still seemed to leave him plenty of time for the many and varied incidental engagements that came his way.

When further speculation on the morning's activities had been exhausted, Karl's manner reverted to normal. With a 'well sod it, let's talk about something more constructive', he reached over to his desk from the table around which we were both sitting and retrieved the stack of papers he had been working on. Charged up with anticipation at what promised to be an invigorating exchange, I emptied my folder in front of me and sorted the contents into separate piles. Past experience of such encounters prepared me to expect a bumpy ride with surprises lurking around every corner.

In spite of this preparedness, Karl's opening comment caught me unawares:

'It's all a nonsense. There's no way the general conclusion can satisfy a fundamental existence condition. If you limit it to where you started out, fine. Hardly earth shattering though. A run-of-the-mill publication in the Journal of Physics, perhaps. Trouble is, as soon as you relax the uniform field requirement the whole justification falls apart.'

I felt a spasm of irritation at the manner in which he appeared to dismiss the conclusion of my weeks of work before even taking the trouble to see it set out on paper; then kicked myself for being caught off balance once again by his customary strategy of provocation as a device for sharpening up minds before a technical discussion.

'Now, wait a minute . . . '

But as I started to speak the uncomfortable thought came to me that his 'fundamental existence condition' could well relate to the consistency test I had yet to apply. That was going to involve many hours work. How could he possibly be so cocksure? Knowing Karl, it was nevertheless worrying.

'Maybe it would be better to start at the beginning,' I said, failing to fully conceal my annoyance. 'There are a number of specific developments you should look at. Then perhaps you'll be able to appreciate the general picture.'

He smiled mischievously, happy as always at having stirred things up, then shifted his chair round to follow better the outline I had prepared. I ploughed through my story, Karl ever attentive, muttering agreement from time to time, occasionally stopping me to check some passage along the way. As we approached a crucial turning point, which led eventually to the unexpected conclusion he had just summarily rubbished, he became quite excited and started scribbling equations on his pad, uttering disjointed, for the most part unintelligible, explanatory comments as he went along. Then, taking my notes, he started reading from where we had got to with intense concentration, putting the occasional pencil tick in the margin, as though marking a student script. I tried to interject a note of clarification at one point, when I saw him stall on a clumsily presented section I hadn't yet got round to cleaning up, but he waved me away, not wanting his concentration interrupted. It was only when he reached the twisted key from which the end result flowed that he turned to me:

'What have you done here?'

I told him. I had adapted a transformation he had used years before in a totally different application we had worked together on at Franklin. The memory of it had come to me in one of those rare and wonderful moments in analysis, which make the tedium of all the rest of it worthwhile. Immediately afterwards on this occasion, and from somewhere else, as though passed to me by a benign tutor impatient at my laggardly progress, had come the idea for the manipulation that rendered it applicable to the problem in hand.

'That's neat,' he said after a long pause, 'very neat,' which coming from Karl amounted to a huge compliment. I had hardly time to feel good about it, however, when he went on. 'But I'm afraid it's where the trouble lies.'

Understandably enough I took some convincing. The discussion went back and forward, the table disappearing under pages of scribbled equations with which I initially sought desperately to refute his arguments and with which he sustained them. Then, when my resistance finally crumbled, our attention turned to trying to circumvent the difficulty or, failing that, to salvaging something from the wreckage.

It was getting late. Both of us needed a drink. I gathered up my things to return them to my room, and we arranged to meet by the main gate twenty minutes later. As I passed the Goldburg Centre I saw it had returned to its normal state, people purposefully coming and going, all lights in the building blazing. The contrasting seediness of the Engineering Science Building toned with my depressed spirits as I made my way through the deserted corridors, questioning my suitability for fundamental academic research. Perhaps I should

45

abandon all this speculative, unfocused nonsense and concentrate on worthwhile practical problems with clearly defined goals – like the people over the way did –, leaving the clever stuff to the likes of Karl who were well able to cope with it. I saw how fickle was the feeling of well-being which had enveloped me the previous evening, and again that morning when things appeared to be going well, only to be swept away at the first obstacle, and this realisation depressed me still further.

Karl, however, was in high spirits as we wended our way towards Soho, stopping at a pub off Tottenham Court Road for the first pint of the evening, which was threatening to be a long one. He went on enthusiastically about my work, making me feel a contender for some sort of Pius XII award. But halfway through the second pint, in the first pub we came to after crossing Oxford Street, his ebullience started to work through to me. And by the time we reached our destination, after one further stop along the way, the evening stretched ahead like a gilded pathway to paradise.

The Goose was experiencing one of its spasmodic lulls in trade, more characteristic of an earlier hour: the barmen chatting contentedly among themselves, grateful for the respite; one of the salesmen of the previous evening sitting morosely at the counter staring into his glass. No sooner had we settled ourselves at a vacant table than Daniela appeared in the doorway, scanning the bar. Seeing us she smiled delightedly and hurried over, causing a dip in the buzz of conversation, a turning of old heads. She was wearing a short leather jacket trimmed here and there with fur, and a long woollen skirt, which in addition to appearing warm and comfortable made no bones whatsoever about acknowledging the soft undulations beneath the surface.

'I looked in twenty minutes ago. As you weren't here, I walked around a bit. Quite an experience!'

'I'm sorry,' said Karl, 'but our discussion took rather longer than anticipated.' Which was true enough, I suppose, but left something out.

'No, I was early. I just couldn't stand it any longer at the Centre. They seem to have gone completely crazy there. Even more so than usual.'

I returned to the counter to get her a glass of wine. When I got back she was still going on indignantly about the Centre. Karl was laughing by now, and she was getting annoyed with him. But while repeating the gist of it to me she too began to see the funny side, and soon the three of us were embarked on a pleasurable journey of speculation concerning the difficulties besetting Grandison and his empire.

It seemed that the present problem revolved around a young Irishman by the name of Sean O'Brien: a biochemist, recruited some years before by Grandison. Karl recalled the occasion:

'I remember talking to someone on the interview panel. They were wetting their knickers at having got hold of him. It seemed he came with quite exceptional recommendations. I remember feeling there was something odd about it at the time, as though his previous employers were very keen to be shot of him.'

'There's certainly something odd about Sean. I was introduced to him in the coffee room soon after arriving from Argentina. Couldn't get any response out of him at all. Even when I told him I'd been working with Di Gregorio. He acted at first as though he'd never heard of him. Then, when it began to appear he should have, he somehow managed to imply he wasn't allowed to talk about such things, as though it was top secret or something. I was only talking about the man, for heaven's sake. And anyway, isn't this supposed to be a university?'

Karl chortled loudly:

'Obviously a well trained member of Trowbridge's team, ob-sessed with the fear that their precious little secrets will be stolen from them. The only secret they should be worried about getting out is how little they know about anything.'

'Well, they're certainly worried now. Threatening terrible things to anyone who tells people outside what's going on: kicked out without references, never work again, that sort of thing. Trouble is, nobody seems to know what exactly it is they're not supposed to talk about. Lots of rumours floating around about Sean, but nobody knows what's really behind them.'

'He's not the one behind the cancer wonder-drug then?' Karl asked mockingly.

'Funny thing is that nobody in the Centre appeared aware of anything like that. They'd no idea of what Sean was working on. He's a complete loner. Doesn't talk to anyone. Not there, anyway. Now people are saying he has been contacting outside companies without telling Trowbridge or anyone else in the Centre. But no one seems to have any idea what it could be about. There was some confusion about how the thing blew up. But now it seems that Grandison was attending some international meeting when he heard talk of a great new discovery that had been made at the Centre. Just the thing he had been waiting for all these years. Trouble was he knew nothing about it. No doubt he managed to bluff his way through, but he was furious with Trowbridge for not putting him in the picture. But then it turned out that Trowbridge didn't know anything about it either.'

The Goose was filling up as Karl set off in high spirits to buy drinks.

'I'm sorry,' Daniela said after a while, turning to fix me with a direct gaze, 'you must be completely fed up listening to me going on about the Centre.'

'Not at all. You and Karl have aroused my curiosity. I can't wait to hear more.'

'Well, I'm absolutely sick of it. Let's talk about something else. Please.'

As though to emphasise her determination on this point, she placed a hand on my knee, then moved it an inch or two up my leg and left it there as I replied:

'Fine. What do you suggest then? Oh, and incidentally, thank you for your greeting this afternoon. It was a nice surprise.'

'It was for me too.'

Karl was in conversation with someone at the bar, a grey haired man in a blue donkey jacket who looked as though he had had a few and was not planning on stopping just yet. The silence following Daniela's last remark was threatening to become awkward. She was the one who eventually broke it by asking how my discussion with Karl had gone.

'Not very well really. He found the fatal flaw. Seems I won't be a contender for the Nobel after all.'

'He has a very high opinion of you, you know. And I don't mean just as a friend.'

'Perhaps that's been a bit dented this afternoon.'

'I doubt it.' And to stress her disbelief in this possibility, she gave my thigh a gentle squeeze.

Further developments were cut short by Karl's return. He apologised for the delay, set down the drinks and settled himself on Daniela's right. She nestled against him smiling contentedly, but without disengaging her left hand nor slackening its grip. Karl appeared well pleased with this arrangement, rekindling my fear of being set up for a consolation prize.

'The fellow I was just talking to is Edward Weatherill, the one who painted my portrait for the Goldburg foyer.'

I had no idea what he was talking about. Daniela on the other hand expressed no surprise as she turned to get a better view of him:

'So that's what he looks like. He must have deteriorated a lot since then. Doesn't look capable of anything at the moment.'

'His eye,' said Karl with mock solemnity, 'is as good as ever it was. It's only his legs that tend to give trouble as the evening progresses.'

The only portrait in the Goldburg foyer was of Ebenezer: a massive, awesome rendering, guaranteed to intimidate visitors, soften them up for Miss Brown. Seeing my look of incomprehension, Karl explained that Ebenezer's portrait had been painted posthumously from a family photograph. He, Karl, was the one who posed secretly in academic robes, to be rendered in vivid colours bearing no resemblance to those of any university in the known world:

'It's all bogus. Bogus to the core. That's what makes it a truly fitting monument for the place. It isn't even Ebenezer. Only the face pretends to be. The rest is me: Karl Dembowski, "Patron and inspiration for the Goldburg Centre" – that's what it says on the plaque.'

From that point on the evening progressed joyously, Daniela's wish for a change of subject being granted several times over, my anxieties evaporating in an alcoholic haze. We might well have stayed on for ever but for Daniela's insistence that we ate. And so we wound our way unsteadily, an entwined threesome, through the teeming thoroughfares to a Chinatown restaurant frequented by Karl. There, over delicious food and Chinese Chardonnay, amid laughter and outrageous speculation, ambitious enterprises were planned and intractable problems resolved – all to be forgotten by the following morning. But the seeds of something more durable, sowed some time before, were brought to germination that evening, the first shoots soon to appear, the early roots to project tentatively into an uncertain future.

Chapter 6

The appointment of Charles Lauder as Director of the Goldburg Centre, though viewed externally as a brilliant coup for the college, was by no means universally applauded within the Centre itself. Things there had become undoubtedly bleak, many of the more able participants having effectively dissociated themselves from its activities and returned to their original departments, with which they had prudently maintained ties. Strangely enough, this seemingly obvious enough failure of the enterprise was not at all apparent to the casual observer, the Centre continuing to receive an exceptionally good press, quite surprisingly in view of the almost complete lack of newsworthiness of its activities: a visit by Dr. X to a quality control laboratory in Barnsley, or an address by Professor Y to a conference on breast feeding in Sweden, would be duly reported in the broadsheets as an event of more than marginal significance; and the occasional entry into the field of the tabloids, typically along the lines of 'dons in sex drug gambol', contributed to keeping the place reasonably well in the public eye. The more-than-casual observer may well have suspected the presence of some manipulative input to this seemingly unwarranted flow of respectful attention, and he would have been right. Hardcastle had no intention whatsoever of letting his brainchild die through neglect. He was seeing to it, in ways strikingly at odds with his much heralded all-open-and-above-board approach to affairs, that at least the symptoms of the malaise were receiving appropriate attention. So far as the root cause was concerned that would have to wait its turn. In the event, this proved to be a mere two years after the completion of the building. Then, with Lauder's inauguration, the full Goldburg project – on which Hardcastle had staked his reputation – was finally to get off the ground.

Those in the Centre who had stuck it out until then were a pretty dull, closed-minded bunch on the whole, not at all disposed to welcoming the arrival of a supremely astute and capable director, keen to get to grips with all aspects of their work and unlikely to be taken in by their posturing. Added to this, the fact that Lauder brought with him the elements of a formidable team of scientists, clearly intent on making waves and turning the place around, provided ample ground for dissension. Lauder, however, dealt with the situation in an unexpectedly conciliatory manner, ruffling very few feathers and soon winning over virtually all his erstwhile opponents. The atmosphere in the place changed markedly for the better, a few deserters drifted back and, most important of all, funds started to flow in from contracts with industrial sponsors anxious not to miss out on what appeared a fertile breeding ground for innovation and discovery.

Hardcastle, whose position and indeed health had been severely compromised by the initially poor showing of his creation, regained the bounce to his step and bored anyone he could manage to corner with interminable assertions of his invincibility. His business acumen, so amply demonstrated with the renascence of Appletons, now all but confirmed with regard to the needs of academia, could soon, he hinted, find application in other troubled areas of public life: the armed services, perhaps? the Church of England? The world, he was wont to state with a cool, direct gaze which defied contradiction, was indeed his oyster, whatever that might mean exactly. Patiently he awaited his call.

Chapter 7

A few days after our dinner in Chinatown with Karl, Daniela phoned to suggest meeting for lunch in the refectory. This gave me something to look forward to during the tedious morning I was to spend in the basement laboratories, guiding third year students through experiments purporting to illuminate elements of my lecture course – which was supposed to provide some theoretical stiffening to the predominantly applied nature of the degree programme as a whole. The trouble was that the experiments frequently failed to work, due to a combination of old and poorly maintained equipment with student indifference and cack-handedness. I was eager to offload the supervision of this class, and with this in mind was currently marshalling arguments to put to Hugh Sutcliffe, the Head of School. Among them would be the opportunity such an assignment could provide for a young member of staff (I had my sights set on just the man) to acquire first hand experience of laboratory practice.

Sutcliffe was particularly keen on laboratory practice. As my class got underway that morning, I was able to observe, through the glass partition separating the physics lab from the remainder of the basement, his massive hydraulics rigs being geared up for action by a technician, presaging the imminent arrival of a visitor he wished to impress. This was effectively the only purpose now served by these antiquated contraptions, some dating from soon after the first world war, which in their various ways caused vast quantities of water (coloured a vivid fluorescent green for further effect) to be hurled through the air with immense force and thunderous noise. In sunken tanks of domestic swimming pool proportions the eerie green liquid swirled menacingly. Karl had once arranged for the show to be put on for a bemused Ben Palmer, joyfully proclaiming as the giant machinery was set in motion: 'Now, that's what *I* call a bloody water feature.'

Spaces around these monsters had been infiltrated here and there by pieces of genuine research equipment. Part of one of these stood directly in front of where I was standing. Behind it, a metal stairway led up to a gantry containing the other part, all visible through the open mesh steel flooring. Things must have been going unexpectedly smoothly for me that morning because I found I had time to watch the antics of Rajmal Ram, an Indian research student, as he prepared to conduct an experiment. Rajmal had been a brilliant undergraduate, and I had been hoping to take him on for PhD research of a strictly theoretical nature. At the last minute, however, he had been snapped up by Sutcliffe with the offer of far more generous funding than I could possibly have raised, financed from a contract with an American off-shore-oil-exploration concern. I was a bit put out at the time but was able to console myself by speculating on the problems which would arise when Rajmal got his hands on equipment. His limitations as an experimentalist had been amply confirmed for me in the very laboratory from where I was now observing him. He appeared to revel in his incompetence in any kind of manual activity, perhaps regarding it the province of a lower caste to that with which he preferred to be associated.

His project involved the elaborate monitoring of a mixture of water and a black, viscous oil as it flowed through a complex circuit of tubes. Drums of the oil, supplied by the sponsoring company, were stacked under the stairway. I watched with interest as he filled a bucket to the brim from one of these, spilling a good bit on the floor as he did so, and then proceeded with it up the stairs, spilling a good bit more as he went. The most interesting part came as he attempted to top up the supply tank through a large funnel mounted on the gantry. Severely underestimating the flow capacity of this device, he carried on pouring as the oil overflowed around him, through the mesh floor and over the equipment and drums below. Serve the greedy bugger right I thought, as with a look of dismay he contemplated his ruined shoes. If he had accepted my offer he could have been simulating the whole thing on the computer – in a one hundred percent spill-free environment.

Daniela looked stunning as she joined me outside the refectory annex, more as though she had emerged from a beauty salon than a biochemistry lab. Slow moving queues stretched before us to the entrance. Partly in view of this, and the fact that I had nothing specific planned for after lunch, I suggested we tried our luck at the Tavola Calda in Charlotte Street, to which she agreed with enthusiasm. She took my arm as we headed down Store Street, very much the image of a couple it seemed, making me wonder about her and Karl, whom I hadn't heard from since that last evening in Soho. He would be leaving for California at the end of the week, returning to the UK a month later, in time for Christmas. What was she going to be doing with herself while he was away? I felt uncomfortable, and not a little excited, as the dangerous territory drew nearer, the keep out signs growing progressively less insistent.

We carried our trays to a corner alcove adorned with a Birth of Venus on the wall and a carafe of plastic flowers on the table. Buon appetito, she said as she unloaded her dishes.

'Buon appetito.'

We munched for a while, and then I asked her what she had been doing since we last met. It turned out that she had viewed a flat in Clapham the previous day, which Karl had found for her through some contact of his, and for which the rent was very reasonable.

'It's on the top floor of a large Victorian house. The only trouble is that to get to it you have to go through the hallway of the first floor apartment below. Two very old ladies have lived there for years. They seemed quite friendly. Very pleased that a woman was thinking of moving in upstairs. It's close to Clapham Common tube, so very convenient for college.'

Even more convenient for Brixton, I thought, with a tinge of guilty anticipation which I hoped didn't show.

'I think I'm going to take it. Do you think I should?'

'It sounds all right, but it's difficult to say without seeing it.' I didn't want to sound too enthusiastic. 'I could come over with you if you want to look at it again. It's not far from where I live.'

'Yes, I know. Would you really? You don't mind?'

I didn't mind at all. At first we arranged to go there from college the following evening. Then some instinct made me put it off to the Friday. It was only later I realised that Karl would be safely en route for California by then, causing me to wince at my unconscious circumspection.

Over coffee she told me that another thing she had done was to go to a show in the West End with Karl and some old friends of his who were visiting from abroad. She hadn't enjoyed it much, nor had Karl, but his friends had been ecstatic, much to his amusement.

'I was really disappointed. I had heard so much about the famous London theatre. But it was all so trivial. Like television soap, in a pretentious, old fashioned sort of way. Mind you, the audience loved it.'

'Much of it is like that, I'm afraid. Earns a lot of money from foreign tourists. There are some good things though, particularly in some of the fringe venues.'

Her eyes lit up, so I went on to say that I would look out for something we could go to together, maybe a lunchtime performance. I used to do quite a lot of that sort of thing with Julie but had got out of the habit. Now seemed a good time to start getting back into it again.

Neither of us felt like returning to college as we were leaving the restaurant. Without making any conscious decision about it, we found ourselves walking north up Charlotte Street, then turning left after a bit and zigzagging our way towards Regent's Park. Although quite cold, it was an unusually crisp, clear day for November, and quite a few people were spending their lunch break walking briskly to and fro along the pathways criss-crossing the grass. We joined them. It would have been nice to sit down on a bench somewhere, but it was too cold for that so we just kept walking. After a while Daniela forgot she didn't want to talk about the goings-on at the Centre and started to do so.

The big news was that Sean could be leaving – to go to MIT of all places. He had tried to keep the whole thing secret, but a colleague of Daniela's, who shared her office, had found the original of a message he had sent left in the fax machine.

'Angela showed it to me. Asked me what I thought she should do about it. I told her to give it back to Sean. It was really nobody else's business. Nevertheless I read it.' She laughed at this admitted limitation to her integrity. 'He had obviously received a firm offer and was just enquiring about a couple of trivial details before accepting it. In the end she decided to take it to Trowbridge. Then all hell broke loose.'

'Does Karl know about this?'

'Oh yes, I told him that evening. He acted quite strangely about it. Laughed a bit of course, as you might imagine. But then he got it into his head that he wanted to see the message. Got me to phone Angela at home on some pretext to see if she still had it. She'd already given it to Trowbridge but had kept a photocopy for some reason. Next day I managed to copy that for Karl.'

Why Karl should take such interest in a simple career move of a junior member of the Centre's staff puzzled me, even given the hoo-ha about his work. I thought he had quite enough on his plate to get on with and put this to Daniela.

'I was a bit surprised at his reaction, but then you can never tell with Karl . . . his thing about the Centre . . . about Grandison.'

She looked uncomfortable for a moment, as though there was something she wanted to divulge but couldn't bring herself to for some reason. She quite often gave that impression. Then she went on:

'Anyway, Trowbridge went straight to Grandison who hauled in Sean for a huge row. Angela was in the office outside. She heard all the threats, the shouting. Then it went quiet. They were in there for ages. She thought Sean looked pretty pleased with himself when he came out.'

The entire Centre was apparently abuzz with the intrigue.

We returned to college with some reluctance, parting at the Centre forecourt where I responded clumsily to her Latin-style proffered cheek. She gave me a cheery wave as she entered the building, and I walked slowly back to my room, my mind whirring with diverse thoughts competing for attention.

On my way I checked my post box. It contained a large envelope addressed to me in Karl's writing. Strangely enough, the work which had dominated my life for months up to about a week before had barely entered my mind since then, as though an unconscious defence mechanism was blotting out that crushing disappointment. Or maybe I had just been waiting for Karl to come to the rescue. It now seemed that he had. The envelope contained a letter and two stacks of stapled A4 sheets, one of only a few pages, the other quite substantial. These were obviously first drafts of papers, the top page in each case consisting solely of a title and the names and affiliations of the authors. The names sprung out at me: P. Harrison and K. S. Dembowski, in that order. I settled myself at my desk and started with the letter:

Paul

It came to me quite suddenly where your transformation could be applied. You will see that the impact should be even greater than you ever hoped for: a truly significant breakthrough, which goes to the root of a problem that has puzzled some pretty clever people for a long time. It also puts pay to that nonsense Galworthy has been spouting all over the place: this really gets him his comeuppance. Watch out for the flying sparks.

Forgive me for springing this on you without consultation. In fact the idea came to me Saturday night, and I spent all day Sunday on it, together with the odd minute I could find since. There are lots of holes that need to be filled in and some promising lines of analysis to follow up in the main paper. The shorter one is fairly complete – only some references to check out and a bit of tidying up to do. This one we should send quickly as a letter to Nature *to lay claim to the main idea before some other bugger does. (I don't really think there is much danger of this at present.) We can decide about the other one later. Think a bit about where best to send it.*

Knowing you well, let me say at once that I don't want any nonsense about who should be first author. For one thing, you did all the ground work and made the vital connections, and it was only bad luck that the generalisation you followed up wasn't suited. It nevertheless led straight to the present application, which you will see is quite free of such problems. Then of course there are the strategic implications.

I'll be in my room most of Thursday afternoon making final preparations for the off. Give me a ring if you can.

Oh, and keep an eye on Daniela while I'm away. I would hate to think of her getting lonely.
Karl

That last line bothered me, had the effect of making me feel uncomfortable, of putting me off turning at once to the papers, which up until that point I had been desperately impatient to read. The fact that he was telling me to do just what I was stumbling towards doing anyway made me feel more guilty about it somehow. What a devious, pathetic creature I was becoming. Yet on reflection it seemed to me it was Daniela who was making the going, was pushing things along. Or maybe she wasn't at all. Maybe she just wanted a friendly companion to introduce her to life in London while Karl was busy with other matters. Maybe.

I folded over the cover page of the short paper and started to read. There were my workings sure enough, but linked in with an additional strand of analysis which bore all the hallmarks of Karl's brilliant originality. Far from merely avoiding the problems with my initial formulation by limiting its area of application, he had succeeded in opening the whole thing up in a way that extended its generality to a vastly larger class of systems than I could ever have imagined possible. There was no doubt at all about the impact it would make. For a start it comprehensively demolished a theory that many in the business had laid great store by. The initial conclusion would be devastating to them; and as the analysis was reported in very abbreviated form, it was certain to cause waves of frantic activity all over the place, stirring any number of people out of their complacency to search for possible errors. I could well imagine Karl's satisfaction at the imminent discomfiture of his old enemy Galworthy, with whom he been battling for years.

I decided to work on this one straight away. It would mean a couple of sessions in the library and no more than a day or two to verify the development, which presumably would at the same time provide a check on much of the fuller version. Then it would be just a matter of smoothing away a few rough edges and submitting it to *Nature*. The other paper would clearly require more work: many references to check out and some analytical sub plots to pursue; as I read on, others of these suggested themselves which could well lead to further substantive applications.

This was undoubtedly the big one. The sensation was that of emerging from an interminable dark tunnel. The light was dazzling. I sat back and closed my eyes and tried hard to consider what Karl had referred to as the 'strategic implications'.

That evening, the newspaper vendor's placards outside Tottenham Court Road tube station bore the legend: London College Cancer Cure. Breaking the habit of a lifetime, I bought an evening paper. Maybe the story had made the front page of an earlier edition, but this was now dominated by revelations of a pop star's wife with a drug problem and the appointment of a new coach for a London football club. Overleaf, competing with an earthquake in South America which had killed some hundred thousand people, was a brief statement to the effect that a dramatic discovery had been made by scientists at London's Prince of Wales College: it concerned a drug that could potentially revolutionise the treatment of many forms of cancer. A Professor Cowbridge was quoted as saying that it was too early to say more than that discussions were underway with a view to setting up clinical trials at a major London hospital.

Chapter 8

Two years after his appointment, and in desperate need of help with the day to day running of the Goldburg Centre, Lauder advertised in the press for the post of Senior Administrative Assistant. Among those responding was Nigel Grandison, then twenty eight years old and with a somewhat suspect degree in biology, which nevertheless gave him some advantage over the other applicants. His references were impeccable; and although Lauder was concerned at his haggard appearance when he first met him – he looked closer to fifty than his stated age – he was duly appointed. Grandison threw himself into his new job with absolute dedication, gradually taking over more and more of the administrative duties, thereby enabling Lauder to engage once again in the academic work he craved and for which he was eminently gifted.

Seen from outside, Lauder remained firmly at the helm, personifying the growing reputation of the Centre in the scientific world. From within, however, it very soon became apparent that it was Grandison who made all the organisational decisions governing the interactions of the various research groups, at first between themselves, later with the rest of the college and beyond. This gradual assumption of control met with substantial resistance to start with, involving Lauder in fierce controversies which he sought to resolve by reason and conciliation. But bit by bit Grandison was able to wear down the opposition, and before very long Lauder was effectively able to withdraw from the scene so far as matters of general administration were concerned. Grandison had made himself indispensable.

It was during this transitional period that the first brush was to occur between Grandison and Karl: a trivial matter which he re-counted to me in the Goose with light hearted embellishments. He had phoned Lauder on returning from California and was surprised to be answered by an officious male voice asking him his business.

'None of yours, I'm afraid. Just put me through to Charles, there's a good lad.'

This response appeared to take the recipient by surprise. After some delay he enquired, in a sullen tone this time, who it was that wished to speak to Professor Lauder.

'Just tell him it's Karl.'

'Karl who, shall I say?'

'Tell him it's Sir Karl Gilchrist from the Goldburg Foundation. I wanted to speak to him about his latest funding application – but don't bother him if he's busy.'

'No, no . . . I'm terribly sorry, Sir Karl. I didn't realise . . . I'll put you through straight away.'

A puzzled sounding Charles Lauder came on the line after a brief pause.

'Hallo?'

'Charles, this is Karl. Who on earth is that monkey you've got answering the phone?'

'That's Grandison,' he replied with a laugh. 'I hope you haven't upset him. Last time that happened it took me half the afternoon to calm him down.' A receiver being replaced sounded somewhere down the line. 'My God, he was listening. That's done it. Never mind. Listen, I'm pleased you're back. I've been wanting to talk to you about that business with Sutcliffe. Seems the old fart has got a bee in his bonnet about . . .'

Chapter 9

The Friday of Karl's departure for the United States was cold and blustery. I set off early for college, intent on finishing off the short paper he had drafted, on which I had been working most of the previous day. It was looking good. At this rate I should be able to send it off for publication by Monday afternoon at the latest. The editor concerned had been alerted by Karl and was expecting it.

I bought two newspapers from the kiosk outside Brixton tube station, mainly to see if they were still running the new cancer-drug story. The day before, following the Evening Standard's 'scoop' of the previous evening, they had all covered it briefly on their inside pages, saying virtually nothing of substance, merely padding out their accounts with old copy of such things as dubious alternative therapies and statistics showing the limitations of conventional treatments. It appeared at first to have run its course; but then I stumbled on a paragraph in one of the financial sections reporting a number of small, but nevertheless significant, movements in certain pharmaceutical company shares, attributable, in the columnist's view, to rumours of revolutionary new drugs for the treatment of cancer. Well, well! Perhaps these were the columns to watch out for, never mind the research literature.

On passing the Goldburg Centre forecourt I became aware that those trying to enter the building were being checked over by two uniformed security guards. These people normally resided in a smoke filled den by the main gate, drinking tea or something stronger, rarely emerging into the open except for the purpose of visiting a nearby pub or going off duty. Karl had always claimed them to be unknowing pawns in a surreptitious medical research experiment on smoking and health – all the more expedient as it was unlikely to suffer disruption at the hands of animal rights activists. Now they appeared sullen and ill at ease at having to do something, squinting dejectedly in the diffuse November light.

An altercation showed signs of developing. Along with a few other passers-by, I stopped to watch, grateful for a touch of street theatre to enliven a dull morning. An elegantly dressed gentleman, with long white hair and a flower of some sort in his lapel, was being refused admission to the Centre. Although unaware at the time of his name and precise function, I had often seen him about the college, standing out by reason of his unusually refined, old-school appearance. This impression was fast evaporating. He was gesticulating wildly now, raising his voice in ill-tempered protest at this unprecedented disruption of his daily routine. It appeared that clarification had been sought from within; and after a while Miss Brown appeared at the doorway, sniffing the air like a carnivore sensing prey. After grudgingly confirming the credentials of the by now enraged emeritus professor of biology (as I later discovered him to be), she returned to her lair to resume guard over the pile of rotting bones left unattended by her desk. Cheered up considerably, I headed for my room, ready now to get back to work.

I picked up with the short paper from where I had left it the day before, adding a few points of clarification, and as a check deriving for myself the progressive steps in the development. This had been going well until some two thirds of the way through when I stalled, finding myself unable to arrive at an intermediate result. This was frustrating, so I decided to give it one more try before phoning Karl. Then I remembered that he would be on his way to Heathrow, driving there in his car with Daniela, who would then bring it back to his garage in Camden. In the back of my mind the nagging thought that something could be wrong somewhere was becoming more difficult to suppress. Then, at last, I did the obvious thing, which was to consult the longer paper. There was the missing step sure enough, with an ingenious argument leading up to it without which it would have been virtually impossible to follow what was happening. It occurred to me that Karl could have intentionally left this out for the purpose of baffling Galworthy, perhaps even goading him into a rebuttal, which could then be spectacularly demolished. You could never be sure with Karl. Or rather, the one thing you could be sure of was that, whatever the game, whatever the stakes, he would play it for fun. His love of mischief never seemed to tire, a further indication of his never having grown up. Given his prodigious scientific reputation this was something rather special, even though irritating at times. Resisting the passing temptation to go along with this view of his intention, I included the necessary line of reasoning. I knew well enough how I, and in general Karl, felt about deliberate obfuscation in the scientific literature.

Just when it was beginning to feel time for a pause, the phone rang. It was Daniela calling from the airport to say that Karl was safely on his way and that she was heading for Clapham. Things had moved since we had last spoken about viewing the flat she had been thinking of taking: having got wind of someone else after it, she had taken it. She was on her way there, and wondered if I could come to help her move some furniture around. In return she was offering a simple lunch – her first try-out of the tiny kitchen. It was already quite late and I had a lecture at four, and needed some time before that to get things prepared. No problem at all. She would drive me back for three-thirty. Karl had agreed at the last minute to leave her the use of his car while he was away. It all seemed very straightforward, very convenient. Karl was barely off the ground and there was I rushing over to her flat. He had told me to look after her though: 'I would hate to think of her getting lonely' was how he had put it. I had it in writing.

The house was in a leafy road running into a corner of the common. It appeared to be the only one around not showing signs of gentrification, the dark green paintwork peeling badly to reveal substantial areas of wood rot, the windows cracked and grimy, the red brickwork in need of pointing and repair. Daniela must have been watching out from somewhere because the door opened as I approached and she greeted me with her usual show of bubbling enthusiasm: running down the front steps to offer first one cheek and then, when I had dealt with that, the other. She was wearing an old sweater, worn jeans and rubber working gloves and somehow managing to look as if she was modelling for a trendy fashion magazine. We walked together up the steps and through the front door.

The ground floor apartment had been divided off from the rest of the house by a flimsy partition, which ran to the boxed-in stairway leading to the floor above. I followed Daniela up, obeying her mimed instruction to go quietly, aware only of a firm rolling softness vacuum packed into thin blue denim. The stairs ended at a narrow landing with a heavily worn carpet and a number of doors opening on to it. On the other side, another staircase led up to Daniela's apartment. As we made our way towards this, the first door we passed opened just enough for a wizened, white-haired head to poke out about four feet above floor level. Daniela greeted it with a convincing display of pleasure and turned to introduce me:

'This is Paul, an old friend of mine. Paul, this is Miss Atkins,' adding somewhat unnecessarily, 'she lives here in the flat below me.'

As I smiled and nodded, the whole process was repeated at another door some way in front of us, except that this time the head appeared some two feet higher than the previous one.

'Hallo Mrs Simpson. Can I introduce my friend Paul. He's very kindly come to help me move in.' Then, to both of them, who by this time had emerged fully on to the landing, effectively trapping us between them: 'I hope we don't disturb you too much moving the furniture about.'

'Oh, don't worry about that my dears, we're both quite deaf you know, we won't hear a thing.'

This, from Miss Atkins, appeared for a moment a welcome revelation, but on reflection quite inconsistent with the available evidence.

'Would you like some tea? We've just put the kettle on.'

'And some biscuits? We always have plenty of biscuits.'

Daniela responded admirably to this twin onslaught, leaving no doubt that at almost any other time the offer would have been avidly accepted, but just now she was preparing lunch for the first time in her new kitchen – and would have to rush because she had left something on the stove.

'Any time my dear.'

'And if you find you need anything: tea, sugar . . .'

'. . . biscuits,' interjected Mrs Simpson helpfully.

'Yes, biscuits. We always have plenty of biscuits. So don't be afraid to ask. It's so nice having a young woman moving in.'

Miss Atkins emphasised both words, *young* and *woman*, in saying this, suggesting the previous occupant to have been an old man whose habits may well have given cause for disapproval. With some difficulty we disengaged ourselves and ascended to Daniela's apartment, which possessed its own front door, half open now at the top of the stairs.

Compared with the rest of the house, the first impression on entering was surprisingly encouraging, all traces of the disreputable old man obliterated in the hasty tarting up process which appeared to have followed his departure. The wallpaper in all the rooms had been painted over in an assortment of pastel shades and all the woodwork gleamed shiny white. Although not very expertly done, the general effect was bright and clean. The furniture too, though very mixed in style, appeared functional and in a reasonable state of repair. Light filtered in from the high windows, which in contrast to those of the rest of the house appeared well maintained and had been recently cleaned.

'It's great,' I said, when we had completed a whirlwind tour, 'and you've got plenty of space. What are you going to do with it all?'

Although having the same number of rooms as my place in Brixton it was altogether more spacious and uncluttered.

'I'll think of something,' she replied with a twinkle. 'Now sit there and read this while I finish getting lunch.'

She indicated a chair and handed me a crumpled sheet of A4 paper.

'Yes ma'am.'

'It's going to be very simple. Next time I'll prepare you something more elaborate.'

She took herself off to the kitchen, which was connected to the living room by a doorless doorway, and proceeded to bang pans and plates, run taps and strike matches in a businesslike sounding way. I settled myself down comfortably and glanced over the sheet she had passed me. It didn't seem to be of any interest at all: just a listing of the staff and post graduate students in the Centre under the various research group headings; their qualifications and positions within the organisation. The whole thing just about filled both sides of the page.

'What the hell am I supposed to make of this?' I called out to her.

She laughed. 'I didn't think anything of it either until Karl found it among my papers. He was fascinated by it, even made a copy for himself.'

I turned to it again. It had a header in small type I hadn't noticed the first time which read: Security classification 3: not to be shown to anyone outside the Goldburg Centre.

'Top secret, I see,' I called out to her.

'Yes.' She laughed again. 'It took Karl quite a while to realise why that was so.'

On hearing that I read on with concentration. The thing that certainly would have delighted Karl was the abundance and variety of job titles, which given the modest size of the work force, if you could call it that, was patently absurd. There were a great many leaders, managers and heads of one sort and another: project leaders, group managers, section heads – other binary combinations (group leader, project manager, etc.) not being ruled out. But if that wasn't enough, and it clearly wasn't, each of these impressive looking designations was at risk of being overshadowed by a similar one with the word senior, even occasionally principal, tacked on to its front end. The rear ends could also be subject to embellishment, generally along the lines of 'with special responsibility for: security, information retrieval, . . . , putting the cat out!' So although conferment of the title 'project leader' could well stir the heart of the recipient's mother, within the organisation itself it represented a status almost as close to the bottom of the pile as it was possible to get.

Yes, Karl would certainly have loved it. But why on earth had it taken him 'quite a while' to uncover the reason for the security classification. It would have fitted in perfectly with his view of Grandison's general paranoia. Another explanation – that it could provide a source of ridicule to outsiders – had to be ruled out as this would clearly not have occurred to whoever it was that had drawn the thing up. I put these points to Daniela, calling to her through the open doorway – at which she then appeared, large spoon and dishcloth in hand.

'There's no way you are going to find out just by looking at it. Karl suspected something, but then had to go off and make enquiries. I'll tell you. It's because many of the qualifications shown there are bogus.'

She vanished for a moment, then came over empty handed and pointed to the name of a senior section leader near the top of the list:

'He hasn't got a PhD. Apparently he started out on one at Imperial, but packed it in after a few months. And that one there . . .

and that one.'

'Why on earth should they do that?' I couldn't imagine what possible purpose it could serve. 'People inside must know about it.'

'You just can't imagine the atmosphere in there. They're incredibly sensitive about qualifications and things like that, mainly because many of the senior people haven't got any to speak of. It wouldn't matter if they were any good, but most of them aren't. And then they get bright, well-qualified people coming in. People they're relying on to do the work – to plan it even, to come up with the ideas. It's no wonder they feel insecure. So they retreat into this self-important fantasy world in which they invent all these management structures and put themselves at the top, so nobody can say they're not in control. They're no better than that lot at Coventry, most of them.'

I could see the influence of Karl in this. Perhaps something in my expression gave this away because she went on:

'Karl says it's like much of industry: Unilever, ICI, the rest of them. People there don't get promoted for technical ability. What they call management skills are all that count in those places. And then the managers are so busy managing and manoeuvring their way up the ladder and greasing the rungs for their rivals that they soon lose what little technical skill they ever had. That's one of the reasons why so little original work ever comes out of those places, in spite of all the talent they recruit. Karl thinks the universities could be going the same way. And now,' she broke off abruptly, 'it's time for some lunch, it's just about ready.'

We sat opposite each other at a small table against the wall, under the window. She had produced a casserole containing a delicious spicy lamb concoction with a variety of vegetables and a bowl of fluffy white rice. Despite her protestations it had obviously taken some time to prepare. No sooner had we exchanged the obligatory buon appetitos and started eating than she jumped up, rushed to the kitchen and returned with an opened bottle of chilled white wine. We talked happily about this and that as we ate and drank; and then I remembered that an interesting looking lunchtime play was to be showing at a theatre pub in Islington the following week, so we made a date for Tuesday. That seemed a long way off, and I was wondering whether to suggest something for the weekend when she told me she had been invited to stay in Sussex with some relations of Karl's I didn't know about: she would be leaving some time on Saturday, returning late Sunday night or Monday morning. This was in some ways a relief. Things appeared to be moving towards a point of irreversible change in our relationship: a jump to an altogether different plane with no way back. Although part (most, all) of me wanted this, something underneath was applying the brakes – not to bring progress to a halt, just to slow it down a bit. This was partly to do with prolonging the safe period of blissful anticipation before the leap, partly to do with Karl, partly out of fear that what was to follow would fail to live up to expectations: would I be a disappointment to her as a lover? as a companion even? The image of Julie floated up from somewhere, hovered around for a while, and then, with some effort, got pushed back to where it had come from.

A little later, to end a brief and not at all uncomfortable period of silence, I told her about the scene I had witnessed outside the Centre that morning involving the security guards and Miss Brown. I did this with the intention of raising a chuckle, but instead provoked an indignant outburst at the heightened security within the Centre itself following the leak of the cancer-breakthrough story.

'Where are they saying the leak came from now,' I asked when I got the chance.

'Oh, from Sean. All of a sudden nobody's in any doubt about that; they're all trying to give the impression they knew about it all along. Sean is quite bullet proof though . . . got everyone eating out of his hand . . . been promoted . . . got his own office . . . and a ground floor laboratory key.'

When I looked puzzled at this last item, she explained that only a limited number of people working in the Centre had official access to the laboratories on the ground and basement floors; and that the main route to these was from the reception area on the first floor, via a door and stairway under the suspicious, ever-watchful eye of Miss Brown. Another more convenient route ran down from the middle of the main first floor corridor, along which were strung out the secretarial offices, common rooms, library and the other general facilities with which the Goldburg Centre was lavishly endowed. The most direct way in from the street, however, was via a door off the main entrance hall on the ground floor – completely bypassing Miss Brown – to which only a very few senior staff members possessed a key. Sean was now numbered among these elite, an unprecedented departure from established practice in view of his lowly formal position in the eyes of his employer, Prince of Wales College. Within the Centre itself, however, he had become overnight – and without so much as a whisper to the college authorities – a principal section leader with special responsibility for something impressive, which Daniela couldn't recall. His behaviour, according to her, had become more obnoxious than ever, every action redolent of his new-found role of star researcher, fulfilling at last the promise and expectations of the whole Goldburg enterprise.

As to be expected, this meteoric rise left many members of the Centre with cause for disgruntlement, exacerbating the rumbling discontent felt over the precipitous closure the day before, for reasons of supposed security, of the route to the ground floor labs from the first floor corridor. The door to this also required a key, issued to the substantial number of persons authorised to use it. Over the years, however, many unapproved copies had found their way into general circulation throughout the Centre, effectively rendering access open to all those who wished to avail themselves of it. Now this perceived breach in security had been closed, forcing those working on the bottom two floors to face a disapproving and aesthetically repugnant scrutiny by Miss Brown, not only on entering and leaving the building but several times throughout the course of the working day.

Added to this, the displacement of a furious senior group head from his private office to a shared one with a mere section leader in order to make way for Sean, together with the fact that a good number of group and section leaders had been around longer and felt they had achieved more than Sean, had the effect of bringing the normally docile establishment to something approaching a state of minor rebellion.

In response to this simmering dissent, Grandison had circulated a letter which came close to apologising for the inconvenience caused by the temporary closure of the access route to the ground floor laboratories. It went on to point out that recent developments, of overwhelming importance for the prestige and future advancement of the Goldburg Centre, had highlighted the necessity for tightened security in these areas, and that work was already underway for the installation of a check point alongside the first floor access door: a cabin which would house a security guard throughout normal working hours. This letter had done little to quell the discontent.

Daniela had also gleaned that problems had arisen regarding the manning of the proposed check point – a predominantly glass walled structure – as a result of the strictly no-smoking policy in operation in all parts of the Centre. College security personnel were sixty-a-day men, almost without exception (in full accord with Karl's conjecture concerning their true function), and Trowbridge had been given the job of resolving this intractable problem. This he was proposing to do by treating their cabin in the established manner for laboratory fume cupboards – used for dealing with noxious chemicals. That is to say, by connecting it to the ventilation duct which subjected the effluent from all these units to an elaborate cleaning process, prior to its discharge into the London atmosphere. Predictably enough, he was encountering difficulties with the college's health and safety authorities. His demeanour, dour at the best of times, was now showing signs of severe strain. What possible objection any rational being could have to the containment of a security guard in a fume cupboard was, he had been heard to complain, quite frankly beyond him.

Speculation on this and related difficulties, and on the delight they would have afforded Karl, continued for a while. Time was running on and the business of moving some furniture around, my supposed reason for being there, had still to be considered. This eventually turned out to involve no more than a minor rearrangement of the bedroom furniture in order to make way for a desk from the living room – all accomplished within a few minutes. Then it was time to go. The washing up, she insisted, could wait until she got back after dropping me off. She had a number of other things to sort out in the flat. No, she was adamant on this point, there was no question of my making my own way to college: she wanted to drive me there. With feigned reluctance, I agreed.

Karl's sports car was quite new: a red MG with a lot of wood and leather inside and a soft top which, if it hadn't been November in London, would have been rather nice to fold down. Daniela looked superb behind the wheel, her hair – which she had worked on for only a relatively short time before leaving the flat – set in an appropriately wind blown fashion.

'You'll tell me won't you,' she had said ominously as we set off, 'if I start driving on the wrong side of the road.'

After that troubled start I had no further worries. She negotiated the traffic quite expertly, and in no time at all we were over Waterloo Bridge, round Russell Square and heading down Gower Street. The lights at the Store Street junction changed conveniently to red as we approached, providing an opportunity for me to slip out, as I then said I would, just a few yards from the college gates.

Then it happened. I put it down at the time to an accident brought about by my clumsiness. On later reflection it appeared just possible that Daniela could have had a hand in it. Whether one way or the other, the how and the why of it, really didn't matter at all. It was simply the fact of it happening that did. On an impulse, as I was poised to leave the car, it came to me that it would be a good idea to kiss Daniela's cheek, in more or less the way Italians are always doing that sort of thing to each other for no particular reason. Although strictly true, that 'more or less' is misleading. What I had in mind was undoubtedly more, but only marginally so. The actual occurrence, however, went well beyond the bounds of intention, amounted to a brake failure of mammoth proportions. With one hand on the door handle, I had swivelled in the seat to make my innocent move. At the critical moment, Daniela must have turned her head towards me, perhaps to say goodbye. The net effect was that my lips, instead of encountering firm chaste flesh, met hers: soft, moist, parted. She made no attempt to pull away and nor did I – not until the lights had changed and a car behind had sounded its horn. Then I tumbled out, slammed the door and watched in a trance as a red sports car driven by a beautiful wild girl accelerated with a throaty roar towards Covent Garden.

The next thing I remembered was sitting at my empty desk, staring into space, vaguely aware that I should be preparing for my lecture to final year engineers but having no inclination whatsoever to do anything about it. I must have stayed that way till close on four o'clock when the phone rang.

'Hallo,' said a soft familiar voice, which could have materialised from the intensity of my feelings.

'Hallo.'

'How are you?' This in a purr, almost.

'Good . . . stunned . . . I don't know. I've been sitting here at my desk, not able to do a thing.'

'Good . . . just think of me then.'

'That's what I'm doing. I can't think of anything else.'

'I'm just thinking of you too. I don't know how I got home. Just that I needed to . . . to call you.'

That fearful leap which I had been wanting to delay (wanting to make) had happened on its own, driven by forces quite outside my control. I was there in unfamiliar territory, a little stunned, confused, but more or less in one piece. Something uncomfortable was coming back to me through the haze, seeping up from the previous level, something that had to be faced:

'What about Karl?' I asked.

Silence.

'You and Karl, Daniela. What about you and Karl?'

'You fool.' She said this softly, affectionately, as one might to a child being unexpectedly slow in resolving a simple puzzle. 'Are you blind? Can't you see anything at all?'

As I was searching for something to say in reply she hung up.

I somehow got through my lecture and returned to my room. I would have phoned Daniela but had foolishly failed to note her number. There was no way to get it now. The best thing appeared to be to stay put. Maybe she would assume I would do that and phone again. To fill a space I got on with the short paper, continuing from where I had left off. It was all downhill now and soon I was lost in it, galloping towards the conclusion. I would finish it over the weekend, send it off first thing Monday morning.

Eight o'clock and still no call from Daniela. Perhaps I had offended her by bringing up the business of Karl. Perhaps the spell was broken and she would want no more to do with me. I couldn't believe that. But then I didn't know what to believe. What did she mean by 'Can't you see anything?'? We were talking about her and Karl. At least I was. What was it I couldn't see?

I collected up some things to take back with me. Maybe I would call at her flat, or maybe call in at the Goose and then go home. I couldn't decide. The Engineering Science block was deserted as I made my way through its corridors and out into the cold night air. On approaching the corner of the Goldburg Centre I saw three figures progressing slowly from the its main entrance, our paths set to converge by the fountain. One was obviously Grandison, another, almost as obviously, Hardcastle. The third, walking between them and doing all the talking with a great deal of emphasis and arm waving, was younger and not immediately recognisable. I veered to the right to avoid direct collision, turning to give a polite nod and a 'good evening' as I passed them. To my surprise this elicited an animated response from the third member of the group:

'Good heavens, it's Paul Harrison, isn't it?' And when I stopped to face him: 'Remember me? Barry . . .'

'Barry Skinner! God, it must be twenty years.'

It was indeed twenty years since we had left school together to go our separate ways: I to Manchester to read mathematics and physics, he to Oxford on a classics scholarship – which signified a stupendous achievement for a boy from St John's. We had met a few times as undergraduates but already moved in quite different circles. Then I took off for California, he for the City, and we lost touch. I had heard a number of rumours of his outstanding success as a business consultant, later in public relations. And although it occurred to me from time to time to try to make contact I had somehow never got round to it. Our exchanges continued for a while, with Hardcastle and Grandison showing increasing signs of irritation at being sidelined. At one point Hardcastle attempted to terminate this untimely interruption of serious business by cutting in with a 'well now, we must be getting along', or something of that sort, but Barry paid him about as much attention as he would have a small child tugging at his trouser leg. Something told me it would be prudent to bring things to a close, so I suggested we met soon to catch up on each other's lives in a leisurely fashion. As he was handing me his card, he turned with a twinkle in his eye to Hardcastle:

'You're witnessing a historic occasion, you know. The meeting after more than twenty years of three contenders for the very first Pius XII award.'

Grandison had turned white, beads of perspiration forming on his brow in spite of the cold. Hardcastle's expression had hardened yet further on discovering himself the only one left out of the secret. He had no idea what was going on and didn't like to be in that position. He didn't like it at all.

'Now, who do you suppose won?' Barry asked him.

Chapter 10

It is twelve years ago now, and some twelve years after he left St John's with the Pius XII award and a couple of mediocre A-levels, that Grandison was to re-enter my life. I had never expected to hear anything of him again. His re-emergence was totally unexpected and, as at that angst-ridden school prize day, decidedly welcome. The setting this time was to be a conference centre in the town of Davos, in the Swiss Alps.

I had finished my PhD at Franklin a few months before and was continuing to work there on a related topic, generously funded from one of Karl's many research contracts. He was to chair a session at the Davos conference in which he had invited me to give a ten minute presentation. In recompense for this I was to receive: an all-expenses-paid week at an exclusive Swiss resort, staying in a luxury hotel noted for its cuisine; a return flight to Europe, which would enable me to visit family and friends in England; and the opportunity to mix with a number of key players in the research area in which I was hoping to find a place for myself. Not, it seemed to me, an alto-gether bad deal. The conference was to open with a formal dinner on a Sunday evening. Karl's session was to be the first, due to start early the following day and end with a post-lunch discussion, leaving most of the afternoon and evening free for poster sessions and what the organisers termed 'informal interactions between participants'. This was to be the pattern for all five sessions, a civilised arrangement with which I could find no fault at all.

I checked into the hotel on the Saturday, in time for a long sleep and some degree of body clock adjustment following the long flight over from Los Angeles. By two o'clock on the Sunday afternoon I had completed the registration formalities and had selected a few slides to show the following day in the course of my presentation: an abbreviated account of a seminar I had already given three times in the United States. Through the window of my impeccably appointed room the snow capped mountains shone brilliantly in the May sunshine. I had intended spending the afternoon exploring the footpaths leading up to them, but in a late change of plan decided instead to check out the swimming pool and sauna in the hotel basement, to which I had seen a bouncy group of trendy young women heading a few minutes before. In view of my recent emergence from the status of impoverished student, it is unsurprising that I was feeling well pleased with myself as I prepared to set off. Then the phone rang.

It was Reception asking if I would accept a call from a Mr Sikorski. After some persuasion I agreed to be put through. It turned out to be Karl, calling from what sounded like Nicaragua, though given the state of the line could just possibly have been the Inner Hebrides. The important thing, which I grasped pretty quickly, was that he would not be in Davos the following morning. Would I mind terribly chairing the session for him? I was hardly in a position to refuse. He would be boarding a plane from wherever he was to Zurich that night and hoped to be in Davos by midday – in time for his half hour presentation, which was scheduled to follow mine at the end of the morning session. If, for some reason, he failed to show up '. . . feel free to carry on for as long as you like'. Thank you!

This was to be my first experience of a major international research meeting. The sessions were to be chaired by persons of indisputable distinction, and the participant list positively bristled with eminent practitioners from all parts of the world. Those in Karl's session were to include a number of high-profile luminaries, including the renowned physicist Anton Baskovich, a prickly émigré

Russian, now settled in Princeton, notorious for his intolerance of anyone and anything that failed to live up to his exacting standards of decorum and scientific rigor. With a muttered oath and sinking heart, I threw my swimming trunks back into the wardrobe and opened the massive volume of conference proceedings, which had been issued to me on registration. Turning initially to my contribution near the end of the opening section, I was reassured to confirm that it appeared to read quite well, the arguments clearly developed and easy enough to follow. Perhaps, on second thoughts, too easy. Could it come over as trivial before this high-powered gathering? This nagging doubt was to intensify as I turned to the preceding entry by Baskovich. Even the title was completely incomprehensible to me, and the introductory section – which, according to the organisers' guidelines, should set out the background to the work in terms readily intelligible to the non-specialist – lost me by the second line. In dismay, I contemplated the prospect of leading the discussion on it in about twenty hours time. The chances of the oral presentation clarifying matters appeared remote: more likely the reverse.

In a cold sweat, I thumbed back through the remaining papers. Though on the whole less obviously opaque than Baskovich's, each would require at least several hours' deciphering, which was presumably what all the other session chairmen had been doing for weeks – though probably not Karl. The bastard! I could just picture his impromptu liaison with the wife of a Nicaraguan oil magnate, or a crofter's daughter on the Isle of Skye: 'No need to rush, my dear. Harrison will take care of things in Davos.' Sullenly, I vowed to get even with him.

The session was to open with a keynote address by Charles Lauder of Prince of Wales College in London, where Karl held a chair. I remembered meeting him briefly some months before when he visited Karl at Franklin. The participant list referred to him as 'Director of the Goldburg Centre', an institution which meant next to nothing to me at the time. His paper, though not in my field at all, looked impressive enough. From what I knew of him, I felt reasonably confident that he would get the session off to a good start. At least that was something. Settling myself at the majestic leather topped desk by the side of the window, and opening the weighty volume of proceedings at the entry following Lauder's, I prepared to defile the heavily embossed vellum writing sheets provided by the hotel management for just such eventualities.

My increasingly desperate attempts to get to grips with the session texts were twice interrupted by telephone calls from the conference office: the first to confirm my willingness to stand in for Karl, who had apparently informed them of this arrangement before asking me; the second to tell me that one of my scheduled speakers, a Dutchman, had cabled to say he would not be attending – in protest at American military intervention in some southern African state. As the conference had been organised by a United States professional body, he felt this an appropriate gesture of disapproval, and enclosed a statement to this effect which he requested be read out at the meeting. His had been one of the three papers I had been making some sort of headway with, having given up on Baskovich's and a Japanese contribution, which so far as I was concerned could just as well have been left in the native language. Things were getting worse. In addition to my problems with technical matters, a hole had now opened up in the programme in addition to that left by Karl, who I very much doubted would make it in time. In smouldering irritation, I added Dutch to Japanese and Russian in my list of least favoured nationalities, leaving the definition of Russian flexible enough to accommodate wherever it was that Karl's ancestors hailed from. Then I tried to contact Lauder, thinking he might welcome some extra time for his opening address, but was informed by Reception that he had not yet checked in.

At the dinner that evening I found myself among a small group, which included Baskovich and another of the speakers of my session who treated him with an obsequiousness bordering on pure farce.

Ignoring completely the rest of us seated around the small table, they communicated together in a curiously one sided manner: the one staring straight ahead, laying down the law on whatever came to mind; the other simply conveying unqualified agreement by means of sharp intakes of breath, contorted facial expressions, muttered phrases of horror and delight, pronounced noddings and shakings of the head, and very probably other bodily manifestations of which I was thankfully unaware. At one point, fairly early on, in what appeared a natural break in this performance, I sought to introduce myself and explain the changed circumstances of our session – only to be cut short by Baskovich with a contemptuous 'we know all about that' and a horrified look from his companion at my temerity in addressing the great man uninvited.

I think it was at this point in the evening that my anxieties peaked, thereafter to subside rapidly as I adjusted to the situation and concentrated instead on the sumptuous banquet being laid before us. This compliance with the stream of events was helped along by the abundant supply of fine wines which accompanied the courses and the conviviality of other members of the group at my table. Some way into the feast, I began to feel sufficiently relaxed to start re-counting the difficulties I was having with my session, due to start in less than twelve hours, making slighting reference to the incomprehensibility of certain of the contributions. This seemed to go down well enough with my new found companions, one or two of whom promised to help out by contributing actively to the discussions scheduled to follow the individual presentations, whether they understood a word of them or not. I was feeling very much better by now. Then, as I basked in the happy realisation that all my previous anxieties had been groundless, I became aware that Baskovich had abandoned the pretence that I didn't exist and was levelling a menacing gaze in my direction. Well sod it, I decided as I helped myself to another generous measure of chateau whatever-it-was that accompanied the seventh course, it's only a bloody talking shop anyway. What the hell do I care.

I awoke early the next morning in a mood of blissful serenity which lasted about three seconds. It was followed by the feeling that someone was inflating my head with a bicycle pump, which I recognised as a symptom of mild alcoholic poisoning, best remedied by further sleep. Then, in a surge of panic, I remembered what day it was, and that in less than two hours the episode which could well end in my abject humiliation and blight my future career was due to start. I lay still for a while, trying to gather my thoughts. There was something that had occurred to me as I drifted into sleep the previous night: a further complication which I had somehow managed to push aside. Now it was bothering me again, though I couldn't remember what it was. Then it came to me: Lauder! Lauder was not at the dinner. I entered the bathroom trying to convince myself that he must have been there, that I'd just been too drunk or preoccupied with other things to notice. And anyway, even if he had missed the dinner, there was no reason to conclude he would fail to turn up for his presentation, certainly not without informing the conference organisers.

I was in the shower, covered from head to foot in soap, when the phone rang, eliciting a Pavlovian response of profound apprehension. Leaving a trail of suds across the plush carpet, I answered it to learn that Lauder had been in a motoring accident on his way to Houston airport the previous morning. The circumstances were still unclear. What there was no doubt at all about, however, was that he would not be attending the conference.

'My God!'

There was something else as well. The secretary from the organisers' office appeared hesitant, as though not quite sure how to put what it was she had to say. It seemed they had received a letter from Professor Baskovich concerning 'the, er . . . arrangements for the session'. It now appeared unlikely that he would be participating.

'I see.'

'We realise this must be very difficult for you, Dr. Harrison. If there's anything we can do to help . . . please do let us know.'

'Thank you.'

So that was it. It was worrying about Lauder, of course; but from the way the information came across it seemed that his condition could not have been all that serious. My session, on the other hand, appeared terminally damaged: no keynote, no Karl, no bloody Dutchman, now no Baskovich, and that very probably meant no his sycophantic disciple. For the eight slots in the programme I had inherited the day before, three speakers remained: a woman from Stanford, the inscrutable Japanese and me. I went over to the window and opened the curtains. The sun was just clearing the distant peaks, the sky blue and cloudless – a perfect day for an early ascent into those mountains; a path to them curved beckoningly out of the hotel grounds immediately below.

After that desperate low, everything changed so fast that my brain for the most part ceased to respond at a conscious level. I performed the tasks required of me blindly, like an automaton, devoid of all feeling. Later I was to learn that this came over as cool competence in adversity, the sort of thing soldiers under fire get awarded medals for.

On emerging from the lift, my mind focussed fully on the problem of locating a cup of coffee, I was met by an agitated conference secretary who had apparently called my room the moment after I had left it. A message had arrived from the Goldburg Centre in London to say that a stand-in for Lauder was on his way and would be arriving at any moment to deliver the keynote address for my session. A mental image of a parachute descending on the hotel lawn tried briefly to gain a hold, only to be rejected with a stern rebuke that this was no time for flippancy. In the meantime, I was to repair to the conference hall to check over the facilities and brief the technician there on the particular requirements of the speakers. I arrived to find Baskovich and his partner of the night before belabouring this unfortunate being with how and when, and in response to what indications, he was to switch on or off which particular device. They glanced up when they heard me arrive, then down again with no sign of acknowledgement. Close by, the Japanese participant stood patiently waiting his turn to add to the poor man's confusion, his arms wilting under the weight of the full mass of conference literature, together with a large quantity of other material with which he was presumably proposing to enliven his presentation. When I went over to introduce myself he smiled broadly and said something which I didn't understand at all but took to be a greeting of some sort, perhaps in Japanese. I smiled and nodded in return, but he repeated what he had just said, his expression quite serious now, and stood looking at me, obviously expecting a reply. I made as though to give one; then, with a great show of noticing my watch, and a gasp, and an 'Oh my God . . . sorry . . . back in a moment,' I hurried from the hall – where things seemed to be sorting themselves out perfectly well without me.

I was quite unaware of the name of Lauder's replacement, speeding on his way to Davos that morning. My first reaction on seeing him from a distance was of shock at his acutely enfeebled state, followed by a wave of selfish concern that he would not be fit enough to deliver his imminently scheduled forty minute address. His uniformed driver helped him out of the black limousine and then hesitantly, with pauses after every two or three steps, into the hotel lobby, where I was waiting to greet him along with John Ogden, the conference chairman. The impression created was of a terminally ill aristocrat being returned to his stately home to die. Then a chord struck and I knew that I had seen him before somewhere, long ago and in a different universe.

His first words resonated with his worn out appearance and the drama of his mission:

'He's dead. Lauder is dead.'

Simultaneous with the shock of this announcement came my realisation of who he was:

'Grandison! Nigel Grandison. What on earth are *you* doing here?'

It must have seemed a particularly stupid and callous thing to say in the circumstances, and Ogden, who had known the name of Lauder's replacement from the onset, gave me a strange look as he took his arm and tried to lower him into a commodious armchair. This attempted manoeuvre had a revitalising effect on Grandison who broke free with unsuspected vigour, complaining loudly that to sit so low would cause untold damage to his already severely injured back. He demanded a high, rigid, straight backed chair – which the ever accommodating hotel staff produced from the banqueting hall – on which he then sat, on high like a pope in audience. Ogden, who knew Lauder well and was clearly shaken by the news of his death, soon made his excuses and left. In ten minutes he was due to open the sessions, after which it would be up to me – and Grandison.

Time was short and there were things that needed saying:

'It's terrible about Lauder, terrible for his family. I met him just a few months ago when he visited Karl Dembowski at Franklin. Quite an extraordinary person. It's just terrible.'

'He was a great man.'

Grandison said this in a way which indicated that the matter was now closed, that there were things of a more pressing nature that needed attention. I suppose I should have been grateful.

'Now, make sure you introduce me as *Deputy Director* of the Goldburg Centre.'

'As you wish.'

'You'll find my slides over there.' He indicated to where his driver was standing, patiently waiting, holding a bulging briefcase. 'They're in order. Please see to it that they're shown that way when I ask for them.'

'I'll do my best.'

'And now I need to use the bathroom.'

As I escorted him there it seemed appropriate to broach another matter which was vying for attention in my mind with the news of Lauder's death:

'This is an incredible coincidence, you know. The last time I saw you was more than ten years ago . . . at St John's . . . when you got the Pius XII award.'

He stopped and turned to me.

'I'm sorry Harrison . . .'

For a moment I thought he was going to deny all knowledge of the event, or perhaps attribute it to a twin brother, also by the name of Nigel; but then he went on:

'. . . but I'm going to have to leave straight after my presentation. I've a number of important appointments in Switzerland before my flight back to London this evening.'

Maybe he hadn't heard me.

The conference got underway in an unusual manner, as was to be expected under the exceptional circumstances. The opening oration started off with the announcement of Lauder's death and a moving tribute to him, followed by a two minutes silence in his memory. He had been a popular figure, well known to many in the audience. The atmosphere in the hall was one of numbed stillness. Ogden went on to express his gratitude to Grandison for his efforts, in spite of severe ill health, in making the arduous journey to deliver the first keynote presentation. He even managed to get in a thank-you for me for filling in for Karl, swallowing the fact that in the limited time at my disposal I had managed to insult both the great Baskovich and Grandison, all but inducing the former to withdraw his participation.

Grandison's keynote was completely out of keeping with the manifestly theoretical nature of the whole conference and bore no relation whatsoever to Lauder's written contribution. But in view of the special circumstances outlined by Ogden, and the speaker's sickly condition, it was received in polite silence and elicited a few bland, not overtly unfriendly, comments in the otherwise virtually empty discussion period that followed.

The format was that of a company promotional presentation, rather than an address to a scientific gathering. A great many slides were shown of the Goldburg Centre: its laboratories, conference rooms, recreational areas, even the forbidding portrait of Ebenezer Goldburg in the foyer. An impressive looking roll of the Centre's sponsors was displayed, which gave no indication, however, of the nature or extent of their contributions. (One of them, according to Karl, when he heard of it later, consisted of a self portrait by the wife of the chairman of the company concerned, elaborately framed at the Centre's expense and displayed in a corridor, facing the women's lavatory.) Then followed a series of lists: of staff and postgraduate students with their qualifications and positions within the organisation; of past, current and projected research projects; of publications and conference presentations; and a mass of impenetrable statistics.

To round things off, he gave an account of what he claimed to be a typical example of the sort of things they got involved with. It concerned a drug for the treatment of a common, frequently fatal heart condition: slides of ambulances, hospital casualty admissions, green clad figures in operating theatres. Then the fundamental research: figures, in white coats this time, looking intently down microscopes and at banks of test tubes and at wiggly lines on video screens. Then the engineering drawing offices, industrial plant and, finally, rows of little yellow tablets in bottles. The only potentially contentious moment came when someone asked him, quite innocently, what exactly the Goldburg Centre's role had been in this enterprise. Through a cloud of vague references to consulting advice and secondment of students, the answer came over as precious little. The questioner – embarrassed at having inadvertently stirred things up, perhaps contributed to the visually evident deterioration in the speaker's physical condition – let it go at that, as did the rest of the assembled company. I thanked Grandison warmly from the chair, and to measured applause he once again moved slowly and painfully out of my life.

After that the session progressed better than I could ever have imagined possible, even discounting my gloom ridden premonitions. Speaker after speaker held the attention of the crowded hall, with animated discussion following each delivery. Even the Japanese contribution came over quite well: the clarity and detail of the projected images largely making up for the total incomprehensibility of the spoken accompaniment. With mixed feelings, I came to appreciate the brilliance of Anton Baskovich. His presentation bore no resemblance whatsoever to the impenetrable text in the conference proceedings – which, it seemed, he had simply dug up from somewhere in order to meet the publisher's deadline. Instead, he ranged freely over aspects of his highly original approach to his current area of research, drawing out links with recent experimental findings – including some reported for the first time in the earlier presentations of the session. The applause that followed his final, flamboyant disclosure was long and heartfelt, only to be eclipsed by that shortly to be accorded Karl – who had arrived in triumphant mood halfway through Baskovich's delivery.

It was with an exquisite feeling of relief that I left the podium, right on schedule, to give my talk: the brief description of a key finding arising from my work at Franklin, which Karl insisted I should publicly lay claim to. One way and another, I just couldn't believe my luck.

Chapter 11

The information initially transmitted to the Goldburg Centre from the hospital in Houston was incorrect: Charles Lauder did not die. The error was perhaps understandable, given the severity of his injuries. He appeared as good as dead on admission, well beyond hope of resuscitation and repair. His survival was due entirely to the enthusiastic intervention of the young medics on duty at the time, eager for early experience of massive surgical procedures, which in the normal course of events would not have come to them till much later in their careers. It was this, rather than any hope of saving Lauder, which drove their actions: to their surprised delight, he pulled through. When fit enough to be moved, he was transferred to another hospital in Texas, and from there, several months later, to a specialist rehabilitation centre in North Carolina. Some eighteen months after the accident, he was able to return to London, resigned to the fact that he would be in need of constant care for the rest of his life. In this respect at least he was fortunate in having a wife willing and capable of fulfilling that role, and an insurance settlement more than adequate to provide for all his financial needs.

From the moment news of the accident reached him, Grandison lost no time in consolidating his hold over affairs. It seemed as if he had been preparing for this moment for years, ardently cultivating Hardcastle, and progressively stepping up the impression that he was the one to reckon with so far as dealings with the Centre were concerned. The fact of his technical naivety only rarely impeded this perception: it represented the norm for many of the more senior people in industry and posed no problem at all with Hardcastle. For the previous two years, Grandison had taken to sending him regular monthly progress reports of the Centre's activities: one side of A4, plenty of spaces, bold headings and nothing in the text liable to cause more than a moment's hesitation to the non-specialist reader; little of any real significance, but plenty of optimistic projections, of links, however tenuous, with pressing problems of the day – just what Hardcastle wanted to hear about and make use of for his own purposes. Though supposedly intended for his eyes alone, the existence of these 'Grandisheets' had become common knowledge and a source of cynical amusement within those departments having interests that overlapped with those of the Centre. To them, the work of Lauder and his immediate associates was what counted there: Grandison, with his far-fetched schemes and machinations, representing no more than an irrelevant – at times amusing, at times irritating – side show. Outside the college, however, a very different picture was emerging.

Lauder and Grandison made an oddly contrasting couple. Although getting on for fifteen years older, Lauder appeared the more youthful, dressed and behaved more casually and exuded an air of fitness and health. He had been a superb athlete in his youth, and in his mid-forties still played a formidable game of tennis and was virtually unbeatable on the college squash courts. Grandison, at thirty, dressed and comported himself as the frail elder statesman, reluctantly prevailed upon to come out of retirement to guide the country safely through its hour of need. When together, on visits relating to research funding applications and the like, it was Lauder who tended to make the going, with Grandison standing by to nod wisely and inject the occasional sober observation. To some, however, the impression that emerged from these encounters was of the young protégé (Lauder) being prepared for eventual office by his benign superior.

Some months prior to Lauder's precipitous removal from the scene, Grandison adopted the title of Deputy Director. Given the ease with which designations of all sorts flourished in that environment, this passed virtually unnoticed. When it seemed certain that Lauder would be gone forever, and that another director would in time be appointed, Grandison applied successfully to Hardcastle to have this position formalised, thereby protecting his future. By the time Lauder had made his first, tentative appearance back in the Centre, the term Deputy Director had effectively come to signify Chief Executive – in much the way the designation Vice Chancellor implies that role in the university hierarchy. For practical purposes, Grandison had assumed full control.

During the period of Lauder's convalescence, the Goldburg Centre underwent changes in direction and organisation, the emphasis turning yet further to contract research focussed on the specific requirements of companies providing finance – and about time too, in Hardcastle's frequently-stated opinion. Much of this work was of little general interest and unpublishable in the respectable research journals. For this reason, Grandison set his mind to the launching of new journals, furnished with amenable editorial boards, not averse to accepting papers that would have stood no chance of surviving critical peer reviewing. This turned out to be easier than expected, a number of publishing companies realising that they could be on to a good thing with specialist publications dealing with currently popular fields of applied research. All the work, both with regard to the burdensome editorial duties and the writing of the articles themselves, would be undertaken by unpaid academics eager for the honour; and these same academics would persuade the university and industrial libraries throughout the world to take out the costly subscriptions. For the publishers, the prospects appeared almost too good to be true. In a remarkably short space of time Grandison had at his disposal two journals, fully controlled by persons he had carefully manipulated into position: the business of notching up

publications for the Goldburg Centre – an important measure of
academic achievement in certain key quarters – was as good as in
the bag.

Chapter 12

That night, after parting from Hardcastle, Grandison and Barry Skinner, I set off down Store Street in a daze, still unclear what to do – whether to call on Daniela in her new flat or go home. I crossed Tottenham Court Road and, on an impulse, turned north; then, after a few minutes, veered left towards Charlotte Street. It was only when I saw the pub that I knew where I was heading. I used to meet Julie there some evenings when she came off work, and for more than a year had been keeping well clear of it. As I entered, my eyes automatically scanned the room in search of her, my mind in the meantime mocking the absurdity of their presumption. But then I saw her. She was seated some way ahead of me, at a table at which we would often sit together. I would have to walk past her to get to the bar – or else simply turn about and leave. As I was deciding between these alternatives, she looked up and saw me, an expression of horror for an instant clouding her features. Then she recovered, giving me an embarrassed smile. I had no choice now but to come up to her – to them: there was a man with her, smartly dressed, dark skinned – Spanish perhaps, or Italian.

'Hallo Julie.' I felt the need to say something more, to offer some explanation. 'I didn't expect to see you. It's the first time I've been here for over a year.'

I could have gone on but felt I had already said too much. What had possessed me to come? Nothing had been planned. For the second time that afternoon obscure forces had precipitated me into an emotional turmoil.

'It's the first time since then for me too.'

She said this softly, looking straight into my eyes, as though not knowing whether to believe me. It certainly seemed too much of a coincidence if we were both telling the truth. Something of this must have seemed a bit odd to her companion, who was looking puzzled and awkward beside her, the atmosphere thick with unspoken senti-ments. She turned to him:

'This is an old friend of mine: Paul Harrison.'

He stood and offered his hand:

'Gino Tozzi. Pleased to meet you.'

'Gino joined us from the Milan office last week. He's staying a couple of months. It's his first visit to London.'

So this wasn't the person she had left me for. What had become of him? I wondered. There was a sad, strained look about her, not just to do with this meeting: something set, permanent. She was aware I had noticed this. We had lived together for seven years after all, shared everything: our hopes, enthusiasms; our anxieties. There was nothing we could hide from one another – or so I had thought.

'You're looking well.' She said this in response to my gaze, in a tone that suggested more a rebuke than anything else. Then, more warmly, as though apologising for the implied bitterness, 'I'm pleased about that.'

I wanted to get away. For months I had been dreading this en-counter, knowing it would have to take place sooner or later. Seeing that she worked quite close to the college, it was surprising it had taken so long. My feelings, however, were rather different from what I had feared they might be. When she had told me she was leaving I couldn't believe it at first. Then I saw something in her I had never been aware of before: a ruthlessness which would serve her purpose, bring her whatever she wanted, regardless of the cost to anyone else. Gradually this view of her prevailed, shrouding all others. I had expected on meeting her to be dazzled by the fulfilment of her ambition, and fantasised in abject misery on the form this would take. It was absurd, it now seemed to me, to have dismissed all the tenderness and warmth I knew she was capable of as covers for an opportunism awaiting its moment. But that is a consequence of rejection, I suppose: well enough documented throughout the ages by all manner of means, at all possible levels. It's just that some people – this person in particular – never seem to learn. What I was feeling now was a blend of contradictory emotions: an element of the old pain of rejection, sharply rekindled at the moment I saw her sitting there; then a tenderness at her unexpected vulnerability – the sadness about her, at which I felt quite unwarrantedly guilty. But all of this thrown out of focus by what had happened a few hours ago that afternoon: by Daniela.

I said I had to go, looking at my watch in a pathetic gesture to suggest some pressing engagement; then, with a nod both to Julie and her perplexed companion, I prepared to leave.

'I'll call you sometime,' she said as I was turning away.

'Yes, do.'

Somehow I managed to leave the pub without knocking into people or other obstacles, in the manner of the early evening drunkard, still in possession of a bare minimum of control. There was no alternative now but to head straight home.

I made my way on automatic pilot, unaware of performing any of the operations involved in getting on the tube, then off it at Brixton. It was only after I had turned into Coldharbour Lane that a sudden, firm grip on my left arm brought me rapidly to my senses, thinking my moment as victim of street robbery had finally arrived. A gruff voice reassured me:

'Miles away, you were. What you been up to?'

I half turned to take in the gnarled features of Johnny Cremer, dangerous looking as ever, despite the hint of a friendly smile.

'God Johnny, you nearly gave me a heart attack.' And then, as I recovered: 'Good to see you. What brings you over this way?'

We had come up to the Prince, an interesting enough pub in its way, which though just down the road from my flat I had somehow got out of the habit of using. Johnny didn't reply. Instead he made a mock-obsequious, after-you-Your-Honour gesture in the direction of the half open door, and without a moment's hesitation I preceded him through it.

I had first met Johnny Cremer years before, soon after returning to the UK from California, a few weeks before taking up my lectureship at Prince of Wales College. The first flat I moved into then was quite close by, in Acre Lane, a road connecting Brixton to Clapham Common. Practically butting on to the house was a strange pub, which I had taken to visiting at odd hours during the day to interrupt the chores of settling in and working on lecture courses in preparation for my new appointment. The strangeness of the place was largely down to the clientele; but as I was new to the area, had been out of the country for over seven years, and away from London considerably longer, I suppose I imagined them typical of working class South London and didn't give it a thought. Exclusively male, almost exclusively white and hard looking, they formed small groups around the dotted about tables and conversed seriously among themselves, with only the occasional dry laugh and exchange between the separate clusters sounding above the burble. As time went by, I started to receive cool, but not unfriendly, nods of acknowledgement from one or other of the regulars during the few minutes I would spend at the bar over my half of bitter. This had become pretty much a regular feature of daily existence in that limbo between Franklin and the start of my new career, and appeared set to continue un-interruptedly over my remaining weeks of freedom. But then, one afternoon, while waiting for the barman to pull up my beer, I was addressed by someone standing next to me at the counter – a tough, rugged looking individual, a type you certainly wouldn't want to mess with or upset in any way.

'Excuse me asking,' he asked, looking me in the eye, 'but you're a burglar aren't you?'

I laughed at first, thinking it some strange joke; then, from his cold expression, realised it wasn't.

'Afraid not,' I said, trying to still keep smiling. Then, as he continued looking at me in silence: 'I'm a teacher actually, or will be when term starts in a few weeks.' Something told me this was a better job description to admit to in the circumstances than university lecturer.

'Are you *actually*?' he said after an uncomfortable pause, mimicking my accent, or perhaps mocking my choice of word. Then, with a chuckle, his features softened. 'Sorry mate. Here, I'll get this.' And he paid for my drink.

This marked the beginning of an unusual friendship developing between me and Johnny Cremer; and the months that followed saw me gradually accepted – as a token oddity, but accepted nonetheless – by the daytime patrons of The Royal Oak. The Den of Thieves would have been a far more apt name. I had stumbled on what amounted to an exclusive club for professional, medium-time criminals; a place where they could relax, float ideas, plan jobs and regale each other with stories of triumphant past achievements and the misfortunes of absent friends. Another thing I learned was that the Oak was frequented by a number of active police officers, effectively ex officio club members, who mixed business and pleasure in easy association with the regulars: exchanging information, doing deals and generally settling into the cosy social ambience of the place. 'All part of the same outfit, you know. Last thing the pigs want is to start winning the battle against crime.' Johnny professed a good grasp of the overall picture. 'Completely scupper their promotion chances, that would: all that lovely money going to the nurses and fucking teachers – sorry mate, but you know what I mean.'

Johnny had changed little over the years, it seemed as we settled at a table in the Prince: a little lumpier about the eyes perhaps, but hard looking as ever. He claimed to be retired from active service now, to operate solely in an advisory capacity to the trade, 'except for the occasional job for the pigs and cloak-and-dagger merchants.' These, he claimed, enabled him to keep his hand well in on the practical side, to maintain his universally acknowledged pre-eminence as master safe-breaker – now, it appeared, by appointment to Her Majesty's Security Services:

'Did one for them the other week in a posh Mayfair pad. God, you should have seen the stuff there. Nearly made me cry to leave it all behind. No idea what they found inside but they seemed very excited about it. Cleaned up afterwards so nobody would ever know.' He smiled at the recollection, the contented smile of the master craftsman. 'So this way I don't lose me touch and still stay clean. Can't be bad, can it?'

It cheered me up considerably meeting him like this. The Oak had long gone to the dogs, it appeared; the old gang long dispersed. He found the Prince more congenial these days, less in contrast with his changed tastes and lifestyle. Someone joined us after a few minutes, vaguely familiar from the old days I thought, though he didn't acknowledge this, and appeared to be waiting to get Johnny alone, perhaps to tap him for professional advice. I decided to leave them to it; and so, with promises to meet up again in the Prince now that he had transferred his allegiance there, we shook hands and I left.

Chapter 13

The following morning I was in the shower when my door bell rang loudly and continuously. My flat occupies two floors above a baker's shop on a busy stretch of Coldharbour Lane, a hundred yards or so up from Brixton High Road. The front door, sandwiched between a butcher's and the baker's, opens on to a narrow stairway leading up to the rooms. All manner of oddballs feel the need to ring the bell from time to time – one of the many features of the place which greatly displeased Julie when she used to live there. The bell continued to ring so I wrapped myself in a towel and made my way over to the living room window on the first floor, from where I could look down relatively unobserved to see who it was. It was Daniela. A little further down the road, Karl's illegally-parked, gleaming MG was attracting the attention of a group of black youths, standing there gawking, as though trying to decide between vandalising or stealing it. Adjusting the towel a little tighter, I descended the stairway and let her in.

'Uh,' she said as I kissed her cheek, 'I like your outfit. But you're all wet.'

She followed me up the stairs, taking advantage of the situation by tugging at my towel as we went. I thought this a bit unfair of her and turned to tell her so, but she just laughed, so I kissed her again.

'Why did you call me a fool yesterday?' I asked after a bit.

'Because you are, and that's what I've come here to tell you. You wanted to hear about me and Karl, didn't you? Well now you're going to.'

We had somehow reached the top of the stairs.

'I think I had better put some clothes on before I hear any more.'

'I think so too. Brace yourself darling. Prepare for the worst.'

She had never called me darling before. My mind had gone completely dead, a blank sheet waiting to be written on. I pulled on some clothes, then went to join her in the living room.

'It's pretty pokey in here,' she said as I arrived.

'I suppose it is. Thank you for pointing it out.'

She was having difficulty suppressing a fit of the giggles, then came out with it straight away:

'He's my father, you fool. You bloody fool! Are you completely blind?'

Then, unable to control herself any more, she burst out laughing.

'Well . . . why in hell's name . . .why on earth . . .'

Massive perceptual readjustments were called for, which I simply couldn't get my head around.

'I wanted to tell you, but you know Karl, how persuasive he can be. He wanted to see how long it would take you to find out for yourself.'

'The bastard!' I was completely at a loss. All I could think to do was to repeat myself: 'The bastard!' Then, in a concerted attempt at originality: 'The bloody bastard!'

I sat down on the sofa and tried to take stock. It took a while for the implications to sink in. When they did however, I realised that the one seeming obstacle to something serious developing between me and Daniela had completely gone – or rather had never existed in the first place. This didn't immediately come over as something to be grateful for; or, if it did, it was clouded over by something else. She was standing at the window, looking at me, her lips set in a tight, amused smile.

'I feel a complete fool. God, how you must have been laughing at me.'

'No.'

She came over and climbed beside me, knelt there on the sofa and put her arms around me, her cheek against mine. We remained like that for several minutes without moving or saying anything. It started to feel all right, then more than just all right. In the meantime, I found myself going back over everything I had witnessed between her and Karl. It all fitted perfectly with her astounding revelation. So much so that I could well accept her incredulity at my dimness. But of course my knowledge of Karl had to be very different from hers. That photo of her as a child, for example: just the thing you could expect to see on the desk of a devoted father. But the notion of Karl in that role had just never occurred to me. He had always appeared quite devoid of any of the trappings of domesticity – in spite of his three marriages and God knows how many other protracted affairs. Then there was the business of his frequently proffered comforting arm and other signs of affection and support for her, which I had misread: all perfectly in keeping with normal paternal behaviour. The one thing which remained odd, however, was the way they completely avoided each other in college. They would only associate together outside, as though there was something clandestine in their relationship which had to be concealed from colleagues. Anybody seeing them together, and knowing Karl at all, would immediately have drawn the same conclusion I had. Realising this made me feel a little better, provided some excuse for my stupidity.

'Do you want to tell me about anything?' I said after an age. 'What you're doing here in London? . . . Anything?'

She disengaged herself with a sigh, and sat cross-legged next to me on the sofa, appearing sad now, as if my words had opened a wound. I took her hand, she lowered her head on to my shoulder.

'It's a long story. Several stories. You'll hear them all soon I expect. There's no time now. I have to leave in a few minutes for Hassocks.'

'Hassocks?' What on earth was she talking about?

'It's near Brighton. It's where Karl's sister Hilda lives. I'm going there for the weekend. Remember?'

The idea of Karl having a sister living in a place called Hassocks seemed unaccountably funny to me. It showed.

'What are you laughing at? They've lived there for years. Her husband was a colonel in a cavalry regiment. He's retired now.'

It was too much. I threw my head back and started to laugh uncontrollably, the tensions that had built up following her disclosure losing their grip, gushing out with my laughter.

'What's the matter with you?' She had shifted her position and was looking straight at me, her face inches from mine. 'He grows flowers now, sells them to florists in Brighton.'

I took her head in my hands and kissed her: first her lips, then cheeks and nose and eyelids and neck; then the small patch of shoulder that was accessible through her jersey, savouring the smell of her, which permeated through the soft, warm wool: a wondrous blend of perfume and sweat and something else that was unmistakably Daniela. Her hands were on my back now, stroking and pulling me towards her; mine moved down her body, to her waist, her thigh.

'There's no time now,' she said, still holding me tightly. 'There will be soon.'

We remained frozen for a few moments, then slowly, reluctantly disengaged; then stood up and embraced again.

'It won't be long,' she said after a while. 'I'll probably stay down there till Monday. They've got horses. I haven't ridden since coming to England.'

The serene image of her in the saddle gave way for a instant to that of the colonel on his stallion, red faced and furious, charging heedlessly with raised sabre across the downs.

'They're nice really. Didn't approve of me at first, but now it seems they can't do enough for me. They didn't have children themselves. And Karl only had me – so far as I know,' she added with a chuckle. 'They seem to want to sort of adopt me.'

'I've got other plans for you.'

'Well they are going to have to wait.'

We kissed again.

'I really must go now. It won't be long.'

'It will seem forever.'

'Well it isn't, and then we'll have all the time in the world.'

Surprisingly enough, Karl's car was still parked intact where she had left it: not clamped, nor towed away, nor stolen, nor vandalised. She climbed in, and with a wave and a blown kiss set off purposefully for Sussex.

I returned to my living room, sat down and closed my eyes. Everything appeared to be happening at once. There were so many things to think about but the only one taking any sort of hold at all was Daniela. I settled contentedly, wallowing in the contemplation of her. I must have drifted into sleep because the next thing I became of aware of was a jolt of anxiety at the thought of losing her, of whatever it was that was happening between us coming to an abrupt end. How could I possibly hope to keep hold of someone like her? What could I offer in terms of a future together? I looked round the room – its pokiness had been evident enough for her to remark on after the first glance. Julie had come to feel the same way about the place. She had wanted desperately to move. I was the one who had insisted on staying put, my doing so probably contributing significantly to our break up. The alternative would have been to sell up and use the proceeds for a deposit on a house in somewhere like Croyden – and then struggle for ever to pay an immense mortgage for the privilege of living in a cultural desert. We had been happy enough in Brixton, after we had bought the place together some eight years ago. Its position made it unattractive then to most potential buyers, so the price was relatively low. Shortly before the time came for me to buy Julie out, I had been fortunate to come into a modest inheritance from the estate of a distant relative, which just about covered my costs. So that no sooner had I got used to the novel experience of having savings than I had to pass them over to Julie, compounding the bitterness of our separation. At least I could console myself with having ended up with somewhere to live in London, with a small mortgage I could afford: quite a rarity then, as now, for someone on a university teacher's salary.

There is something quite special about life in Brixton which makes almost anywhere else pallid and dull by comparison. Most of the time it's a vibrant, anarchistic melting pot, throbbing with good-natured vitality and colour: the market a bustling island of cultural diversity and free entertainment, the air filled with loud music and irreverent, jocular banter. The mood on the streets can change though, can take on an aspect of foreboding and danger as at the flick of a switch. Street crime is rife, much of it related to the drug trade, the plight of addicts desperate for a fix. In addition to the random targeting of vulnerable individuals, lethal warfare between rival drug gangs was becoming an ever increasing feature of the Brixton streets. Julie and I had lived in Coldharbour Lane long enough to feel part of the scene and therefore relatively safe from the attention of prowling muggers. There is something to be said for this attitude, because an air of confidence, of fitting in, certainly provides some degree of protection. We had never suffered any trouble ourselves, but friends visiting us had. So far as Julie was concerned, the crunch came when her boss and his wife were robbed at knifepoint, in broad daylight, yards from our doorway. He had expressed interest in visiting us to see for himself some of the colourful venues Julie liked to describe to her colleagues. They came up from their country home in Surrey, decked out as though for a visit to the opera. The idea had been to have a drink at our place, then a meal in a local Indonesian restaurant, then on to a gig at the Fridge. They arrived at our door white faced and in shock: minus a Rolex, a diamond broach, some three hundred pounds in cash and all trace of desire for further exposure to ethnic subculture.

I went over to the window and surveyed the street. The betting shop directly opposite was in full swing; the punters, the backs of their heads visible through the top of the painted glass front, juddering excitedly as they watched a relayed event on the video screen. I had once witnessed a police raid on the place: plain clothed officers gathered outside, trying unsuccessfully to look unobtrusive, waiting for the big race to get underway; then, when all inside were fully engaged, storming in to emerge moments later with a huge, struggling, dreadlocked black man, who was bundled unceremoniously into an unmarked vehicle and whisked away before anyone had time to realise what was happening. You don't need television here if you have a taste for that sort of action. Below me, a middle-aged Asian couple were peering intently into the shop next door, the one on the other side of the baker's from the butcher's – not a candlestick maker's, but a place which for over two years had displayed the same scant selection of dull, unfashionable clothing, and was generally regarded locally as a front for something altogether more exotic. I had never seen anyone inside it. As I watched with interest, the couple appeared on the point of ending this unbroken record. Then, as though at a signal, they turned away simultaneously and melted into the passing stream. A few yards across the street to my left, on the corner with Railton Road, a sizeable group of Afro-Caribbeans was gathering noisily, its members jostling with each other outside the pub – the notorious Atlantic –, waiting for it to open. One moment it was a carefree, buoyant scene, marked by raucous laughter and the playful exchange of insults; then, quite suddenly, for no apparent reason, the mood changed, became heavy and threatening, polarising the players into distinct groups, causing passers-by to cross the street, even turn about and hasten anxiously away. I saw a knife appear in someone's hand, the blade glinting in the feeble morning sun; then another. The taunts and insults rained louder, were for real now, the whole scene set to explode. I thought about calling the police, was about to do so in fact, but then the atmosphere began to subside: knives were put away, shouted exchanges declined to the normal level, and the doors of the Atlantic opened to admit its customers.

I couldn't imagine Daniela living here, returning alone at night through the dark streets. Then it occurred to me that I had never felt this concern for Julie, taking it for granted that she would be well able to cope, was in fact immune to such dangers. Remembering her strained appearance of the night before, I felt a spasm of guilt at this, at taking her for granted in general. Her feelings for living here had changed as she had changed: from the game young student I had first met to the woman approaching thirty, seeing life slipping away, watching her contemporaries getting on with the business of raising children, feathering conventional nests in bourgeois suburbs: growing up; settling down. The problem it now seemed had been me all along – at least that was how it had to be in Julie's eyes: I could hardly blame her. It was just that the life she had come to crave was not for me. She had realised this, even if I hadn't, and had taken the necessary action. My injured stance could no longer survive objective scrutiny.

Chastened, my thoughts returned to the present. Where did this introspection leave things now? What possible future could there be for me with Daniela? I could find no answer; it was uncomfortable to dwell upon. Better just to focus on her return to London on Monday and play it from there. The thought of her enveloped me for a while. Then, reluctantly, I moved to my desk and prepared to start work on the final stage of the first of the two papers I was writing with her father.

Chapter 14

Soon after he had been brought back to London, arrangements were made for Lauder to pay his first visit to the Centre. He arrived in the late morning, supported by his wife. A reception committee, consisting of Hardcastle, Grandison, Trowbridge, Miss Brown and other long serving members of the Centre staff, was there to greet him. It was an emotional occasion, if somewhat awkward at first as a result of nobody being quite sure just how to play it. But then Lauder settled himself at his desk; and after thanking everyone for their kindness and support informed them in a trembling voice of his firm intention of gradually resuming his duties as director. This declaration appeared to come as a surprise to Hardcastle, who probably had other plans in mind by then. Under the circumstances, however, he could do little else but join in the general euphoria. Grandison, in particular, was ecstatic, his obvious delight all but overwhelming him. His abiding fear had been of a newly appointed director usurping his painstakingly acquired position. With Lauder back at the perceived helm, his continuing supremacy appeared assured.

Lauder's subsequent actions were true to his words. The following Monday he arrived at the Centre shortly before ten o'clock accompanied by his wife. He made it known that he wished to speak to each of the group leaders in turn in order to become fully conversant with the work in progress. His previous secretary had moved on, and so he appointed another member of the secretarial team to this role – one with whom he had worked well before. At first he came in for two days a week, soon to be extended to three. His scrutiny of the research was turning out to be extremely thorough. Following an introductory meeting with a group leader, he would work his way down the entire group with one-to-one discussions with all its members. These exchanges were long and probing, and copious notes of them were dictated to his secretary, to be later collated into comprehensive reviews. Before the first group had been fully dealt with news of its ordeal travelled rapidly through the others, promoting a great deal of soul searching and frantic preparation. Lauder's mind, it was quite clear, had remained as sharp as ever. His intention, it was equally clear, was to focus it on directing at first hand all aspects of business within the Goldburg Centre. Feelings differed widely on the desirability of this unexpected intervention.

Grandison, in particular, was more than a little put out by Lauder's involvement with the full spectrum of the Centre's activities. He had previously concentrated on those projects with which he had a direct interest – in the main those deriving from the ones he had set up himself soon after his initial appointment. But these had dwindled during his absence, several of the key players having accepted offers from elsewhere. Now it appeared he wished to apply himself more generally – to interfere, so it seemed to Grandison, with everything. 'Why on earth couldn't he just get on with his own academic work as before and leave the rest to me?' he thought.

Another major setback for Grandison concerned his relegation to second fiddle in the unfitness stakes. Throughout his life, he had been accustomed to receiving special consideration and attention as a consequence of his poor health and enfeebled condition. Now this all went to Lauder. It was making Grandison ill. The longer it went on the more ill he became, until it reached the stage where it was difficult to tell from appearances which of the two of them was in the poorer physical state. This didn't seem to help matters at all: Lauder continued to receive all the respect and sympathy for brave persever-

ance in adversity. Grandison felt himself completely sidelined in this regard.

Lauder, in turn, was also far from happy at the situation he was gradually uncovering. The more he probed the more unhappy he became. The powerful theoretical base, from which much of the earlier work of the Centre had stemmed, and on which he had laboured hard in establishing, had all but eroded away. In its place he found a mishmash of projects, which beneath a cloak of high-flown jargon and naive justification amounted to very little indeed. He blamed himself for having allowed things to deteriorate to this level – a process which had clearly started some years before his enforced departure. The embarrassment he felt at his neglect of the broader picture, in favour of what he now saw as self-indulgent absorption in his own scientific work, was all the worse for the dawning realisation that he now lacked the strength to turn things around again.

Other things bothered him too, adding further to his discomfort. There was, for instance, the matter of the Wednesday seminars. Lauder had instituted these soon after his appointment. They had flourished, becoming a key event in the college calendar. Open to anyone, they regularly attracted distinguished visitors from outside, some of whom would travel long distances to attend. Lively discussions would more often than not follow the presentations, which were delivered by carefully chosen visiting academics and scientists from industry, as well as the occasional member of the Centre staff and other departments within the college. These were still operational but had changed beyond all recognition. Now closed to all outsiders, they consisted in the main of bland reports of current experimental investigations by junior researchers. Probing questions involving any hint of criticism of the work were frowned upon in the discussion periods that followed. In fact, it was to stop such, what Grandison felt to be, morale-damaging interventions that the curtains had been drawn. Lauder was horrified at the dullness and smug cosiness that prevailed in the first seminar he attended following his return. The contrast with the previous forum for critical debate and exchange of ideas was more than he could stomach. Again he blamed himself for allowing it to happen – although this time the changes had all been brought about during the long period of his involuntary absence.

And then there was the question of internal appointments to permanent positions within the Centre. A number of these had been made since Lauder's accident on the basis of Grandison's private recommendations to Hardcastle. They all involved fixed contract staff who had been producing dull, unimaginative work for years. What criteria had been used to select these over the heads of other obvious candidates – both from within the Centre and, more usually, from outside – of self-evidently superior ability? Lauder put this to Grandison one evening while waiting in a low, depressed state for his wife to arrive to take him home. 'Unstinting loyalty to the Goldburg Centre' was the reply. In Grandison's view this was the one and only criterion worth considering. Clever people who had not absorbed the culture of the place only caused trouble: it had happened before, he was determined it should not happen again. Lauder was feeling too exhausted to argue. His condition had been deteriorating of late, not helped at all by contemplation of the seemingly undrainable morass into which he found the affairs of the Goldburg Centre had become immersed.

Chapter 15

I worked fairly solidly on the short paper throughout that Saturday afternoon. As a result it was as good as finished by early evening, leaving me what was left of that day, and all the next, to get through before Daniela's planned return on Monday. A phone call to my parents, who had both retired and lived in North London, took care of the Sunday. I had been neglecting them, my mother told me truthfully, so I was pleased to accept their invitation to lunch the next day, and planned to lure my father, who had taken to getting out less and less, to their local that evening. One of the films showing down the road, at the Ritzy, looked promising, so I decided to try for an early performance. On my way there I called in at the Prince for a half, looking round to see if Johnny Cremer was there. He wasn't. And when I got to the Ritzy all the seats for the film I wanted to see had been taken. So after no more than a few seconds' hesitation I headed for the tube.

A problem with the Goose is the uncertainty of where a chance exposure to it may lead: this can sometimes count as an attraction. My intention that evening had been for a single leisurely beer to pave the way for a curry, or perhaps a bowl of noodles, somewhere in that general area. As I stood at the bar waiting to be served, a cultured, if rather too carefully articulated, male voice sounded off to my left – to no one in particular, so it seemed at first. Then it became apparent that he was addressing me:

'So he's buggered off again to America, lucky sod. Only way he gets away with it, I suppose. Never stays in a place long enough to get caught.'

I turned. Edward Weatherill was standing beside me, uncharacteristically drinkless I noticed. I had never spoken to him before but had often seen him in there – once or twice with Karl, to whom he was presumably referring. I smiled and nodded in sincere agreement. The barman had come over to take my order.

'What are you having?' I asked.

'A pint of Guinness would go down well, thank you. I'm stuck here waiting for my wife. Stupid cow's late as usual.'

While the drinks were being poured, Edward was joined at the bar by a tall, frighteningly thin, worried looking man with a mop of untidy grey hair and a shabby pullover dotted about with lapel badges supporting improbable causes: another Goose regular, who had been pointed out to me as Edwin Bloomfield – a painter who after years of scarcely scratching together a living was currently enjoying a run of phenomenal success. Edward greeted him in a manner which struck me as offensive:

'Painted your arsehole yet?'

Bloomfield, however, appeared neither offended nor surprised. He smiled knowingly before replying:

'Not yet. How about you?'

'Not bloody likely! I'm thinking of doing another one though.'

'Really? Anyone I know?'

Without waiting for a reply, Bloomfield turned abruptly aside to collar the barman, who having given me my change appeared set on a speedy withdrawal to the far side of the house. Grudgingly, he served up the requested glass of house claret before taking off. Edward made the introductions:

'This is Edwin Bloomfield. Sorry, but I don't know your name.' Then to Edwin: 'He's a friend of Karl Dembowski's.'

'Paul Harrison,' I said, shaking his hand.

'You're not a scientist, are you?' He seemed puzzled by this possibility.

'Yes, I'm afraid I am.'

'Oh dear,' he said, after a moment's hesitation. 'Well, never mind. I actually got a note from Karl this morning, from the States. He's going to miss my opening at the Buckingham next week. Pity that. He's always good value on those occasions.'

Edward was starting to look uncomfortable. He leaned awkwardly on the bar, then noticed something in the body of the pub over to our right and turned to me:

'Those people over there seem to be leaving. Try to grab their table if you can. My legs are beginning to play up again.'

He said this in a way which implied I was aware of this condition of his: an old war wound perhaps, sustained in action far exceeding the call of duty. I took my three quarters full glass over to where he had indicated, and managed to slide into the chair the previous occupant was just leaving; then to assure another customer that the other vacant seat was indeed spoken for. Edward joined me a minute or two later bearing two full glasses. He appeared to have recovered his bounce, the first pint having seemingly done the trick.

'You're probably wondering what that was all about,' he said as he settled into his chair, adding mysteriously: 'Your friend Karl up to his pranks again.'

As I sat looking bewildered, he reached into his breast pocket and came out with some crumpled pages, one of which he handed me.

'See what you make of this,' he said.

It was a letter, which started off with a 'Dear Edward' but was clearly a mailshot to artists asking for contributions to a charity auction. The letterhead was of a Cork Street gallery and was signed by some notable with impressive looking appendages on both sides of his name. It started by going on at some length about the goodness of the cause and how successful previous outcomes of this annual event had been. *The theme this year*, it then announced, *is gardens*.

116

Having got that out of the way, it branched off into a protracted consideration of the inspirational role gardens play in all our lives, eventually coming to the point: *Please, please do try to make this year's auction the most successful ever. Send a small painting, or other art work, of maximum dimension no more than twelve inches, based on a garden: either your own garden, or else some other of which you are particularly fond.* There was a bit more, but nothing that seemed to be of any consequence. I handed Edward back his letter.

'Well, what do you make of that then?' he asked me, smiling expectantly.

'I don't know really,' I answered truthfully. 'Seems a bit twee to me, that's all. What on earth am I supposed to make of it anyway?'

He appeared irritated at my response; then, on looking at the page I had returned to him, his expression changed.

'I'm sorry. I seem to have given you . . .'

But before he could throw any light on the matter, the pleasant buzz of convivial conversation, to which we were contributing, was overlaid by an indignant, booming female voice – 'There you bloody are!' –, which caused a number of male drinkers in the place to pale anxiously for the time it took them to realise the target was someone else. Almost the only one not to turn a hair was Edward. She came over to him, striding menacingly:

'What the fuck do you call this?'

'Listen, you stupid bitch, I told you quite clearly . . .'

'You told me you'd be in the Clarence. That's where I've fucking been. Then on a wild goose chase over half of fucking London.'

'Listen will you. I said I'd be in the Clarence *lunchtime*. Right? *Lunchtime*, you deaf cow. I never go to the fucking Clarence in the evening. You know that perfectly well. What the fuck are you playing at?'

'You fucking listen to me . . .'

They appeared in for a long haul, neither showing any sign of letting up. I sat frozen throughout the initial onslaught and counter attack, trying hard to appear unconnected in any way with Edward, fearful that at any moment the woman's wrath would turn on me. Then, on an impulse, as they both paused for breath, gathering resources for phase two, I stood and offered her my seat. The look of utter contempt with which this was received told me that, as usual, I had misjudged things. Edward, however, was quick to spot a further possible weapon for his armoury:

'This is Paul, a friend of Karl's. You realise you're making a fucking exhibition of yourself in front of him.'

'Don't fucking come that one with me. I can tell you something else . . .'

I stood there more exposed than ever; then, at an opportune moment, slipped off to have a leisurely pee, leaving them heavily at it. When I returned, things had calmed. She was seated in my chair with a drink in front of her and addressed me quite civilly as I came up to them:

'Don't take any notice of us, dear. Just a routine domestic squabble, that's all. All over now.'

Edward didn't seem so sure:

'I told you quite clearly . . .'

'Edward! Enough. OK?' And then to me: 'I'm Sarah; married to this one here,' indicating Edward, who was sitting impassively, planning his next move. 'There's a spare chair over there. Why don't you grab it.'

While I was doing this, her attention was drawn elsewhere. She turned to Edward:

'Did you see who just walked in? It's that tight cunt Benjamin. On the scrounge again, no doubt!'

Benjamin was short and chubby and wearing a suit a couple of sizes too small for him which had seen better days. He waddled his way to the bar, where he greeted Edwin with a great show of surprised delight, as though for a brother long thought lost at sea.

'This should be interesting,' said Sarah. 'They're both as tight as nuns' twats. Any bets on who buys a round?'

Edwin was looking distinctly unhappy, his glass almost empty. Benjamin, beside him, was going on emphatically about something, with a great deal of arm waving and facial expression.

'Before you interrupted us,' Edward began, with a critical look at his wife, who for a moment gave signs of becoming dangerous again, then relaxed, 'I was beginning to explain to Paul about Karl's latest escapade.'

Sarah brightened considerably on hearing this. She was really quite attractive, I noticed: a good twenty years younger than Edward, maybe more. Quite heavily made up in a tarty sort of way, which blended in well with her choice of language, giving an edge to the plummy accent and decidedly confident bearing.

'You listen to this,' she said to me, completely calmed down now, smiling encouragingly at Edward, all trace of previous bitterness gone, 'it's fucking marvellous.'

It appeared that Edward had taken Karl along with him to a gallery in Cork Street, where he had some business to conduct with the owner – concerning a nude portrait of his wife, which Edward was hoping to be commissioned to paint.

'Quite a tasty little piece,' interjected Sarah. 'Puts it about all over the place. Only one who doesn't know about it is her old man. Now he's paying to advertise her wares.'

She gave a hearty guffaw.

'Now look here,' Edward was clearly unhappy at his wife stealing the best lines, 'who's telling this fucking story, eh?'

'Sorry darling, I'll button up now, promise. But the whole thing's fucking marvellous.'

Edward drank deeply from his glass before continuing. It turned out that on arrival at the gallery they had been approached by a harassed looking assistant who, on seeing Edward, had come over to ask a favour. He had prepared an important letter on the word processor, which had to be sent out to a large number of people. For some compelling reason, which remained unclear, all hell would break loose if he didn't catch the next post with the first batch. Nobody was around to give it a final, independent check. Would Edward mind just casting an eye over it before he printed out the multiple copies? He handed him a draft. Karl, helpful as ever, also took a look at it, spotted a small typing error and watched with interest as the correction was made on the machine. There was some confusion over precisely what happened next: Cecil, the gallery owner, had arrived in a filthy mood, screaming for his employees to hurry to him for urgent consultation; Edward thought it best to postpone the business discussion until things had calmed down, and slipped out of the way into the print room; Karl, so he claimed a couple of days later, remembered a pressing engagement and left. When things had settled, Edward was able to negotiate very favourable terms for his commission, and the gallery assistant just managed to catch the post with the first batch of letters.

'This,' said Edward, producing the crumpled sheets from his pocket and carefully selecting one to pass me, 'is one of them.'

It looked at first sight exactly the same as the one he had shown me a little earlier. Soon, however, the differences became apparent. *The theme this year*, it now read, *is arseholes*. Sarah was reading it with me, shrieking with laughter at the account of the inspirational role these play in our lives; then breaking off in mid shriek to read aloud the bit that, in her view, broke all records for aptness and brilliance:

'Send a small painting – this is fucking marvellous – *based on an arsehole: either your own arsehole, or else some other of which you are particularly fond.'*

Tears were running down her cheeks now, making quite a mess of her face. Edward too was chuckling away, but not uncontrollably.

120

There was a serious aspect to all this which he felt the need to impart:

'Amazing those machines, you know,' he said, with a look of wonderment. 'It seems that by just pressing a button you can change one word for another everywhere it appears.'

For perhaps the first time in his life, an appreciation of the phenomenal advances of modern technology had got through to him. It was a humbling experience which was going to take some getting used to.

I went over to the bar to buy drinks. Edwin was looking more miserable than ever there. His glass appeared as near empty as when I last saw it ages before. He was clearly in need of a drink, but knew that buying one would mean also buying one for Benjamin – who was still there next to him, looking a little concerned perhaps, but not yet entirely without hope. Edwin raised his glass to his lips, then replaced it on the counter with no detectable reduction in its contents. On seeing me trying to catch the barman's eye, his features brightened a little:

'Oh Paul,' he said, reaching inside his pullover, 'I meant to give you this before.' He handed me a small envelope. 'It's an invite to my opening at the Buckingham next Wednesday. Hope you can make it. Pity Karl won't be there.'

I thanked him as I gave my order, feeling the need to offer something in return.

'What are you having?' I asked him, being aware as I did so of Benjamin stiffening at his side.

'That's very good of you. I'll have a glass of claret, thanks very much.' He turned to the barman to specify the particular variety he had in mind. It sounded an expensive one.

'So you're a friend of Karl's,' said Benjamin, manoeuvring himself round Edwin. 'I'm Benjamin, by the way.' He offered his hand. 'Karl's probably mentioned me.'

'Is that it then?' asked the barman. There was no way out now.

'What can I get you?' I asked Benjamin, silently acknowledging defeat.

'Oh, I'll have a scotch and soda. Thanks very much. I see there's a special offer on doubles.'

Sarah, who had been watching all this from afar, greeted me reprovingly when I got back to the table:

'You utter prick! How could you fall for all that? Don't say I didn't warn you about them.'

'Well, he gave me an invitation to his show . . . the opening next week. I couldn't very well . . .'

'Huh,' she snorted, 'anyone can walk into those things. And there'll probably be a pay bar in any case.'

'Yes,' said Edward, 'and he's probably negotiated a cut of the takings, if I know Edwin.'

They were both in good moods now, past hostilities completely behind them, quite resigned to having missed the appointment that seemed so vitally important a short while before:

'It makes no fucking difference anyway,' Sarah remarked philosophically. 'If they're really interested in getting you to do it, they know where they can bloody well find you.'

Edward disengaged his glass from his mouth to nod in agreement. There was a settled look about him now. Nothing was going to shift him. The talk returned to Karl, whom Sarah appeared to take a suspiciously keen interest in. But it was Edward who brought up the matter of the posthumous Ebenezer Goldburg portrait:

'When he heard I'd got the commission – I've a feeling he may have had a hand in that somehow – he absolutely insisted on posing for the body. He was completely the wrong shape. Sarah had to pad him out with cushions and things. Remember that?'

'I certainly do,' said Sarah, smiling contentedly.

'But he was still about two foot too tall.' Edward was looking indignant at the memory of it. 'Caused me no end of difficulties. If I'd had someone like . . .', he waved his arm in the approximate direction to where Benjamin was just draining his glass, '. . . like that little fat cunt over there, I'd have finished in half the time and made a better job of it.'

'But you made a marvellous job of it.' Sarah was waxing sentimental now. 'Everybody loved it. And Karl was so happy at being able to help out, bless him. It was really quite touching.'

It must have been an hour or so later that Sarah announced their intention of going on to their club – some artists' haunt in Chelsea.

'Why not come along with us,' she said, 'It's quite pleasant there and the bar doesn't close for ages.'

'I really do need to get something to eat.' It had already been quite a session. The prospect of extending it was not without appeal, but I was starving.

'Oh, then you must come. The food there's excellent. You two wait here while I hunt down a taxi. We can share the fare. I've a feeling that this is going to be a really good night.'

Chapter 16

By the time I got into college on Monday I had just about seen off the hangover sowed the previous Saturday evening – which had somehow managed to stretch to include a good slice of Sunday morning. My mother, seeing me later that day, ascribed my haggard appearance to overwork – a perennial concern of hers, previously with regard to my father, now in view of his unquestionable success in overcoming this inclination apparently transferred to me.

I had a nine o'clock lecture, which got me in early and left the rest of the morning free to print out copies of the short paper and send them off to the journal. I also faxed a copy to Karl in Franklin – he had specifically told me to do this *after* it had been submitted, not wanting to be tempted into suggesting modifications. When this had all been taken care of, I found I still had an hour or so to kill before lunch. Time to focus uninterruptedly on Daniela. She should be returning any time now; I had made quite a good job, it seemed to me, of filling in the period of her absence. Settled at my desk, I tidied up the file on the completed paper, then closed my eyes. Almost immediately, the phone rang:

'Hallo Paul. It's me. How are you?'

'Better now I'm talking to you. No, I'm fine. How are you?'

'Fine too. It's good down here. I've done a lot of riding, which is great. Quite a change from London.'

There was something a little distant in her manner which concerned me for a moment. I asked her:

'Can you speak? You sound a little . . . constrained.'

'No, not really. I'm phoning from Hassocks. I just wanted to tell you that I'll be staying here tonight. They have some guests coming they want me to meet.'

'I see.'

'I'll be leaving first thing in the morning. I'll call you soon as I get back. In plenty of time for our theatre date.'

'You haven't forgotten then?'

'How could I? But I must go now. I'll see you soon.'

'Not soon enough. Bye darling.'

'Bye for now.'

Although it was perfectly obvious that Hilda, and perhaps the colonel, was within earshot, I still felt a little let down at the brevity and lack of intimacy of that exchange. It was ridiculous of me, I knew full well; just an indication of my insecurity and how much appeared at stake.

I headed for the refectory early, well before the crowds could be expected. As I carried my tray over to the tables, I spotted a lone figure I recognised seated at one of them and went over to him.

'Mind if I join you?'

He looked up and beamed cordially:

'Paul! What a pleasant surprise. We haven't spoken for ages. What have you been up to?'

Tony Mulgrave was a strange soul. An exceptionally able and prolific physicist, who had published seminal papers in his field, he now devoted himself exclusively to matters of college administration. Such transfers are normally associated with those possessing little talent for academic work. No one could begin to claim this of Tony. Karl had tried to persuade him against the move when it was first mooted, pointing colourfully to the unedifying company he would be forced into close proximity with; he was also concerned at the loss to his department of one of the few remaining major players on the international research front. But Tony persisted, feeling the need, for personal reasons, for a complete change of direction. He was now widely regarded as a beacon of sanity up there, tempering the more injudicious, often plain barmy, schemes of Hardcastle's before serious damage could be done; even spoken of as a possible successor when Hardcastle decided, perhaps with some encouragement, to move on.

'Actually, I've been working on something with Karl,' I said, in answer to his question. 'Just sent off a short note on it to *Nature* this morning.'

This appeared a more appropriate choice from among the set of 'what I had been up to' than my other recent escapades.

His look of interest was quite genuine. He too had collaborated with Karl in the past, and could hardly have failed to have been stimulated by it. I told him a little about the work, but on starting to go into some detail saw his concentration fade. He had withdrawn from the game quite some time ago. Other problems of an altogether different nature exercised him now. Our conversation drifted over further areas of supposedly mutual interest before settling, unexpectedly for both of us, on the Goldburg Centre. How exactly this came about remains unclear: it probably started with some reference to Lauder, the sadness of it all and the loss his departure represented for the college as a whole. Then I think I made some passing mention of the Sean O'Brien affair, inadvertently giving the impression that I knew more about it than the very little I in fact did. Tony lit up considerably at this point. It turned out that he had got himself heavily involved in that business, and clearly wanted to talk about it to a disinterested, but not totally uninformed, third party. We had finished eating and the place was beginning to fill up. A small group of people we both knew appeared to be heading with their trays towards our table.

'Let's go somewhere quiet for coffee where we can talk,' he said; and with that, and a nod to our approaching colleagues, we got up and left.

He led me to a small, pleasantly furnished room in the block that housed Hardcastle's suite, the Registrar's office and other administrative departments of the college. It was unoccupied. In an alcove stood a machine, which made what turned out to be quite reasonable fresh coffee. We took our cups to a sofa and low table by the window and sat for a moment or two in silence before Tony spoke:

'How did you get to hear about the O'Brien affair? It's all very hush-hush as you must know.'

I realised that I was going to have to play this carefully. Tony's involvement was clearly at the very highest college level; I was intensely curious to find out what lay behind it. Daniela could hardly be named as my source; nor Karl for that matter, whose views on Grandison – and the Centre in general now that Lauder was gone – were common knowledge. It was obvious that Tony wanted to talk, so a good half the battle was already won. I just had to take care not to sound any alarm bells.

'Well, from a number of people really. Postdocs in the main, those working in the labs around him. They'd been warned not to talk, but you know how it is after a few beers in the Marlborough.'

I thought this sufficiently plausible and vague. In fact it went down better than I could have imagined:

'I know. They're the ones who seem to be more in touch with what's going on than anybody. I think it's to do with their lack of any permanent status in the place. People at all levels, including secretaries and the like, feel they can talk to them freely, without fear of any comeback.'

Another silence followed in which it seemed to me he was weighing up the wisdom of revealing something. I felt the need to get things rolling:

'How on earth did you come to get involved in all this?' was all I could think to say. 'It's a bit outside your usual area of activity, isn't it?'

On asking this, I realised I had no notion whatsoever of what his usual area of activity might be.

'Not really,' he replied. 'Anything to do with Hardcastle's . . . ' – I think he was about to say something disparaging, then changed his mind – 'with the college's interests . . .' He looked me straight in the eye, paused and then started again: 'Seems this could be the really big one, you know. The problems though . . . the problems are enormous. They seem to be homing in from all directions.'

'I can well imagine you having problems with Sean O'Brien. He's a very peculiar customer by all accounts.'

I was taking a risk now. Something that Karl had said in passing a week or so before – in the Goose, I thought – came back to me. I blurted it out as though it had been my impression all along:

'Something seemed strange to me about his appointment here; the way his previous employers spoke so highly of him and yet made no apparent attempt to hold on to him.'

'I know,' he replied with emphasis. 'The real problem though is with the job he had before that: with ARC Pharmaceuticals. He foolishly signed agreements when he joined them without seeking legal advice. They bind him to secrecy on what he learned there in a singularly restrictive manner, and prevent him working in related research areas for years: effectively prevent him working at all. That was the root of his problems with Carsons – the firm he was with before coming to us. Our lawyers are working on it. Seems it can be claimed that his employment rights have been unjustly violated. But who knows where it will end up.' Then, after a pause: 'There could be millions at stake here, you realise.'

These revelations, so far as they went, could well explain Sean's obsessive secrecy concerning his work. Also Grandison's behaviour at times. The story could be beginning to unfold. All I had to do, it

128

seemed, was to inject the occasional appropriate comment and sit tight – and hope that Tony's motor, well wound up now, wouldn't snag. He was looking at me with an expression that suggested he was again weighing something up. Eventually he put it to me:

'I've set up a small working group to look at all aspects of this business. We meet at short notice – not usually the whole group, some only get asked occasionally, when it seems appropriate for one reason or another.' He paused for a moment. 'How would you feel about becoming an occasional member?'

This was more than I had bargained for. I felt a small tremor of excitement, well concealed I hoped, and let the silence persist for a while before answering – truthfully for a change:

'I don't really know if I would have anything useful to contribute. What I know of the business is just based on hearsay and speculation – and what you've just told me. I've no expert knowledge at all to offer.'

'I know all that. We've no shortage of so-called experts – many with fixed views and vested interests. Just occasionally though it can help to tune into the opinions of disinterested outsiders. I think you could be useful there.'

It came back to me at this point that my interest in the matter had been driven by Karl's unconcealed contempt for Grandison and, by implication, anything coming out of the Centre under his direction. If I was to be drawn into the Sean O'Brien affair, as Tony was now proposing, I would clearly have to put all that behind me. The problem of conflicting loyalties was bothering me, making me genuinely undecided about whether to accept his invitation.

'Perhaps it would help if you could put me a little in the picture. I'm completely clueless about what's involved.'

He looked at me steadily for a while before replying:

'Have you any commitments this afternoon? You don't need to rush away?'

'None at all. I'm as free as a bird.'

He looked at his watch, hesitated for a moment, then made up his mind:

'Very well then. I'll try to be brief. The general situation as I see it is this.'

What he went on to tell me wasn't brief at all. I had the feeling that he desperately needed to sound off about the whole business – preferably to someone with his scientific background, who spoke his language. Not for any technical reason, but just so as to feel at home. He probably missed that in his newly chosen career. With considerable vehemence, strikingly at odds with his customary manner of quiet objectivity, he began by outlining what he saw as the appalling record of the cancer treatments at present on offer.

'If you're unfortunate enough to contract the disease the alternatives are pretty bleak – unless it turns out to be one of the very few varieties that conventional medicine can handle. If it's not, and the chances are it won't be, the oncologists will still try to persuade you to let them treat you with phenomenally expensive poisons, which they know can at best just keep you alive a few more months. It's a multibillion pound business this. And these jokers, for all their posturing, are little more than technicians, doing the bidding of their masters: the pharmaceutical giants. They're the ones who provide all the facilities – and the perks that go with the job: like conferences in the Bahamas, where when they're not swanning around the bars and beaches you'll find them arguing frantically over whether the addition or increased dose of some ingredient to the toxic brew increases life expectancy by a week or so. It's an unholy alliance; made to look respectable by constant reference to the great God research.'

I had never seen him like this before, and realised that I didn't know him at all. It occurred to me that some personal experience, a tragedy somewhere in his life, could be driving his bitterness, and I wondered how much longer he would go on before getting to the matter in hand. Not that I was in any hurry. What he was saying was striking a distant chord, stirring up a memory of something long forgotten, a vague unease buried in the past. When he started up again, it was heartening to realise there was to be more of the same to come. The O'Brien business could wait. There was plenty of time.

'I've had reason to look a bit into what they call research. A basic problem here is that the ethos of their training is quite opposed to the whole idea of it. Medical students are brought up on a vast diet of facts, which have to be learned and accepted unquestioningly. Much of their coursework consists of simply regurgitating it all, any attempt at originality in interpretation being speedily jumped on as an impertinence. And then, when they qualify and get their first hospital jobs, immense pressure is put on them to "do research" and publish. Just like that. With no training, or feeling for how to go about it at all. The utter triteness and ineptness of much of what gets into print has to be seen to be believed.'

He looked up at me, his mouth contorting into some semblance of a smile.

'A few years back, a student of ours in Physics decided he wanted to switch to medicine. Bright lad; just completed his second year. Decided in the end to finish it off and then start again from square one in medical school. He picked up a first and did just that. Used to call in to see us when he had a moment. The only problem he was encountering was with the blandness of the assignments – that and the criticism he came in for when he tried to inject a note of analysis into his reports. He decided in the end to carry on more or less as he felt he should – as he had been trained to – and just live with it, and accept being marked down and railed at. He's a GP now, good one by all accounts.'

'I think I met him once, in Karl's room. Peter something . . .'

'Pete Stanford, that's him. But I'm sorry, I'm going off at a tangent. I'm suppose to be filling you in on the O'Brien saga. It's just that it meshes in with other things . . . things that have bothered me for quite a time. I don't know how relevant it all is . . . '

131

'Do carry on. I'm finding it interesting.'

I was worried, as I said this, that it could sound patronising.

'It corresponds to feelings I've had myself,' I added, partly to be on the safe side.

Tony's expression reassured me. He smiled, rather more fully this time, before continuing:

'The real problem though is financial. Nothing untoward about that. But what is special in this case is the way that massive, quite impenetrable financial barriers prevent any new initiative getting off the ground: rule it out of play almost from the start. And all helped along of course by the pathetic acquiescence of the clinical so-called researchers.'

Bits and pieces of what he then went on to describe had already managed to filter through to me. But the overall picture he painted tied these and other unexpected strands together into a depressingly convincing picture of institutionalised failure. Chemotherapy drugs were a thriving, multibillion pound business, in the firm grip of the international pharmaceutical companies – themselves key components in the economies of all the world's developed nations. The licensing of a new cancer drug, perhaps one showing considerable promise in laboratory and animal tests, was subject to the results of extensive clinical trials, presided over by a regulatory body, which included, and relied to a large extent on the expert advice of, representatives of the major pharmaceutical companies themselves. The early stages of safety testing and registration could cost in the region of fifty million pounds, and many promising candidates – the overwhelming majority of them, in fact – would be destined to fall at the last fence. On this basis, the final outlay in bringing a new product on to the market could well turn out to be closer to ten times that figure. What this all meant was that small players, even quite big small-players, didn't get a look in; and so far as the big players were concerned only a truly mass-market product could stand any chance whatsoever of recouping development costs, let alone of making a profit. Against this, the mass-market products at present on offer were making enormous profits – despite the fact they had come to represent perhaps the most abysmal and long running scientific failure of modern times.

'I'm a firm believer in a free market in these as in most matters,' he added, perhaps to reassure me he was no closet revolutionary, sitting there waiting for the capitalist system to collapse. 'The profit motive undoubtedly provides the engine for getting things moving. What we have here though is blatant protectionism, dressed up and presented as "safeguarding the patients' interests".'

'But what about all the research the drug companies engage in? Are you saying they're blocking new developments? We're always hearing of novel ones coming through . . . being tested.' Karl's reference to sheep's bollocks and larch bark came back to me as I was saying this. 'There was one in the news only the other week. And what about all the clinical trials. They're still going on aren't they?'

'Oh yes. They're still going on all right. You should see the proposals for new ones. Some of them read like evidence produced at the Nuremberg trials: calling for terminal case volunteers to test the toxicity of some new ingredient for the brew; requirements being a life expectancy of a couple of months; trial to be terminated on the death of a second participant, and so on, and so forth. Probably put over to the desperate souls and their loved ones as a last hope: a state-of-the-art discovery that might just . . . you never know . . .'

He was looking tired, dispirited again; then, with an effort, pulled himsclf together:

'There's plenty of work going on all right. Trouble is it's just tinkering with the same old discredited approach, as though there were no real alternatives. Very good they are at dismissing other suggested lines as unproven, unscientific.'

'So where does O'Brien's work fit in to all this?'

I thought it time to move him on before he started running out of steam again. He smiled apologetically.

'Yes, I can see you must be wondering where all this is leading. The problem with the current approach, as I understand it from the experts, is that it basically treats all tumours the same way: just kills off cells regardless. That's what satisfies the mass-market condition, justifies the development costs. The alternative is targeted therapy: targeted on specific genetic mutations that give rise to a particular tumour. Experts are pretty well agreed that this is the way forward. Trouble is that each treatment has to be designed for a relatively small number of people, each drug having to go through the full testing and registration procedures: it simply isn't economically feasible. Especially when the drug companies are making a killing, quite literally as it happens, on what they have going already. Effective targeted treatments would undermine all that. And the oncologists would have their work cut out: monitoring a vast variety of advanced procedures, instead of just doling out much the same to everyone and recording how long they take to die.'

He paused. A painful memory, it seemed, was once more gaining a hold on his concentration. I responded quickly this time:

'And O'Brien?'

'Yes, O'Brien. I'm coming to that.' He smiled, having rapidly regained his composure. 'Seems he moved straight from university into a job with ARC Pharmaceuticals. There was apparently some family connection involved. His academic record wasn't brilliant, but it appears he really took off once he got there. The atmosphere in the place seemed to suit him, at least initially. It's an unusual company.'

What followed was an account of the activities of this enterprise, an offshoot of a merchant bank, which had been able to assemble a formidable team of scientists and to attract immense sums of venture capital from wealthy investors prepared to accept the high risks involved in the development and exploitation of potentially phenomenally profitable advanced pharmaceutical products. A significant and fast growing proportion of their activities concerned the targeted treatment of certain specific forms of cancer. To this end, they were drawing on fundamental research – which they were partially funding in a number of universities – directed at identifying differences in the genes of tumour and healthy cells, thus tackling the problem at its root.

Sean had stayed with them for a little over three years, working in a team with some of their ablest people – who had been attracted there by high salaries and a stake in the company's fortunes. He joined when the cancer drug development project was just beginning to get off the ground. And by the time he left, a first new-generation drug, targeted on a somewhat rare and always lethal form of cancer, for which no treatment of any sort was currently available, had passed the initial stages of development and had been submitted for registration and testing. Others, it seemed, were to follow. Predictably enough, problems were being encountered with the regulatory board, which the company attributed to the hostile reaction of members with established pharmaceutical company affiliations. The battle was by now being waged at the highest political level – involving at least two government departments and, it was claimed, 10 Downing Street itself. But even in the event of a successful outcome of these initial skirmishes – which could lead to tests being carried out on a small number of volunteer patients – the prospect of these, by their very nature limited-market, drugs becoming generally available remained virtually zero. Only a radical overhaul of existing funding mechanisms and procedures could bring about a change. This had to be what ARC Pharmaceuticals was gambling on: the hope that a dramatic demonstration of the benefits of a new treatment would arouse public awareness, force through political action.

'To get back to O'Brien. All was going well for him until he started having ideas of his own about which lines to follow up in the project. As you said yourself, he can be an awkward customer at times. Seems he fell out first with the team leader, then with the rest of them. He eventually handed in his notice and moved straight into Carsons – a niche biotechnology outfit with which he'd apparently been negotiating for some time – to the predictable fury of ARC Pharmaceuticals when they got to hear of it. But they got their own back all right: threatened legal action on the basis of agreements he had signed on joining, without fully understanding the implications, and had subsequently forgotten about. Carsons too, it was hinted, could have found themselves liable for crippling damages. They couldn't get rid of him quickly enough. Which is how he ended up in the Goldburg Centre.'

'And which is where the story begins, so far as we're concerned.'

I said this in response to his, what I took to be, well-there-you-are-and-that's-it nod of the head, with which he sat back and went quiet, as though having changed his mind about confiding in me further. Having listened to him patiently for nearly two hours, I wasn't going to let him get away with that so easily.

'So what on earth has he been up to in the labs since then? The people around him don't appear to have a clue. If it's a continuation of his cancer work with ARC Pharmaceuticals then you've certainly got problems, from what you've told me of his past employment agreement. Just what is it you're asking me to get involved in here?'

This, just to remind him he had asked me to join his working group. It seemed, however, that I had misinterpreted his gesture. Sean, he went on to tell me, was indeed still working on a cancer drug, targeted on a very common and lethal tumour. The approach he was using was quite different to that with which he had been involved at ARC Pharmaceuticals. Different too from the one he had once tried to get them interested in without success. It was as a result of what he saw as this snub that he decided to leave when a suitable opportunity arose, and it was then that he covertly approached Carsons – who immediately showed interest. In the meantime, another breathtaking idea had come to him. It was based on some current university research, on which an ex-colleague from student days, with whom he had maintained close contact, was engaged. He explained the bones of this to Carsons, with the result that within a few weeks he was on their payroll.

'You now know what happened there. As a result of that he's been pretty cagey about his work in the Centre. Grandison's very supportive, as you can imagine. And Hardcastle has a merchant bank positively breathing down his neck with proposals to fund development – at least through to the Phase 2 trials. If these go the way some are anticipating, public response could well drive the government to intervene. With elections coming up in eighteen months, this could be seen as just the thing to turn things around for them.'

On my way back to the Engineering Science block, I passed a group of young people with surveying equipment taking measurements around the Goldburg fountain. For a moment it seemed as though Grandison's plans to replace it were starting to materialise, but then I realised they were engineering students on a coursework assignment.

As I approached my room, the phone began to ring. Thinking it could be Daniela, I dropped my keys in the fluster of trying to get the door open; then, on managing that, launched myself across the room to my desk. But it was a male voice which answered my greeting: Karl's.

'Paul, hallo. I found your fax waiting for me when I got in. Paper looks great. How's everything else there?'

But before I could answer, or even work out where to start, he went on:

'Can't talk now. I'm already late for a meeting. Great things happening here, which I'll tell you about some other time. One thing though, quite unconnected with all that, which might interest you. That fax of O'Brien's to MIT: it was never sent. Nobody in that department's ever heard of him. Bright lad that Sean. Wasted in Grandison's outfit, don't you think? Must fly now. Speak to you again soon.'

Chapter 17

The attempt by Lauder to regain control of the Goldburg Centre was short-lived, his detailed probing into the activities of the various research groups ending soon after he had finished with the third one. Whether what he was uncovering contributed to his deterioration was impossible to say, but his initial spirited efforts left him deeply depressed, and after little more than six months back at the Centre, he suffered a severe relapse from which he never recovered. For a while he maintained the illusion that he would eventually return, but this time it was not to be. Severance terms were agreed, and he was persuaded to adopt, upon retirement, the unusual title of Honorary Director of the Goldburg Centre. This move was only partially motivated by a desire to acknowledge his unstinting services in promoting the reputation of the Centre within the international academic community and beyond – although this was the direct thrust of Grandison's case to Hardcastle when Lauder's final departure was being considered. Shallowly buried in his proposal however, for Hardcastle to dig up for himself, lay the suggestion that an absent (unpaid) Honorary Director of distinction, together with a dedicated Deputy Director of proven administrative ability, could be quite adequate for the efficient furtherance of the Centre's affairs. As Hardcastle was encountering pressing problems with college finances, taxing even his legendary prowess in such matters, the prospect of saving the very considerable salary of the Goldburg

Centre's Director (rumoured to exceed even that of the Student Health Centre's dentist) was unlikely to go unheeded.

The outcome could hardly have been better for Grandison. The setback he had experienced with Lauder's valiant attempt to resume control on his return from convalescence was now more than compensated for, his de facto reign receiving added legitimacy. Celebration would have been inappropriate under the circumstances. Instead, the occasion was marked by Grandison suffering a near collapse in his office, complaining of severe pain in his right leg and being rushed to hospital with a suspected thrombosis. Nothing was discovered, and he returned to college a week later looking even more the worse for wear. He was accompanied this time by his wife, a large matronly figure, who had never been seen before by most people at the Centre, and was thought by those that saw her on that occasion to be a private nurse or specialist carer hired to assist in his recovery. This misconception was quite understandable in view of how their relationship appeared to outside observers. Her sole concern it seemed was to minister to his every need, and she continued to escort him to college and collect him when required, at whatever hour that might be, from that day onwards. In this way the tradition established by Lauder's wife was confirmed and elaborated upon. On arrival, she would adjust the position of his chair and get him safely installed on it at his desk; then see to it that his phone and other essential objects – which always included a water jug, glass and assorted bottles and packets of tablets, together with other things of which he would inform her grumpily – were all within easy reach; then check the room temperature and humidity and confer with Annabel, his secretary, with regard to any special requirements for the day.

Mrs Grandison – her first name, like so much else concerning Grandison, remained a mystery or closely guarded secret – looked about the age her husband appeared to be; which meant that either she was a good bit older, or else had also aged prematurely, perhaps out of consideration for how he might have felt about any obvious disparity in this regard. In fact the former was the case. She had been a long-standing friend of his mother, having met her at their local church, at which they both actively participated in various fund raising and other social activities. Mrs Grandison senior had been impressed with the way the future Mrs Grandison junior mixed in with the generally much older volunteers on these occasions, as well as the devoted manner in which she had cared for an elderly relative up to the time of his death. Although the idea of her son marrying anyone at all would have been hard for her to come to terms with, when the relationship blossomed she found it difficult to voice any real objection; and when their intention to wed was formally announced, she was able to console herself with the thought that things could very well have turned out considerably worse. Flightiness was a vice for which she felt a particular abhorrence and considered endemic in modern women: probe as she might, she could find no trace of it at all in the future Mrs G junior. As she explained to the vicar in the course of preparations for the ensuing nuptials, 'Nigel is going to need a steady, mature woman to look after him when I am no longer able to do so.' The fact of the near ten year difference in their ages did not seem to her to pose a problem: rather the reverse.

It was frequently remarked upon by the Centre's secretarial staff that Grandison's physical condition appeared to improve markedly each morning following his wife's departure. He would rise from the chair into which he had been so carefully lowered, and go about his business, if not exactly striding manfully, at least showing little more in the way of overt symptoms than could be attributed to a minor sport injury. His abiding preoccupations were with the image of the Centre as viewed from afar and its smooth, trouble-free functioning as felt from within. However, there lurked somewhere beneath the surface the realisation that something more was required if the ambitious expectations for the place, so effectively fuelled by Lauder, were to be realised. The reputation of the Centre was still riding *high, in spite of the withdrawal of virtually all the people responsible for establishing it. This could not continue indefinitely. There was little chance of anything of significance emerging from the present well-oiled, smoothly functioning machinery without something else – somebody else – entering into the picture. Such considerations never came even close to influencing his upbeat public pronouncements on the work in progress, even less the contents of the Grandisheets transmitted to Hardcastle. They very probably only rarely surfaced in his own consciousness. When they did, however, they would perturb his delicately held together illusion that the work of the Centre was truly at the leading edge of scientific progress. Given his condition, it appeared unwise to dwell upon this notion. Instead, he contented himself with the vague thought that sooner or later, in accord with no more than the law of averages, something truly earth shattering would emerge. Not from the appointment of an established researcher, who would very likely want to take full credit for any breakthrough discovery, but from a young, eager recruit, with a latent talent which would bloom in the cultural environment so painstakingly put together and nurtured in preparation for such an eventuality.*

Chapter 18

I was in my room on the morning following my session with Tony Mulgrave, having finished a ten o'clock lecture and in the midst of preparing another for the late afternoon, when the phone rang. It was Barry Skinner, returning the call I had made to his office a few days before, when he had been out of the country on some business assignment:

'Hi Paul. I just got back from Sweden last night and I'm off to the States on Friday. Any chance of us meeting for lunch before then? What about Wednesday? That's tomorrow. It seems to be pretty well the only slot available. Thursday's out, and then I'm off.'

I could hear anxious voices swelling in the background, urgently calling for attention.

'Yes, that should be fine. Shall I call at your office? How about twelve-thirty?'

'Better make it one. No, one-fifteen. I've an appointment here at quarter to. It could take twenty minutes or so. Do you know how to get here?'

'I'll find it. Looking forward to seeing you. It's been a long time.'

'Me too. Must go now. Panic stations here. It's always the same when I go away.'

A woman's voice sounded hysterically from the melee; then a man's, angrily trying to calm her.

'I'll leave you to it. Best of luck. Bye for now.'

'Bye.'

No sooner had I replaced the receiver than Daniela phoned from the Centre to say she had just got back. We arranged to meet by the Goldburg fountain half an hour later – in good time to get to the theatre pub for the pre-show lunch, which came as part of the package in the ticket price. I had last been there some two years before and was looking forward immensely to this return visit. The play was by an Irish-American journalist, who had risen briefly to fame a while back with a book on corruption and sheer lunacy within the flourishing born-again-Christian movement: a disturbing and carefully researched account – according to some – which had succeeded in unifying a number of extreme religious and right-wing political groups in vitriolic condemnation. Little had been heard of him since, giving rise to speculation that he had been murdered by one of his enraged enemies. The play represented his first attempt to resurface in another guise.

Daniela was waiting for me by the fountain, buttoned tight into an elegant, black coat; multicoloured scarf wound about her neck; hair jutting out determinedly from under a fur beret.

'I'm sorry,' I said as I approached, taking in her ill-tempered expression. 'Have you been waiting long?'

In fact, I was a good ten minutes early myself.

'No, I just couldn't stand it any more in there. I don't know what I'm going to do. That Trowbridge is a complete idiot; knows absolutely nothing. How on earth did he get into that position? Let's get out of here.' Angrily, she took my arm. Then after a moment or two forced a smile. 'Sorry. It's good to see you.'

As we headed for the main gate, I sensed her body gradually unwind. She didn't want to talk about what had upset her – not immediately, anyway; no doubt I would hear all about it soon enough. As we made for the tube, I told her what I knew of the author of the play we were going to see. She remembered something of the fuss over his book and squeezed my arm in contented anticipation:

'You don't know how much I need to escape from all the rubbish and trivia I seem to have sunk in.'

I wondered, as she said this, whether her stay in Hassocks had been all she had implied to me when she had phoned; then, with a mental shudder, whether I too was to be included in her general disillusionment. Maybe she sensed this because she stopped in her tracks, swivelled round and gave me a look of worried longing which lasted for as long as it took for our lips to come together.

'Oh Paul,' she said a moment later, 'what are we going to do?'

I was floating now, oblivious of everything else, basking in the wonderful feeling that the voyage could really be starting, the tie ropes disengaging from their moorings, ready to be thrown clear of the quay.

'Lots of things,' I replied, when I found my voice. 'First we are going to have lunch, then see a show, then we're coming back here to go through the motions of working for an hour or so' – I was being pedantically practical now, the course set, only trifling details requiring attention – 'and then we're going home . . . together.'

I could feel her body stirring through her coat, tightening at first, then relaxing.

'Does that sound all right to you?'

'Yes, it does.'

We continued on our way, hand in hand, the air crisp and clear, the future stretching bright before us. It was then that Daniela started to tell me of her reasons for coming to London, for getting away from home. As I had suspected, there was a man involved: the painful ending of a long relationship. While an undergraduate, she had started an affair with a young lecturer in the arts faculty of her university. They had become formally engaged a short while later – to the delight of her mother. He was very bright and handsome and from an extremely wealthy, influential family – 'All the girls in my year were jealous. It was considered a great coup' – which made it all the more difficult when it fell apart. It had lasted throughout her student years and into her first teaching appointment. Then she found he had been playing around, had suspected it for some time and tried to ignore it: 'But then he didn't seem to bother hiding it from me. Seemed he wanted me to know, to admire him even for being so sought after; wanted me to accept it. I think I tried to for a while, then couldn't any more.' She had felt completely alone in her misery, parents of no help at all; so she had turned to Karl, who had assumed the role in her life of a wise, fun-loving uncle to whom she could always turn. Although rarely around, he was always contactable and responsive. 'He had never taken to Carlo – same name, almost,' she gave a sardonic chuckle as she said this. 'Probably saw in him something he didn't much like in himself. Had plenty of advice to offer though – some of it quite helpful.' It was Karl who had suggested she got away for a spell, advised her how to go about it. 'He actually fixed things so that I got this year at the Goldburg Centre. God knows what Grandison would do if he learned of the connection.' As Karl's feelings for Grandison and the Centre were never in doubt, this appeared a strange choice at first – as well as testifying to his undercover manipulative skills. But his reasons turned out to be not entirely selfless. 'I'd just love to get you installed in that place,' he had told her quite early on, 'you may be able to do me a favour or two while you're there.' She smiled affectionately to herself at the memory of this; no trace of bitterness, no sign of objecting to being used. 'He's a rogue as you know, but he has his good points. And anyway, I'm well used to him now. Maybe that's what helped me put up with Carlo for so long.'

We had reached Angel. As we alighted from the tube, she added something to her story which I didn't want to hear at all, which sent a small tremor through my body:

'Carlo wrote to me last week. Claims he's a changed man . . . desperately unhappy . . . wants me back . . . wants us to get married.' She smiled distantly. 'Promises everything . . . not to look at other women again . . . ever.'

She had said all this in what could pass for a relaxed, matter-of-fact manner, as if it was somebody else's affair she was taking an interest in. I tried to match her tone:

'Do you believe him?'

'Doesn't seem very likely does it? But yes, I think he means it at the moment. He's woken up to the fact that I've gone . . . never thought that could happen. Now he's desperate to get me back. Not a state that's going to last if he's successful though.'

'Have you written back?'

'Oh yes. I always reply promptly to letters. Told him I would think about it. There's no hurry because for now I'm definitely staying put – if I can stand it any longer at the Centre.' Again the sardonic chuckle. 'I've got another eight months here.' She turned to look at me. 'Who knows what could happen in that time?'

'Who knows?' I agreed.

I felt the urge to embrace her, there on the platform, deciding on balance against it. Instead, simply taking her hand as we made our way through the grimy, subterranean caverns, then up and out on to the street. In the silence that had descended on us, I pondered the similarities in the emotional upheavals we had each undergone at around the same time: the end of long, loving relationships; my recent encounter with Julie matching somehow her receipt of Carlo's letter. Maybe what was taking place between us was simply growing out of a shared experience of loss. Julie's drawn features when we had met just days before, her troubled 'I'll call you sometime' as I had turned to leave, the feelings we had had for each other for so long. All this came back to me as we continued on our way, hand in hand still as the weather changed, through the now blustery streets. Maybe Daniela in her silence was lost in thoughts of Carlo: weighing up the possibilities of a reconciliation, of a return to a rich, familiar landscape among friends and family: the chic apartment in town, the country acres with the fine house, stables for the horses. Weighing this against a life of relative squalor with me in Brixton. Some

146

choice! What of the idyllic voyage on which we had set out minutes before? Would we even manage to clear the harbour?

We arrived at the pub. The dining area was crowded, an expectant, excited buzz filling the air as the time for what was to be the first public performance of the new work approached. It was difficult to talk much over lunch as we had to squeeze on to a bench at a long, crowded table. Instead we just ate and looked at each other and took in the ambience of the place until it was time to go into the theatre – a large, converted basement, painted out completely black; the ceiling a mass of suspended black lighting equipment; the three-quarters-round stage merging with the front row benches. It looked both intimate and businesslike. Daniela was clearly impressed. I could feel her excitement as we made our way across the stage to unoccupied seats over on the far side.

Once settled, we turned our attention to the spectacle of the place filling up – often an entertaining prelude to the show itself in such venues. The audience was predominantly young, but by no means exclusively so: a mix of trendy students, exotically got up arty types, businessmen in suits intent on making the most of the extended lunch break. All in high spirits, newcomers making their way across the stage, others weaving between those already settled to the remaining unfilled places. A very feeble old man – his face set, perhaps surgically, in a delighted grin – was being led by a fierce, somewhat younger woman in tweeds to a place which, she insisted loudly, had been reserved for them at the front. Sufficiently intimidated, the occupants squeezed over to accommodate them, causing an elastic deformation to propagate through the first row. Quite close to where we were sitting, an impromptu performance by an acutely embarrassed American tourist – unquestionably identifiable as such by his tartan trousers (on closer inspection, a patchwork of several tartans) – was drawing out a spirited audience response. In skirting the stage, it seemed he had made contact with one of the assembled props, a floor lamp of unusual design, sending it off balance. With a display of some agility, much appreciated by the packed house, he had managed to catch it before it hit the floor, but was then unable to reposition it. Try as he might, it would start to fall each time he let go – to a crescendo of gleeful cries, applause, catcalls. A stage hand materialised from somewhere to come to his rescue – to further applause, acknowledged with a deep bow. Daniela was loving it. I could feel her excitement mounting up to the moment when without warning the lights faded to total darkness; then on again, almost immediately, illuminating just the stage. The play had begun.

An altogether stunning production was to unfold before us, portraying in just one hour to the minute a desolate, compelling, occasionally absurdly funny view of the human condition: the two male characters, Younger and Older, delivering their lines for the most part from their respective beds – positioned symmetrically at the back of the small stage; between and high above them, a huge clock ticking away relentlessly, at times the only sound breaking the stillness; the beautifully crafted dialogue progressively increasing in tension as Younger fearfully anticipates the future, Older despondently laments the past. Moments of hilarious allusion to current events and personages peppering the bleakness – drawing loud, relieved laughter from the otherwise spellbound audience. Disjointed at first, then gradually gaining a terrifying coherence as the two seemingly independent soliloquies converge, and the huge minute hand approaches the hour when the mounting tension is set to explode. A gong sounds deafeningly as the moment arrives, the lights fade to nothing, then blaze up to reveal just two actors at the footlights, smiling and bowing.

Daniela was on a high as we emerged from the theatre, out into the cold:

'God, that was really something. I feel purged somehow. Sounds silly, but it's true. As if all the shit I have had to put up with has been flushed away.'

We were heading back to the tube, walking arm in arm, slowly adjusting to the world outside.

'And did you know . . . the one who played Younger . . . he was in that rubbish I saw in the West End last week with Karl and his friends. He must be in it tonight. I don't know how he can stand it after this. Oh Paul, we must do this again. It was wonderful. Such a change from all the crap I've seen since I've been in London.'

I felt no desire at all to return to college, felt positively repelled by the idea. As though reading my thoughts or, more probably, simply in harmony with them, Daniela stopped and turned to me:

'Let's do something else now. I just can't face Trowbridge after this. Anything but that.'

It was just past three o'clock. I had a lecture at four. A telephone booth had magically positioned itself beside us. We entered without a further word being spoken and, pressed against her, her fingers caressing my neck, her teeth nibbling at my right ear, I arranged with the school office to post notice of the cancellation.

'We're terrible,' she said, as we emerged from the cocoon, out on to the street, 'bunking off like this.'

'I know. It means bed for both of us I'm afraid, without any supper.'

We spoke little on the tube journey to Clapham, sitting contentedly holding hands at first, turning from time to time to gaze at each other, taking in the fact that a fateful decision had been made, that life was never going to be the same again. Daniela was looking different: softer and deeply relaxed, all signs of the tension, which had seemed so essentially a part of her, banished without trace. But for me the mounting excitement at what was in prospect was starting to cycle in my mind with the enormity of what was at stake:

memories of Julie surfacing intermittently like warning blows; of the utter incredulity with which I had first reacted to her departure; the abject misery of loss and rejection which was to follow. It was a dangerous course on which we were now embarking. Daniela had been watching me, reading my thoughts. 'Relax,' she said softly, nuzzling at my cheek, oblivious of fellow passengers facing us from across the aisle, 'everything is going to be all right from now on.'

A fierce wind was blowing through the entrance of Clapham Common station, bringing in sodden leaves from the common from the huge piles accumulating outside in the street. We trudged through them as though through mud, a fine rain falling almost horizontally, pounding our faces and bodies. Daniela looked at me and laughed, happy as a child on holiday, then started to run. I gave chase, soon catching her under an awning where we embraced; then, heedless of the rain which was pouring down in buckets now, we set off slowly, arm in arm, along the remaining hundred yards or so to our destination. We entered the hallway soaked, puddles forming beneath us on the worn linoleum, water running down from Daniela's matted hair over her face. She grinned, and with exaggerated gestures motioned me to follow her quietly up to the first floor landing. This we managed to negotiate undetected. Then, as we mounted the final staircase, the sound of a inquisitive door opening behind us sent us scurrying into the flat.

The first sensation on entering was of gratifying warmth, in stark contrast to conditions outside.

'You've turned the heating up,' I said. 'It feels wonderful in here.'

'Yes,' she replied, smiling mischievously, leaving no doubt that she had planned this early return.

'You wicked little . . . '

But I wasn't able to finish because her lips were on mine, our soaked clothing squelching between us. She laughed as we disengaged and started to unbutton my coat.

'We must put our clothes to dry in front of the radiators,' she said. 'It shouldn't take long.'

'There's no hurry anyway.'

'No, none at all.'

We helped each other do this, being quite thorough about it. It took quite a long time.

What happened immediately afterwards could by no stretch of the imagination be regarded a technical success. Things had got underway agreeably enough, even exquisitely so. But as the crucial moment approached, shallowly buried anxieties started to resurface in me. For a while they appeared to be gaining the upper hand, seeing to it that nothing at all was going to happen. And when in a desperate counter offensive they were overcome, banished in one irrepressibly triumphant surge, it was all over almost as soon as it had begun. We lay together entwined, in silence. I couldn't remember ever feeling so overwhelmingly at peace. From somewhere outside of myself came the demand that I should say something, apologise somehow; but the loving tenderness of Daniela's expression when I turned to do this told me it was unnecessary: nothing needed to be said. So we simply adjusted our embrace and continued to lie together in a delicious torpor, which it seemed would never end.

It was Daniela who eventually spoke. Maybe I had dozed for a few moments, my conscious state so relaxed, so close to sleep, that it was difficult to tell. For a while we exchanged endearments, words and half formed phases with which we gradually returned to earth. Then she asked about Julie, about my feelings for her now that the initial pain had had time to heal. Karl had obviously told her of this: she was aware of the time scale, of the way it had finished. I told her what came to mind of the affair (Is that what it had become? Simply an affair?), in particular how it had ended; how the intense pain had lasted for nearly a year, until quite recently, after meeting her –

Daniela; of the occasional twinges that still persisted, the unfocused feelings of regret for the loss of something of great value; but that it now seemed to belong to a past life only vaguely remembered.

'It follows pretty well what happened with me and Carlo: seven years of thinking this was for ever, then the sudden end.'

'I know. I wondered if that was what brought us together. Maybe it was, but so what. We could just view it as the necessary paths to each other. And you?' I felt anxious as I asked this. 'How do you feel about it now? Does it still hurt as much?'

She didn't reply. Instead she manoeuvred herself on top of me and kissed my lips. My hands moved down her back. I felt my body awakening under the pressure of hers, responding to the feel of her softness under my hands.

'That's good,' she said, smiling lovingly, kissing me again, but adding when I went to make a definite move: 'Not yet. Wait a bit. It's too soon.'

We rolled over on to our sides as though glued together and lay serenely face to face. After a while she started to talk about her home in Argentina, about her mother and stepfather and Karl. Strangely enough, it seemed there were no bad feelings between them. Karl would phone often and visit two or three times a year, staying with them where he was always welcomed – in particular by Daniela whom he pampered extravagantly. This aspect of Karl came as a revelation to me, seemingly quite at odds with his apparently cava-lier treatment of wives and mistresses. 'He used to send money to my mother, before she married Pablo' – an older, comfortably off widower; they had met when Daniela was an infant and had married shortly after her fourth birthday. She remembered well her initial hostility to him, and still had feelings of guilt about this. For although somewhat distant and reserved, he was a kindly man, with no children of his own, who always treated her with great affection, as if she was indeed his own daughter. He and Karl got on well enough together, there were never any problems there. Altogether,

her childhood had been an extremely happy one. She had gradually come to regard Pablo as her father; Karl was something else, something special, a bonus that set her apart from her friends, gave an added dimension to her life. From the age of twelve she would often spend a week of her school holiday with him in California, flying out on the ticket he would post to her:

'He really spoilt me . . . the beaches, films, restaurants . . . buy me clothes and things. I never wanted to go back home.'

It seemed to me that, as always, Karl had somehow managed to get the best of both worlds – in this case keeping his freedom while at the same time enjoying the delights of parenthood. The truly impressive thing was that he achieved all this without causing resentment to those left to shoulder the burdens. Anybody else and they'd be for it; but for him: oh, it's just Karl, bless him – as Sarah had put it the other day.

'It was terrible when I arrived in London.'

Daniela had stirred herself, adjusted her pillow, then sank back down, putting an arm around my waist.

'Karl was at Franklin, I knew nobody here. He'd got someone to find me a room – on the second floor of an old house in Camden Town. I could hardly even manage to lift my suitcase. People are so unhelpful here . . . the taxi drivers . . . everybody. I don't know how I got it up there.'

I made a sympathetic murmur, backing it up by stroking her shoulder and pressing my leg more firmly against hers.

'There was just about room to fit my case in the space next to the bed. I had to climb over it to reach the grimy washbasin under the window.'

I raised myself on an elbow so I could kiss her forehead, then her lips.

'I just laid on the bed and cried.'

I had pulled away to look into her eyes.

'Why on earth had I come here? Was I mad or something? Oh Paul!'

We kissed again, and then there was nothing in the world that could stop us, or so I thought. I was wrong.

When I became aware of the hammering my first thought was that it was Miss Atkins – or more likely the other one, the tall one – banging on the ceiling below with a heavy broom handle, or perhaps a pneumatic drill, borrowed for the occasion from the road gang in the next street.

'What the bloody hell! . . . '

But then I realised it had stopped.

Daniela was starting to giggle.

'It's us,' she said when she could get it out. 'It's the bed . . . on the floor.'

Then I remembered being aware of the occasional bump earlier on. This time we appeared to have hit the resonant frequency of the floor structure.

'I hope they haven't got a crystal chandelier down there.' – I had in mind the one in my grandmother's house, which would shed its cut-glass lozenges at the slightest disturbance – 'What the hell are we going to do?'

Daniela, however, had things well under control. She had taken the duvet through to the living room and thrown it over the massive old sofa. Then she fiddled with the knobs on the television, eventually tuning into an indoor tennis tournament and turning the sound on full.

'Just to be on the safe side,' she said as she came over to me, glowing in her nakedness.

The room vibrated to the pounding of ball against racket and court, like a metronome for brief periods; then cutting out and starting up again. It took a bit of getting used to at first. Then I ceased to notice it.

'Why don't you slip out and buy a bottle of wine while I prepare some supper.'

It was getting on for eight o'clock. We had showered together and dressed. It felt as though we had always been together like this. I couldn't remember ever feeling so good, so settled and complete.

'Is there anything else you need? Sainsburys will still be open. I'll be going there anyway.'

'I think I've got everything . . . maybe some fruit . . . oh, and some decent bread if there's any left; what I've got here is a bit old.'

My coat felt quite dry and warm now as I kissed Daniela good-bye, making quite a performance of it, as though leaving for the front with a good chance of not making it back. I carefully opened the door; then, after closing it even more carefully behind me, crept down to the first floor landing.

But the sensors had been finely tuned this time. Before I was even halfway across to the main staircase the last door opened to reveal Miss Atkins with Albert, her ancient cat, hanging from one arm. She was giving me a strange, direct look, which had the effect of stopping me dead. Then she spoke:

'You've been very naughty, you know.'

What on earth could I say to that? I waited in silence for her to continue.

'You left the living room light on all last night. We saw it from our kitchen. You'll be sorry when you get the bill.'

In the normal course of events I would probably simply have thanked her for pointing this out, maybe even explained that I wasn't there the previous night, so that this wasteful extravagance was all down to Daniela and that I would speak to her about it. But there was nothing normal about the way I was feeling just then.

'Oh, we leave it on for Benjamin,' I said, searching for inspiration, then finding it in her bemused expression. '*Benjamin*: Daniela's iguana. It likes to sleep during the day and prowl about at night.'

She was looking puzzled, eyes narrowing suspiciously.

'With the light on he settles down quite well. Lets us get some sleep for a change.'

'I don't know what Mr Catchpole will have to say about that,' she said, presumably citing the landlord. 'He doesn't allow pets in the top flat. It's in the contract.'

Albert was looking distinctly unhappy, his back legs hanging freely, his middle gripped between her body and left arm, over which his front half was leaning, as though over a ship's rail in order to be sick. He struggled, causing the grip to be tightened and his unhappiness to increase.

'Oh, Mr Catchpole was delighted. "That should solve the security problem," was how he put it when we asked him. Well, you're not going to have any trouble with an intruder when you've got an Argentinian iguana on the loose. Not unless he's not worried about losing an arm.'

Her expression indicated that a message of sorts had got through.

'I'm afraid I must dash to the shops before they close. We need meat for Benjamin. You probably heard him banging around frantically earlier on. If I don't find some soon no cat in the neighbourhood will be safe.'

I don't know about Miss Atkins but Albert understood me perfectly. His struggling turned frenzied, all his claws came out, his jaws parted to emit a piercing howl and reveal his few remaining teeth; and it was all his mistress could do to get him back in the room with the door safely closed behind them before he could break free.

Let that be a lesson to any female, nonagenarian midget who thinks she can mess with me tonight, I thought, as with a bouncing stride I set off for the shops.

Chapter 19

I awoke the following morning from a long, untroubled sleep to find Daniela there beside me. She was lying on her back, her head inclined a little in my direction, apparently still asleep; but when I kissed her very gently on the forehead she smiled and, without opening her eyes, rolled over on to her side and put an arm around me. I couldn't imagine a more perfect awakening. Later we showered and dressed, breakfasted leisurely on coffee and toast and set out, hand in hand, for college. A full day stretched ahead for me: three lectures that morning, lunch with Barry Skinner, what would be left of the afternoon to work on the second paper I was writing with Karl, and then, in the evening, Edwin Bloomfield's opening, to which I was taking Daniela – eager and excited at the prospect of further exposure to the cultural life of the city.

It was a cold morning but dry and crisp, the grass on the common tinged with frost and splattered with white blobs, which took a second glance to identify as seagulls, masses of them, which rose together as we watched to swoop and soar and wheel against the powdery blue-grey sky.

'It's days like this that make me long for somewhere warm, like the beaches in California.' Daniela smiled to herself at the recollection. 'Karl and I would spend hours on them. He used to go on about the waves, the way they broke as they approached the shoreline, making currents for the surfers, throwing up mountains of foam. There was one place where that happened way out at sea and he asked me once what I thought about that. I would have been about twelve at the time. I told him there must be a submerged island there. He was delighted.'

'That fits, you know. It would have been a few years before I started on my PhD at Franklin. Karl had got involved in this mad proposal with some Californian entrepreneurs to rebuild a sea bed somewhere around there. Their idea was to improve the surfing conditions; seemed there could have been millions in it; but it turned out to be hopelessly impractical, and would probably have been an environmental disaster as well. I'm sure Karl was aware of that all along, but the idea appealed to him, particularly as it represented a way-out application of some theoretical work he'd been playing around with for years. The time he spent on it wasn't wasted. It led on to countless other things – one of which provided funding for my PhD. So you see, you and I were linked even then, even before I had become aware of your existence.'

'Karl never talks to me about his work. Nor do you, come to that.'

She was smiling as she said this, squeezing my hand and drawing closer to me.

'Shall I tell you about the sea waves then? Carry on from where Karl left off?'

'That's going back a long way. But, yes; why not.'

We had stopped at the main road on the corner of the common, waiting for the traffic lights to change.

'Well, it all started with something a couple of British mathematicians had come up with years before: a stability theory for wave motion. You know, you look across the sea and it's covered in waves, just moving along, minding their own business, the water jigging up and down in crests and troughs with no foaming, no breaking. That's what you call stable wave motion. OK?

She nodded.

'Then somewhere, generally on the approach to the shoreline, this all breaks down. The regular pattern fails: water at the crest, instead

158

of subsiding symmetrically, races on to crash down somewhere ahead, leading to all the dramatic effects you see on a good surfing beach – where, as luck would have it, the sea bed just happens to be well shaped for the purpose; but it could probably be a lot better, of course. Anyway, the delightfully simple thing that came out of the original theory was that instability – where a wave goes unstable and breaks – occurs at the place where short waves (those with the peaks closest together, which for stable behaviour travel faster than all the others) get overtaken by the long waves (those with peaks a long way apart). As the speeds at which short and long waves travel are well known, and both depend on the sea depth, it becomes a very simple matter to predict the depth at which breaking should occur. It soon became apparent that these predictions were spot on. This lent credence to the basic theory, which Karl was able to generalise to describe all manner of complex wave behaviour, and which had potential for the design of an optimal sea bed geometry for whatever conditions you may want to create on the surface. That's what these Californian guys latched on to.'

'I can see Karl really taking to that,' said Daniela with a quiet laugh. 'Playing God as usual; trying to go one better.'

'Well, that's one thing, I suppose. But the practical thing that came out of it all was closure for the set of equations which now forms the basis for the best available computer code for simulating wave motion. Ironically enough, the main current use of this high powered tool is for animation effects. You know, a typical Walt Disney scene: pirate ships fighting it out in a storm, waves battering them, breaking over the decks, that sort of thing. All simulated automatically now, leaving the animators free to concentrate just on the characterisation.'

'Again, just up Karl's street! He's always taken an interest in crappy special effects films. I simply regarded it as just another facet of the little boy in him that refuses to grow up.'

A little later, standing crushed together on the crowded tube, Daniela started to tell me of her exasperation at Trowbridge's interference with her work at the Centre:

'I wouldn't mind at all, in fact I'd welcome the opportunity to have a proper discussion about what I'm trying to do. It's not that difficult to understand. But whenever I speak to him about it I get that blank, dead fish look; you know, when someone hasn't understood a word you're saying to them. So I go down a level and try again. Still no trace of comprehension. So I give up. Then he starts making inane comments and suggestions that bear not the slightest relation to my work. He's completely out of his depth. He should be working in a supermarket or something, seeing to it that the shelves are properly stacked. He'd be good at that. He's very conscientious: puts in the hours, is the first to arrive in the morning, never leaves till late at night when everything's been tidied up, always at Grandison's beck and call – you should see the way he runs up to him when he's called, like a great, stupid dog.'

We had to change trains at Kennington, managing to get seats this time before the carriage filled; then watching the odd assortment of morning passengers, very different from those of the night, filing in to sit, stand and lean, dead eyed and blank, passively waiting for the working day's drudgery to begin. When after several failed attempts the sliding doors managed to close on the heaving mass inside, Daniela went on to tell me about her latest brush with Trowbridge, one she was working herself up for a serious row about. It concerned equipment, vital to her work, in one of the ground floor laboratories. She had got the necessary clearance to use this from time to time when the need arose, but now he was making trouble, trying to stop her going down there altogether. It seemed that the problem stemmed from Sean, who worked mainly in the adjacent lab but was gradually spreading his tentacles all over the place, claiming exclusive rights to whatever he could lay his hands on.

'Nobody knows what he's up to – certainly not Trowbridge, for all his pretence of being in charge. He's obviously been given instructions to see Sean gets whatever he wants. They seem terrified he'll pack up and leave. He's really got them . . . what's the phrase I heard the other day? . . . over a barrel.'

'Maybe they worry too much about him being wanted elsewhere.'

'What makes you say that?' She looked at me expectantly. 'Do you know something I don't?'

'Yes, I think I do. I've been waiting to tell you about it but it seemed there were better things to talk about since you got back from Hassocks.'

'I know.'

Her shoulder pressed against mine and her hand gently squeezed my wrist as I told her of Karl's enquiries concerning the supposed offer from MIT. She looked puzzled for just an instant:

'The crafty, scheming little shit. That fits perfectly with what I've always felt about him – without any clear reason until now.'

'Worked a treat though, didn't it?' I laughed as I said this but she clearly didn't want to see the funny side. 'Karl was quite impressed,' I went on. 'He thought it showed a creative streak in him he hadn't been aware of before.'

'He would,' she replied, angry at first; then, after a few moments, squeezed my hand and gave a wry smile.

'Perhaps it would be better to just keep this to yourself for the moment. Don't say anything to Angela, or to anyone else come to that. You haven't heard the main bit yet.'

I started to tell her about my session with Tony Mulgrave. She cut in at the first mention of his name:

'I remember Karl speaking about him years ago. They worked together for a while, were quite close. Then something happened to him. I think it was to do with his mother getting ill, then dying. He had some sort of breakdown. Karl was quite upset about it. I remember it well because he missed coming to stay with us before the term started at Franklin, staying on in London instead, trying to help Tony sort himself out.'

'Well he seems well enough sorted out now; even spoken of as a possible successor to Hardcastle.'

As I said this, I wondered again about Tony. Something of his account of Sean's work had bothered me at the time and I was reminded of this now without being able to pinpoint what it was. It didn't quite hang together: something was missing. Perhaps things would become clearer, I had thought afterwards, when I got to attend one of the working group meetings. But now I wasn't sure this was ever going to happen: Tony's manner when we parted had somehow conveyed the impression that he could have had second thoughts about involving me. I couldn't really blame him. As I had told him at the time, there was little I had to offer for their purposes. But I was not to wait long for my unfocussed misgivings to crystallise: Daniela had spotted the problem on hearing my potted account of Tony's story. We were approaching Tottenham Court Road when she asked the question, which I immediately kicked myself for not having asked Tony at the time:

'Where are these mysterious financiers getting their information from? If you say it's Trowbridge or Hardcastle then forget it. They can't be that stupid. There must be somebody else involved. Some supposedly reliable source that tells them they're on to a winner.'

'You're right. You've just put your finger on the thing about the whole business that's been bothering me: the credibility of the work, who it is that's making the judgement.'

Something else she had said a short while before was stirring up another misgiving I had had with Tony's story:

'Tony's mother . . .' I turned to face her. 'Was it cancer she died of? Can you remember?'

'Yes, I think it was. In fact, I'm quite sure it was. There was something about the treatment she was receiving. It's coming back to me now. Tony was getting involved. I think he insisted on changes at some point. And then she died and he blamed himself. That was something Karl was always trying to reassure him about: that he did what any intelligent, concerned person would have done in the circumstances.'

We had surfaced by now, emerging from the station into the traffic jammed streets, exhaust fumes and exhaled breath condensing in rising clouds through the cold air.

'I'll show you a short cut to college,' I said, guiding her into Great Russell Street. 'Well, it may not be actually shorter but at least makes a change.'

We passed scruffy cafes and souvenir shops, the trade union movement's Congress House, with its Soviet style sculpture – exultant male figure leaping to the assistance of a supine comrade (getting the lazy bugger out of bed and back to work, perhaps); arriving eventually at the massive, cast iron gateway on the left, into which we turned, traversed the forecourt, the Grecian portico, and entered the building. Then across the vast courtyard, on through a maze of corridors, staircases and galleries; stopping as the mood took us to view exhibits; exiting finally through the door in what a visiting Dutch professor had famously, and without facetious intent, described to colleagues as the backside of the British Museum. Malet Street stretched before us, its right flank dominated by the forbidding, modernistic edifice of Senate House, headquarters of the University of London; to its left the eastern boundary of Prince of Wales College, its main-entrance-bearing south face peering out a mere twenty yards ahead.

'It's a particularly good route if it happens to be raining,' said Daniela.

I agreed with her:

'A lot of people find it useful. So long as they don't think of introducing admission charges. They'll find their visitor statistics tumbling even more than they could possibly have imagined if they do.'

I was working at my desk later that morning when the phone rang. It was Tony Mulgrave in buoyant mood. He had just heard from the head of the legal team looking into the agreement Sean had signed with ARC Pharmaceuticals, and was bursting to tell someone about it. Apparently it was full of holes. On the basis of expert advice, the college's lawyers were now convinced they could get the whole thing thrown out.

'This really changes everything.' He was exuding confidence now, a new man. 'What with this, and recent developments on the political front, it seems things could really be rolling.'

Chapter 20

Grandison's hands-off approach to the research of the Centre was not without danger. A noteworthy occurrence, which permanently scarred him, concerned an American postdoctoral researcher recruited by Lauder shortly before his car crash. It was actually arranged through Karl, who was approached at Franklin by the young man, Stan Shultz, who knew of his links with Prince of Wales College and was keen to experience a spell of living and working in London. He had just been awarded his PhD for a notable piece of work, which had been supervised by a high-flying colleague of Karl's from the Department of Biosciences there. Shultz's credentials were impeccable: he clearly had a brilliant career ahead of him and was being wooed at the time by a number of American universities, vying with each other to secure his services. It was his misfortune to arrive when the Goldburg Centre was going through the state of turmoil that followed Lauder's accident, and to be assigned by Grandison to a group quite happily engaged in abysmally low-level contract research for a manufacturer of canned food products. He protested, at first politely, later more forcefully, but Grandison, disconcerted by what he saw as his authority being brought into question, stood firm. As a result, Shultz transferred himself to the library and concentrated instead on delving into the voluminous literature relating to his fields of interest, in preparation for serious programmes of research in the future, intermittently writing to other university departments in the country to offer seminars on the work he had done at Franklin, which was just beginning to appear in the scientific journals. By way of breaking the monotony of these solitary pursuits, he took to attending the weekly seminars, entering with vigour and incisiveness into the ensuing discussions. These interventions did not always meet with universal approval; the crunch came when a member of Trowbridge's team, who had reported some experimental findings with which he appeared well pleased, revealed himself, under questioning by Shultz, to be completely unaware both of the theoretical background to the work and of other recent investigations into effectively the same problem. Trowbridge's attempt to come to the rescue only led to his own ignorance of his supposed field of expertise being held up for public display. Grandison, who had arrived late to the meeting, but not late enough, turned white with fury at what he regarded a treasonous attack, and subsequently took various steps to see to it that such a thing could not occur again. An immediate one was to call in Shultz to tell him he was no longer welcome in the Centre; and, as he appeared to be contributing nothing to the programme to which he had been assigned, the best thing he could do would be to move on as soon as possible.

This led to the first major clash between Grandison and Karl, who had just returned to London following a two month stint in California. Shultz had come to see him in a highly distressed state, telling him of the difficulty he had been encountering in engaging in any worthwhile research, and of his recent clash with Grandison. Confirmation of the seminar incident was not difficult to obtain. Viewed objectively, this amounted to little more than the pointing out by Shultz of things that should have been obvious to any serious investigator. Karl lost no time in calling on Grandison to inform him, in characteristically direct terms, of the total unacceptability of his stance. He demanded he apologise to Shultz and arrange for him to discuss with members of Lauder's team where his undoubted talents could best contribute to their researches. Grandison, more than a little ruffled at this outside intrusion into the Centre's affairs,

166

at first insisted coldly that it was nobody's business but his own. But when Karl exploded and threatened to take the matter further, he realised that his singularly precarious position would thereby be brought under the spotlight, and with bad grace he caved in. After Karl had left, he summoned his wife to fetch him immediately. The following morning she phoned to say that he was unwell and would require a period of complete rest, after which he was not seen again at the Centre until midway through the following week.

This incident marked the onset of hostilities with Karl, regarded by Grandison as representing a discredited academic elite: feckless individualists of no relevance to the systemic progression of scientific research; eccentric purists, hostile to any attempt to contain their isolated explorations within a management structure capable of meeting stated objectives. Karl, for his part, saw in Grandison just another example of the dead hand of bureaucracy: stifling individual imagination and initiative; reducing the once fiercely idiosyncratic academic to a cog in a banal machine; chasing funding for its own sake and producing nothing of originality. In a nutshell, taking all the fun and meaning out of the game.

Chapter 21

The offices of Reisenberger, Day and Skinner are to be found in an elegant cul-de-sac off Oxford Street, where they occupy the entire ground floor of a comprehensively gutted Regency mansion: of the original building only the facade remains. I entered from the street into the reception area to be confronted by what can only be described as a glamorous blond seated behind a low counter. Her demeanour promised untold delights if I could just get through the simple initiation test she lost no time in subjecting me to. Behind her, a glass partition revealed an open plan office in which five or six designer-clad young persons of all sexes were making a very good job of staring intently at computer screens and otherwise giving the impression of urgent, stimulating activity.

'Hallo there,' she said with an alluring smile. 'What can I do for you this morning?'

A number of possibilities came to mind.

'I've come to see Barry Skinner. Maybe I'm a few minutes early.'

'What's your name please?' I told her. 'You don't appear to have an appointment. I can't find anything here.'

She was thumbing through the pages of a heavily scribbled upon notebook, not as though in any way searching for my name, rather to make clear to me that I stood no chance at all, so forget it.

'Well, he's expecting me at one-fifteen. Why don't you just phone to tell him I'm here.'

'I can't do that.' She appeared quite shocked at the thought of it. 'He's with an important client. What did you say your business was?'

'I didn't.'

'Perhaps you had better fill in your details here.'

She had produced a pad and was indicating, with a beautifully manicured, green lacquered nail, a blank row on the open page. This called for my name, company, business, contact name and other things as well.

Before I could get round to invoking some right-to-privacy legislation, perhaps throwing in the Geneva Convention, Barry appeared from somewhere behind her escorting his important client: a small rat-like individual of Middle Eastern appearance, sporting a shiny-new, brown-velvet-collared camel hair coat. Seeing me, Barry smiled warmly and came over to shake my hand.

'Paul! Good to see you. Sorry if I've kept you waiting. Why don't you go up to my office – Melinda will show you the way. Make yourself at home. I'll be with you in a couple of shakes.'

Melinda smiled coyly, then gave me a look as she led me away which implied that, against all the odds, I had somehow made it; so that it was now just possible . . . perhaps some rainy Monday afternoon, when there was nothing much else going on . . . but not to bank on it.

'I'm incredibly impressed,' I told Barry when he joined me no more than five minutes later. His office featured a good deal of gleaming chrome and leather, tastefully blended with a number of extremely expensive looking antiques. 'You don't mean to tell me that a third of all this is actually yours?'

'Closer to half, as it happens. When it was all Charlie Day's he simply added the name Reisenberger for effect – very important in this game. Then when I bought in we decided to keep it. God, you haven't changed a bit – now that the initial shock has worn off.'

'Just what I was thinking about you.'

Apart from the natty clothes, styled hair and not unattractive laugh lines around the eyes, there was still very much of the irreverent undergraduate look about him that I remembered well. He went over to an elaborately carved oak cabinet, possibly dating back to William the Conqueror, perhaps once one of his treasured personal possessions, and opened it to reveal a dipsomaniac's dream hoard of bottles, glasses and related accessories.

'I've booked at a place in the City I sometimes take clients to for chinwags in reasonable privacy. Not flashy at all, but the food's OK. What would you like to drink now?'

'Whatever you're having will be fine.'

Over Camparis-on-the-rocks we began to feel our way, somewhat awkwardly at first, into what common territory we could find. The awkwardness evaporated remarkably quickly, was gone in fact by the time we had finished that first drink. I had been looking forward to this encounter, but worried that it would have to be rushed on account of Barry's crowded work schedule. However, as we passed Melinda, on our way to the Mercedes and chauffeur waiting outside, he turned to her:

'Sam can deal with anything that comes in for me this afternoon. I won't be back till late. Paul and I have a lot of catching up to do.'

The restaurant was in a discretely lit basement, which emanated a persuasive impression of wealth and influence. This was largely due to the clientele: predominantly male, middle-aged and of generally unhealthy appearance, seated around the small, well spaced apart tables, all quietly engaged in matters of great moment: insider deal-ings, multimillion pound takeovers, arms sales to repressive regimes, assassinations of troublesome heads of state, not to mention more transparently illegal ventures. A waiter greeted Barry as might an old family retainer and we were escorted to an alcove with a table laid for two, but containing enough plates, cutlery and especially glasses to accommodate a small concert party. As we were settling down, a notably sinister arms dealer at a table some way off gave a friendly wave in our direction, which Barry returned.

'That, believe it or not,' he told me, 'is the bookies' favourite for the next Archbishop of Canterbury. If it comes off we could well do some good business there. He's concerned about their image. Talking about a full makeover if he gets the job.'

We then got talking about old school colleagues, although both of us had hardly kept up with that side of things. One fellow, a near contemporary, had gone into politics, entered parliament as a conservative MP, then got kicked out at the next election. Another one was in jail for fraud. These amounted to the most significant exchanges in that general category. I was particularly keen to hear of his dealings with Grandison but something told me not to rush this; likewise with Hardcastle. We had just about got through the first bottle of wine, however, when without any prompting Barry embarked on a trail of reminiscences which it appeared could lead naturally into his dealings with Prince of Wales College and the Goldburg Centre.

'It's donkey's years since Charlie Day got the Appletons contract. He's getting on a bit now, Charlie, but in his day no one could touch him. People still go on about what he did before that for the dairy products industry, in particular the yoghurt thing. Worked absolute wonders, not only for Charlie and the business but the profession as a whole.'

As I looked at him uncomprehendingly, he went on:

'Don't you know the story? My God! I thought everybody did. You know, after the Second World War . . . the huge emphasis on dairy products . . . just the thing to sort out the nation's health. Milk for school kids, pint-a-day all round, lashings of butter, cream and cheese for everyone: a land flowing with fat and cholesterol. Then years later the backlash: people dropping off the perch all over the place clutching their chests. And not just the workers; not just another of your unfortunate industrial diseases culling the hoi polloi.

171

It was captains of industry this time, the rich and successful disproportionally targeted: this lot here.'

His arm swept to encompass the huddled clientele, earnestly swilling wine from enormous goblets, stuffing rich food into bloated red faces.

'This was serious. Something had to give.'

It did, he went on to explain. The dairy products industry was huge; vast amounts of money were at risk, not to mention the political fallout which would have followed its collapse. It hovered for a while, then started to totter, consumer confidence eroding by the day. Charlie Day was consulted, at first on a relatively minor aspect; later, when his strategy was seen to yield results, more and more. In the end he was running the whole show, subcontracting to well tried specialist operators where necessary.

'There was no instant solution. Public confidence had to be rebuilt. This takes time, has to be approached from every conceivable angle. That was where Charlie really scored over all his rivals – and, my God, there were enough of those. Big fish as well.'

The waiter had brought more food and Barry ordered another bottle. Looking around it occurred to me that I might have been somewhat off target in my assessment of our fellow diners: nothing really sinister about them at all; just going about their legitimate business in a civilised manner; no harm at all in that. Sounds of controlled jollity erupted from somewhere behind me, people toasting and congratulating each other on the conclusion of a deal.

'The first thing he did was to see to it that the other side of the story got told: the nutritional benefits of milk. There was plenty of evidence around for that.'

He paused to transport a cube of cream coated veal to his mouth.

'It was just a matter of emphasising it, getting it reported in the press and everywhere else. Charlie had that side of things well sewn up. He even set up a small journal, regularly publishing summaries of current research articles into nutrition and other health matters.

Got it sent out to thousands of health workers and the like throughout the country – the Dairy Council are still doing this. Each issue contains something or other showing what a good thing dairy products are – sandwiched between unrelated items that could be of interest to those people, so as give some sort of impression that it isn't purely self-serving.'

'Where on earth does all this research originate from?' I asked. 'Where is it published?'

'Oh, all over the place. It's no secret any longer that medical research can be used to show absolutely anything. Charlie was probably the first to make use of this fact in an organised way. If you were to come to me tomorrow asking for independent research showing that a diet of stinging nettles and corned beef is the key to sexual potency and longevity, my guy who deals with that side of things would come up with half a dozen supporting articles in seemingly respectful journals by the next day. The health food manufacturers have no difficulty whatsoever in finding research to support anything they produce. The only trouble is that it's just as easy to show the contrary: that vitamin C and green cabbage are bad for you, for example. You're a physicist. What you guys think of as research bears no relation to this medical stuff: anything goes there. There's no consensus at all, and nobody's the slightest bit bothered.'

What he was saying meshed in well with Tony Mulgrave's view, I thought, as the waiter came over to refill our glasses. Barry took a sip, murmured approvingly and carried on:

'But his really brilliant coup was to spot the potential for yoghurt – virtually unheard of here at the time – and push it to the limit. It's only milk, for Christ's sake, with a few bugs growing in it. And yet within a year or two Charlie had everyone, starting with the dyed-in-the-wool vegetarians and other health freaks, gulping it down as if they'd discovered the elixir of life.'

'You mentioned Appletons a while back,' I said, when I had finished laughing. 'Were you involved with them at all? I only ask because it seems that Hardcastle made his reputation there. It's commonly believed in college that that's what got him appointed rector.'

'Most of it was before my time. Charlie was the one responsible. All Hardcastle did was raise the money to pay him. I keep an occasional eye on them now, see that the press get fed the good news, that type of thing. Same with the Goldburg Centre. Charlie passed that over to me too when we went into partnership, though between you and me it's a pain in the arse, which we only continue with for old times sake – for Hardcastle's sake to be precise. No money in it for us to speak of.'

I thought at this point to ask if he knew anything about the O'Brien affair, was involved with it in any way, but, as he hadn't mentioned it himself, thought better of it. Maybe later. A natural break occurred as we chose the dessert, after which the conversation turned to more personal matters: his recent divorce, which I was able to cap with my break with Julie. He was now reasonably settled with someone else, and I confessed to the possibility of something new starting for me, though I didn't feel comfortable about being too specific at this stage. We nevertheless made vague plans to meet up as a foursome sometime. Then, inevitably, the Pius XII award came up, always good in the past for a chuckle and a rehash of the speculative considerations advanced at the time. This reminded Barry of an interesting bit of news:

'Did you know that Ignatius has left the order?'

'You're kidding.'

'Not at all. He occasionally temps for a firm of business consultants in the Midlands. We've even used him ourselves once or twice. Last time was only a couple of months ago. I met him briefly with his sister – who, believe it or not, looks just like him. They live together now in a council flat in Birmingham.'

I tried for a moment to imagine Ignatius without his grubby cassock and dog collar, then gave up.

'Did you question him about the award? . . . Oswald's lead up to it?' I asked instead.

'No time. But maybe some other day. He's keen to get more work. Seems he lives largely off his sister's pension. He's a shrewd old bird, quite useful in his way. Would you like to meet him? Easy enough to arrange.'

'No thanks. You know, I met Grandison at a conference in Switzerland ten years after he left school. I tried to talk to him about St John's, the Pius XII award and all that, but he wouldn't respond at all. And when I meet him now it's the same. Not that I would dream of trying to bring that up again, but I see him mentally shying away in anticipation. It's strange, don't you think? Did you see the way he responded when you joked about it that evening? With Hardcastle? What do you make of him now? You must be involved with him quite a bit if you're looking after the Goldburg Centre's interests. How do you get on with him?'

There! After holding back all that time, I had jumped in feet first. Did I imagine it or did Barry look a trifle uncomfortable for just a moment. If he did he rapidly recovered, summoning the waiter to come over, and ordering two glasses of a vintage Sauternes he had sampled the week before.

'You must try this,' he said as we waited for it to arrive. 'Yes, he's a strange fish. But totally dedicated to putting the Centre on the map. You have to admire that. It also makes life a lot easier for me.'

He said that last bit in a way that made it quite clear he wanted to change the subject.

'Ah, here it is.'

The waiter had arrived with an opened bottle from which he proceeded to pour into two of the remaining glasses.

'Oswald's in a home, you know,' Barry went on after tasting and signifying approval. 'Gone completely gar-gar, so they tell me, poor chap, though apparently quite happy and contented.'

175

Something came to me quite suddenly then, with a certainty which defied reason and explanation.

'That holy picture,' I said, 'the one of Oswald at prayer. You faked it didn't you?'

I had sometimes wondered about this before, but now, after the passage of more than twenty years, there was absolutely no doubt.

Barry chuckled good-naturedly, took another sip from his glass and looked me straight in the eye.

'What do you think of it, eh?'

'Marvellous, bloody marvellous.'

An enveloping sweet richness, hints of marmalade, exotic spices, something precious . . .

'How did you do it?'

'Easy enough, even then, if you have access to the facilities. They still keep popping up all over the place, you know. If only I had a penny for every copy that's been made. In Italy he's an Abruzzese hermit who conversed with snakes and wild beasts; in Ireland some bloodthirsty monk; God knows who else he passes for. Some people have absolutely no scruples.'

As we were leaving, weaving our way around the tables, Barry exchanged greetings with a number of remaining diners, stopping once or twice to do this more thoroughly, interspersing light-hearted banter with seemingly urgent matters of business. A quintessentially British way of doing things, I thought with approval: the casual greasing of the wheels of commerce by able, amiable denizens of places such as this; the making of momentous decisions affecting the lives of millions to the accompaniment of the good things of life. What a splendid way to do business. What a shining example to hold up to the world.

Chapter 22

After leaving the restaurant, I asked Barry if he would drop me off at Oxford Circus, which is on a direct tube line to Brixton. I felt the need to flake out for a while, certainly there was no point in trying to work on the paper. When I got home, I phoned Daniela, arranged to meet her by the Centre entrance that evening, in good time for Edwin Bloomfield's opening, then collapsed on the sofa. I must have dozed for an hour or so and awoke feeling terrible. A shower and a strong coffee helped a bit, and then it was time to set off. Some people, I thought, as I headed down Coldharbour Lane, are always doing this sort of thing: people like Barry and those others in that restaurant; they probably regard it as a normal part of the working day. Perhaps I'd been missing out somehow. On the other hand, on careful consideration, perhaps not. Though I had to admit Barry looked all right on it, but then you certainly couldn't say that for most of the others. Flaccid considerations of this type occupied my mind for the remainder of the journey, were pretty well all it was capable of.

I arrived at the Goldburg entrance just as Daniela was emerging from the building, looking exceptionally stunning. We kissed, rather sedately in view of the presence of colleagues heading home and workmen in overalls leisurely contemplating the fountain; these then took to making notes on clipboards and conferring earnestly among themselves. Could it be that plans for its removal were really taking shape?

'It's not far is it?' Daniela asked as we were approaching the gate. 'Can we walk? I could do with some air and exercise after spending all day in the lab.'

'Why not. I need some too.'

Winding our way towards Cork Street, I told her of my afternoon with Barry. This got quite involved as the whole background needed filling in and I had difficulty getting the order right, giving the story some sort of coherence. There were so many strands: St John's, the Pius XII award, Grandison, the Goldburg Centre, even Hardcastle. I left the Oswald holy picture bit for later: a treat I knew she would enjoy.

'But this is amazing.' She had been questioning me all the way through my muddled account, trying to untangle the knots. 'Do you think he's involved in the Sean business in any way?'

'I'm sure he must be, but that's delicate ground. He didn't mention it so I thought it best not to bring it up. He seemed a bit cagey about his dealings with Grandison in general. I suppose that's understand-able if they're in the middle of something. Anyway, the last thing I wanted to do was appear too interested.'

It dawned on me as I was saying this that any worries I might have had about divided loyalties had completely evaporated. All I wanted was to get to the heart of what was going on; and, whether or not I was to attend Tony's workshops, I was with Karl one hundred percent, I decided, regardless of what other motives he might have. There were three of us in this: Karl, Daniela and me. It was impossi-ble to imagine more perfect partners in any venture.

I was still in this unusually decisive, upbeat mood as our route brought us alongside the Goose, where we managed to resist the magnetic attraction of its open doorway – through which, however, I caught a glimpse of Edward Weatherill, propped up at the bar, his legs still apparently holding up well for seven-thirty.

'If only we had more time,' I said sadly as we walked passed, 'but we're late as it is.'

We arrived at the gallery together with a smartly dressed couple, potential buyers by the look of them, just as the door opened to let someone out. There was quite a crowd inside, standing around in groups, holding glasses and talking loudly, nobody so much as glancing at the paintings, which lined all available walls, including those of the corridors and stairways leading to a mezzanine and basement. We entered a room looking around for familiar faces, seeing none at first. Behind a table in a corner, a waitress was filling glasses with something fizzy from a large jug. Then I became aware of Benjamin, standing in front of her, patiently waiting.

'Thank you so much,' he said as a glass was passed to him, 'I'll just take another for my friend if you don't mind.'

He made off happily, clutching them both, not responding to my nod as he passed, either not noticing me or, more likely, seeing no need in the present circumstances to bother with social niceties.

Daniela then suggested we examine the paintings, a seemingly eccentric thing to attempt to which I nevertheless agreed. Slowly we made our way round the exhibits, taking in those parts not completely obscured behind guests lost in animated conversation: tenor and bass notes overlaid with soaring sopranos, exclamations and peals of laughter intermittently raising the decibels. The sound track in the next room was much the same, but contained an additional strident note which struck me as familiar:

'Paul . . . '

Sarah's voice boomed from the far wall, against which she had been conversing noisily with a small group, which included a strikingly good-looking young woman, exotically got up and an obvious focus of attention. A much older man, with a shiny, embalmed look about him, was standing proprietorially beside her, his face set in an expression of profound disapproval.

'. . . come over and join us, there's someone here I'd like you to meet.'

'Who on earth is that?' whispered Daniela as we picked our way over to them.

'Sarah, Edward Weatherill's wife.'

'Looks more like his daughter, or granddaughter even.'

'I know, she's quite a girl though, I think you're going to like her.'

Daniela didn't look too sure about that.

'Well! What have we here?'

Sarah was eyeing Daniela approvingly, if somewhat suspiciously.

'This is Daniela, a friend of mine.'

'*Very* nice! A friend eh?' Her eyes narrowed: 'Haven't I seen you before . . . with Karl Dembowski?'

God, this was getting complicated. On hearing Karl's name, the look of disapproval on the face of the embalmed one intensified.

'You could well have done,' said Daniela, 'I've known Karl for years.'

'I see,' said Sarah knowingly; then, turning to the group: 'This is Paul Harrison, he's also a friend of Karl's.'

Brief introductions followed, ending with: '. . . Cecil Uttley and his wife Fritzy. Cecil owns a gallery a few doors down the road. He also runs a charity auction that was very much in the news a short while ago.'

She laughed heartily on getting this out, as did Fritzy and others in the group; Daniela, to whom I had told the tale, chuckled; Cecil's stone-faced countenance hardened yet further.

'Oh, come off it Cecil, crack it a bit. Where's your sense of humour?'

Any reply he may have wished to make was blocked by the arrival of a waitress bearing a tray of glasses.

'Champagne anyone?' she asked.

'Champagne!' exclaimed Sarah derisively. 'Tesco's Spanish plonk more likely.'

She nevertheless helped herself, as we all did, including Cecil, without any modification to his sombre expression, clearly firmly set on not enjoying himself.

'You haven't by any chance seen my old man?' Sarah's abrupt change of tack perhaps indicating she had decided to let Cecil off the hook. 'He should have been here ages ago.'

I hesitated for a moment, weighing up whether or not to admit having seen him, but before I could come to any decision Daniela had chipped in:

'He was in the Goose half an hour ago, we saw him as we passed on our way here.'

'Oh my God! That means he's been there since lunchtime. Fit for nothing again tonight.' She laughed as she said this, her anger of a split second earlier disintegrating as suddenly as it had formed. 'Which leaves me with the usual fucking problem of getting him home.' She drank from her glass without seemingly finding fault with its contents. 'Usual bloody story. Well, I'll face that one later.' Her glass was empty now, she was looking around for a source of replenishment. 'Bit bloody slow in passing the stuff around aren't they?'

'I do hope he makes it here,' said Fritzy, who had clearly been storing something up and had moved to centre stage to deliver it. 'I haven't seen him since he finished my portrait. Thank heavens that's over and done with. If I'd known what was involved, I don't think I would have agreed to go through with it.' She didn't say this as though she meant it somehow. 'Although the final result is rather good, don't you think so Sarah?'

'Brilliant, bloody brilliant. *Very* erotic. Should do you no harm at all when it gets seen around. Fritzy is trying to make it as a model,' Sarah added for my, Daniela's, and everyone within earshot's benefit, 'doing quite well actually. Just reached the point when she needs that little extra push.'

'The positions he got me into while trying to decide how to do me.' Fritzy had clearly in no way finished with her account, was just warming up to it, her voice gaining in volume, holding the attention of everyone around, quietening them down appreciably. 'I didn't know *what* to think at first. You should see the sketches! Doesn't believe in leaving much to the imagination, your old man. But I do have to say, he was always perfectly charming. And *very* persuasive. I don't think I would have done it for anyone else.'

'Yes,' agreed Sarah, smiling away at the memory of something, 'he hasn't lost his touch in all these years. Especially when he's working on something that turns him on.'

'Yes, and getting paid five grand into the bargain.'

Cecil, having aggressively broken his vow of silence, immediately found cause to regret it:

'Now come off it Cecil. You know perfectly well you got an exceptionally good deal there. The duchess of Westmoreland paid more than double that for a formal portrait – of which, incidentally, you grabbed a fat commission for doing bugger all. And that only took five sittings.'

'God knows how many I had.' Fritzy gave Cecil a cold look before continuing. 'I don't suppose he had her climbing naked up and down a step ladder.'

'I don't suppose so either,' said Sarah. 'For one thing she's nearly seventy . . .'

'Said it would help me relax before sitting. You know, I really think it did.'

Daniela squeezed my hand. She was smiling happily when I turned to look at her, clearly enjoying herself as much as I was. I felt a sudden urge to have her to myself, to take her off somewhere. We appeared to be the only ones in the room still wearing coats.

'Is there a cloakroom here?' I asked Sarah, 'it's getting quite warm in these things.'

'Downstairs, you can't miss it. And don't leave a tip in the bowl when you go back to collect. Just give something to the girl if you want to when nobody's looking, or else Hamish will simply knock it off her wages, tight sod that he is.'

There was nobody in the cloakroom, all the hooks loaded, other coats forming piles on the counter and chairs to which we added ours. Having done this, it seemed appropriate to take advantage of being unexpectedly alone together among all that soft fabric, lining the walls inches thick, but this was soon interrupted by the sound of someone thumping down the stairs.

'Shall we go home?' I said, as we straightened our clothes.

'Yes, soon. But while we're here let's quickly take in the rest of the pictures. I'm quite impressed with what I've seen so far.'

I had to agree with her. There was undoubtedly something night-marishly compelling about them, their nature-defying use of colour: blood red skies over yellow oceans, blue woodlands exuding menace; everyday scenes of conventional domesticity overlaid with a haunting sense of impending doom.

'Is he mad do you think?' Daniela was staring at a purple dog, which you just knew was about to savage the green child standing passively watching with its indigo mother. 'They're so strong and obsessed. It would be easy to imagine them being painted in a lunatic asylum.'

'I don't think so somehow.'

I was thinking of Edwin, duelling with Benjamin over the price of a drink, behaviour that could be thought obsessive I suppose, but not quite in the way she was implying, more in the tight-as-a-nun's-twat category of Sarah's scheme of things.

'That's Edwin over there, isn't it?'

Daniela had paused to indicate his presence as we were easing our way into another room from a crowded corridor. He was locked in serious, hushed conversation with two men, one of whom I had seen just before, weaving his way arrogantly between the assembled groups, receiving respectful nods from almost everyone, most of which he chose to ignore. Whatever it was that was going on between him, Edwin and the other one appeared of the utmost gravity, Edwin's face revealing a concern far in excess of what could conceivably be attributed to anything as relatively mundane as mere art. It could be that the one I hadn't noticed before was a doctor, explaining to him his condition was inoperable, but that if he took things easy he might just about be able to hang on for another week; or perhaps it was being put to him that the protocol of the occasion required that he treat everybody present to a slap-up dinner some- where expensive.

Further speculation was cut short by a loud disturbance, marking the arrival at the gallery of Ben Palmer and Edward, both much the worse for wear, Edward testifying convincingly to this condition by falling over immediately on entry, thereby impeding both the egress of guests who had had enough and the arrival on the scene of Sarah, who, having correctly interpreted the kerfuffle, was hastening to his assistance.

Her voice, tinged with an unaccustomed softness – 'Are you all right, darling?' – rang out above the general commotion, at first giving me some cause for concern over Edward's well-being: but only for a moment.

'Of course I'm bloody all right. Just get me up will you, you stupid cow.'

Also heading purposefully in his direction, people respectfully making way for him, was one of Edwin's co-conspirators, the putative doctor of my imagination, now seemingly intent on showing off his professional skills. As usual I had got it wrong. This one, it turned out, was Hamish, the gallery owner, concerned solely with maintaining decorum and showing he had matters under control. (The other one, I was to learn later, was a noted art critic, whose varied response to greetings provided a clear indication of the greeter's current pecking order in the art world hierarchy.)

'Perhaps we should help,' said Daniela.

We were quite close and the people around appeared rooted in silence, only Ben trying ineffectively to help Sarah get Edward to his feet. Hamish was standing commandingly beside them, giving useless advice in loud, confident tones.

'Oh piss off Hamish.'

Sarah was even more than usually unprepared to accept any nonsense. She had secured a firm hold of Edward's left arm and I went round to relieve Ben on the right flank.

'Yes . . . that's right. One, two, three . . . ups-a-daisy.'

'Careful now!' This loudly from Edward, not it seemed unduly grateful for our efforts. 'Look what you're bloody doing will you.'

Hamish, giving a very good impression of being unoffended by Sarah's directive, led the way to an inconspicuous alcove, where we lowered Edward into an armchair, in which he rapidly recovered his composure and asked Hamish to fetch him a drink:

'Not the piss you're doling out for the occasion, if you don't mind. Just get me a drop of that single malt you've got locked away in the safe.'

Ben too appeared to be in a somewhat improved state, even going so far as to apologise to Sarah for Edward's condition, which he put down to his (Ben's) cause for celebration, to which Edward had sportingly agreed to participate:

'Seven bloody years it's taken. I'd completely given up hope of ever getting anything, and then in the post this morning comes this fat cheque. I just couldn't believe my eyes.'

'What the fuck are you talking about Ben?' asked Sarah, not unkindly.

'The fountain! The Goldburg fucking fountain . . .'

Ben paused for a moment, looking somewhat confused, as though he couldn't quite believe what he was saying:

'They're going to start it up again. Christ knows when, but it's all agreed. Paid me off into the bargain. Mustn't tell anyone though . . .

sworn to secrecy and all that. They don't want the press getting wind of it, not after what happened last time.'

'If I were you,' said Sarah, 'I'd get that cheque cleared pretty smartly – like first thing in the morning when the banks open.'

'Oh, I've done that already. Thought it would dissolve in my hands if I didn't. Straight to the NatWest soon as it arrived, before telling anyone. Watched while they piped it aboard.'

'Well, then there really is something worth celebrating.' Sarah was looking quite excited at the prospect. 'Edward,' she said, turning to him. '*Edward!* Wake up for Christ's sake.' Then, to us: 'Fancy making a night of it?'

I became aware of Daniela's arm encircling my waist.

'We'd have loved to,' I said, 'but I'm afraid there's something else we've arranged to do.'

'I'll bet there is,' said Sarah, understandingly.

Chapter 23

A short time after the incident with Shultz, the Goldburg Centre was targeted by a practical joker who almost succeeded in causing severe embarrassment. An announcement had been prepared for insertion in the 'positions vacant' columns of a number of newspapers and journals advertising postdoctoral posts in the Centre. It ended with a standard rubric in small print stating that the place operated an anti-discriminatory, equal opportunities policy, so that applicants would be judged regardless of race, religion, sexual orientation, or any other characteristics which a less enlightened employer might well baulk at. Annabel had prepared the piece for electronic transmission to the agency that dealt with such matters. She had printed a copy which remained on her desk for the day or so it took her to get round to checking it. When she had done this, and had satisfied herself that all was well, she proceeded with the transfer. What arrived at the agency, however, differed from her printed copy, the rubric having deviated somewhat from the standard form. It still set out to reassure potential applicants of the open minded objectivity of the selection procedure, but now did so by drawing attention to the rich diversity of present Centre personnel. These were said to consist predominantly of members from severely disadvantaged minority groups and to include ' . . . a fair sprinkling of social outcasts and sexual deviants of every conceivable persuasion'. Publication was only halted at the last minute as a result of action by an unusually vigilant member of the agency staff: she telephoned Annabel. After that the heavens opened.

An emergency meeting was rapidly convened of the college's Equal Opportunities and Sexual Harassment Committee, and a painstakingly thorough investigation set in motion. The misdeed must have occurred between the times of the unadulterated version being printed by Annabel and its corrupted rendering being received by the agency. It was during this period, Grandison came to realise with mounting excitement and indignation, that Karl had come to plague him about the Shultz business. Annabel, under close questioning, could not recall having seen him leave, and so would very probably have been out of her office, through which visitors to Grandison had to pass, when he left. This, so far as Grandison was concerned, clinched it. To others, to whom Grandison confided his suspicion, the idea of Karl spotting the printed copy on Annabel's desk, locating the file on her PC, then composing and keying in the alteration – with Grandison liable to enter the room at any moment from one side and Annabel very likely to do so from the other – appeared implausible. He nevertheless refused to budge from his view, even when it was pointed out to him that the file was held on a server, readily accessible from any terminal in the general office, which was used by countless people having ample time to devise and execute the deed. The only outcome of the inquiry was the intro-duction of security measures, which considerably inconvenienced a large number of people going about their innocent business without offering much in the way of an impediment to further illegal inter-vention by a determined hacker.

Chapter 24

Karl did not return to England for Christmas as had been planned. He was obviously up to something big at Franklin, hinting at this but not wanting to be drawn further while whatever it was remained unsettled – which was anyway how I came to interpret his untypical reluctance to go on about whatever it was. He eventually got back to college in time for the start of his main postgraduate course in mid-January. Daniela had met him at Heathrow, returning his car to him more or less in one piece, and it was arranged that the three of us would meet up in the Goose one evening a couple of days later. When the time came, Daniela and I arrived first, found somewhere to sit and settled down to await Karl's return from some undisclosed business appointment – or perhaps, you could never completely rule it out, amorous engagement.

Looking at Daniela seated there, contentedly waiting while I returned from the bar, I couldn't believe my good fortune. We had been together now for getting on for two months, alternating the nights in accord with some unconscious formula between Clapham and Brixton; lunching together in the refectory or somewhere else close to college; spending the evenings and weekends shopping, cooking, going to the cinema or to a show of some sort or out for a meal; a lot of the time simply lazing around, talking about everything and nothing; suppressing nagging thoughts that this was too good to last, that the ending would be too painful to contemplate. Six months remained of her contract at the Centre; we hadn't got round to considering what would happen when it ended, as though mentioning it would bring it nearer, ignoring it constrain it always to the far distant future.

Karl arrived in buoyant mood, taking in the contents of our glasses from the doorway and heading straight for the bar.

'We're going to have to get into the habit of drinking a lot more now he's back,' said Daniela, with resignation tinged with affection.

'I haven't forgiven him yet,' I replied, 'nor you come to that.'

Her arm was resting on my knee, she gave it a squeeze.

'Well, now's your opportunity to have it out with him.'

But Karl gave me no chance for that, even if I had wanted one, acknowledging our togetherness with a half smile, then launching into an enthusiastic assessment of the acclaim, and in particular the distress to certain people, set to follow the appearance of our short piece in *Nature* – accepted now and due out any week. The next much longer paper was pretty much complete, the one after that well underway, and still my mind was grappling with new twists and applications, which appeared endless now that the conceptual barrier had been breached.

'Changing the subject for a moment, how's young Sean O'Brien getting along these days? Any new developments there?' Karl paused for a moment, though not as if expecting a reply, before continuing: 'I had a rather interesting discussion the other week with an ex-board-member of Mencken's which brought to mind the little fellow. You know, I really think it's about time we gave serious thought to finding out just what it is he's up to.'

I glanced at Daniela before replying, receiving an encouraging smile.

'It so happens there is something there we've been waiting to talk to you about. There've certainly been developments, though we're still very much in the dark. Quite by chance I've managed to get myself involved. The whole thing's being taken pretty seriously by some people.'

I went on to tell of my chance meeting with Tony Mulgrave and what it had led up to, Daniela chipping in here and there with observations of her own and filling in details I had overlooked: my afternoon session with Tony; his delving into the morass of dubious cancer drugs and their marketing; alternative research developments, in particular with relation to Sean's work at the Goldburg Centre; the upbeat way our encounter ended; the prospect of attending his working group meetings, whose precise purpose was still obscure. Karl listened attentively, only interrupting to ask if we knew the name of the company Sean had first worked for, where he had cut his teeth on the targeted cancer-drug programme.

'ARC Pharmaceuticals,' I replied, 'a venture capital company . . .'

'Precisely,' he cut in, a knowing smile lighting his face. 'That's the chain: ARC Pharma, the Goldburg Centre, Mencken. No prize for spotting the weak link.'

He went silent, lost in thought for a few moments, then apologised for the interruption and asked something about Tony's workshops.

'He only invited me to one just before the place closed for Christmas. It was cancelled at the last minute because Grandison was ill or something; anyway he couldn't attend and that was that. I haven't heard anything since. Perhaps I won't be invited again.'

'Probably clashed with his monkey gland therapy.' Karl had rapidly reverted to normal. 'Why not phone Tony to ask about the next one. You don't want to get overlooked by default; though I'm surprised he asked you in the first place, knowing of your association with me.'

'I thought you were supposed to be on good terms with him. What happened?'

'Nothing happened. We still are on good terms. It's just that he knows well enough my opinion of Grandison. He used to share it at one time. But since the poor sod is always having to deal with him officially now, it appears he's come to terms with his previous well-founded views. Makes life easier for him that way I suppose.'

There was something in this which brought to mind Barry's remarks concerning Grandison: the admiration he came close to expressing coming as a surprise to me at first, later to be put down to simple business self-interest.

'I don't think I'll phone. If I get invited, OK. But it's going to be bad enough as it is feeling like a spy with Tony, without pushing myself on him. That would really make me feel uncomfortable.'

Karl laughed before replying:

'I'm beginning to give up hope of you ever developing healthy criminal instincts. A few would do you no end of good you know.'

'He's perfectly all right as he is,' said Daniela, giving me a tender look. 'I've got quite enough criminal genes for both of us, thanks to you.'

'So you have my dear. Maybe you could use your influence on him then.'

'I'll think about it. And, incidentally, I clearly remembered Tony Mulgrave's name when Paul first mentioned it. I still haven't completely forgiven you for not visiting that time, when his mother died. Selfish I know. Probably down to those genes.'

'Well I was sorry about that too, probably more than you imagined. Didn't seem I had any choice though. You know, he never really got over that business. For a time I thought he was going to do himself in. Which doesn't make him the ideal candidate for dealing with all this, does it? Though I can understand his views on the pharmaceutical industry well enough. We talked it through long into the night on numerous occasions. At first he thought of trying to get involved at a practical level. You know, unearthing the significant statistics from under the garbage: real success rates and costs, that sort of thing; putting the true picture firmly and transparently in the mass-public domain. But that sort of thing requires an extremely clear head. Emotion doesn't help at all, can leave you wide open in fact – especially with that lot: they never miss a chance to rubbish opposition for being emotional. Unscientific, unproven are other words they're fond of coming out with when criticised, as though they don't apply to their own assertions, in spite of obvious enough evidence to the contrary. A major problem to consider though, to never lose sight of in fact, is that they've some pretty big guns up there, and absolutely no inhibitions about using them when they feel threatened – as my chum from Mencken left me in no doubt about.'

My previous misgivings about Tony's objectivity fitted well with Karl's account. His tone of voice had changed now, habitual light irreverence giving way to a quite uncharacteristic seriousness of manner, which surprised me, and Daniela come to that, blocking any thoughts we may have had of adding anything more. Instead we just sat there, waiting in silence for him to continue.

'Let me refer to him as Henry. What I'm going to tell you will make it easy enough for you to identify him if you want to. I just don't want to go broadcasting his name around. There's certainly no doubt about his fear of what he told me getting back to his old company chums.'

Karl had lowered his voice in saying this. He stopped for a moment to drink from his glass. Daniela and I moved our chairs closer. I glanced round to see if any untypical customer was within earshot, then smiled mockingly to myself at my absurdity. Karl continued:

'I have to tell you that it wasn't altogether a chance meeting. Rumours of trouble at Mencken's, and possible political ramifications, had been floating around the bio groups at Franklin for some time. They're one of the world's leading producers of chemotherapy products. It occurred to me that the fuss surrounding O'Brien's work – you know: Hepplewaite's visit to the Centre last November with the pharmaceutical company big wigs and all that – could be in some way connected. Then I noticed that Henry was down to speak at some duff conference in Florida and on an impulse paid up the fat registration fee and trotted along.'

I had to smile at this typical example of Karl's approach to matters that attracted his interest. He had a seemingly infallible instinct for spotting advantage in the most unlikely places and diving in to reap it. It appeared that he knew that Henry had left Mencken – a Swiss pharmaceutical company, one of the biggest players on the international scene – under something of a cloud a year or so earlier. There had been some talk of insider dealing, which had come to light and was then blamed for wrecking a planned merger with another pharmaceutical giant, which had been all set to go through. An inquiry had cleared Henry of any overt wrongdoing, but he was nevertheless persuaded to retire from the board on exceptionally generous terms – or so it was reported somewhat indignantly in the financial press.

'Now what reason could there be for such generosity? Well, it could simply be a case of "poor old Henry's gone and got himself into a bit of a mess; could happen to the best of us; it's not as though Mencken are going to miss the odd million or two – even though the merger he fucked up leaves us deeper in the shit than ever, with no shovel around this time". Doesn't quite ring true somehow though, does it?'

He turned to me, eyebrows raised.

'Well, put like that, no, I don't suppose it does.'

'So what else could it be?'

He went on rapidly, not risking another banal response:

'Two rather obvious possibilities come to mind: either he's taking the rap for someone else – Klaus Berger perhaps: "Merger Berger", their chief executive; or else he knows too much to be set loose with a hulking great chip on his shoulder.'

'I remember years ago, you telling me you met Klaus Berger at Franklin.' Daniela was leaning forward in her chair, a look of concentration on her face. 'Something to do with them funding a project

194

of Di Gregorio's. You got yourself invited to some fancy dinner they were putting on for him: part of the buttering up process. I seem to remember you being quite taken with him.'

'Too right I was. And who do you think he brought along with him on that occasion?'

'I suppose it has to be Henry.'

Karl gave me an ironic, there's-a-clever-boy nod. In response, I decided to air a piece of recently acquired knowledge, which appeared at odds with what he had been saying:

'What makes you say Mencken are in trouble? I thought they were supposed to be doing very nicely just now; that the failure of the merger turned out to be for the best in the end.'

Not a normal focus of interest for me, all this stuff. It was just that since getting involved in the O'Brien business I couldn't resist scanning the financial pages of whatever newspaper came to hand for references to the pharmaceutical industry. There are some fascinating snippets to be found there, when you get the hang of what to look out for. Some of them, it now occurred to me, could come in useful for throwing out in a seemingly knowledgeable way at Tony's workshops – in the unlikely event of my being called to attend any of them.

'I didn't quite say that, as it happens,' said Karl rather smugly, 'but it's true nonetheless. They're spending a lot of money putting over the contrary view – successfully it would seem. In fact they have very severe problems, which could be at the very heart of the matter so far as we are concerned. I'll get on to that in a moment.'

'Well before you do, let me get you a top-up.' Our glasses were empty.

Daniela was grinning away happily.

'This is better than the movies,' she said, as I prepared to set off for the bar.

'But you haven't heard anything yet,' said Karl.

'I know. But I can feel the tension slowly mounting, like in a good film. I hope you're not going to let us down. I'd hate this to all end in an anticlimax.'

Karl didn't reply. They were both still sitting there in silence when I returned with the drinks. He waited until I had settled before starting again:

'So yes, I had met Henry briefly before. Another thing I knew was that interesting rumours about him were floating around usually well informed circles concerning his rather exotic tastes in certain activities. I felt if I could only get him alone for a while; perhaps shepherd him off to some place where he could indulge himself a bit . . . well, there's no knowing what other indiscretions he might feel like owning up to after that.'

Daniela bubbled over on hearing this:

'It's getting too good to be true. So you've managed to work in a sex angle. A rather sordid one too it seems.'

'Oh, I wouldn't say that. Everyone to his taste. All pretty harmless anyway, so far as Henry is concerned. But I'll spare you those details for now.' Daniela's face fell a little. 'There are other angles to consider – and by no stretch of the imagination harmless ones this time.'

Karl was looking even more pleased with himself than usual. He was a skilled raconteur, enjoyed that role, had us really hooked and knew it. Taking his time, he started by describing the background against which the activities of Sean O'Brien could conceivably be viewed. The first bit meshed in pretty well with Tony Mulgrave's remarks to me a couple of months before: that a general problem being faced by the pharmaceutical giants – which Henry had apparently gone on at length about before being induced to turn to specifics – had come about as a consequence of the growing number of small, well funded, niche biotechnology companies. These, by their nature, tended to draw in the brightest of the young scientists emerging from the universities, attracted by the free, academic-style environment – their work often firmly tied in with those of university departments and research institutes – together with the prospects of a substantial share of the profits from any developments to which they contributed. On the whole, the problem was more an irritation than a real threat to the big players, whose strength lay in the large number and wide diversity of their products, which made them relatively insensitive to the occasional damage done by a successful competitor for an isolated slot in the market. The pressing problem besetting Mencken, however, had come about as a result of its foolhardy over-reliance on chemotherapy drugs for cancer – at one time the seemingly guaranteed mega money earners, which had carried it to unrivalled heights. Now this was all being threatened by a growing number of (in the words of Klaus Berger, as reported by Henry) 'smart-arse pigmy concerns pretending to be getting to grips with the root causes of the disease'.

The potential problem had been identified years before. Diversification was the obvious long term remedy, but time could be running out. A rapid way of achieving this was by means of a suitable merger or takeover. It was this perception which had led to the shake up resulting in the appointment of Klaus Berger. He had previously established something of a reputation for himself as a skilful manipulator in that field, having successfully overseen a number of such operations in widely diverse commercial sectors – not all of which, it turned out, had resulted in unions blessed with prolonged periods of sustained prosperity. That, however, could very well be put down to others. Berger liked to see his role as that of marriage-broker: preferring, after seeing to it that a union had been sealed, to move on, suitcase bulging with big ones, leaving the subsequent chore of guidance-counselling in other hands. This time though he had come severely unstuck: the merger had failed. A scapegoat had been identified and paid off; but that still left Berger in place, unwanted elsewhere, with a huge problem which was growing by the day. At first he had little idea of how to deal with it; but in such a large, multinational organisation expert advice is always close at hand. With no escape route, no alternatives in sight, he was learning fast.

'Try to put yourself in their place.' Karl was in his element now. 'Billions are at stake. Your patch, which you've lorded over for almost as long as you can remember, is being threatened by piddling newcomers busy developing weapons which have the potential for doing you untold damage, even putting you out of business. You wield enormous power and influence, have no scruples whatsoever, and millions are at your disposal. Well, what are you going to do about it?'

The Goose was filling up. The anonymous buzz of innumerable conversations – peppered with the occasionally distinguishable word or phrase, the shrill peal of laughter – growing in volume, filling the air. Karl had paused to acknowledge a friendly wave from some-where over by the bar. He had been away for two months; it seemed more than likely that someone or other would come over to join us, to feel the need to acknowledge his reappearance on the London scene.

'And so, what then?' I asked, anxious to get him going again before the inevitable interruption. 'I suppose the odd, fatal road acci-dent wouldn't be beyond their resources. Anything far short of that is going to be a bit of an anticlimax after your build up.'

A little playful provocation, I thought, would not be amiss in the circumstances, but I was surprised at his measured response:

'*All* possibilities were considered. You have to remember that these people operate in areas of the Third World where that sort of thing and much more are the order of the day. You should have heard Henry when he really got going – after a rewarding experience and a few post-coital snifters: "They'll stop at absolutely nothing to block them . . . tens of millions available for the purpose . . . people have been killed before for getting in their way." When that last bit slipped out it had the effect of sobering him up pretty quickly: "For God's sake forget I said that. I don't know what came over me." The interesting thing is that he was reporting discussions at first hand. He could hardly have reacted adversely at the time. It's only now he's out in the cold that he can afford to act shocked. An interesting example of institutionalised insensitivity, don't you think?'

'Presumably they settled on something less dramatic. But we still haven't yet heard who it is they're so worried about. Or have we?'

'You have indeed. And it looks very much as if a key passage of the drama is being acted out under our noses.'

'So it's ARC Pharmaceuticals then?'

Daniela was looking quite excited as she said this.

'Indeed it is. They're the prime worry just now it seems – now that the other one, Demorest, another Swiss company, has been forced into receivership. That was a relatively easy thing for them to arrange over there. Here they're having to tread rather more warily. Some political considerations, stoked up it seems by clever lads at ARC Pharma, appear to be giving them a load of trouble, causing a lot of sleepless nights for Berger and his mates at Mencken.'

Again, this seemed to fit in with Tony's story, and at the same time shifted the play away from Sean and the Goldburg Centre to an altogether vaster pitch. It occurred to me that perhaps we should talk to Tony, share what knowledge Karl had acquired, and try to decide together on where to go from there. I put this to him.

'Certainly we should talk to him,' he replied at once, having clearly been considering it, 'but now is not the time. Before we do that we need to be quite sure of ourselves. We haven't got anything like a coherent picture yet. What we do know is that Mencken will stop at nothing to protect their interests. What exactly they're up to at present is anyone's guess, but you can be quite sure they're up to something. Henry only spoke directly of the early stages of their assault: the infiltration by handsomely rewarded placemen of the regulatory body overseeing clinical trials and the rest if it; and freely applied threats of hugely expensive litigation to frighten off busybodies. But he hinted at more sinister strategies they had employed in the past and were desperately gearing up again in readiness. The main question for us is where, if anywhere, young Sean figures in this. It just seems too much of a coincidence that all the fuss surrounding him now – Frank Hepplewaite's visit with all those pharma big wigs, the security precautions and the rest of it – is unrelated to Mencken's problems. They're the ones who have everything to lose if he really is on to something, and a lot of people know it.'

Karl broke off to acknowledge a wave from the bar, making me think for a moment that we were to be joined by others, but he managed to put that off with a see-you-in-a-moment gesture before continuing:

'And there's another thing to consider. A view seems to be gaining ground that Sean was the real prime mover behind ARC Pharma's initial success. I'd like to bet a small fortune on that being Grandison's opinion.'

'Gaining ground where?' Daniela came out with this in a burst of angry incredulity. 'And what on earth does Grandison know, for Christ's sake? You know perfectly well he's incapable of making an informed judgement on this.'

'Only too well, my dear,' said Karl, smiling reassuringly, 'but someone could be making it for him. And anyway, I'm simply repeating to you what I've heard and hazarding a guess at Grandison's reaction to it. As to where the notion is gaining ground, I can only vouch for the biological sciences people at Franklin. The fact it has got there would indicate it's pretty widespread I would imagine.'

'I can't believe that Sean is on to something significant. It just doesn't ring true. The conversations I've tried to have with him . . .'

'I know all that, and you're probably right. But we don't *know*. And, perhaps more to the point, others don't know either: Tony for one. As I've said before, what we need to do is get an objective assessment of just what young Sean has done, what he has achieved. That's what we need to put our minds to.' He was looking hard at Daniela as he said this.

'He keeps everything locked in a massive safe, his log books, everything,' she replied distantly, as though her mind was elsewhere. 'Apparently it was moved into the lab from Registrar's ages ago. There was a huge fuss about who should know the combination. According to Angela, Sean wouldn't hear of Trowbridge or anyone else . . . What's the matter Paul?'

'You never told me this.'

'What, about the safe? Sorry, it simply didn't occur to me. I just took it for granted . . . What on earth's the matter with you?'

My mind was reeling.

'Suppose I could get it open – the safe I mean. How long would it take you to make the objective assessment Karl's asking for?'

'Don't be stupid.'

'No, I'm serious. I'm only smiling at what Karl was saying about me earlier, about not having developed any criminal instincts.'

'What, you think you can get hold of the combination then?'

They were both looking at me as though I had gone mad.

'No, nothing as mundane as that . . .'

Chapter 25

It was a source of continuing disappointment to Hardcastle that the inauguration of the Goldburg Centre had passed without ceremony or acclaim. This was undoubtedly due to its inauspicious beginnings: the general confusion, absence of direction and bad feelings which had marked its gradual emergence – together with the withdrawal of Max Warlberg and the lacklustre image of his replacement – providing little incentive for anyone wanting to draw attention to its existence. Lauder's preoccupation on assuming office some years later was to be on the substance of the task ahead of him. To this he devoted all his considerable expertise and effort, with eventual noteworthy success. By this time, however, it was too late to celebrate the Centre's foundation: some other milestone would have to be put in place for a related purpose. But any thoughts Hardcastle may have had along those lines would have been shattered by Lauder's incapacitating accident.

For Grandison, ever on the lookout for promotional opportunities for the Centre and himself (a combination for the most part fused in his perception to a single entity), the idea of an imposing monument rising from the concourse fronting the Centre forecourt came to him one afternoon, while being driven round Trafalgar Square by his wife – on their way to Victoria for an appointment with his chiropodist. It was to become an abiding obsession. The particular site he had in mind for the purpose was of significance because a roadway separated it from the Centre and its forecourt, thereby lending to the impression of it as a general college amenity area, rather than an integral part of the Goldburg Centre itself; a prominent Goldburg Monument there would do much to dispel this irritating misconception. When he judged the moment opportune, Grandison aired the proposal within Hardcastle's hearing, hoping he would bite. He did, subsequently coming to believe the idea to have been his all along.

That the monument should take the form of a fountain was down to Hardcastle's wife. All her life a devoted monarchist, with a consuming interest in the royal family, it was a matter of particular pride to her to be married to the rector of Prince of Wales College at a time when the heir to the throne bore that very title. She yearned for the day when she might be presented to him in person, relentlessly belabouring Hardcastle for his seeming inability to bring this about. One morning, while adjusting her curlers at the breakfast table, she was to learn of plans for a Goldburg monument. Excitedly, she put it to him that Prince Charles should preside over its inauguration – only to be informed that that was exactly what he had had in mind all along. She then pointed out, as a matter of possible relevance, that the prince had recently been instated president of The Fountain Society: an institution with the sole aim of encouraging the proliferation of water features throughout the length and breadth of the realm. Hardcastle remained silent while this fresh information fused with his current plans, then merely grunted non-committally; but by this time the idea – his idea – of a Goldburg fountain had become firmly rooted, and his mind engaged immediately in scheming for its realisation.

When he got round to raising the matter with Grandison, however, he was surprised, and not a little irritated, to detect a coolness in response which he could not for the life of him understand. A fountain, so it seemed to Grandison, in so far as he had views on such matters, represented little more than a symbol of tranquillity and oneness-with-nature, which was far from what he considered appropriate in the circumstances. How could such *passive imagery convey the thrust and dynamism with which the Goldburg Centre would shortly impact on the unsuspecting world? What he had in mind was something along the lines of that thing outside the trade union place over the way, only several times bigger: a dramatic personification of the Goldburg Centre (bearing, he could imagine in his wilder moments, a passing resemblance to himself) raising to its feet a moribund and protesting Prince of Wales College. Cautiously, and in spite of soundly based misgivings, he outlined in the most general possible terms the bones of his feelings on the matter to Hardcastle, whose response was predictably terse:*

'Bollocks! That sort of thing went out with the ark. And anyway, who's to say a fountain is incapable of making a powerful impact, eh?'

Although that last bit was said without thinking, it awakened a distant memory, which rapidly surfaced and overflowed:

'I think I might be able show you something that should disabuse you pretty smartly of that notion.'

It was not since soon after taking office at Prince of Wales College, in the course of a supposedly fact-finding tour of experimental research facilities, that Hardcastle had had reason to visit the laboratories of the School of Engineering Science. The thing that came back to him now, one of the few things on that visit which had made any impression on him at all, was the thunderous display of water power put on for him in the basement of the building by Hugh Sutcliffe, then a lecturer in hydraulics, later to become Head of School. (His only other memory of that occasion was of the remarkable resemblance Sutcliffe bore to a goat, a characteristic he was apparently quite comfortable with, subsequently enhancing it with a straggly grey beard.) Hardcastle immediately phoned him to enquire whether the equipment in question was still operational; and, on learning that it was, to arrange for a demonstration the following day. The event proved an unmitigated success for all concerned:

Sutcliffe and his elderly technicians, overjoyed at the chance to show off, before distinguished and clearly enthralled observers, the might of their ancient and much loved machinery; Hardcastle, smugly delighted at having so decisively made his point; Grandison, the doubter, won over completely to the previously unimagined potential of water power as a potent analogy for the Goldburg Centre and all its soon-to-flourish works.

Chapter 26

It was a matter of relief to me to have been interrupted straight after my, what must have appeared, strange reaction on learning of the existence of the safe in the Goldburg Centre basement – an event which endowed the recent reappearance in my life of Johnny Cremer with almost mystical significance. A moment's reflection, however, revealed the immense chasm separating the potential resolution of the question of precisely what Sean had been up to in his work, which Johnny's unique expertise appeared capable of facilitating, with its practical implementation. Our relationship, after all, although warm enough so far as it went, was based on an appreciation of the quite different social worlds we each inhabited, both happy to take distant, outsiders' views of the other's sphere of activity – an attitude which provided mutual illusions of escape from the confines of our separate existences. Like going to the pictures in a way, though on a personal, interactive level. What had passed through my mind in that moment of revelation involved a merging of these worlds. I had no idea what Johnny's reaction might be to this; nor, come to that, in what manner I might approach him. So I was glad of the interruption, which gave me a chance to think a little before opening my mouth again. As it turned out, that phase of the evening was brought to a close rather earlier than anticipated, and before the question could be reopened, due to Karl having to go off somewhere in a hurry for some reason. We left the Goose together, separating from him soon to take the tube back to Clapham. Before parting, Daniela invited him to supper there later in the week.

'I'll look forward to it,' he replied with a grin, 'and especially to hearing how Paul intends breaking open that safe.'

Spot on as usual, I thought – as I responded with a promise to try not to disappoint him – even when he thinks he's joking.

As soon as we were alone, Daniela put an arm firmly around my waist and asked what the hell I was on about. I started to tell her about Johnny, the circumstances under which we had met years before, his professional activities, our recent encounter in Brixton. There were too many people pressed up close to us on the tube so that much of this had to wait until we were in the open again, making our way along the side of the common.

'But this is incredible,' she kept repeating, clearly thrilled at the possibilities that had opened up. 'Do you think he will help us?'

Not a moment's hesitation, I noticed with pleasure, at the prospect of risky, decidedly illegal action: Karl's daughter to a T.

'I don't know. I need to think carefully how to put it to him. He'll certainly want to know what we're about. I'll have to be perfectly honest with that. Any dithering and he'll smell a rat straight away. He's razor sharp. And, in any case, that's the only way I could possibly play it with him.'

Daniela was running with it now, there was no holding her back:

'You must get in touch with him as soon as possible. We should stay in Brixton for a while, that way you can keep calling into the Prince until you meet up. Probably better if you go alone. I'll get details of the safe: make, model number if I can find it. Oh, and I'll photograph it. I've got an old Polaroid camera somewhere among my things. Oh Paul! This is so exciting. Do you really think he will be willing to help?'

The next morning, after travelling to college with Daniela, I found a note in my post tray from Tony Mulgrave and hurried to my room to open it. It was the long awaited invitation to a working group meeting, which had been hastily convened for the following afternoon and would be addressed by a member of an ad hoc Ministry of Health committee concerned with government policy implications of recent developments in cancer research. I sat back in my chair and closed my eyes. Things seemed to be moving fast on all fronts, forcing me into an ever more committed position, awaking an excitement quite unlike anything I could remember having experienced before. After what seemed a sufficient period of daydreaming to get on with, I moved the bulging file from the side of my desk to its centre and folded back the cover.

I had been working steadily on the first long paper, going through the pleasurable final tidying up stages prior to submitting it for publication, when there was a tap on my door. It was Hugh Sutcliffe, looking very spruced up, an operation which had in no way detracted from, perhaps even further enhanced, his goat-like appearance: beard neatly trimmed, as though in preparation for the County Show. His eyes as they met mine revealed that shifty look which signified he was either about to butt you or ask a favour: to fill in for him, perhaps, at some tricky college meeting, something which could require hours of preparation simply to avoid the risk of being made to look a complete nincompoop. Knowing the signs well enough, I maintained an air of silent coolness: looking up, pen in hand, as though interrupted at a crucial moment of some taxing development. Just a pose though: capitulation never really in doubt.

'Sorry to bother you, I can see you're busy.'

He waited for me to deny this, or else express pleasure at the prospect of a break from whatever it was I was busy at. When neither were forthcoming he went on regardless:

'It's just that a rather awkward situation has arisen which requires some urgent action on our part. It could turn out to be quite serious for the school. All a result of that stupid accident in the workshop.'

'Accident?'

I had no idea what he was talking about. Later I was to discover that a second year student had sustained a cut finger, requiring two stitches, while participating in a newly instituted 'workshop practice module' – introduced in response to demands from an industrial member of an accreditation board, clearly distressed on discovering that engineering graduates in his company appeared unable to operate a lathe. 'His own bloody fault,' according to Ted, the genial, racist workshop-supervisor. 'A lot of people from that part of the world are just not adapted for practical work. Not their fault really,' he had gone on, contradicting his assertion of seconds before, 'it's simply not in their genes.' Although the part of the world referred to remained unspecified, it occurred to me that it was a good thing that Rajmal Ram – Sutcliffe's accident prone Indian PhD student – had graduated before this innovation had come into force: it could well have put pay to a brilliant future career.

The 'awkward situation' had arisen as a result of the official en-quiry, which had followed notification of the accident. Previously regarded as no more than a matter of form, this had been conducted by a new, dead keen and raring-to-go member of the college's Health and Safety committee. Apparently put out by Sutcliffe's reluctance to acknowledge the gravity of the incident, he had widened his investi-gation: first to include other workshop practices, later to encompass all points of possible contact between man and machine throughout the school. His damning report threatened severe consequences if effective action to tighten safety procedures was not forthcoming:

'We're to be inspected by the Health and Safety Executive. They have the power to effectively shut us down if they consider safety standards to be inadequate. We've got a month to put things in order before the visit.'

Having first cocked things up by his arrogant high-handedness towards someone he regarded as being of no consequence, Sutcliffe was now busy offloading the burden of putting things right. In addition to dealing with matters regarding the physics lab, he wanted me to oversee the whole exercise:

'Ted will look after the nitty-gritty of course, but he can be a bit tactless and offhand at times. I'd like you to take overall charge and deal with the inspectors when they come. I know you're good at that sort of thing.'

If he thought this attempt at what he imagined to be flattery would serve its purpose my expression told him otherwise. He had obviously prepared himself for this eventuality, adding:

'I think when all of this is sorted out would be a good time for Dobson to take over your physics laboratory module. Now that you've got it up and running, it would be a good opportunity for him to get some practical hands-on experience – if you feel happy about that, that is?'

When he had gone I basked for a while in satisfaction at the effective deal just struck: the troublesome lab class was to be handed over to someone else without my even having had to broach the matter; consideration of safety issues could wait till the paper I was working on had been finished and despatched; I returned to it with renewed vigour.

The next day, a few minutes before the appointed time, I arrived at the room Tony had booked for the meeting. Only he and the invited speaker were there, poring over some documents. Tony waved to me in a friendly enough fashion as I entered, then carried on with his private conversation. Gradually others started to arrive, some of whom I was on nodding terms with, others I vaguely recognised, and one or two I couldn't recall ever having seen before: twelve or so of us in all, including four or five senior members of the Goldburg Centre. Some ten minutes after the meeting was due to start, Tony muttered something about having to wait for Grandison:

'He's definitely coming. I confirmed it with him a couple of hours ago.'

We waited awkwardly in near silence.

The eventual arrival was announced by a loud knocking on the door, which then opened to admit a small procession led by Annabelle, carrying a briefcase and stack of manila folders; following her was a small but strongly-built junior member of the Centre staff, bearing aloft – as though an item of religious paraphernalia, his expression radiating pride at being the one chosen for the task – the special chair of robust construction employed by Grandison to accommodate his fragile back; then Grandison himself, hunched and limping heavily; and finally, a further female employee of the Goldburg Centre, whose function appeared to be to fuss over Grandison, substituting for Mrs Grandison during working hours. When, after a number of false starts, a satisfactory position had been found for the chair and Grandison had been installed on it – in a commanding position, a good nine inches above everyone else in the room – the entourage prepared to depart. This was interrupted by Grandison complaining loudly of the cold, throwing as he did so an accusing glance at Tony for his thoughtlessness in subjecting him to this additional hazard to his delicate health. The surrogate Mrs Grandison responded promptly, calling out that she would fetch his overcoat and making off in haste to do so, leaving her companions at a loss over whether to follow her through the door or await further possible demands from Grandison, seated imperiously now, surveying the room and its occupants. His overcoat eventually arrived and was carefully draped over his shoulders and the back of his chair as though a ceremonial robe. The entourage departed, and Tony with little further ado introduced the speaker.

I listened with close attention to the story as it unfolded, trying to read between the lines, to second-guess where he was leading us with his meticulously prepared presentation. The government was determined, he told us at the start, to do everything in its power to facilitate research from whatever quarter into the effective treatment of cancer – which, he acknowledged, had been making disappointingly slow progress along established lines. A major problem to confront, however, concerned the large number of pressing claims from all over the place, many sincerely made and fervently believed in, all crying out for painstaking investigation and testing. These ranged from naive but passionately held beliefs in herbal and other so-called natural remedies to recent advances in fundamental high-tech research. Practical mechanisms whereby alternative treatments could be rigorously tested were simply not in place, and if they were would cost tens of millions of pounds each time to implement. Quite apart from the cost were the ethical considerations of subjecting volunteers to procedures almost certain to prove ineffective. The major drug companies alone it seemed could afford to finance the testing of products having the potential to lead to profitable outcomes. This was being seen by an increasing number of citizens to be blocking more promising developments. So much so that the government, ever mindful of its obligations, and well informed by focus groups of growing public disquiet, was determined to facilitate a more broad based approach to the battle with cancer. The committee on which he served had been set up explicitly with this purpose in mind.

In what was clearly intended for repeated presentation before diverse audiences, he gave examples of supposedly bogus cures which had been the subject of widespread acclaim: simple herbal recipes attributable to the North American Indians, Chinese mushrooms, antioxidant enzymes and others. An unusual one derived from experiments conducted on goats subjected to high pressure conditions, in a research investigation into the bends – the decompression sickness suffered by deep-sea divers. Goats, it appears, share many physiological properties with humans – a disclosure which, to the speaker's evident surprise, gave rise to loud, sustained chortles from the hitherto sober audience. It seemed that a number of these unfortunate creatures suffered from tumours which appeared to shrink, in some cases disappear completely, after repeated exposure to the compression/decompression cycles. Such was the excitement at this discovery that a venture capital company took the decision to invest large sums of money in seeking to exploit it – with predictably disappointing consequences. Many such improbable examples had arisen, would certainly continue to show up from time to time, and could generally be dismissed with a minimal expenditure of effort. Relatively recently, however, a highly advanced scientific approach was giving real cause for optimism, and at the same time illuminating the immense problems involved in developing potentially epoch-making discoveries into marketable products. The present audience was well aware of the problem, which had now come to represent the focus of the committee's activities.

Having got the general introductory material out of the way, the speaker turned to the particular concern of the working group: the development, drawing heavily on current advances in genomic research, of drugs targeted on specific tumours. There appeared little doubt that this was the way forward. He dealt at length with technicalities, losing me for much of the time. What was to emerge eventually was that the old problem remained: that of filtering out approaches of real practical utility from among the many lines being pursued – a task which was growing ever more intractable as a result of confidentiality considerations in the highly competitive environment in which the work was being carried out, and the complexities of the research procedures involved. The government was neverthe-less determined that an efficient mechanism be put in place to separate potential winners from the also-rans. With the establishment of such a mechanism, legislation could be tailored to promoting the selected few, with the government even entering into partnership and loan arrangements to assist small successful enterprises, for whom the burden of development costs would be clearly prohibitive.

Although put over with great panache, there was something about the arguments which on reflection appeared to pose as many prob-lems as they sought to address: questions concerning the impartiality of the chosen experts, for example, given the extent to which the international drug companies operated hand in glove with so many clinical and academic professionals; the selection of the few, with the corresponding rejection of the many, at a relatively early stage of development, well before the preliminary clinical trials, which would provide the first real indication of a drug's effectiveness. I sensed that one or two others in the audience may have shared these and other concerns. But such considerations were to be swept aside by the speaker's subsequent disclosure, which took almost everybody present by complete surprise:

'You may all be wondering why this meeting has been called, particularly at such short notice. Nothing I have said so far would appear to have the ring of urgency about it – just the report of another think-tank discussion, which may or may not result in action of some sort. Well, it turns out that this time things have progressed with phenomenal speed. A decision has been reached at the highest level to accelerate matters by instigating a pilot experiment before a fully tested procedure has been set in place. Nine seemingly promising developments have been scrutinised in an attempt to single out potential winners. Following an exhaustive investigation, two have been so identified. One of them, you will no doubt be delighted to learn, emanates from Dr Trowbridge's team in the Goldburg Centre.

The predominant reaction to this announcement was indeed one of delight, members of the Centre staff vying with each other in ever more outlandish, self-congratulatory contributions to the ensuing discussion. Grandison in particular, though clearly well aware in advance of what was coming, appeared all but overcome at this long awaited affirmation of the Goldburg Centre's eminence in the scientific world. His eventual response was measured however, simply thanking the speaker and expressing regret for Trowbridge's absence, due to important matters he had to deal with concerning specific arrangements for the next stage of the new drug's development.

My mind in the meantime was wrestling with imagined reactions and perplexities: of Daniela's face when she would learn of the elevation of Trowbridge to research stardom, and that the credibility of Sean's researches had been verified by experts; and the fact that Sean's name had not been mentioned, when it was perfectly clear to everyone present, except perhaps the invited speaker, that whatever it was that was causing the excitement had to be entirely down to him. What the hell was going on? I noticed two others looking uncomfortable, not joining in with the general euphoria. In particular Frank Mendellson, a well regarded pharmacologist from Biological Sciences, who asked a fairly innocuous question at one point concerning the criteria by which the experts had come to their decision, only to be sharply rebuked by Grandison for rocking the boat, bringing up sensitive matters which were best left to people in a position to understand them – which was a bit ripe, I thought, coming from him. Mendellson closed up at this, looking more uncomfortable than ever, and my thoughts turned to what Daniela's reaction might have been, had she been there. I felt myself getting angry, largely on her behalf, and the welling of a desire to do a bit of boat rocking myself. Tony appeared withdrawn and distant, had opted out of his role of chairman, allowing a free-for-all to develop. A lull had followed Grandison's ill tempered put down which I found myself attempting to fill:

'I don't quite know why Tony asked me to this meeting . . .'

I got to my feet having said this, in defiance of Grandison's sarcastic, barely muted 'nor do we' and accompanying sniggers from his acolytes.

'. . . but since I'm here let me say how delighted I am that things appear to be going so well. Since speaking to Tony some time ago, I've been taking a keen outsider's interest in cancer research developments . . .'

It was Tony's turn to look uncomfortable now. I barely knew what I was going to say next. For some obscure reason, my mind had been searching for the name of the Swiss company Karl had spoken of, whose researches had long been bothering Mencken, and which had been closed down: it wouldn't surface. I carried on, praying for inspiration, expecting to peter out embarrassingly:

'I was interested to hear the speaker refer to nine developments which his panel of experts investigated. I wonder . . . could he tell us who the other winner was?'

'I'm sorry . . .', the speaker glanced at Tony sitting glumly beside him, 'but until the formal announcement has been made . . .'

'Presumably it has to be ARC Pharmaceuticals,' I cut in rudely, but what the hell! And in that instant, the name I had been searching for soared from somewhere and I uttered it before it could escape again: ' . . . now that Demorest have been put out of business.'

The fact that foreign companies could hardly have come under the panel-of-experts' remit was of no consequence given what, as I realised belatedly, had been my barely conscious intention all along. It was a reaction I was seeking from the speaker: some indication he was aware of, perhaps even a party to, Mencken's concerns regarding these two specific enterprises. A momentary hesitation was all I was looking for, an awkward flutter in an otherwise seamless delivery. What occurred went far beyond my wildest imaginings, the impact obvious to everyone present, causing a silence to descend on the room, an abrupt halt to the euphoria. The speaker had turned the colour of chalk, his expression as he regarded me in stunned silence one of surprised, undiluted fear: the truant schoolboy with a sick note apprehended on emerging from the cinema; the trusted employee caught with his hands in the till. All eyes were on me now, Tony's switching to the speaker then back to me again in evident puzzle-ment, others fixing me with unconcealed anger: the gatecrasher behaving with predictable vulgarity, stirring up trouble among the invited guests.

Tony had come out of his stupor and was regaining control. The look he gave me was not unfriendly but clearly intended to shut me up. He said something about the extreme sensitivity of what we had been privileged to hear in advance of a formal announcement, and implored us to keep it strictly to ourselves until it entered the public domain. The speaker beside him, collecting himself with visible effort, nodded vigorously at this, as did Grandison from his throne, his features contorted in anger and indignation. The meeting was brought rapidly to a close, leaving me feeling an outcaste, but happy enough nonetheless that a further piece of the jigsaw was finding its way into the still far from clear picture which was relentlessly beginning to emerge.

Chapter 27

Following my unwelcome intervention at Tony's meeting, I headed back to my room and tried to phone Daniela, getting through instead to Angela. She told me that Daniela was working in the basement and not likely to return to her lab for an hour or so, as she had managed to gain access to equipment she had been trying to get hold of for weeks. I left a message to say that I would be in my room until she finished and for her to phone me there. This arrangement suited me fine as I wanted to get on with the paper, then take Daniela out somewhere to talk about the fresh developments over a drink; she was going to need one.

I had been working away steadily for some time when the phone rang. The woman's voice, when I answered, was not Daniela's and asked me to hold. After a brief pause, Grandison came sharply on the line:

'I want to speak to you Harrison.'

'Anytime Nigel.'

It was probably a reaction to that 'Harrison' which gave rise to my almost unheard of liberty of addressing Grandison by his Christian name: an impromptu signal that I was not going to be intimidated. It appeared to take him by surprise, delaying his response by several seconds. When it came, it seemed the tone had softened somewhat. He was clearly in an extremely worried state, suppressing with difficulty his natural tendency to dominate, to go on the attack.

'I had to leave straight after the meeting. Not feeling too good. My wife came to fetch me.' I had assumed up to then that he had been speaking from the Centre, that it was a secretary who had made the call. 'I just wondered . . . could you possibly call here this evening. It's important that we speak. Very important.'

I had never heard him sounding so conciliatory, almost pleading.

'Where exactly is here?' I asked, reasonably enough.

'What?'

He sounded irritated at my question, the old Grandison straining to emerge from under the covers.

'I've no idea where you're speaking from. And in any case I've got something on this evening.'

I had always assumed he lived in some dormitory fringe area of the outer suburbs, somewhere like Cheam or Pinner. In fact it turned out that he had a house just down the road from college, in Bedford Square, where he was calling from. I was intrigued by this; also of course by what it could be he wanted to speak to me about, but I thought it wise to maintain an offhand manner. Eventually I agreed to call on him sometime later, refusing to commit myself to a precise time, giving the impression I had a busy schedule and would try to fit this in as best I could; drawing some satisfaction as I hung up from my gamesmanship.

Daniela phoned at about seven sounding pleased with herself. Her work was going well and, as I learned later, she had got details of the safe and had photographed it. She was also dying to hear about the meeting I had attended. We met by the fountain and I explained as I escorted her to the tube why I would have to part from her for a while.

'He probably thinks he can scare you with threats like he does everyone else. But it will be interesting to hear exactly what it is he has to say.'

I had given her the bones of how the meeting had gone, my late contribution and the reaction to it – details to follow.

'I'll go home and cook,' she said. 'I need to do something like that. It'll help me unwind. Then when you get home we can celebrate.'

'Isn't that a bit premature?'

'Oh Paul! Whatever happens, we've plenty to celebrate. Haven't we?'

We had stopped walking and edged into the doorway of a shuttered up shop.

'You're right,' I said a little later, 'it's only a game this thing we've got ourselves into. It's good fun at the moment but it doesn't really matter a damn. I love you Daniela, that's all that matters.'

'I know. And I love you too.'

'I'll get away as soon as I can. And I'll try to bring a bottle of half decent wine with me.'

But as I left her, the memory of Grandison's intimidating 'I want to speak to you Harrison' floated up again. It's only a game, I repeated to myself as I retraced my steps, it doesn't matter a damn.

When the door opened in response to my knock, I thought at first I had come to the wrong place: to a private clinic perhaps, or a hospice. Assorted crutches protruded from some sort of umbrella stand in the hallway, and a distinct smell of disinfectant emanated from around, or perhaps from, a large matronly figure regarding me suspiciously from the other side of the half open door.

'I've come to see Nigel Grandison,' I started hesitantly, getting no response. 'He's expecting me.'

It took some time, but the message eventually got through:

'The Deputy Director is resting at the moment. You will have to wait.'

For a moment I thought she was going to close the door in my face, but then she seemed to change her mind, opening it reluctantly. She was dressed almost entirely in a tone of grey that could have been chosen to match her hair: thick stockings, woollen skirt and a well upholstered blouse, on which was pinned a heavy watch. Her hands were wet, I noticed as she dabbed them on a white apron, as if she had been interrupted while attending to a bed bath, or perhaps – my mind racing merrily now – to the enactment of some yet more intimate matronly function.

'You can wait in the drawing room.'

She said this as she was leading me along a corridor to the back of the house, passing on the way a staircase fitted with one of those mechanical devices you see pictures of in dentists' waiting room magazines – used for transporting seated persons, generally depicted as being of the female blue-rinsed variety, between floors.

The room she left me in had all the appearances of a hospital-ward day-room, for which some, but not excessive, effort had been expended to make look homely: a blue, polished linoleum floor; an assortment of comfortable chairs, some plastic covered, all sporting crisp, white-lace antimacassars; framed prints of well loved paintings – two Constables, a Monet and others of that ilk, hanging symmetri-cally, suspended by chains from a picture rail. To the right of a chintz curtained window, isolated in the far corner, a television set emitted colour and action but no sound. I sat facing it, trying at first to lip-read the young presenter. Soon tiring of this, I closed my eyes and reflected upon the strange manner of Mrs Grandison's reference to her husband.

She had, I had to concede it, a problem there. 'Nigel', or for that matter 'my old man' were clearly out the question. 'Mr Grandison', the only formal form of address to which he was entitled, sounded almost as bad given the eminence of his position in the Goldburg Centre. The trouble was that he possessed neither a doctorate nor a professorship, in spite of being frequently addressed as Doctor or Professor out of ignorance or deference and never complaining about it. So the problem was there all right, but the solution, 'Deputy Director', still seemed a trifle clumsy, the deputy bit not helping at all. Did her use of it extend to private exchanges? I wondered: to situations involving her in getting her hands wet?

Further speculation was cut short by an ominous, rumbling noise and vibration which filled the room, returning me rapidly to the here and now. Was it an earthquake? – unusual for London, but not unheard of. Or a heart attack? For an instant I wondered if it had been wise to throw out all that religious baggage foisted on me at St John's. The next thing to grip my attention was the television; I couldn't believe this but it was starting to levitate, no question about it, the patterned wall paper behind clearly delineating its steady upward progression; for a physicist this was particularly difficult to come to terms with. Then I realised it was not just the television but the floor – or at least the section of floor, a meter and a half or so square, on which the television was standing. With some relief I saw that this was not levitating at all but formed the top of a box-like structure rising up from below, and stopping just short of what would otherwise have been a destructive collision of television and ceiling. The low rumbling ceased abruptly, to be replaced by a tone of higher pitch as a motorised wheelchair bearing Grandison emerged from the now stationary lift and entered the room.

He was wearing some sort of heavy bath robe, and I thought at first he had discarded his artificial leg, but then saw it tucked awkwardly behind him. His vehicle made a sharp left, then accelerated towards me quite fast, stopping precipitously a foot or so in front of my chair.

'Thank you for coming Harrison,' he said angrily, his tone lacking all sense of gratitude. 'Perhaps you can tell me just what it is you're playing at?'

It was, I had to acknowledge, a good question. There seemed no conceivable reason why the affairs of the Goldburg Centre should be any of my business. If Sean was on to a winner, something that would seed a revolution in the treatment of the most dreaded class of diseases known to man, then wonderful: a cause for universal rejoicing and celebration. And if not? Well so what! Grandison would emerge with egg over his face and the affairs of the Goldburg Centre would settle back to normal. Why should that be any concern of mine? Or Karl's, come to that? Or Daniela's? These were my first reactions to Grandison's assault as I sat facing him, his pale, strained features fixing me with a cold stare. I had to remind myself of the limitations of this portrayal however, of the wider implications of the affair which Karl had uncovered, and to which the three of us were committed to unravelling. Everything it seemed hinged on the credibility of Sean's discovery: of who it was that had vetted it and pronounced it kosher. Grandison's faith must surely stem from someone other than Sean himself, or Trowbridge. Why the secrecy if the case was as watertight as he obviously believed it to be?

These well worn considerations flashed for no more than a few seconds through my mind, after which it turned to the question of how best to play things from there. Grandison was a bully, accus-tomed to getting his way in everything and unused to opposition. Any sign of accommodation on my part would only be seen as weakness, further encouragement for his hectoring, and get nowhere. So, for pragmatic reasons, I decided to simulate anger myself and confront him head on. That way there appeared just a chance that, in the heat of the moment, he would reveal something or other that would throw further light on the matter.

'Now look here Grandison, I'm by no means alone in having reservations about O'Brien's work. None of the people competent to judge it appear to have any idea what he's up to. And from what little they know of him personally they find it highly unlikely that it could be of any consequence whatsoever.'

Grandison had turned whiter still. A noise behind me signalled the arrival of Mrs Grandison, alerted it appeared by my raised voice, ready to interpose herself between her husband and the dangerous intruder she had so recklessly admitted to his presence. Grandison didn't appear to notice her. He was almost beside himself with rage.

'Who have you been talking to?'

I could hardly cite Daniela, nor Karl for that matter.

'Never mind who I've been talking to. You know perfectly well that any number of people in Biological Sciences would be perfectly able to pass judgement on the work. Who on earth are you relying on? Don't tell me it's Trowbridge. He hasn't a clue what's going on there, and he'd be incapable of judging it if he had.'

There! I'd done it now, got carried away and gone further than intended. I was hyped up though, beginning to enjoy the unfamiliar role I had managed to cast myself in; it seemed a pity to end it just yet:

'If it was just you and the Goldburg Centre I really wouldn't give a damn. But there's the college to consider. A debacle like this looks like turning into could cause untold damage. I have every right to be concerned, along with a lot of other people.'

My God, did I really say that? It sounded like Sutcliffe in one of his habitual pompous outbursts. The thought of that brought a smile to my face, no doubt adding to Grandison's perplexity as he regarded me with a strange glint in his eye. I met his gaze in silence, which he eventually broke, surprisingly quite calmly, his anger, though still visible enough on his face, held in check. Any thought I may have had of goading him into a heated indiscretion was clearly misplaced.

'Look Harrison, I can assure you that O'Brien's work has come under the closest possible scrutiny: both from the Ministry of Health committee and the consultants acting for the company which is now funding the project – and will be funding the clinical trials. We're talking millions here. Do you really think they would be proceeding as they are without cast iron assurances? Hardcastle is right behind us in this, sees it as vindication of his faith in the Goldburg Centre. He's not going to take kindly to interference from you or anyone else. I don't know what it was you were alluding to this afternoon, but you seem determined to cause trouble. Well neither you nor anyone else is going to get in our way now. It's the moment we have all been working for.'

'I'm delighted to hear it. All you have to do then is divulge the name of the company involved and the names of the experts who vetted the project and all the doubts will be resolved. When are you going to do that?'

'Go away Harrison. Go back to your theories and equations. It's the real world we're dealing with here. You're completely out of your depth. I was talking to Sutcliffe about you the other day. He's quite disappointed in you, you know. After all the expectations you brought with you, the glowing references from Dembowski and others. Seems it has all come to very little.'

Mrs Grandison escorted me to the door. As I was about to step through it, a slamming noise from behind made me turn my head. Grandison had emerged from the room I had just left, on foot, walking quite well under the circumstances. I hurried away. With any luck the wine store at the end of Windmill Street would still be open for business; otherwise I would have to call in at the Goose.

Chapter 28

Hardcastle and Grandison, all previous differences satisfactorily resolved, now threw themselves with vigour and determination into the Goldburg Fountain project. The first problem involved finding a sculptor of sufficient reputation prepared to collaborate in a multi-disciplinary programme with specialist engineers. The brief was for a truly dynamic landmark for the Goldburg Centre and college as a whole. Names were suggested to Hardcastle from various contacts, and the matter raised by him at Academic Board – in the presence of Karl Dembowski, who nevertheless refrained from contributing to the subsequent discussion. Following that meeting, the name that kept impinging on the eyes and ears of Hardcastle from diverse authoritative sources was that of Ben Palmer: Royal Academician, sculptor of note and just the man, it seemed, with the vision and ability to bring the project to a triumphant conclusion. Hardcastle was particularly impressed, on meeting him for the first time, to learn he was fully conversant with Sutcliffe's hydraulic machinery, and had long toyed with the notion of incorporating such visions of naked power in an art installation of dramatic impact. Various outline schemes were discussed, involving Hardcastle, Grandison, Sutcliffe and Harvey Denton – a professor of control engineering from the school. In due course, Ben was commissioned to come up with a conceptual design, on the basis of which Hardcastle would seek funding.

In order to get this commission, which could then lead to the truly substantial one for the full realisation, Ben had had to swallow many misgivings about the project in general:

'Do they realise the problems they're letting themselves in for?'
he asked Karl, not for the first time, over a pint in the Goose. 'The
golden rule for water features is to get the water up there somehow,
using a cheap, reliable irrigation pump for instance, and then let it
cascade down under gravity. Once you start pumping with great
force through nozzles and the like, particularly in the sort of quanti-
ties they're talking about here, costs go through the roof, mainte-
nance becomes a perpetual headache, and you're lucky if you can get
the thing working for a quarter of the time it's meant to. I should
bloody know.'

He went silent having said that, his mind's eye in the meantime
scanning defunct installations up and down the country, testifying to
the years it took the golden rule to evolve in his consciousness.

'Look,' advised Karl reassuringly, 'the whole thing has been
clearly set up as a multidisciplinary project. That's what sold it to
Grandison and Hardcastle in the first place. Just make sure your
contract leaves all responsibility for the functioning of the machinery
itself firmly in the college's court. Then all you need concentrate on
are the aesthetic considerations.'

'That could be easier said than done,' said Ben, prophetically as
it turned out.

While Hardcastle was engaged in persuading reluctant potential
sponsors that their long term interests would best be served by
coughing up – an excercise he had lost none of his legendary prow-
ess in over the years –, Sutcliffe and Denton worked on the complex
flow system for the distribution of water from a giant submerged
pump between the six vertical tubes, through which it was to be
propelled with massive force towards the heavens. Sutcliffe's role in
all this amounted essentially to negotiating with manufactures of
pumps and valves, with whom he had collaborated closely over many
years, for the provision at knock-down prices of obsolete stock he
knew they had stored away somewhere and forgotten about;

Denton's involved the design of the computer control system, which in accord with a flexible programmable sequence would be capable of varying the distribution of water at predetermined time intervals between the six spouts. Much was to be made in the publicity blurb, which accompanied all stages of the project, of the supposedly state-of-the-art nature of the techniques employed.

Hardcastle's success in fund-raising surprised even himself; and Sutcliffe's approach to equipment manufacturers resulted in an agreement to sponsor the project to the tune of virtually all the necessary pumping and control valve hardware – available from stock as a result of modest overproduction on a colossal Middle Eastern oil refinery contract years before. So far as Ben was concerned the net result was that he would have at his disposal more funds than envisaged in his wildest dreams. His original design was enlarged and much elaborated upon, to the mounting excitement of Hardcastle and, in particular, Grandison, who was increasingly coming to regard himself the architect of this major addition to the London skyline.

As Ben worked on the fountain, so Hardcastle and Grandison set about making arrangements for its inauguration. Prince Charles was approached through the appropriate tortuous channels, and a date agreed at which he would be both able and willing to officiate. A company of public relations consultants, with whom Hardcastle had had previous satisfactory dealings, was contracted to coordinate the complex business of interactions with the media; they also advised on the physical requirements for the ceremony itself, proposing a seating arrangement for VIPs on a platform close to the fountain, which would offer the ideal angle for photo shots and television coverage. Months before the event, its organisation and speculation on its wider significance were to become Grandison's overriding concerns, eclipsing matters of security and research in the Goldburg Centre, which had previously held prominence, alongside personal health considerations, in his world view; as the day grew nearer, *these concerns deepened, etching new worry lines over the sagging pouches of his tormented features. Hardcastle, in stark contrast, appeared rejuvenated by his success in getting the project off the ground and, in particular, of securing the services of the Prince of Wales for the opening ceremony; basking in self-satisfaction, he received his wife's new-found devotion to matters of his comfort with imperious detachment; happily, he stepped back to allow Grandison fill in the details.*

Chapter 29

It was on the crowded tube, one morning nearly a month after my confrontation with Grandison at his home in Bedford Square, that Daniela reminded me of Johnny Cremer's expected return any day now from a top-secret working holiday somewhere exotic. I had learned of this after having almost given up hope of ever making contact with him, my frequent appearances in the Prince continuing to draw a blank. Then, after something like a fortnight of trying, I recognised an old associate of his seated at a table there, in a small group which stood out as being singularly out of place among the predominantly young, bubbling clientele – the major component of regulars who provided the Prince with its distinctive ambience. 'Yeah, budding thespians and bloody Brixton poets,' had been Johnny's response when I had remarked on the striking dissimilarity to his old haunt in Acre Lane, 'but makes a nice change, don't you think, now that I'm a reformed character?'

Well at least I was getting warmer, it seemed, as I set my mind on what to do next. I could hardly interrupt the obviously private discussion being conducted in hushed tones over the table by hard looking middle-aged men, from outward appearances devoid of any indication of having followed Johnny into early retirement from professional wrongdoing. The fact that they were pushing back the pints with commendable enthusiasm, however, provided the potential for a one-to-one encounter; and, sure enough, members of the group soon started availing themselves of opportunities, arising from dead spaces in their deliberations, to slip off for a while. My target appeared to have the bladder of a carthorse, but patience prevailed, and I was eventually able to insert myself next to him at the urinal, weighing up how best to introduce myself. This turned out to be unnecessary as, after a sideways glance in my direction, he came out with:

'You're Paul aren't you, a mate of Johnny Cremer's?'

And then I learned that Johnny was on a mission for his new sponsor – regarded by his companion with deep suspicion:

'If things go wrong those people don't want to know. Leave you right in it. And the money's peanuts after what Johnny's used to. But it's somewhere nice and sunny apparently, so he's worked in an all-expenses-paid holiday while he's at it. All right for some, I suppose.'

'You're right,' I said to Daniela as the train pulled in to Tottenham Court Road station. 'We'd better call into the Prince this evening.'

She was staying in Coldharbour Lane for most of the time now, having managed to transform the flat in a matter of days, throwing out much of the accumulated junk and installing potted plants and many other pleasant features. After my initial lone sorties to contact Johnny had proved unsuccessful, she had started coming with me to the Prince, quite taking to the place: 'It's like a breeding ground for future patrons of the Goose,' she had observed perceptively, 'for when some of their youthful earnestness has worn off.'

The previous few weeks had been busy ones for both of us, serving to take our minds off the O'Brien affair, which appeared to have entered a static waiting phase, preparing perhaps for the great leap forward which would astound the world. Needless to say, this was not how it appeared to Daniela, convinced as ever of Sean's duplicity and technical incompetence – second only to that of his superiors at the Centre. Her own researches had been making rapid advances from the time she had started collaborating, unknown to Trowbridge, with a group in Biosciences. She had been working hard, intent on bringing things to some sort of a conclusion before the end of her contract, just five short months away. In the meantime I had got myself entangled in the unbelievably convoluted operations involved in satisfying the relevant authorities that all was safe and secure throughout the School of Engineering Science laboratories and workshops. The visit from the Health and Safety Executive had fortunately been postponed, as a result of the indisposition through illness of a senior inspector: one Terence Onions, a Yorkshireman, famed for his inordinate pig-headedness in the execution of his duties. There was always a chance, I had thought optimistically, that it could be serious; not that I wished him permanent harm of course, just something to put him out of action for a year or so.

With regard to my own work, the appearance of the short piece in *Nature* had led to the high-profile response Karl had predicted: widespread interest and gratifying comment, together with a surge of indignation from predictable quarters, which had rapidly died down as the message took hold. Galworthy had maintained his silence so far but was reliably reported to be unimpressed, sullenly preparing a rebuttal, to which I looked forward with equanimity. The first full paper had been enthusiastically acknowledged by the editor concerned, with a promise to accelerate the reviewing and publication processes; and I had already received invitations to present the work at universities in Australia and the USA. All in all a notable leap in my standing in the academic stakes, to which I had yet to come to terms.

We had seen rather little of Karl since his return from California some weeks before. He had come to supper at Clapham a couple of times, but apart from that had appeared elusive, clearly absorbed in whatever it was he was brewing up at Franklin. In fact he was there now, having compacted his physics course by fitting in extra lectures and delegating sections to postdocs. He had been delighted to hear of our intention to break into Sean's safe, and I could see him filing away for future reference my connection with Johnny Cremer.

'I'm sorry to be of so little help,' he had said at one point. 'You'll understand soon enough the reason for my evasiveness. It's not in my nature at all as you both know. Anyway, you seem to be managing things well enough without me.'

It was certainly strange; yet another imponderable, along with all the others that were conspiring to turn my life inside out. Not that I was complaining, not by any means.

As we emerged from the station, Daniela went over to the news-vendor to buy a paper.

'I know,' she said, smiling at my puzzled expression, 'but I saw something in this over someone's shoulder in the tube.'

We stopped so she could rummage through the pages until she found the picture that had caught her eye: of a painting depicting a nude and well-endowed female form sprawling provocatively on a velvet chaise longue. "Von Da Bar!!!" ran the headline, mystifyingly enough, until we read that the painting was of the model Amanda Von Fredricks, which explained all with commendable economy.

'I was right,' said Daniela excitedly, 'it's Fritzy.'

And when I got round to examining the face I had to agree with her, no doubt about it.

'So that's where she gets the Fritzy from,' she went on. 'The Von Fredricks must be her maiden name, or that of a former husband.'

'Or maybe a nom de guerre,' I added, remembering her present husband's embalmed look of disapproval at Edwin Bloomfield's opening some weeks before. 'It says here that she's much sought after, but doesn't specify in what capacity.'

It went on to say that the work was representative of a fashion-able trend for wealthy men to commission nude paintings of their generally much younger wives, the present example emanating from the brush of the distinguished portrait painter Edward Weatherill, whose recent depiction of the Duchess of Westmoreland was currently on view at the National Portrait Gallery.

'Good for Edward,' I said, delighted for him for the publicity, 'but it's going to be a bit of a disappointment for the punters who flock there expecting something like this.'

As Daniela started to fold away the paper it came to me that something I had glimpsed there related obliquely to Karl. The sensation appeared stronger than could be attributed to mere acknowledgement of the approval he would undoubtedly have felt for Edward's technique and subject matter.

'Just a minute,' I said, taking the paper from her hands. 'There was something else there . . .'

Another headline, competing in succinctness with Fritzy's, stood out from an adjacent column some way below: "Pope's Big Bang Beano".

That was it. The text went on to report – in familiar idiosyncratic style, posing few problems for the inattentive reader – supposed celebrations in the Vatican at the recent retraction by an acclaimed physicist of a previously held view, which had been rapidly gaining ground, that the 'Big Bang', rather than signifying the beginning of the universe – the moment of its creation by God, according to those, like the Pope, given to thinking in such terms – in fact occurred at an unexceptionally ordered location in space-time: neither a beginning nor an end; corresponding to a universe which had always existed, would always exist; is simply there, here, infinite yet bounded. A view of things more or less in keeping, give or take a few esoteric details, with what most would have been quite happy with, may even have regarded as pretty well self evident, before the dawn of science; later to re-emerge in the guise of a profound hypothesis from the highest echelons of the scientific community; incomprehensible to virtually everybody else, and seemingly inconsistent with the orthodox notion of a divine whim being responsible for getting the whole thing off the ground.

'No prize for predicting Karl's view that the bugger's been heavily leaned on,' I said, on deciphering the gist of the news item. 'Did he ever talk to you about his work at Franklin with Alain Brumi on all that stuff?'

'Not really, no. But I seem to remember hearing Bruni's name mentioned some years ago. Karl was very pissed off at the time. I think it was to do with Bruni not agreeing to publish something they had done together, and then someone else getting in first, or Karl thinking that that could happen. But he never wanted to talk to me about his work. You know that.'

'Yes, of course. You're right though: he did fall out with Bruni at one time, but it didn't last long. He has always had a great regard for him, and they soon patched up their differences. They had come to the conclusion, years before anyone else, that the Big Bang represented just another point on the continuum: a rather special one, of course, but still ordered, still obeying the same physical laws as everything else. You know . . . it all comes down to that business of the critical mass: if there's enough mass in the universe, gravity will eventually stop it expanding, start pulling everything back together again – right up until it's all effectively concentrated at a point . . . ready to explode again . . . restart the whole bloody business. In which case our conception of the birth of the universe in fact relates to just one position on a cycle which repeats itself indefinitely. Bruni has been working for years on those billionths of billionths of a second before the explosion: on the precise mechanism that sets it off. Karl has long been obsessed with a related problem . . . trying to calculate the total mass of the universe from first principles. At one point he thought he had shown that this must exactly equal the critical mass, that any other quantity would be inconsistent, would fail to satisfy certain essential conditions . . . Trouble was that it wasn't one hundred percent: there always remained something not quite complete, not quite resolved. He keeps going back to it whenever he can find the time, convinced that the missing element is there somewhere, just waiting to be uncovered. The stakes are truly enormous . . . you can't begin to imagine the impact . . .'

235

'Actually, he did say something to me about it, now that you mention that. Or rather, it was about the reaction of fundamentalist religious groups to the things he was getting into.' Daniela laughed to herself at the memory. 'I suppose you could class the Vatican in with them.'

'Well, they're certainly extremely sensitive about the whole issue . . . biding their time . . . working out how to react if the worst comes to the worst and the notion of a moment of creation goes completely out of the window. Memories of the mess they got themselves into over evolution are making them very wary this time: they don't want to look ridiculous again, taking a stance that ends up only being accepted by a few certified nutters. They certainly don't want that happening again.'

We called into the Prince that evening on our way home. There was no sign of Johnny, nor of any of his cronies, and so after a drink at the bar we decided to go for a curry somewhere close by. Later, on arriving home, Daniela suggested I went back to see if he had shown up, and with some reluctance I agreed. She had brought some journals back with her, which I knew she wanted to look through and so would be quite happy to get rid of me for a while.

'Don't be long,' she said as I kissed her, 'unless you meet him, that is. If you're late I'll know that you have.'

I didn't think it very likely. But, in fact, I saw him as soon as I walked in: perched on a high stool in one of the small, distinctive stalls which continue the line of the bar through the long narrow space running to the back of the building. He was alone, looking suntanned and out of place, standing out from the bustling mass sprawled around cluttered tables on a rich assortment of chairs and worn sofas; others standing in languid groups; a few young women in flowing cottons, with strings of beads and other ornaments, seated in simulated abandon on the floor; all it seemed talking at once, laughter and the drone of excited conversation all but blocking out the piped seventies music. Johnny seemed pleased to see me.

'I'd just about had enough of this place,' he said, smiling ruefully. 'What are you having?'

We chatted away about nothing in particular until he brought up the matter of his busman's holiday in the Caribbean, the little job he had just done for his new friends:

'Piece of piss it was. Don't know why they had to involve me. A smart lad with a junior DIY kit was all it needed.' He appeared offended for a moment at the thought of this, but soon brightened up. 'Worried about the clearing up afterwards, I suppose. But it's quite a place. You should give it a try some time. And the black girls! . . . God, I've never seen anything like them.'

'What, not even here,' I said, meaning Brixton, not the Prince, which despite its location was patronised almost exclusively by young, chattering class whites.

He laughed; then, as though choosing to misunderstand me, went on to expound a bit of local history:

'Used to be the Black Prince you know, back in the days before the darkies moved over. Had a big picture of one of them hanging outside; fearsome looking brute, covered in gold and gems with a great black beard – like something you see now coming out of the Atlantic. It was as though whoever it was that thought that one up could see it all coming. Then the landlord at the time, it's years ago I'm talking about, had it changed by deed poll to The Prince. Changed the picture too – to the Eyetie that's up there now. Decided to keep it foreign without tearing the arse out of it this time.'

The Eyetie in question bore more than a passing resemblance to a well known portrait of Machiavelli. I thought of mentioning this, then decided it was perhaps time to change the subject completely.

'I think we could be in business.'

I had let myself in and crept up the stairs. Daniela turned her head expectantly from the sofa, an open journal on her lap, others and a wodge of handwritten notes forming an untidy heap beside her. Loose papers fell to the floor by her discarded shoes as she leapt to her feet and rushed over to embrace me.

'I thought you must have found him, but tried to persuade myself you hadn't to avoid disappointment. Let me clear up, then you can tell me all about it.'

She gathered up her papers, then went to fetch a bottle of wine. We snuggled together on the sofa for a while and then she gently disengaged herself and poured two glasses.

'Well?' she said as she handed me one, 'what's my clever boy managed to arrange then?'

I started to tell her. It had all gone better than I could possibly have expected. Johnny had been very amused at first at my request, but not unduly surprised at the general problem:

'It's amazing what gets locked away in safes. People seem to think the things inside must be valuable, but it's often the opposite: rubbish they don't want anyone to know about. Can come as a bit of a disappointment that, when you've been to all the trouble I have at times – in the old days, of course.'

As regards the safe itself, when he heard the make he could hardly contain himself:

'They went out of business years ago: when it got around they could be opened by a kid with a tin-opener, almost. The same people operate under a different name now and claim to have something better on the market.' Nothing he was particularly impressed with though.

'The only slightly bothering thing,' I went on to tell Daniela, 'is that I'm going to have to do it myself.'

This was certainly a source of worry, in spite of Johnny's firm assurances.

'He's going to explain it all and lend me some equipment. "Piece of piss" is how he described it: "For a bloody physicist should be even easier than that".'

'Did you tell him there's also going to be a biochemist on hand?'

'No I didn't. I'm meeting him tomorrow morning at nine in a shop in Acre Lane – where he keeps the gear he's going to lend me. God Daniela! What have we got ourselves into?'

The following morning I walked with Daniela to the tube, then bought a paper to read over coffee and toast in a cafe by the station: killing time before my appointment an hour later. I had Daniela's Polaroid photo of the safe, though Johnny didn't seem to think it necessary. He had gone on at length about how easy the operation was going to be: something about being able to see the cogs actually lining up in place as the combination dials were rotated. But I hadn't understood quite how this was possible and felt that there could very well be difficulties for the uninitiated, which may not have occurred to one with his long experience and expertise.

Time was dragging: still half an hour to my appointment, which was only a five minutes' walk away; so I made my way to the market, progressing through the open and covered parts, noting for future reference what was on offer in the way of food, clothing, hardware and potentially useful services – like the vacuum cleaner spare parts and repair stall, the tailor who would take on anything from replacing buttons to making a suit. Then back across the High Road to Acre Lane; past several greasy spoons doing a fair trade; a betting shop from which a young black man emerged, squinting self-consciously in the daylight; newsagents stacked high with brightly coloured magazines, catering for all tastes; a barber getting his place ready for customers; coming eventually to my destination.

The grimy window was stacked high with decrepit looking television sets interspersed with other electrical junk. Behind this could be seen more of much of the same, all but filling the body of the shop.

A badly printed notice informed of spares available for all makes, of guaranteed repairs, of cash offered for old sets. I entered with some difficulty, between laden shelves lining the narrow space behind the door; into the dingy, dimly lit interior, from which there appeared no way out other than that through which I had come in from the street. From behind the clutter at the back, I heard a voice; then an arm, followed by a head, and finally a whole body, emerged into the space some way in front of me. He was small and slight, a mere wisp, and so able to manoeuvre with relative freedom through the tiny spaces between the heaped shelving. His glasses were large with thick lenses, which appeared misted over; his brown overall reached all but to the floor, as though bought long ago in anticipation of a growth spurt which had never materialised.

'Yes?' he asked irritably, clearly annoyed at the intrusion. 'What do you want?'

'I see you sell televisions,' I replied, unclear how to proceed further, 'but I don't need one just now.' He stared at me, impassively. 'I've come to see Johnny Cremer,' I went on.

'Never heard of him. Who are you anyway?'

'My name's Paul. Johnny told me to meet him here at nine.'

'Never heard of him. Just wait a minute will you.'

He withdrew sideways, in the direction from which he had come. I waited in silence, taking in the dust covered muddle which looked quite unsaleable, as if it had been there for ever. After what seemed an age his voice sounded again:

'You'd better come through.'

When I reached the back of the shop, I saw with relief that a passageway through the piled debris was just about negotiable by persons of normal build. I followed this to a door which opened on to a small workshop, where the advertised repair operations could conceivably be carried out.

'Just about got the kit together for you,' said a familiar voice.

Johnny was standing with his back to me at a bench, fiddling intently with something.

'Come and have a look at this,' he said, not taking his eyes off whatever it was. 'I think you're going to like it. It's my very own customised peeping Tom.'

What he showed me was a control box fitted with knobs and a small LCD screen. A fine cable protruded from it, which turned out to contain two fibre optic transmission lines: one for sending light to a tiny probe at the far end of the cable, the other to bring the illuminated image back for display on the screen. I was beginning to understand how it could be possible to 'see the cogs and line them up'.

'All you need to do is drill a hole about two inches below the combination dials and pop this in.' I produced Daniela's photo. 'Yeah, just about there.' He marked the point with a pencil. 'One of the cogs on each wheel has a bit missing, so that when they're all lined up and in place the door is free to open. What you do is just line up the cogs with the missing bits anywhere you can see them clearly. Then take the probe out – you've finished with that now – and rotate all the numbers down one click. Try the door. It won't open first go, so you go down another click and try again. And so on until you're there. That way you always keep the cogs lined up right until you're home. Piece of piss.'

The principle was certainly clear enough, but there remained a mass of detail which I wanted to be absolutely clear about. I needn't have worried though. Johnny had set up a small test rig for me: a sealed metal cylinder into which I cut a hole with the charged up hand drill he was providing with the kit – which all fitted neatly into a smart 'executive-style' brief case. By rotating the inserted probe, I was able to see all the internal features of the cylinder displayed clearly on the screen.

'Very clever. Have you patented it?'

He laughed; then went on to explain some points of detail, sketching quite skilfully what to look out for in the actual lock itself. We could do with someone like him in the school, I thought, to run that workshop practice module among other things. The clarity of his instructions would have been difficult to better.

'It probably won't be till Thursday next week,' I said. 'Is that OK?'

On Thursdays Miss Brown finished early, in order, so it was generally believed, to attend classes in advanced unarmed combat or some such lethal pursuit. Whereas on other days she would often hang around till all hours, even return unexpectedly, perhaps in the hope of surprising transgressors, on Thursdays she would depart at four and never be seen again till Friday morning. It seemed a good day to choose for our escapade.

'No problem. Take care of the kit though. And keep it to yourself. OK?'

The following morning, Daniela and I set off early for college from her flat in Clapham, arriving at the Centre concourse to find the Goldburg fountain discharging modest quantities of water, more or less evenly distributed between its six spouts. Passers-by slowed down or stopped for a while to take it in, and a small group, over on the far side from us, stood rooted in earnest discussion as they watched the flow.

'My God, he's looking smugger than ever. Who on earth are those people with him?'

I looked again over at the group Daniela was staring at, seeing immediately what she meant. Sean was standing there imperiously, surrounded by four or five very attentive, smartly dressed men, who wouldn't have looked out of place in that restaurant where I had lunched with Barry. As we watched, he turned abruptly and set off, walking briskly across the walkway to the Centre forecourt, his escort trotting to catch up, two of them flanking him when they had done so, questioning him respectfully it seemed as the group made its way up into the building and out of sight.

'Now what do you make of that?'

She clearly didn't expect an answer. Instead I took her hand as we followed in their direction, kissing briefly on arrival at the entrance, then parting reluctantly to go our separate ways.

Chapter 30

The sensational happenings at the fountain's inauguration were so extensively reported on television and in the press, and relayed relentlessly throughout the world, that little purpose can be served in repeating them here. However, certain general consequences of the misadventure – minor disaster, hilarious farce, call it what you will – were to emerge well after the media spotlight had been turned off and deserve at least passing consideration.

Undoubtedly, the most generally significant of these concerned the future appearance of the royal head, up until that day exhibited in public lushly endowed with hair, henceforth to appear bald-patched and polished, in full keeping with family tradition, marking out its bearer, for the first time in the eyes of some, as a credible future monarch. It could hardly have turned out otherwise following the televised and copiously photographed devastation of his pains-takingly assembled hair arrangement in the torrents of descending water. It has to be said at this point that the prince's demeanour during and following his ordeal greatly endeared him to the public at large, significantly raising his approval-rating in the opinion polls. His subsequent good-natured chuckles and asides at the press photographs and crude accompanying captions – Baldy Prince Charlie, Hair to the throne, *and the like – further adding to the credit earned by his stoical behaviour amid the general panic which for a short while enveloped him on the VIP platform.*

Among the few who followed the prince's dignified example,

maintaining a frozen stance throughout the duration of the deluge,
were Hardcastle and Lady Hardcastle: the latter's elaborate and
ridiculously expensive (according to Hardcastle) hairdo rapidly
coming to resemble (again according to Hardcastle) a drowned rat;
her professionally made-up face running with streaks of black and
colour like something that had gone off on a wet fish stall.

Less creditable was Grandison's reaction as it became clear
something was going seriously wrong with the planned rhythmic re-
distribution of water between the six spouts: his look of terror
evident for the world to see in the earlier photographs of the event;
his blurred image in the later ones, as the first waters struck the
platform, indicating a speed of departure which some estimates put
in the Olympic sprint class. His wife, who had been watching from a
less prestigious but dry vantage point, rushed to his aid, escorted
him with difficulty into the Centre building and from there, by un-
known means, away. She phoned the next morning to declare his
condition serious. Many weeks were to pass before he was to be seen
again in college.

A truly positive consequence of the whole business, in addition to
that regarding Prince Charles's standing with the public at large and
the implanting of the names of Prince of Wales College and the
Goldburg Centre firmly in the minds of tens of thousands who would
otherwise never have heard of them, came about as a result of
Harvey Denton's careful observation of the patterns of instability,
which became evident a few minutes after the prince, with due
ceremony, had depressed the switch which triggered the giant pump
and set the fountain in motion. The programmed sequence had been
set to divide the bulk of the flow equally between three of the six
spouts, the lesser remainder equally between the other three; then,
after each half minute of operation, the conditions were to be
reversed, causing the three higher penetrating jets to fall to the level
of the three lower ones and vice versa, the whole cycle repeating
continuously. Denton, along with other informed observers, soon

became aware of the classic symptoms of incipient instability: the oscillations progressively growing in magnitude, the higher jets reaching ever higher, the lower ones ever lower. He was surprised at first, having he believed fully accounted in his design for all the complex dynamic interactions which could occur, his expertise in this field being exemplary, the subject of worldwide acclaim. But it was not until the onset of the secondary instabilities, first identified by the gradual increase in height of one of the two central jets at the expense of all the others (the one, as luck would have it, closest to the VIP platform and, as was subsequently discovered, inclined from the vertical a few degrees in its direction), that his interest was well and truly awakened. A number of baffling phenomena commanded his attention, such as the curious double bleep occurring spasmodically in some of the weaker jets, suggestive of some complex high-order interaction, never to his knowledge previously reported upon. But it was the uneven growth-rate pattern of the dominant jet (repeatedly falling, then increasing in height by progressive, at first seemingly random, length-increments) which he came to realise with mounting excitement held the key to the whole problem. Far from being randomly distributed, these increments, he now saw, had to be related to one another in accord with a dimly recollected conclusion to a strictly analogous problem, encountered some years before and shelved for want of a practical application.

Entranced, his mind switched from the physical reality unfolding before him to its mathematical abstraction, oblivious of the frantically escalating activities of the press photographers and television crews directly in front of him, the growing unease on the celebrity platform through the fountain beyond them. He saw instead the sober arrays of the state-variable formulation, the sparsity of the transition matrix crying out accusingly for his neglect of factors clearly in need of consideration. As the dominant jet soared yet higher – approaching its final limit as the others faded to nothingness, and a blustery gale which had been circling undecidedly all morning found at last a propitious channel along the thoroughfare between the tall buildings and struck decisively from behind –, his thoughts turned from the time- to the frequency-domain: to unexpected bimodalities in the power spectrum density function, to unprecedented migrations of poles and zeros in the complex plane. It was at the precise moment that the waters broke over the platform, as though the screams of terror and panic stricken chaos had somehow released a mental blockage, that inspiration dawned. He hurried away, oblivious of the sirens as fire engines and police reinforcements rushed to the scene; through hordes of jubilant students, who had been confined by officious security personnel to vantage points far from the area of devastation. On reaching his office on the fourth floor of the School of Engineering Science, without so much as a glance from his window at the frenzied activities unfolding below, he set to work.

His resulting paper (H P N Denton, 1987. Applications of a revised Hoffmeyer-Neiland algorithm to model based control strategies for systems exhibiting multiple Leperrier interactions. Int. J. Adv. Autom. Cont*., vol. 344, pp.1134-1153) came in due course to be considered a watershed for major new developments in non-linear control theory, elevating its author, already a respected international authority, to undisputed dominance in his exacting field.*

Chapter 31

On the morning of the fateful Thursday, I travelled to college as usual with Daniela, feeling the adrenalin starting to flow as we entered the main gate. We had stayed at Clapham the night before, discussing until quite late the precise arrangements for the break in. Security regulations now decreed that the ground and basement floors of the Goldburg Centre be vacated by eight o'clock every evening and the access doors locked. The fire escape doors from the ground floor laboratories, however, could still be opened from inside the building. And one of these, the one in the corner close to the Malet Street boundary, was situated well out of range of the security cameras which had recently been installed in the area. It thus appeared a suitable choice for my proposed illegal entry late that night, and subsequently as an escape route for both of us on completion of our mission. What made it particularly convenient was Daniela's acquisition of a key to the nearby gate into Malet Street itself; she had learned of an illicit copy of this in the possession of a colleague and had managed to appropriate it for long enough to get a copy cut. What a team! Wasted in our present occupations it seemed.

The greater part of my day was to be occupied much in the same way as many others in recent weeks: in seeing to it that all the regulations regarding safety and health in the school laboratories and workshops were being rigorously enforced; and, perhaps more importantly, that all the paperwork testifying to this undeniably worthy condition was in order and available for inspection. Following a promising relapse, Inspector Onions had managed to confound medical opinion by making a full and rapid recovery, and was reputedly raring to go on his first assignment since his all too temporary incapacitation. Friday of the following week had been definitely decided upon for the Health and Safely Executive inspection. Much remained to be done in preparation for this crucial event, and I was experiencing difficulty in giving it my undivided attention. Certain related matters nevertheless helped me get through much of the day, for which I was grateful.

Daniela and I lunched separately. She left the Centre in the afternoon, ostensibly for a visit to the dentist, expected back later to continue working in the basement lab. The plan was that she would return with Karl's car and Johnny's briefcase some time after six; then go through the motions of continuing with whatever it was she was supposedly doing, finishing off shortly before eight; having then bade farewell to anyone still around, she would proceed to the loo and lock herself in a cubicle. There was some risk here but, on the basis of careful observation of her colleagues' behaviour at around that time of day, she was reasonably confident of evading detection. In the meantime, I would work in my room until nine, leave college by the main gate, where the security guards were well aware of my spasmodically late working habits, then head for a restaurant in Charlotte Street for a leisurely supper. At ten-forty-five, as near to the dot as possible – we had synchronised our watches – I was to be at the fire escape door, having re-entered college through the Malet Street gate with the aid of Daniela's illicitly acquired key; at precisely that time she would crack open the door. As a fallback, in the event of my not being there, she would remain in place and open up again fifteen minutes later. Then I could set to work.

Thus far everything went exactly to plan. I entered the building at ten-forty-five and we made our way together by torchlight to the internal, ground floor laboratory containing Sean's safe. Daniela had covered the only small window – in the door to the corridor – with paper and masking tape; then, when we were safely inside, she taped over the cracks around the door. When this had been completed to her satisfaction she turned on the light.

'How do you feel?' she asked, as I stood there frozen, heart pounding dangerously against my rib cage: she could hear it, I felt sure, from across the room.

'OK,' I lied. 'And you?'

'OK too. Let's get on with it then.'

She appeared quite composed, quite unfazed by the enormity of what we were doing. I, in marked contrast, felt a trembling in my stomach and knees, I wanted to shit; the safe, there in front of me, stood massive and unassailable; the whole escapade a dream: a mad, confused dream.

'It's only a game,' she said softly, putting her arms around me, 'and we're winning. We can't quit now, not while we're winning. Let's get it over with, then we can go home.'

Slowly, as though drawn by a weary deity, the black cloud lifted: the bad moment passed, my confidence returned. I kissed Daniela, then went over to Johnny's case, laid out for me on a table alongside the safe. The drill was ready for use, the short bit in place: 'The length's just right: go in up to the chuck. It's as silent as they come: diamond tipped, self lubricating, the lot.' Johnny had prepared everything meticulously for me. A centre punch and hammer, held in place with Velcro, nestled beside the drill. I took them over to the safe, carefully positioned the punch and dealt it a hefty blow.

A deafening chime – as though of an immense cathedral bell summoning the faithful of a sizeable diocese – reverberated around the room.

'Jesus!'

We stood rooted in silence as the echoes died. Even Daniela had lost her composure, had turned a deathly white.

'It's all right,' she said after what seemed forever, 'there's nobody around.' She was recovering rapidly. 'Anyone who heard it would just think . . .'

What she thought anyone would just think was never disclosed, because at that moment the silence was broken by the distant sound of a door being noisily unlocked and opened. We resumed our frozen stances. Then the light came on in the corridor outside. I could see this through the paper Daniela had taped over the window. What a pair of plonkers we had turned out to be. Perhaps it would be best to stick to physics and biochemistry after all – if we ever managed to get out of here alive.

Heavy footsteps of someone descending the stairs from the first floor sounded through the stillness. Then a voice – loud and bestial, devoid of any vestige of human feeling: Miss Brown's voice – called out from some way off:

'Is anybody there?'

Daniela looked at me, forcing a tight smile, shrugging her shoulders in mute resignation. My immediate reaction was to look around for a weapon: a loaded Kalashnikov perhaps, stashed away somewhere for emergencies such as these. Then I went over to Daniela, ready if necessary to defend her to the death with my bare hands. The footsteps had stopped. Another voice, far away and indistinct, had shouted something to which Miss Brown replied:

'Well, you could have told me.' She sounded angrier than ever. 'I thought you were asleep somewhere.'

This provoked a discernibly furious, but otherwise still incomprehensible reply. She started to retrace her steps, muttering menacingly; the light in the corridor went off and a door slammed. We couldn't believe it: the danger appeared to have passed.

'Let's get out of here.'

I had replaced the offending hammer and punch in the case and was closing the lid.

'But we're in the clear now. If that drill is as quiet as you say it is, our problems are over. What's the matter with you?'

'But . . . after that . . . they'll be listening. It's madness to risk it now. We can come back another time, when it's safe, when we've had a chance to . . .'

'If you think that after waiting for you in this place for three hours I'm going to give up now, when everything's set to go . . . you must be mad. We'll wait till twelve-thirty. Everyone will be away or asleep by then. From what you told me it'll only take fifteen minutes to open the thing. What's the matter with you?'

I was thinking of that play we had gone to only the previous week: Macbeth, at the Young Vic. Quite a moving portrayal it had been of a man having the sense to change his mind when the enormity of what had been contemplated finally got through to him. But could he convince her? After that he had never stood a chance.

It was just coming up to ten to one, ten minutes late by Daniela's reckoning when, with the merest whisper of a groan, the door of the safe swung open. It was a truly wonderful feeling: akin to winning the Irish Sweepstake say, with the added satisfaction of knowing it had been achieved by hard won expertise and long, patient planning. Daniela enveloped me in a firm embrace, my earlier attempt at feeble capitulation completely forgiven. Then it was time for her to get to work.

There was not a lot inside: the bottom shelves were completely empty; Sean's log books, six substantial hardback volumes, occupied the high top shelf; below them, to the left, some half-dozen folders containing loose sheets, neatly stacked; and next to these a pile of journals, topped with a smart looking box file. Nothing more.

'Seems the work of a well enough organised individual,' I said, receiving a withering look in response.

'I'll start on the logs.' She took them in her arms. 'Have a look in that box file. It could be something interesting. This lot's probably going to take a while to make sense of.'

She seemed a little put out at this, as though having forgotten that opening the safe was just the beginning so far as she was concerned. A fear of mine, which I hadn't conveyed to her, was that the outcome could prove indecisive. Given the breathtaking build up we had just participated in, this could present a painful anticlimax.

'OK. But first I'm going to tidy up a bit.'

This was to involve removing all trace of the break in. Johnny took this phase of the operation very seriously and had given careful instructions on how to proceed. As Daniela settled at a desk, I mixed a tiny quantity of resin with which to fill the hole. The safe was an old one with a number of scratches and small rust marks here and there over the surface: easy enough to disguise the damage as another of these. When I had finished, I called Daniela over to admire my handiwork.

'Brilliant,' she said, somewhat unappreciatively. 'I'll have to speed up a bit with the logs. It's all painstakingly pedestrian and dim-witted, full of quite unnecessary detail. I'm going to have to start skipping sections. Nothing of any consequence whatsoever so far.'

'Well, I'll have a look in that box now. If there's anything I can do to help you, just shout.'

But I was the one to shout, just as soon as I had lifted the box from the pile of journals, revealing them to be not scientific publications at all but porn magazines, about twenty of them.

'It's going to take me quite a while to wade through all these,' I said; 'God! Come and look at this one.'

It must have been getting on for three-thirty when Daniela's patience finally yielded a definite result. She had prepared herself well beforehand, genning up on recent developments in cancer research and in particular the fundamental work underlying them; in addition to the published literature, she had drawn on personal contacts with people working in these and closely related fields. Initially, her probing into Sean's reports appeared to be getting nowhere, yielding merely a succession of what amounted to little more than routine undergraduate laboratory assignments, reported with a seriousness of manner which confirmed her initial impression of his technical naivety. Then, about eighteen months back, he had embarked on what Daniela was able to identify as a more or less straight application of the early approaches employed by ARC Pharmaceuticals. The animal tests, however, must have come as a disappointment to him: some initially promising results – which, if taken alone, could be used to engender slender grounds for optimism – followed by others, which turned out to be either ambiguous or unambiguously negative. This had gone on for some time, the work clearly getting nowhere. Then, abruptly, the reporting was to undergo a dramatic transformation.

'Look at this, Paul.' Daniela's voice broke a long silence in which I was having difficulty keeping awake. 'I should have started at the end, it would have saved a lot of trouble.'

He appeared to have flipped completely some six months before, as though having suffered some mental trauma. The layout of the log appeared unchanged: each daily entry starting on a new page, the date carefully underlined, the small neat writing set out in short paragraphs interspersed with sketches of what could be taken for molecular structures and reaction pathways, the occasional table of experimental conditions and results. But now the content, previously naive in Daniela's estimation, had turned to pure gibberish. One paragraph, written as a letter in the to-whom-it-may-concern mould, consisted in painfully effusive references to himself: his brilliance as a researcher and entrepreneur, his undying determination to succeed. Others went off into childish fantasies: of evil forces set on his destruction, against which he must remain forever vigilant; of benign beings acting on his behalf, providing him with the wherewithal to

254

defeat his enemies. This continued, day after day, occasionally punctuated with rambling reports of experimental investigations, which Daniela pronounced meaningless, as mad as the rest of it. Some later entries, echoing the first indications of his breakdown, could have been the result of some quack self-assertion course: constant reiteration of the certainty of eventual recognition, of the fame and fortune which would one day be his.

I felt a sadness for him growing as I read on, guilt at our intrusion into the world of his personal demons. The box file had yielded an opened packet of chocolate biscuits, two rather desiccated apples and a few envelopes addressed to him, with Irish stamps on them – apparently containing letters from his mother: the name Mrs H R O'Brien written on their backs. The porn mags were mainly of the specialist spanking and bondage varieties, well thumbed through by the look of them. Daniela had been singularly unimpressed when she had come over at my request to check these out: 'She doesn't seem to be enjoying that very much,' had been an immediate comment. 'No, nor does he by the look of it,' I had replied. 'Obviously a serious business for both of them.'

'What are we going to do now?'

Something in my tone must have conveyed the guilt I was feeling, prompting Daniela to reply defensively, as if in response to criticism.

'We had to find out, Paul. It's not just Sean, he's only a pawn in all this. He obviously needs help. But what of the people who are encouraging him, leading him on? Not Trowbridge and Grandison: they haven't a clue about anything, they're totally in the dark. What about the others though? The experts and financiers supposedly backing this crap to the tune of millions?'

I went over and hugged her, feeling some resistance, a stiffness in her response which I had never experienced before. It was un-warranted but understandable: we were both dead tired by now, her previous dislike of Sean making it easy to see this outcome as a gloating victory, which I was viewing with sanctimonious disapproval. This wasn't true at all; and the moment would have passed, would have been completely forgotten but for what we were to encounter later that morning on returning to Clapham.

For the moment, decisions had to be made swiftly. There was a photocopier in the next room which Daniela had the key to and we had thought of using. But that would take an age. I proposed an alternative:

'Why don't we just take his last year's log. That would provide concrete evidence for what has gone on: the earlier straight crib of the ARC Pharma procedures and the point at which he lost touch with reality. If we put everything else back carefully he might not even notice for a while. And what if he does? He's going to find the game is up soon enough anyway. I can't see that it makes much difference.'

So it was agreed. We put everything back in order, noted the combination settings, then returned them to those we had recorded on arrival. The only sound as we left the building was of a tranquil gurgle from the Goldburg fountain, left gently flowing overnight. Hand in hand, we skirted the corner of the forecourt, keeping close to the wall, then out through the gate into Malet Street. Karl's car was parked close by, and within minutes we had driven through the deserted streets and were back in Daniela's flat, exhausted but well enough pleased with ourselves.

She was in the bathroom when the phone rang. It was just coming up to four-thirty. My immediate thought, understandably enough I suppose, was that this must be connected in some way with our misdeed. I answered in trepidation. But it was a woman's voice sounding distressed, asking for Daniela in Italian. Even before she got to the phone I knew something was seriously wrong. Daniela was controlling herself with difficulty, her voice in the mouthpiece unconvincingly reassuring.

'It's Pablo. He's had a stroke. A bad one by the sound of it. Mamma doesn't think he is going to survive.'

I went over and held her in my arms. She felt stiff and unresponsive, her mind totally focussed on what she had just heard, on what to do next:

'I have to get back. I have to see him. Oh Paul, it may be too late.'

With difficulty, I persuaded her to come to bed. First thing in the morning we would phone a travel agent, get her on the first possible flight. There was nothing to be done at the moment. Sean's log book lay on the table next to the phone. Her eyes took it in then turned to me, her face blank, expressionless, tears starting to trickle down her cheeks.

Chapter 32

I awoke on Friday morning after no more than about three hours sleep feeling surprisingly refreshed and alert. Daniela lay beside me, her intakes of breath pulsing irregularly as though the anxieties of the previous night had invaded her dreams. I crept out of the room, closing the door carefully behind me, and made for the phone. The earliest direct flight to Buenos Aires was on Saturday afternoon, others involving complicated connections saving at best a few hours. The agency, deducing urgency, quoted an exorbitant price for the open return, reluctantly agreeing to hold it for no longer than one hour. At least that would allow Daniela to sleep a little longer before I would have to wake her to obtain approval.

Some time after I had hung up, Karl called from California. He had been in contact with the hospital to which Pablo had been admitted and wanted Daniela to know that his condition was less critical than her mother had been assuming, and that there was every hope he would pull through. In the meantime there was much for us to talk about, and when I got round to replacing the receiver the time limit set by the agency had almost expired. Daniela agreed sleepily to the proposed arrangements, which I confirmed without further delay and then attempted to persuade her to try to sleep a little longer; but she insisted on sticking to our original plan for her to continue working as usual in the Centre in case something should blow up there. So after breakfasting on black coffee we set off for college. Karl was to phone back that evening at around eight, when she would be able to question him directly on Pablo's condition.

As we were getting ourselves ready, and later on the tube, I told her something of what I had just learned from Karl. He had somehow managed to pursue his investigations into the Mencken/ARC Pharma imbroglio – not by reference to Henry this time, whom he thought it best to leave out of things for his own good – but by tracing back to source the rumours concerning Sean's supposedly dominant role in the ARC Pharma drug development programme. How exactly he had been able to do this remained unclear but would have certainly have involved a fair degree of subterfuge and flair. Anyway, he had first been able to establish beyond doubt that, far from being a key member of the research team, Sean had been regarded, almost from the onset of his appointment, as completely incompetent and would undoubtedly have been got rid of much earlier were it not for a family connection with one of the directors. Rumours to the contrary, he had been able to verify, emanated from two key individuals unequivocally associated with Mencken, one still in a senior position there, both having gone to extraordinary lengths in attempting to conceal their roles in the affair.

Communication with ARC Pharma on this, and indeed most matters, had been inhibited by the delicate political considerations relating to the sought after reforms in procedures and funding mechanisms for drug validation; and, perhaps even more so, by fear of reprisals on the part of the directors and senior employees, who had become aware of a data bank of dirt and plausible innuendo on them, ready to be unleashed in the event of a perceived threat. Karl had documented the evidence for this, such as it was, and was returning to London the following Thursday. Our findings on Sean's work in the Goldburg Centre complemented well what he had uncovered of the broader picture, providing concrete evidence which no amount of arm waving would be able to gainsay. Tonight we were to discuss strategies for moving the whole unhappy affair towards some sort of a conclusion.

Daniela was still stunned by the news from home and suffering from lack of sleep. These were the reasons, I persuaded myself, for a small but perceptible coolness towards me, which I had never experienced from her before. As she was leaving the next day for an indefinite period, this was particularly distressing, and it was taking considerable effort on my part to ignore it, as seemed the best thing to do. In addition to everything else, we were both anxious to learn if things were normal in the Centre: whether Sean had become aware of the missing log, and if so what his reaction had been. Daniela managed a weary smile as we were about to separate by the fountain.

'I'm sorry to be like this,' she said. 'It's not fair on you, I know.'

'My God Daniela, you don't have to apologise. I know what you're going through. What I don't know is how I'm going to exist without you after tomorrow.'

Karl phoned that evening as planned and spoke reassuringly for a while to Daniela, who appeared clearly relieved: Pablo's condition had continued to improve, the immediate danger seemingly past. It was good that she was to see him but the urgency no longer existed. She could relax and enjoy her visit home.

'I'll put you through to Paul,' she said, not wanting to talk about anything else while her concerns for Pablo were still uppermost in her mind, 'he'll tell you how things stand now with the Centre.'

Nothing untoward had occurred there, Sean still giving every impression of working away diligently, striding around as usual as though he owned the place, clearly unaware his number was up, his lone fantasy world destined for imminent destruction. The question remaining for us, which we had had little chance to discuss, was how best to follow up our devastatingly successful initiative. Regarding this however, Karl had everything under control:

'There's no need for either of you to admit to any involvement at all. I've already spoken to Tony, arranged to meet him Thursday evening, soon as I get back. Told him what it's about without giving details. Understandably enough, he seemed surprised to hear from me on this, but not at all unfriendly. I think he was beginning to have grave doubts himself about the whole affair.'

'How are you going to explain getting hold of the log?' I asked, having been wondering about this, now that the break-in was unlikely ever to be discovered.

'No need. That's quite irrelevant. It could have simply been left lying around so far as anyone else is concerned. It'll certainly give Sean something to think about, but what can he possibly say? Poor sod! Someone quite close to him must have been involved, someone who knew his weakness, how easily he could be manipulated. Anyway, it'll all be in Tony's court soon. He should be well able to deal with it. We can just sit back now for the most part and watch.'

Both of us were feeling pretty well exhausted that evening, and Daniela needed to sort things out for her departure the following afternoon. She had told Trowbridge of her impending absence, its reason, the uncertainty of when she would be able to return: 'He's a cold fish. No trace of compassion, just moaning on about the disruption this was going to cause to the project – as if he had any idea at all of what I've been doing there. Seems he's waiting for me to produce a paper he can add his name to. Keeps on about that: the pathetic creep. I don't know how much more of it I can put up with.'

While sympathising unreservedly, this last comment caused a tightening in my gut, an addition to my growing concern for how she would react to her homecoming. I was well aware of letters from Argentina never referred to: from Carlo, without doubt. And from things she had let slip, I knew her mother was hoping for reconciliation there, a return to the prospect of a good society marriage, a prosperous, settled life for her close by, the envy-tinged approval of neighbours. Once again the confluence of this unanticipated return home with the first and, so far as I could remember, only trace of discord in our relationship awakened fears which had lain dormant from the time we had come together: what sort of life could I offer to compete with what she was effectively being asked to reject?

The following morning we made love drowsily, barely emerging from the slumber which had overtaken us no sooner than we had hit the mattress the night before.

'Come back quickly Daniela,' I murmured as we lay entwined. 'Come back soon.'

She didn't reply; instead snuggled closer and kissed me without opening her eyes.

Later, on arriving at the airport – where we had driven uncomfortably in Karl's car, squashed in among Daniela's cases – I felt my apprehensions again taking hold: that a phase of life was ending, the fear that she would never return. Why, I thought darkly as her luggage was being checked in, was she taking so much back with her?

At the entrance to the departure lounge, she broke the silence which had settled awkwardly over us:

'It won't be long Paul. Don't look so worried, you're making me nervous.'

'I'm sorry. I've got so used to you always being around. It's going to be lonely at home without you.'

We embraced and kissed and then she was gone. I was to return Karl's car to his garage in Camden; then try to think of something to do with myself for the remainder of the weekend.

On arrival at college the following Monday morning, I called in at the school workshop to see Ted. The Health and Safety Executive visit was just four days away now and much still remained to be done. Far from 'looking after all the nitty-gritty', I was having difficulty getting him to move at all on a number of glaringly obvious items, all in urgent need of action. Terence Onions, according to

Dobson, was determined to prove to the small part of the world he inhabited that sickness had in no way blunted his razor sharp awareness of potential danger, however slight; nor his praiseworthy determination to see it all but eliminated, regardless of cost and inconvenience. Why was it, it occurred to me, as I waited for Ted to emerge from the store room or wherever else he was hiding, that Dobson, along with everybody else, appeared so familiar with Onions's doings and reputation? Even Karl, when I had mentioned in passing on the phone that I was preparing for a Health and Safety Executive visitation, had observed: 'not by Terence Onions, I hope – for your sake, that is.' I began thinking that perhaps Sutcliffe had singled me out for the present task as being the only one never to have crossed him before.

Ted appeared eventually, looking sheepish.

'Everything well in hand,' he said coming up to me. 'The lads will be clearing up the basement tomorrow afternoon. Rajmal is on holiday, thank the Lord. Won't be back till Monday. It's going to take a while to clear up his mess.'

At least that was some good news. The state of Rajmal's rig and the surrounding area was a constant source of dismay to everyone – regardless of safety inspection considerations. He had lately installed a steam supply, so as to be able to conduct his experiments at high temperature: '. . . preparing to pour boiling oil over the invaders,' was how Ted had viewed this development, 'in full accord with his tribal traditions, no doubt.' Although possibly anthropologically off target, this observation reflected a general, genuinely felt concern.

Other lesser matters still remained in need of attention:

'You haven't got that guard on the band saw, I see. Has it arrived yet?'

'Not to worry. The manufacturers have promised it first thing tomorrow morning; I've just been on the phone to them.'

He was looking decidedly shifty as he said this. Further points of detail were, I was assured, also well in hand. Unconvinced, I left and made my way to my room.

I had tried to phone Daniela the day before. From what I could understand from her mother, she was asleep the first time; and when I called again later that morning there was no reply. I would try again in the afternoon.

In the meantime, there were a number of 'hazard assessment' forms which required chasing up. One of these had to be completed and signed by someone accepting responsibility for each student laboratory project. As a number of these made use of the same rig, often related to more than one course module, it could be unclear at times who exactly should be deemed responsible. This convenient ambiguity was widely invoked as reason for non-completion of a form, such evasions being understandable enough in view of the difficulties entailed. Almost all the experiments involved risks no more severe than those encountered in unadventurous everyday life, each having to be ascribed, with detailed justification, a hazard rating in a numerical range from one to ten. Boiling an egg, for example, would score relatively low: two, say, or three. Whereas clandestine sex (with a neighbour's wife, for instance) would undoubtedly score high, at a level for which the additional demands of constant super-vision and full protective clothing would take a carefully worded exclusion clause to circumvent. I spent most of the rest of the morning tracking down and imploring people to fill in the remaining blanks:

'If in doubt,' I would tell them, 'put down anything; if Onions disagrees we'll simply go along with him and change it;' adding optimistically: 'That should keep him happy.'

Daniela was out when I called in the afternoon. I tried, in my few words of Italian, to enquire after Pablo, but her mother was unable to understand me; nor could she when I tried to explain I would call again later; after which followed a brief spate of further unintelligible exchanges before I hung up.

Although far from happy with how things were going with the impending inspection I decided there was nothing further I could do about it at present. Seated at my desk, I wondered about Daniela: where she was, what she was doing. Then I opened a file that lay in front of me and read through some analysis started half-heartedly a couple of weeks before: another strand stemming from the work with Karl, which promised a further elaborate twist to the seemingly never ending saga. Yes, I thought to myself as I got to the end of it, this should keep me busy for a while; then, ruefully, addressing my thoughts directly to Daniela this time: right back to where I was at before you burst into my life and took it over.

I set off from Brixton early the following Friday, not happy at all at the thought of what was in prospect. Karl had arrived at college straight from the airport the previous afternoon, and I had gone to his room with Sean's explosive log book to brief him before his meeting with Tony. He was looking exceptionally pleased with himself, showing no signs of jet lag, and suggested we met in the Goose later that night. 'I'm not going to be late,' I had told him, quite firmly; 'I'm going to need an exceptionally clear head for Onions in the morning.'

Changing at Stockwell, on to the packed-to-bursting Northern Line, I became aware of an unpleasant waft in the carriage, reminiscent of itinerant fairgrounds of my youth. Onions! it came to me after a few moments: greasy, fried fairground onions. Unable to conjure up an accessible soothsayer to interpret this supposed omen, my mind turned to the matter of that surname: How on earth does he put up with it? My head was heavy from the effects of the previous night with Karl, my uncharitable thoughts targeting the focus of my frustration over the past weeks – quite unfairly, I tried to tell myself: Onions may yet turn out a paragon of affability and sweet reason; you can't go through life believing all the malicious rumours you hear. It was no use: imbedded prejudice winning through as usual. Anyone in his right mind would have changed it years ago. Though probably not a lot of good in his case: he'd only have gone for Longbottom or some other such northern absurdity.

I got off at Tottenham Court Road, the initial encounter with Onions just minutes away, my mind turning again to uncomfortable speculation on the likely consequences of the whole thing ending in complete disaster. My spirits started to rise a little as I crossed Great Russell Street, the result of a hazily glimpsed silver lining, which faded tantalisingly before I could fully take it in. I was well on my way up Store Street, within sight of the main college gate, by the time it reappeared, fully visible this time and well defined: the one certain outcome of abject failure would be that I'd never be asked to do anything like this ever again.

Chapter 33

Such was the confusion following the extraordinary happenings during the Goldburg fountain's inauguration that the manner of Grandison's departure from the VIP platform, which suffered the full force of the deluge, passed almost unnoticed. Fortunately for him, the press and television cameras and the attention of the reporters themselves were fully focussed on the Prince of Wales; so that Grandison's remarkably agile antics – as he projected himself from the platform and thence into the arms of his wife, who had rushed forward from the barrier behind which the less important persons had been herded – were never recorded for posterity. He was nevertheless to suffer dearly for his improvident overexertion.

The news first reached Hardcastle a couple of days after the event, still recovering from his experiences and rocked by the sudden elevation of Prince of Wales College to television stardom and front page interest in all the nation's newspapers, as well as a good many overseas ones. Grandison had phoned him from hospital, his voice barely audible, as though a last breath:

'It's my leg. They're trying to save it but it doesn't look good. I feel so helpless here, leaving you to cope with everything. I'm so sorry, Sir Charles. I just don't know what to say.'

'Just concentrate on getting well again, Nigel. Don't worry about us, we can cope. Could be worse.'

In fact, Grandison's misfortune was just the thing Hardcastle needed to pull himself together, to provide him with a strategy, now that Grandison was safely out of the way, for dealing with the disaster. He experimented at once on his wife, at whose bedside he had taken the call:

'I warned him about putting too much reliance on those people: bloody so-called engineers and that piss artist. But would he listen? Would he buggery.'

Lady Hardcastle did not reply. She hadn't spoken since her ordeal, had taken to her bed and remained there, her dreams in shatters. Doctor Kavanagh from the Health Centre had prescribed sedatives and expressed optimism for her eventual full recovery.

'As if I didn't have enough to contend with,' Hardcastle mumbled ill-temperedly as he parted from her to attend to his official duties. His mind lightened somewhat as he left his residence, heading for the administration block. *Well, at least no one can say I didn't succeed in putting Prince of Wales College on the map,* he thought as he reached the building, acknowledging no contribution from Grandison this time. *Must talk to Charlie Day about how best to play this one.* And with a laugh to himself, and a bounce to his step, and a cheery greeting to the girls in the outside office, he entered his sanctuary and set about leafing through the papers which had accumulated on his desk in his absence.

It was getting on for six weeks before Grandison was to reappear at the Centre, accompanied, with even greater dedication and concern than previously, by his evermore solicitous wife. Amputation had emerged the only feasible option, and he was having to adjust to the temporary artificial limb with which he had been provided, while arrangements were being made in Sweden for a truly state-of-the-art replacement. He was greeted with something almost approaching warmth by the quite humourless Trowbridge, who had substituted for him and had been forced to bear the brunt of the for-the-most-part good-humoured mockery and innuendo, the persistent demands of the media as they played out for all it was worth the most news-worthy of farces to have come their way for decades.

The Centre secretaries were notably impressed at the manner in which Grandison bore his new affliction. He seemed calmer, more relaxed, affected little by his additional burden: the limp more pronounced perhaps, but not too different from before, so that it passed virtually unnoticed. 'And think what it will be like when he gets his new one,' they would whisper to one another as he walked past, 'he'll be better off than ever.'

The one thing guaranteed to upset him though, to give renewed cause for concern for his physical well-being, was any reminder of the circumstances of his humiliation. He would brood over this at his desk, turning over in his mind the progressive decisions leading to the disaster, the persons responsible who had now cut and run, leaving him to face the ridicule one-legged and alone. Hardcastle was clearly identifiable as a major culprit:

'I told him from the start that a fountain was quite unsuitable, but would he listen?' he asked his wife for the hundredth time. 'Once he gets an idea in his head, no matter how imbecilic and unsuitable, there's no shifting him.'

But others were equally to be found fault with. Harvey Denton for one, who quite happily admitted:

'. . . my fault entirely. Should have realised when Ben decided to chop different lengths off the spouts that it was going to influence the output dynamics. Fascinating problem, you know . . . the way a relatively small imbalance in the drag interactions . . .' and so on, at length, losing everyone almost before he had started.

And that stupid goat Sutcliffe . . .

But then he discovered, inadvertently, from snatches of an over-heard conversation between two of the Centre's postdocs, that Ben Palmer had been seen in the company of Karl Dembowski, in a low pub of all places, laughing with him in evident conspiracy. That *clinched it. In seething indignation he confided his discovery to Hardcastle, whose response was totally unhelpful:*

'Forget it Nigel. The past is past. Look to the future. And remember: the world's eyes are on you now; just see to it that the Goldburg Centre gives them something to marvel at next time.'

Chapter 34

I was to meet Onions in Sutcliffe's room at nine-thirty, the whole business scheduled to occupy all the morning and a good part of the afternoon. Sutcliffe was to offer some initial conviviality, a playful butt perhaps, before making his excuses and handing over to me. This arrangement was to get things off to a bad start, Onions clearly put out at being fobbed off with other than the head man:

'You'd think he'd have taken my visit rather more seriously – dashing off like that on some pretext,' was how he put it to me, almost as soon as we had been left alone together. 'He doesn't seem to realise how serious this could turn out to be for the school.'

For a moment, I considered the prospect of playing on this theme of Sutcliffe's deficiencies as a means of establishing some sort of bond between us; perhaps throwing in some jocular reference to the short rutting season for the species, with heavy consequent demands on him at this time of year; but then I thought better of it. First impressions of Onions – initially confused by the feeling, soon to be discounted, of having seen him somewhere before – suggested the marked absence of a sense of humour, and cautioned against any hint of familiarity. There was something distinctly odd about his appearance, perhaps to do with the way the component parts, though on the whole unexceptional when considered in isolation, appeared ill-matched, as though put together hurriedly from leftovers at the end of a batch assembly process: a large, heavily built trunk supported on short legs tapering down to tiny feet, which he maintained always well apart, even when walking, as though to compensate for the precarious balance resulting from the small area of contact with the ground; the head, also small, but perched on a thick neck which matched the body, topped with a shock of mousy hair, which I first took to be a wig of simple construction – the strands all falling symmetrically from a high central point to produce a tea cosy effect – before deciding that nobody would make one like that, except perhaps for sale in a joke shop. A cluster of ball pens and other implements protruded from his breast pocket; from behind heavy, dark-framed glasses tiny eyes stared suspiciously, on the constant lookout it seemed for sources of dissatisfaction, ever ready to take offence.

'I thought perhaps you'd like to start with a quick tour of the labs so as to get an idea of the general picture. Then you can decide what you want to look at in more detail.'

This seemed to me a reasonable enough approach to kick off with, left him free to play it however he wanted when he had some grasp of what was involved. I was quite unprepared for his immediately hostile reaction:

'What I want, and I hope you're going to provide me with, is an account of the school's philosophy with regard to safety and loss prevention: the extent to which it permeates the teaching programme as a whole.'

'Well, I can only speak for myself . . .'

'I was afraid of that. It's just not good enough, not good enough at all. It's what I wanted to talk to Sutcliffe about, but he's apparently got more important things to do, or so he thinks.'

'Look, you're going to meet Ken Dobson over coffee later this morning. He deals with safety and loss prevention in his second year course to all engineers. You can ask him about . . .'

'Well for one thing, I don't drink coffee, and for another you don't just tuck away safety in a course, which very probably nobody takes a blind bit of notice of, and then wash your hands of the matter. Do you know how many man hours were lost in the industrial sector last year due to accidents in the workplace?'

He had hit the nail right on the head so far as Dobson's course was concerned – a dead loss, according to those few students who bothered to turn up after the first couple of lectures.

'No,' I replied in answer to his question, trying hard to look interested. 'Tell me.'

Terence Onions, it rapidly became apparent, was a man with a giant sized chip on his shoulder who had taken considerable pains to manoeuvre himself into a position of some power, which he used in attempts to assuage the frustrations which life, justifiably enough in the circumstances, had seen fit to bestow upon him. Later, in the common room, he had let on to having been rejected as a young man for a degree course at Prince of Wales College, a humiliation which still rankled after what must have been well over twenty years. My colleagues, gathered glumly around the table, made an excellent show of expressing shock and indignation at this grotesque misjudgement.

'Best thing that could have happened, as it turned out,' Onions had gone on. 'Went to Manchester instead; wonderful course it was; never looked back since.'

This declaration provided me with an opportunity to put my foot in it:

'Really,' I responded with animation, 'I went to Manchester, read Physics with Mathematics. What department were you in?'

It turned out he hadn't gone to the university at all, but to some institute no one had heard of from which he obtained a diploma. The silence following this disclosure was broken by Dobson coming to the rescue:

'I think we could learn a lot from some of these polytechnics and other places. They seem more able to adapt to the changing needs of society than we do.'

Everyone went through the motions of more or less agreeing with him.

The remainder of the morning, while by no means problem free, had not gone nearly as badly as expected following Onions's opening onslaught. I was soon to realise that there was little of substance behind his bluster and was able to devise a reasonably effective strategy for dealing with him. This consisted in agreeing whole-heartedly with everything he said, then talking rapidly about the purpose and theoretical background of the particular experiment under consideration, using opaque technical terminology wherever possible, with the contrived assumption that he was understanding me perfectly, that only a complete ignoramus could fail to. It didn't work every time, but enough to get by on: the blank look on his face as he nodded in feigned agreement a pleasurable indication that I had him in tow, was gradually asserting control. The visit to the work-shops, which brought to a close the largely satisfactory pre-lunch activities, went off without a hitch, Ted having overcome his habitual inertia and moved decisively to put his house in order: all equipment guards fitted and an abundance of protective clothing in evidence – even the tea boy sporting safety spectacles as he stood over the kettle waiting for it to boil.

I felt I could afford to relax a little, allow my mind to wander to the other encounter which was to have taken place that morning, thoughts of which enabled me to keep the tussle with Onions in per-spective. This was initially to have involved solely Tony Mulgrave and Sean, with Grandison and possibly Trowbridge scheduled to put in an appearance half an hour or so later – with very probably a crash team bearing full resuscitation equipment standing by. Karl and Tony had had their planned meeting the previous evening, the gist of which had been conveyed to me soon after in the Goose. Also present had been Frank Mendellson, invited by Tony at Karl's request after hearing from me of his independent, if hesitant, stance at the ill-fated gathering some weeks before. Although obviously a difficult situation for Tony, he had been won over by Karl's careful exposition of what had been uncovered of the underlying conspiracy, and Mendellson's damning assessment – reflecting long held suspicions, amply confirmed by the appropriated log book – of Sean's research. What had made things a little easier for Tony to swallow had been his growing feeling that something was seriously wrong with the whole business, with the objectivity of Grandison's and Trowbridge's enthusiastic advocacy of Sean's achievements, and indeed their competence to judge them. This had been for the most part suppressed as a result of the apparent willingness of a venture capital company, acting on impeccable expert advice, to commit tens of millions of pounds to funding further developments. Although the reason for this willingness still remained unclear, the possibility that Mencken could be behind it provided sufficient grounds for suspicion that something rather more could be involved than would be apparent to the innocent observer: his past probing into the dealings of the pharmaceutical industry leaving him under no illusions regarding their integrity where their interests were concerned. Karl and I had planned to meet the following day, by which time the early fallout from the affair would be making itself felt, curiosity and some anxiety in the meantime exercising a tantalising hold over me.

And if that wasn't enough, there was the ever present question of Daniela invading every unoccupied moment of my consciousness. I had eventually managed to get through to her on the Tuesday, had spoken to her a couple of times since, being aware each time of some artificiality in our exchanges which I had tried to put down solely to her concern for Pablo – making slow progress, no clear indications yet of how reversible his condition, of how soon he would be able to return home.

Onions had managed to recharge his engines of hostility over lunch, making much of the few minor irregularities uncovered during the course of the morning, giving rise to concern that one or other of my colleagues would lose patience with him, provoking a breakdown of the uneasy truce I had taken pains to establish. Then things took a decisive turn for the better as a result of the intervention of Bob Crowe, a thermodynamicist who, it turned out, had been raised in a Yorkshire village close to the small town where the Onions dynasty had its roots. The two of them were soon well at it chewing over past glories: the opening of the first gas works in the area by Alderman Onions, great-uncle of Terence, an event still spoken of with reverence by the older inhabitants; the stolid defensive attributes of a local batsman ('. . . two full days at the crease and never a chance given.'); the unrivalled excellence of the local brew. Bob had quickly cottoned on to what was required of him and was playing it for all it was worth. If only, it came to me as I watched them, I had thought of setting up a meeting with Hardcastle. In addition to satisfying Onions's desire to confer with top brass, both could have derived pleasure reminiscing over long past discomforts joyfully endured: of whippet races on the frozen moor, weekly baths in the coal bucket. I kicked myself for not thinking of this before. But it was nevertheless with the feeling that a satisfactory conclusion to the business was well in sight that I led Onions away from the common room restaurant for the last leg of his tour of the laboratories.

The first premonition of the disaster that was set to occur came to me as I opened the door from the stairway to the upper basement, which contained a number of small laboratories and led to the gantry, through the open mesh steel flooring of which could be viewed Sutcliffe's giant hydraulics rigs in the basement proper. An intense hissing noise, soon to be identified as a sizeable leak of high pressure steam from somewhere below, greeted our arrival, condensing clouds of vapour wafting through the floor some way in front of us.

'What in hell's name is going on?' demanded Onions, clearly aroused by the expectation of discovering a serious malfunction, an opportunity to harangue and prescribe, just what he had been searching for unsuccessfully all morning.

At that moment I became aware of Rajmal Ram, complete with overflowing bucket, ascending the stairway from the basement. In vain I tried to direct Onions away from the scene, towards the labs lining the far wall, but realised almost immediately that there was no hope whatsoever of deflecting him now.

'I'm going to get to the bottom of this,' he declared, the call of duty stiffening his shoulders, intensifying the determination in his eyes.

Cautiously at first, as though concerned that his tiny feet could slip through the steel mesh of the floor panels, he made his way towards the spot where Rajmal had materialised in front of us, like a genie from a bottle, surrounded by rising clouds of vapour. His face lit into a huge grin on seeing us approaching, no doubt due in part to a flawed assessment of the brownie points he was to be awarded for cutting short his vacation.

'Just what is going on here?'

The officiousness of Onions's demand was completely lost on Rajmal, who won my guarded admiration by proceeding to answer him with a well articulated account of the imponderables encountered in the transport of non-isothermal, highly non-Newtonian, two- or even three-phase corrosive mixtures through hundreds of miles of twisted undersea pipeline:

'. . . some truly fascinating theoretical problems are thrown up when you start to look into it in detail. Things you would never think of at first. For instance . . .'

'I'm not talking about that. What about this steam?'

'Steam?'

He looked genuinely puzzled for a moment. The clouds were getting denser now, the hissing more intense.

'Oh, don't worry about that,' he said, when eventually the penny dropped. 'Only a temporary lash-up to see if the thing works . . . leaking a bit, that's all.'

'I think it might be an idea to turn it off, Raj,' I said, trying hard to sound calm, matter-of-fact. 'Get Ted to send someone down to fix the leak.'

But Onions was fully wound up now and set to go. Muttering aggressively to himself through clenched teeth, he strode to the stairway, from under which the steam appeared to be issuing, and started his descent.

What happened in the next few seconds, and its immediate consequences, belong to that rare but nevertheless familiar class of human experiences, which rely for their existence on such an improbable coincidence of seemingly unrelated events as to render them inconceivable in the telling. The totally unexpected component in what was to befall was Grandison, whom I had observed making his way across the basement towards the bottom of the stairway, just as Onions was approaching it in the opposite direction from the top. How he came to be there, and what precisely were his intentions, I was never to learn, but I certainly figured in them as was clear from his enraged cry of 'Harrison! I want to talk to you', which stopped Onions in his tracks some third of the way down and precipitated the ensuing calamity. I was later to learn that the confrontation with Tony Mulgrave had turned bitter beyond even the most pessimistic of forecasts, and had ended with Grandison storming off in an uncontrollable rage, seemingly blaming me for having engineered the collapse of his dreams. There he was now, seething at the bottom of the stairs, prompting Onions to turn sharply in order to see for himself, perhaps contribute some further expression of disapproval to, the object of his indignation.

What Onions had failed to take into account, however, was the oily condition of the steps, with the result that he found himself

278

performing considerably more than the intended half rotation. Viewed dispassionately from above, there was a certain elegance, something of the ballet, to his initial pirouette; but this impression was almost immediately dispelled by the ungainly gestures that followed as, panic stricken, arms flailing wildly, he sought for some rigid structure to which to attach himself in order to stabilise his condition. In this he was successful, if only momentarily. A vertical tube, well positioned for the purpose but unsuitable in other respects – it was the as yet uninsulated high pressure steam line to Rajmal's rig – ran down close by to the basement floor, and this Onions somehow managed to clasp hold of with both hands. Letting go an instant later, he projected himself down the stairway with great force and an ear-piecing howl, moving almost horizontally to start with, or so it seemed from where I was watching from above. A massive control panel, belonging to one of Sutcliffe's antiquated machines, and bearing a profusion of protruding dials and valves in angular brass with an abundance of sharp corners and other unpleasant features, stood a few feet in front, directly in line with Onions's trajectory. Should he have continued with his course he would have undoubtedly done himself serious injury. Fortunately for him however, Grandison was there to block his path, to stop him dead in effect: Onions's forward momentum being transferred to Grandison, propelling *him* backwards into the control panel, the overall effect providing a somewhat muffled demonstration of the principle of Newton's cradle.

'Get Ted to send down the first aid team and call an ambulance right away.'

As Rajmal scurried away to do this, I hurried down, almost slipping on the greasy steps, to render what assistance I could. Onions was on his feet by now, waving his hands about and shouting. He looked different without his glasses, which lay broken on the floor beside him. My initial impression of recognising him from somewhere returned more forcefully, but there was no time to dwell on it.

'There's a cold tap in the corner over there. Get your hands under it and keep them there. And shut up. Can't you see what's happened here.'

Grandison was out cold, lying half on his side at the foot of the control panel. There had been a sickening thud as he had struck it which had made my stomach turn. A small pool of blood had formed on the floor beside him, but not from his head as I had first fearfully imagined. Years before, I had attended a rudimentary course in first aid which had included the business of stemming bleeding in just the situation I now found myself in. In near panic, I tried to recall the procedures. His right trouser leg was torn and blood soaked; easing it carefully up to the knee revealed a gash on the calf, some two to three inches long, from which the blood flow had practically ceased. No sooner had the relief at this taken hold that it came to me with a rush that this was the leg I had always assumed had been amputated some ten years before.

Unbelievable as it may sound, though testifying to my charged and confused condition at the time, my instantaneous reaction to this discovery was one of marvel at the astonishing developments in prosthesis technology which had made the deception possible. This notion was rapidly to give way to the more rational one that I had simply got the leg wrong: that it was the other one, the left one, which had been removed. It was as I was testing this hypothesis, discovering it to be as erroneous as its predecessor, that Ted and a businesslike looking entourage, bearing a stretcher and other appropriate items of equipment, arrived to take over.

I stood watching in a daze, bewilderment at my discovery overshadowed by contemplation of the lifeless form of Grandison, lying surrounded now by quietly occupied crouching forms; distant, intermittent protestations of Onions the only sound breaking the stillness.

Chapter 35

'He's going to be alright, just concussion as far as I can tell. We've dressed the leg but it could probably do with a couple of stitches. The ambulance should be here any moment now.'

Ted had already soared in my estimation, making me feel guilty at having doubted his commitment earlier on. For a while I had wondered at his apparent lack of interest in the miraculous reappearance of Grandison's leg, the whole episode of its loss being common knowledge, his stoical resilience in the face of the affliction a frequent source of comment and admiration. But when we found ourselves alone for a moment, he gave me a sideways glance and murmured under his breath:

'Probably have to send it back to Sweden for repair.'

In the meantime, Grandison was starting to stir, looking pretty terrible, but not it seemed, when I got round to giving due consideration to the matter, significantly more so than usual. When his eyes opened and started to give signs of focusing, I thought it prudent to absent myself in order to avoid the risk of the sight of me impeding his recovery. My tactical withdrawal from that potential source of disharmony was, however, to launch me straightway into another: with Onions, the final outcome of which was to prove unforeseeably satisfactory – though not before the passage of a further unpleasant period of hostility.

'You're not going to get away with this, you know.'

Onions was seated on the edge of the bed in the first aid room, both hands heavily bandaged, giving the impression of a boxer in white gloves indulging in verbal aggression as a prelude to the real business, about to start any moment. Ted stood thoughtfully by as I took the brunt of these preliminary skirmishes.

'The whole place is a total disgrace, the basement an absolute death trap. It amazes me that nobody's been killed there before now. I'll be making my report as soon as I get back.'

This sort of thing had been going on for some time and I had given up all thought of trying to win him round, thinking instead of trying to persuade Sutcliffe to go over his head, to put in an official complaint about his manner and objectivity. There were plenty of witnesses around to testify to that. A pretty forlorn hope perhaps, and not at all a good idea in principle, but what possible alternatives were there?

Then something extraordinary happened: it came to me quite suddenly where it was I had seen Onions before. It was the glasses which had caused the initial problem; without them there was absolutely no doubt at all. At first this revelation appeared totally irrelevant to the matter in hand. But gradually the bones of a villainous plan began to take shape in my mind. I needed time to think through the implications, assess the damage in the not unlikely event of the whole thing turning pear-shaped. What I was contemplating could well be construed a serious criminal offence; the habit seemed to be growing on me, faster perhaps than even Karl would have considered healthy.

It was at this point that Ted, stung by the thrust of Onions's criticisms, which he rightly felt could in many respects reflect badly on himself, and probably dismayed at my apparent abandonment of the struggle – I had gone silent, lost in urgent thought –, embarked on a seemingly futile counter offensive, claiming the basement laboratory to be a model of good housekeeping and safe practice, potential hazards clearly labelled as such for all to see – including the temporary steam line which he, Onions, had unfortunately, for reasons best known to himself, felt the need to take hold of:

'Look, Mr Onions. In fairness, now that things have calmed down a bit, let me take you back to have another look. I know there was a steam leak, but these things do happen when research equipment is being worked on. It's been fixed now, and there was never any real danger. Just come and see for yourself. In all fairness, I'm asking you.'

Against all the odds, with bad grace and marked reluctance, Onions allowed himself to be led away, leaving me behind, grateful for the opportunity to think something through. By the time they had returned, with Onions in a more hostile mood than ever, I had more or less decided to chance my arm.

'Just what sort of a fool do you take me for? You must realise this makes matters considerably worse for you. A deliberate conspiracy to cover up and mislead. Cleaning up that oily mess and sticking that notice on the steam line. Just what do you take me for?'

At least no one could accuse Ted of not trying, I thought, as I decided on my response, to pave the way as it were for the follow-up:

'You don't really want me to answer that, do you?'

We had reached Sutcliffe's room, where Onions had left his cloth cap and other prized possessions. He was looking at me in furious disbelief as I unlocked the door with the key Sutcliffe had handed me while giving notice of his intention to keep out of harm's way until the coast was clear.

'Just what do you mean by that remark?'

The redness of his thick neck had spread to his face. He looked almost beside himself with rage. My heart was pounding danger-ously, the fear that I was embarking on a doomed course growing by the second. Nothing for it though but to carry on, and the hell with it!

'Come inside Onions, then you can pick up your things and go off and write that report.'

I opened the door and almost bundled him through, speechless now, perhaps a tinge of concern at my body language, the abrupt change in my demeanour as I hyped myself up for a new role. He was standing quite still, watching me in silence, his fury giving way to puzzled indignation as I decided that the time had come to let rip:

'You don't remember me, do you? Last November, in that pub in Soho? I was the one who tried unsuccessfully to warn you off what you were obviously up to.'

'What are you talking about?'

For all his indignation, a note of hesitancy had crept into that response, a hint of concern. He had been quite drunk at the time, would surely have come round later remembering fragments of what had taken place; horrified no doubt, the more so on speculation concerning the bits he could no longer remember. At least that was what I was banking on.

'I think you know perfectly well what I'm on about: your little jaunt with a rent boy: Tommy Rawley by name, aged fifteen . . . alias Michelle . . .'

The colour drained completely from Onions's face on hearing that last name, any thought he may have had of denial, of calling my bluff, completely abandoned. I had no idea of Michelle's real name, and he was certainly a good twenty years old, a one time promising welterweight boxer, according to Malcolm, the Goose's sublimely tolerant landlord, '. . . before he got in with that lot'; certainly well able to take care of himself.

'The victim of a serious assault a few days after he went off with you. You may be interested to know that the police are particularly anxious to trace his contacts.'

Onions was trembling all over by now, it seemed he might fall. Taking his arm, I helped lower him into a chair. He looked pitiful sitting there, shaking his head in disbelief that this could really be happening to him:

'I had no idea . . . no idea at all. It was terrible. You've got to believe me. I thought it was a woman, a grown women. I never even imagined anything like that . . . not until . . . Oh my God!'

He took his head between his bandaged hands and shut his eyes. My immediate instinct was to call it off, to put an end to his misery, but I managed to restrain myself. Just a little bit longer, I thought, maintaining a stern air of silent disapproval. He opened his eyes for a moment to take in my expression, then closed them again. Almost time, I felt, to start offering a touch of reassurance:

'I think I can just about believe you. The trouble is there are a lot who wouldn't. The police are under enormous pressure to draw up a register of suspected paedophiles. They're certainly not the slightest bit interested in claims of mistaken age estimates. Last thing they're interested in.'

'Oh my God!'

He had started to tremble again, quite violently this time.

'Look, don't worry. It was a million to one for me to have been there when it happened.'

'Nothing happened.'

'It doesn't matter one way or the other. I'm not going to say anything anyway. So far as I'm concerned this is the end of the matter.'

The look he gave me changed gradually from cringing fear to, well . . . yes, love: sudden, late blossoming love. He started to rise, giving every indication of intending to embrace me. Adopting the nearest I could manage to a severe magisterial tone, I was just able to dissuade him:

'Just see to it that you behave yourself in future, that's all. Now you had better get back up north and start writing that report.'

Passing by the school office on the way to my room, I found a note in my post tray from Tony Mulgrave asking me to phone him. It was well after six by then and I wondered whether he would still be in his office.

'Hallo Paul. Thank you for calling. I thought it a good idea to have a word with you. To warn you really that Grandison appears to have it in for you . . . your intervention at that meeting a while back . . . and what has happened since . . . this afternoon to be precise.'

'I know. He came to find me in the hydraulics lab, got himself involved in an accident there. He's in hospital now . . . No, nothing serious: a bit of concussion and a small gash on the leg – you know, the one we all thought had been amputated years ago. Probably requires a stitch or two . . . '

Tony sounded fine, as though a great weight had been lifted from his shoulders. Knowing of my association with Karl, he must have suspected me of being involved with him in the affair more than had been let on, but no trace of resentment was evident from his manner. What he went on to tell me though, to warn me about, made my heart sink, was just about the worst news I could have imagined. Hurried enquires had apparently been made that afternoon in the Goldburg Centre, a number of factors being held up together for view from the standpoint of the disastrous revelations still to be fully absorbed: Daniela's close association with myself; her frequent presence in the ground floor laboratories; the coincidence of her sudden departure with the mysterious migration of the crucial log. Two and two had been put together and, despite a number of errors and omissions in the intermediate steps of the calculation, the correct answer arrived at. Alongside the prevailing currents of bitterness and recrimination, of wounded vanities and vanquished dreams, a bridge had been comprehensively burned: there seemed no prospect of her ever being able to return.

Desperately, I tried to contact Karl, but he was nowhere to be found; I needed to talk to him about Daniela, the fix we had landed her in, what could be done about it. Next, I tried to call Daniela in Argentina, getting through to her mother, who gave a complex account of her current activities which I hardly understood a word of, this failure to connect coming over as something of a relief however, as I was at a loss how to disclose the interpretation being put on her absence in the Centre. What a mess! There appeared no way out.

In dejection my mind turned to Sean and Grandison. No sense of victory there, nothing to gloat over: their pipe dreams of glorious acclaim collapsing into emptiness, the full realisation of abject failure. However absurd and unsympathetic the dreamers, contemplation of their downfall only added to my increasingly depressed state. I could think of nothing to do with myself, eventually deciding to kill a couple of hours by walking home to Brixton. Maybe that would help unjumble my thoughts, throw up a suggestion for an effective course of action. It was just as I was about to start on my way that the phone rang: it was Karl.

'Thank heavens you called. I've been trying to get you for ages. I really need to talk to you. It's about Daniela. Seems we've landed her right in it with the Centre.'

'I know. And I need to talk to you too, about something else . . . ' He didn't sound very concerned about her, '. . . about a number of things, in fact. Can't tonight. Are you free tomorrow? Late afternoon, say about five? I'll be in my room. Oh, and incidentally . . . I've had another thought on the stability problem . . . another rather different application of the general idea. I think you're going to like it.'

How he could turn his mind to all that stuff at a time like this was beyond me. He was clearly in a great hurry, but I just managed to prevent him hanging up:

'Listen Karl, there's something else I think you ought to know.'

'Can't it wait till tomorrow?'

'Well it could . . . but I think you should hear about it before then. It's about Grandison's leg . . .'

Chapter 36

The following day, shortly before the appointed time, I arrived at Karl's room in the Physics Department. Being Saturday the college was almost deserted, the only sign of life issuing from the main gatehouse where loud drunken deliberations were in progress on the apparently partisan behaviour of the referee in the previous evening's televised football match. Karl was working away at his desk, giving every appearance of having been at it for a long time. He nevertheless seemed well pleased to see me, and with little hesitation stopped whatever it was he was doing and started to tidy away the papers and other clutter piled in front of him.

'Well,' he said, on completing this to his satisfaction, motioning me to a chair and coming round to settle himself in another, 'it seems there are a lot of things we need to talk about.' Unusually for him, he appeared serious and restrained, signs of fatigue evident around his eyes.

'I know,' I replied, grateful at last for a chance to talk constructively about what had kept me awake most of the previous night. 'Daniela's the one who's really been landed in it. What are we going to do about that? I can't think of anything else. It's driving me mad.'

'Don't worry. It will settle itself in time. In the meantime there's something else . . .'

'Look Karl, you don't seem to realise how much this means to me. I'm not interested in hearing about anything else. Just what the hell are we going to do about Daniela?'

'Try to be patient for a moment.' A flicker of irritation, almost immediately dispelled, crossed his features. 'I've been up to my neck for months now in a mountain of issues which have somehow all managed to come to a head at the same time. Some of this you know about, but now you need to know more. Then when you've got the overall picture perhaps we can start to think how Daniela can fit into it. OK?'

While saying this he had leaned forward, fixing me with a steady, determined look, which I knew well enough signified that there was little point in trying to shift him. With effort I held back, responding with silence. After a few moments he settled on his chair, lightened the atmosphere with a chuckle and engaging smile, and launched into his story. I had the feeling I was to be in for a long haul.

'Two seemingly unrelated strands had been attracting my casual attention for some years; recently they started to come together. At first I put this down to my overactive imagination, seeing links where none existed, the coincidences too improbable to bear serious consideration. Then things started to happen which gave body to these ghosts, forcing me to pursue them seriously, devote quite a bit of time to the whole business. Which was particularly inconvenient, as it happens, because something else, something quite big, was going on and calling for every bit of my attention – but I'll come to that later.' He paused, lost in thought for a moment. 'The first strand you know all about: Grandison and the Goldburg Centre; the vast chasm separating the hype from verifiable achievement. It wasn't a personal matter, you know . . . at least not to start with.' His expression relaxed on making this qualification. 'OK, so things took on a different hue later, but the basic issue had always been about standards and values, about academic control. It's a battle that's been going on for years and it's being lost; and yes, Grandison had come to epitomise the whole sorry saga for me. But the main battle started well before that and was rather less focused. It's to do with the encroaches of what you could call the detached management

289

syndrome: the belief that the top people don't need to have any understanding, even at a relatively superficial level, of the technical content of whatever it is they are there to manage. They leave that to their underlings, and as a consequence have to live with the wool being forever pulled over their eyes when special interests, of which they remain for the most part unaware, come into play. So you have the successful grocer brought in to run the railways, the rag trade tycoon appointed to see through reforms in the educational system. They get away with it for a while; but then when things go wrong you're left with the unedifying spectacle of the top man claiming complete ignorance in his defence, shunting responsibility on to those below and exiting in indignation. This is established practice for politicians, we're quite used to that; provides for good family viewing and makes bugger all difference anyway. But it can prove disastrous in other fields. For the universities it spells the end of the road so far as independent scholarship is concerned.'

The silence which for a moment followed this pronouncement was broken by the sound of a car backfiring outside, in Gower Street.

'Not Grandison shooting himself, I hope.'

I said this instinctively, perhaps in an attempt to move Karl on to what for me was undisputedly the main track.

'No such luck. People like that show remarkable resilience, are completely oblivious of their absurdity. It's a source of great strength to them. He'll even ride out the miraculous reappearance of his leg, you'll see.'

He started to laugh having said this and I was soon joining in; the whole elaborate business of the deception and its uncovering was indeed hilarious, too bizarre to have been credible had it not been for what I had witnessed with my own eyes.

'With hindsight, I should have suspected as much. It fits perfectly with his playing the disabled card at every turn. And what about his wife? She must have been in on it from the start.'

It occurred to me here to admit to my early association with Grandison: St John's, the Pius XII award. That I had never done so bothered me, seemed unaccountably withholding on my part; then I decided that this was not the time. I would see to it soon enough; also enlighten him on Grandison's relationship, such as I had been able to observe it, with Mrs Grandison.

'No, the thing that first concerned me about Grandison was the growing preoccupation with secrecy in all aspects of the work of the Centre: growing as his influence grew. A good number of projects were being conducted jointly with teams in the Science Faculty. At times this was seriously impeding progress, and was a source of continual irritation and complaint which I and others were having to deal with. Charles was sympathetic and took effective action when advised, but when he departed from the scene the whole thing turned impossible. Very occasionally the need arises to keep quiet for a short while about some development or other; but genuine academic research, in whatever field, is characterised by people talking freely with other interested parties, exchanging ideas and advice openly with enthusiasm. That way things move forward, people get to trust each other, become aware of what's going on in other places, are able to respond to it, can seek help from like-minded souls. The Goldburg Centre is simply rotting within its self imposed isolation.'

'Why your interest in what was going on in the basement labs then? Getting Daniela installed there? Not that I'm complaining about that.'

'Two birds with one stone is the answer to your second question. She needed to get away from Argentina for a while and that was something I could arrange – on the quiet, of course; and yes, while we were at it, why not take a peek at what was going on down there? The epoch-making activities in the basement laboratories – of which absolutely nothing could be divulged – had become Grandison's prime justification for special treatment in all manner of funding and other college matters. Hardcastle had supported him heavily at first,

291

but lately appears to be backing off. He seemed to opt out of the O'Brien business some while ago, as though a warning of sorts had got through to him: left it all to Grandison, who had jumped in up to his neck. I was curious – you could probably put it stronger than that – to find out if there really was anything of significance going on down there. I very much doubted it. Frank Mendellson, the nearest we have to an authority in that general area, certainly had his doubts too, but he's not the type to stick his neck out: yearns for a quiet life does our Frank. The problem is very much the one I was on about earlier: Grandison's ignorance of the basic work he is supposed to be leading, and his consequent inability to make sensible decisions about almost anything that concerns it: his reliance on Trowbridge a case in point; his being completely taken in by Sean's nonsense another.'

'Daniela was able to see through them almost at once. That must be the case for many of the people they recruit. What's the matter with them?'

'Nothing at all. All they want is experience – on paper, if nothing else – and recommendations and other help in finding jobs after their contracts in the Centre come to an end. Grandison's very good at that sort of thing, and only too willing to help those who are prepared to suck up to him. Greatly impresses personnel managers and the like.'

Daniela, I recalled, had quickly come to realise this as well. What on earth did Karl mean about fitting her into the picture? It was clear he had something up his sleeve, but there was no point in trying to hurry him in his present mood. After the briefest of pauses, he started up again:

'Sean was the one I was more worried about. Couldn't predict at all how he was going to react. In fact, once he had got over the initial shock, I think he was probably quite relieved it was all over. The pressures he had been under must have become intolerable, even for a scheming blockhead like himself. What started out as a simple case of wishful thinking and self-deception, fuelled by snippets he had picked up at ARC Pharma – where, as you now know, he was considered a complete dunce, foisted on them by his director uncle – became strongly reinforced by the glowing regard paid him by Grandison – big boss of the famed Goldburg empire. At first this could be put down to ignorance on Grandison's part, taken in as he was by Sean's cunning self promotion, the glowing references and the fact that he came from Carsons – a state-of-the-art concern, if ever there was one, famed for a whole range of vastly profitable biotech innovations; helped along no doubt by the equally duped Trowbridge. It must have seemed that this was just what they had been waiting for: someone with the potential to put the place on the map. They probably had some reservations to start with, Sean being far from the first on whom they had built up hopes. But then other factors intervened to convince them beyond any shadow of doubt that they had really picked a winner this time. And Sean himself was drawn up to the next level of the fantasy game being created for him by very persuasive people. Which brings me to the second strand of the tale: an altogether bigger issue which for years appeared completely unconnected with the pathetic power politics of the Goldburg Centre. But there you go.'

Karl paused, settling back in his chair and throwing a questioning glance in my direction. I could think of nothing of any consequence to say, so too settled back in silence, waiting for him to continue.

'As you know, Physics and Biosciences at Franklin work together quite a bit, there are some strong ties there. We tend to meet up pretty frequently for lunch in the faculty club, talk about this and that, at times connected with the work, more often just idle chatter. Remember Dan Carella? Exotically turned out guy with mad staring eyes and a mass of frizzy white hair?'

I did indeed. He had stood out as the token eccentric, throwback from a previous hippy age, quite incongruous among the body of staid, conventionally attired men and women who made up the faculty during my time there. He and Karl got on well together.

'Something of a loose cannon,' Karl continued with a chuckle, 'and very unpopular, it turned out, with representatives of certain pharmaceutical companies who were funding some of the department's research. I had innumerable long conversations with him, particularly after that business with Tony Mulgrave – his near breakdown following his mother's death. Just mention drugs or, in particular, drug companies and he's off: there's no holding him. He's compiled a huge dossier over the years of pharmaceutical company malpractices – quite often blatantly illegal ones: concealing evidence of dangerous side effects of their products, even bribing doctors with massive sums not to reveal these; ghostwriting supporting articles to appear under the names of supposedly impartial medical experts, who are then paid generously to not deny authorship; paying exorbitant lecturing and consultancy fees, which can effectively double a doctor's salary for a matter of a few hours work; and countless other things. He's accumulated a mountain of evidence for the extent to which the gravy train has permeated the medical profession as a whole, buying anything from silence to vociferous support.

With regard to the research, drug company influence can be overwhelming, particularly when it comes down to clinical trials of potential products. In spite of the rigorous guidelines in place, these procedures can be riddled with subjective elements. Doctors, who have been extravagantly courted with gifts, research support, handsomely remunerated conference participation in exotic locations and the rest of it, get to feel the urge to present their results in the most positive manner possible. They may not even fully realise they are doing it: you know, finding reasons with hindsight why the odd bad point or two on the graph shouldn't have been there in the first place, so that the overall trend looks better, can be fed to journalists and others as a great step forward, something with the potential to bring relief to thousands. Difficult things to track down these claims, but Dan reckons to have done so, to have hard evidence of widespread tampering with research results, particularly as it happens in the field of cancer research, where the stakes are truly enormous. What Tony Mulgrave had uncovered with regard to the treatment his mother was receiving fell well within the range of normal suspect practice. More recently, Dan has been taking a close interest in the dirty trick campaigns which certain of the larger concerns have been pursuing in order to protect their patches. It was his tales of these, and in particular his perplexity at the upbeat publicity being given to a small Texan company initiative in a cancer research programme which colleagues of his in the know could see no reason whatsoever for taking seriously, that suddenly caused me to reflect on the possibility that the mysterious goings-on in the Goldburg Centre could be in some way connected.'

'And that's when you decided to investigate for yourself?' I asked, to fill the pause that followed.'

'Yes, indeed.' Karl was looking tired now, closer to his age, as though a struggle of sorts had ended and he could let go. 'Though God knows how I managed to fit it in with other things going on at the time. It was an uphill struggle all the way, until Henry came on the scene. Then, with something concrete to latch on to, an insight into the whole improbable campaign started to emerge. The full picture is still far from clear, but enough has come out to form a pretty good idea of what they're up to – together it seems with some of the other big players in the game. Basically, their idea is to neutralise the efforts of ARC Pharma, and one or two other small operators, to convince the population at large that new drugs, resulting from fundamental research into the root causes of cancer offer real prospects of a cure. In the end it all comes down to political considerations: if enough people come to believe this then the government may find it sufficiently in its interest to act decisively. Their problem is that this would mean committing large sums of public money and instigating radically alternative funding and validation procedures – both potentially hazardous undertakings, given the massive co-ordinated opposition which would be unleashed by the pharmaceutical giants through their paid-up experts and financial backers. So it's a delicate balance we have here, from which the government senses danger and would far rather keep its distance. Mencken decided to help them along a bit with this hands-off approach by taking a leaf out of ARC Pharma's book and setting their sights on appealing directly to the public: providing a spot of negative input for the focus groups to get their teeth into with regard to these newfangled, so-called-advanced scientific approaches to the problem. Given their influence and the resources they were prepared to commit, it appeared to them a one-sided contest.'

'So what are you saying exactly?' I broke in, my tone betraying a growing unease. 'That Sean and others were promoted as sure losers? A bit over the top that, isn't it?'

'Not at all, no. Because what we're talking about here is the carefully engineered manipulation of public opinion – in this case to back up other direct pressures being brought to bear; the nurturing of a natural cynicism for all claims of wonder cures emanating from anywhere other than established household-name pharmaceutical company sources. It's a complex business this: that of forming an opinion in such matters. No conscious involvement at all on the part of the recipient; simply a matter of those neural networks working in accord with fixed laws to determine what weights to give the multifarious inputs . . . gradually homing on to a settled entrenched view which reason and argument are going to find very difficult to shift. Religious beliefs are formed that way, feelings of patriotism, of prejudice in all its guises; of faith – that much vaunted, impenetrable barrier to rational thought. Political and religious leaders down the ages have understood intuitively the forces at work here and used them, often with astonishing success. But now the fundamental mechanisms are being unravelled, and mass communications enable vast audiences to be reached, to be bombarded with information that has been carefully crafted to produce the sought after effect.'

This all sounded very much in harmony with Barry's description of his working practices, giving rise to a feeling of guilt at my amused reaction on hearing of them.

'Sean's is only one of a number of related investigations being groomed for the purpose. As it happens, they've got rather more than they bargained for in this case. What they were after was a well hyped up wonder drug, which after initial promise is shown to come to nothing – along with all the others. Now they must be racking their brains for how to salvage something from the fiasco. They're also very probably considering how best to compensate Grandison, keep him onside in the event of any ensuing unpleasantness, though that shouldn't be too difficult for them.'

Vying with a sense of incredulity at Karl's unfolding exposition was a welling anger; both at the sickening Machiavellianism of the alleged perpetrators and at Karl's composed, matter-of-fact delivery, betraying no trace of disapproval for the despicable campaign he was describing.

'But how could they be so sick?' I exploded angrily. 'Everyone knows what is at stake here . . . the suffering . . . the devastation of so many lives.'

Karl's expression, as he turned to face me, managed to convey sympathetic understanding of my response, while at the same time declaring emotion to be unhelpful just now; time enough for that later, when the full picture has been put in place. It was unfair of me, I realised almost at once, to attribute callousness to his seemingly light hearted exposition: just Karl in his habitual analytical, one-thing-at-a-time mode; each 'thing' to be impassively examined and carefully highlighted before passing on to the next, the lighter the brush strokes the better, all emotion held in check.

It took a while, but I eventually had to come round to accepting the story he had put together from what turned out to be a vast accumulation of material from widely diverse sources. A difficult part for me concerned the sheer scale of the sums involved, the millions invested in backing programmes heralded as being at the leading edge of pioneering research: programmes carefully chosen for being certain to be seen clearly to fail. Karl, however, had been able to establish that a good proportion of the initial investment could be protected and recouped by creative accounting; actual losses offset against tax; and that, enormous though it appeared, the overall cost of the operation amounted to peanuts compared to the sums flowing in worldwide from the sale of established, for the most part abysmally ineffective, chemotherapy drugs – whose whole future could be seen to be coming increasingly under threat. Given the company's influence in every conceivably relevant sector – clinical, academic, political, industrial, financial – it had every reason to be confident of eventual success in its overall strategy.

'It's getting late,' Karl said at last, drawing the subject to a close, at least for the time being. 'You don't have to rush off anywhere?' I smiled and shook my head. 'Because there's something else I want to talk to you about. Something that might go down better over a pint. I think we could both do with one.' He seemed to stall for a moment, wistfully taking in the piles of papers on his desk; then with a shrug got back into gear: 'I'm going to leave everything here for the morning. An interesting situation has arisen which throws up a number of possibilities you may well like to think about.'

No sooner had we passed through the main gate than Karl started to tell me about the negotiations being conducted at Franklin, which he had been so cagey about for months. It appeared that a major new initiative was to be launched there: a new research institute, funded from an enormous private-foundation endowment, together with sponsorships from a number of major industrial companies. A large plot of land, adjoining the Franklin campus, had be acquired for the purpose, and work was due to start any day now on the construction of the sumptuous new complex, due for completion within a matter of a few months.

298

'A sort of Goldburg Centre,' I said, in the lull that followed this announcement, 'with knobs on.'

'Exactly,' he replied with relish, going on to tell me that the appointment of the director to lead the new enterprise would be announced the following week.

'Yes,' he said smiling to himself, as though at the ludicrousness of it, 'I'm afraid it's me. I must talk to Edward about getting my portrait painted for the foyer.'

As we headed for the Goose, Karl proceeded to describe his plans for the new venture. It sounded on the face of it too good to be true, the prime driving force coming as a reaction to the all too evident decline in open-ended, curiosity-driven research in favour of the goal-orientated varieties, sponsored by concerns possessing commercial or other special interest in the outcomes. Although this trend was widely acknowledged to be stifling all but the short term exploration of well trodden ground, with consequently gloomy implications for general progress and innovation, it appeared unstoppable: directing the most gifted graduates away from their natural habitat of fundamental inquiry into applied areas where finance was more readily available. Karl had been instrumental in seeding this massively funded initiative, aimed at restoring and strengthening the base for pure research in a number of key areas; bringing on board any number of eminent personages from academia, the oil and electronics industries, the State of California in general. A major carrot had been the perception of immense prestige in being associated with what was envisaged to become one of the world's foremost centres for fundamental scientific research.

'Three Nobel laureates have already expressed interest, including Baskovich – who sends his regards, by the way. And this is only the beginning. Quite a bit of horse trading going on regarding staffing, but I've seen to it that I maintain effective overall control.'

We had just about reached the Goose when Karl stopped and turned to me.

'I was thinking it might be about time you returned to pure physics, if you don't mind my saying so. Not that you've ever really left it, of course. But, you know . . . doing your own thing full time . . . none of that tiresome business of courses and lab classes for engineers. Anyway, something for you to chew over.'

A tide of confused emotions washed through me on hearing this. The problem however, impeding full appreciation of what was in effect on offer, remained Daniela. I tried to put this to Karl, but he chose to ignore it, just keeping on about the new institute: the superb facilities it was going to provide; the unbelievably generous research funding, initially for five years, with every prospect of it increasing substantially thereafter; the stimulating environment resulting from free interactions among some of the world's foremost scientists:

'You wouldn't believe the responses I've been getting,' he went on, looking me straight in the eye, just managing to suppress a grin: 'Di Gregorio was one of the first to bite; he'll be recruiting almost immediately, as soon as the formal announcement has been made.'

Something appeared different about the Goose, an air of general festivity seemingly uniting the normally separate groupings.

'My God! I'd quite forgotten,' said Karl, as he took this in, 'it's Malcolm's birthday. We almost missed out on the party.'

As we made our way to the bar, I noticed Michelle and her friends engaged in animated conversation with a bevy of smartly dressed business types – lunchtime clientele by the look of them, come back for the special occasion. She looked over for a moment, taking in my appreciative gaze and responding with a coy wave, which Karl noticed and felt the need to comment on:

'Not having ideas in that direction, are you?'

'I suppose you could say that, in a way.'

'Really? Tell me more – bearing in mind of course that I speak as a potential father-in-law.'

'I haven't told you about my session with Terence Onions yesterday, have I?'

'No, but now you're changing the subject.'

'Not at all. The two are incontrovertibly linked: intimately you might say. I think it's about time you were wised up on this one.'

Predictably enough, Karl reacted warmly to the tale:

'You seem to have come on beyond my wildest expectations: safe breaking, blackmailing a public servant . . . What next? You're wasted at Prince of Wales College, you know. Time to consider a move up the ladder, don't you think?'

Malcolm had materialised from somewhere behind the counter looking contented, if a bit bemused. As he approached us, Karl took a pen from his pocket and scribbled something on a scrap of paper.

'A long term one this,' he said, handing it over, 'but if you've got a few bob going spare you might like to put them there for a while. Never know your luck. Happy birthday Malcolm.'

'You know I've always been a sucker for insider information.'

Malcolm was smiling happily as he folded the paper and put it in his breast pocket. 'Thank you Karl. I'll probably take you up on it. What are you both having.'

The tip, I was just able to make out as it changed hands, consisted of two words: ARC Pharmaceuticals.

Just then a loud female voice expressing joyous relief burst on us from a few feet away:

'Thank heavens I've found you. I was hoping against hope you'd be here.'

I turned to see Fritzy advancing towards me, beaming delightedly; but it turned out to be Karl she had in her sights:

'Karl darling, I'm so sorry about last night. I just couldn't, couldn't get away at the last moment. You can't believe the scene just as I was leaving. But that's it now. Over and done with at last, thank God. Never again. Never, ever again. Oh darling!'

She embraced him passionately, giving rise to a dip in activity around us, a momentary reduction in noise level through which a mumbled 'lucky bugger' sounded from somewhere close by.

Probably my imagination, but did Karl look just a shade embarrassed? If he did, it passed almost immediately. Partially extricating himself, he started to make the introduction, only to be stopped by Fritzy:

'Oh, I know Paul,' she said, turning to me with a charming smile, 'What have you done with Daniela? I've been hoping to meet her again.' Then to Karl, suggestively: 'An old friend of yours, I believe. Beautiful girl!'

Explanations, which appeared necessary at this point, were thankfully interrupted by an inharmonious rumbling from the far side of the house, the refrain gradually to be taken up by everyone present: '. . . happy birthday dear Ma-al-colm, happy birthday to you'. Applause, raised glasses, demands for a speech.

Malcolm, pulling himself together with difficulty, was admirably succinct:

'Just two things I want to say: Thank you all for coming along and all drinks on the house for the next fifteen minutes.'

More applause, followed by the inevitable for-he's-a-jolly-good-fellow, accompanied the surge to the bar – which coincided, as it happened, with the arrival of Sarah, looking angry at first but brightening up considerably on seeing us:

'You haven't seen my old man by any chance? Should have been here ages ago. I left him with Ben in the Clarence at lunchtime. God knows where they've buggered off to.' Then, after a pause, in which the singing and cheering rose in a crescendo to a discordant climax: 'Well, sod him then. He's old enough to take care of himself. Get me a glass of white wine, will you Paul, while they're still giving it away. Whoops!' – this in response to someone pushing past her to get to the bar. – 'Look where you're bloody going will you. Clumsy sod! You know, I've got a feeling this could turn out to be a really good night after all.'

I was beginning to think so too. But then the thought of Daniela came hurtling back, making me feel guilty at being there without her amid all this jollity. Karl was at the bar, getting everyone's drinks, passing them back as they were poured, Fritzy beside him glowing as though with pride of possession. He was well old enough to be her father. How does he bloody manage it? Apart from anything else, where does he find the time?

It was in the midst of these musings that it came to me what I had to do. What was the matter with me for not thinking of it before? First thing Monday morning I would head for that travel agency and book on the next available flight to Buenos Aires. There was nothing I was doing at college that couldn't be postponed for a week or so. And even if there had been? It was simply a matter of priorities, and nothing – there was absolutely no doubt in my mind on this point –, nothing came before Daniela. I would phone her after buying the ticket. She could meet me at the airport. God, it was all so simple. Having got that out of the way, I felt lighter, able to appreciate for the first time the events of the last few months; it was as though all my life had been in preparation for this period. Able also to suppress the horrendous thought that my arrival would be an embarrassment for her; that she had already moved on – or back, rather: back into the life she had so impetuously abandoned.

A harsh bellow from close by brought me back to the present:

'There you bloody are! What the fuck do you call this?'

Edward's somewhat sheepish look was rapidly turning to one of aggression. It was a set piece performance they had put together over the years, a comforting ritual around which they conducted their lives:

'Listen, you stupid cow; ask Ben what we've been bloody doing. Two fucking commissions I've managed to negotiate – almost.'

303

Karl turned from the bar, where he held a strategic position next to the pumps:

'What are you two having? Guinness?'

'That'll do fine,' said Edward, Ben Palmer at his side nodding in agreement. 'Two pints. God, what a day. Could really use a drink after that one, eh Ben?'

I was going to miss all this, I thought, if I ever got round to moving to California.

Postscript

Standing at the window of my old room, looking through it into the Centre reception area across the way, it seems as though nothing at all has changed in over two years, since the time of the Sean O'Brien debacle and the miraculous reappearance of Grandison's leg: two agitated visitors to the Centre peering apprehensively at Miss Brown, seated sullenly at her desk; a distant, subdued burbling bearing witness to the continuing smooth operation of the Goldburg fountain. It occurs to me to confirm the validity of these two pronouncements from the far window of the adjoining store room, almost immediately deciding it to be hardly worth the effort. Instead just standing here, staring into space, turning over in my mind the developments and changes that have taken place since those seemingly far off days.

Sean returned to Ireland almost immediately after his crushing exposure – an event he had somehow managed to interpret as a revelation from God, further evidence of His mysterious ways of moving. On arrival, his mother arranged hasty consultations with a bishop – another influential relative – and within a matter of months Sean had been installed in a seminary, in preparation for a new career, less susceptible than the previous one to the intrusions of objective judgement.

Julie, rather than calling as promised, had written a lengthy letter which I found myself quite capable of taking at face value without rancour or distress; it wished me well and expressed regret for the pain she had caused, necessary though her action had been. She had

305

become pregnant soon after leaving me, the result of an affair which had been going on for quite some time, and of which I had been completely unaware. It had all ended precipitously and she had lost the child, had felt this a punishment for her duplicity. Things had continued to go badly for her after that but were now showing signs of looking up: a developing relationship with an Italian colleague, which I had witnessed the beginnings of in that pub in Fitzrovia; an imminent transfer to Milan; talk of marriage, a new start in life. I replied warmly, expressing the hope we might meet again some time when all the dust had settled. It had been too easy: a simple tidying up of what has already become a distant memory.

Barry Skinner's affairs had clearly been going from strength to strength when I saw him last – almost a year ago now; a hurried meeting this time over coffee in the common room, before he was to fly off to Zimbabwe to discuss the possibility of some business with the Mugabe government. He had been quite excited over recent exploratory encounters with the Conservative Party which, after two crushing General Election defeats by the now thoroughly discredited Labour, he felt could well be in with a real chance next time. Their pressing problem, however, was their new leader: widely regarded, even among many of their most dedicated supporters, as a smug, self-seeking, thoroughly unpleasant dissembler: someone at whose approach small children and domestic animals would take off in distress. Barry's brief, which he was throwing himself into with glee, was to put him over as sincere and cuddly. 'If they win – and given the hole Labour have dug themselves into over Iraq and that joker in the White House, there seems a good prospect of that now – then Reisenberger, Day and Skinner could well find themselves at the leading edge of shaping national policy. I think I could quite enjoy that.'

For a while, I continued to run into Johnny Cremer from time to time in the Prince. Then he started coming in less, as though tiring of the place, which had never seemed to suit him anyway, perhaps simply provided a breathing space between phases in his life. Before long we ceased to connect at all; though I still half expect to be apprehended some dark night, to hear again his harsh voice reassuringly mocking my anxiety.

An obituary in the Times some months ago effectively rounded off a news story of a short while before, reporting the discovery of the body of a retired pharmaceutical company director in his Mayfair flat. Despite some controversy at the inquest, the coroner had eventually returned a verdict of death through natural causes. The obituary made some reference to the deceased's depressed state following his retirement from the board of Mencken, precipitated, it appeared, by allegations of insider dealing, which had wrecked a proposed merger with another pharmaceutical giant.

As for Mencken itself, its fortunes following a brief period of uncertainty, subsequently to be decisively attributed to hostile innuendo and false rumour, appear to have resumed their steady ascent. Klaus Berger received his knighthood for 'services to industry' in the wake of this resurgence, then promptly retired, expressing the desire to apply his undoubted talents in hitherto, for him, untested waters; his subsequent appointment to the post of Rector of Prince of Wales College, following Hardcastle's unexpected resignation for personal reasons – not widely accepted in college as in any way attributable to his, possibly facetiously reported, desire to spend more time with his family – nevertheless coming as some surprise.

One of Sir Klaus's first acts on taking office had been to acknowledge Grandison's de facto status, promoting him to Director of the Goldburg Centre and seeing to his nomination for a CBE in the following New Year's Honours List. I could imagine only too well Mrs Grandison's exultation at these developments: 'The Commander of the Order of the British Empire is resting. You will have to wait.' The much diminished deputy directorship passed to Trowbridge in lieu of a requested increase in salary, to his evident satisfaction.

Tony Mulgrave contrived to perform a timely about turn shortly before Berger's appointment had been made public, returning to Physics as Head of Department, a move welcomed by Karl as facilitating plans he was concocting for a joint venture involving a couple of research groups at Prince of Wales College and his new institute at Franklin. Tony has also managed to get himself actively engaged with ARC Pharmaceuticals in their political struggle, satisfying earlier aspirations to engage in this area of activity. The company's first targeted cancer drug is now apparently all set to undergo the vitally important Phase III trials, funded in part from a substantial inflow of venture capital following its conspicuous success with Phase II. The sought after political process is still seen as an uphill struggle however, though shares in the company have soared, making me wonder whether Malcolm had been wise enough to take up Karl's birthday present tip of a couple of years ago.

Against all the odds, Karl and Fritzy are still very much together; Karl, for the first time I can recall, professing his philandering days to be over, even talking of raising a family. More than talking, in fact: Fritzy's quite exceptional body just beginning to display the faintest suggestions of additional elegant curves in the central region. She has been causing quite a stir at Franklin: exuding charm and glamour, with that touch of foreign class which keeps the natives drooling; presiding with Karl over his flourishing empire.

Her condition, I suspect, is to a fair degree down to Daniela. They see a lot of each other, living in the same community and having many interests and friends in common now. When Daniela became pregnant Fritzy was the first to be informed; I remember well her immediate look of shock rapidly giving way to surprised delight. It wasn't long before Karl, having clearly been worked on, started giving hints of a radical shift in his personal philosophy.

Daniela is looking wonderful: still two months to go before the birth and glowing with health; delighted as well to be working with Di Gregorio once again, on a project which has quite restored her faith in pure research. I feel bad about leaving her to attend a conference back here at Prince of Wales College – arranged ages ago, before her condition had been confirmed. She was to have accompanied me, but then insisted I came alone; in the meantime taking the opportunity to pay a last visit before the birth to her mother and Pablo – fully recovered now –, both delighted at the prospect of a grandchild, which largely makes up for us having insisted on a very private wedding last year: just them, Karl and Fritzy, and another couple of friends who turned up at the last minute to watch us sign away our lives to each other.

It seems strange to be back in my old room, temporarily vacant following occupation by a visitor on sabbatical from a university in Canada – who also, as it happened, rented our flat in Brixton. We decided to keep this: lettings arranged by the college accommodation office taking care of expenses and even providing a few bob into the bargain. If things work out as Karl intends we may well be spending regular periods back there, something we are both looking forward to as a nostalgic contrast to our new life in California.

Tonight I will be paying my first visit to the Goose for getting on for a year. I phoned Sarah, who promises to be there with Edward and to drag others along for the occasion. Predictably enough I've been missing the place, and other aspects of life in London. But then there have been compensations, massive ones come to that; and already, after four days and just two to go, I can't wait to get back to Daniela: missing her far more than anyone or anything I have ever missed at any time in my life.